Heroes of the Rising Moon

A Novel by

J. Schimschal

Heroes of the Rising Moon is the fifth novel in the Darken Realm ®
series of books and is the sequel to The Devil's Utopia, Ruins of
America, Iron Messiah, and Prophet of Sorrow

Heroes of the Rising Moon

Published by Fossil Ridge Books Inc.
P.O. Box 33218
Northglenn, CO. 80233

ISBN 10 0-9777327-4-6
ISBN 13 978-0-9777327-4-6

Published in the United States of America

Acknowledgements
This book is dedicated to Ella. May your life always be filled with wonder.

About the Author

J. Schimschal is the author of the Darken Realm series of books. He lives in the western United States with his family. Additional information can be obtained by visiting **www.darkenrealm.com**.

Prologue

The prize of all prizes has finally been found. Nova 7, the legendary mercenary team has liberated the most powerful weapon ever developed by mankind from a heavily protected underground vault. The protector of the ruins, a fearsome machine born by the ancients gave chase to the mercenary team. Confronting the metallic menace, Nova 7 defeated the foul machine and passed into the wilds of America.

Pushing eastward through the interior of the continent, Nova 7 finds themselves travelling through a domain in which time has forgotten. Passing through silent towns, the northlands have been abandoned by humankind for hundreds of years. Beasts and creatures born from sinister nightmares now stalk the dark forests of the north.

The final leg of the long journey is at hand. Nova 7 pushes forward with fervent intensity to meet their destiny. As they struggle forward, their future and the fate of the American continent has never been more uncertain…

Chapter 1
The Forest of Glass

The mid-day sun shone brightly on the open field. Gray stalks of wheat had been battered by the cold weather and driven into dormancy. Banion plodded slowly through the field. As he did, he smiled, briefly lost in the moment. The fields were definitely planted by a farmer; rows and rows of wheat grew for many acres. Looking around him with a sense of familiarity, he knew that although the fields had been planted, the tenants had long since passed on. Weeds and other harmful plants had begun to take hold of the field.

As he walked amongst the tall gray stalks, he caught sight of an abandoned farmhouse. He moved towards the building slowly, as if in a slight daze, walking dreamily in the warm sun. When he reached the perimeter of the abandoned homestead, he shouldered his weapon and stepped toward the front door.

The timbers of the farmstead were spotted and the white paint had mostly peeled off the weather-worn wood. Beneath the battered coat of paint, gray timbers peeked out like a layer of grime. Banion reached out to feel the worn wood, finding the timbers smooth to the touch. As he succumbed to a sense of nostalgia for his former life, a chill suddenly rolled down his spine, cooling his body in the warm sun. Blinking, he sensed a presence. He turned to his right, catching sight of a flash of white. Stunned, he trembled briefly. There was something familiar about the flash of color and movement. Feeling that he was losing his mind, Banion returned his gaze back to the worn house before him.

His mind was spinning. Banion looked at the worn gray timbers and felt his past abruptly invade his senses. As he rubbed his hand across the wooden beams again, they felt just like home, or rather, his former home. The house and open field reminded him of his ranch and the house he had shared with his wife long ago. As he reminisced, the flash of white stung his mind once more. Blinking again, he felt that he was losing his mind. Half crazed, he stumbled toward the last sign of movement.

"Don't go," he said softly. As his mind began to seek the familiar, he was drawn into a vivid, waking dream. Moving quickly, he rounded the corner of the building. In the distance, beyond the fields of wheat, was a form garbed in a white flowing dress. Long dark hair flowed down her back. He stumbled toward the image, his heart aching and his mind driven into a strange frenzy.

Disappearing into the tree line, Banion rushed forward to reach the strange woman escaping into the forest. The faster he moved, the further she escaped, a distant vision, a mere wisp amongst the dense trees. After a few minutes of chasing the wraith, he stopped and scanned the foliage in frustration.

"Hey!" Jared grabbed his shoulder. As he whirled around, Banion looked like a crazed madman. Grasping Jared roughly, he grabbed his throat with his left hand. Like a flash of lightning, his right hand closed around a silver revolver. In the blink of an eye, Jared was staring down the revolver's barrel.

"Hold on! It's me!" Jared said in alarm.

Tani had rushed upon the scene and shouted at Banion, "Hey! Banion, calm down!"

Banion's savage, angry demeanor changed instantly as he realized that he was nearly throttling the tribal. "You startled me," he said in a dull tone, blinking heavily. With a harsh push, Banion threw the tribal back.

Frightened by the encounter, Jared took a step back, raising his hands in the air. "We called out to you but you didn't answer. We thought something was wrong. I wanted to make sure nothing was wrong."

"I'm fine," Banion said quickly, turning his attention back to the forest, scanning the tree line.

"You don't look fine," Tani commented. "Did you see something? You're all pale and pallid like a ghost."

"I thought I saw something," he stuttered back, still looking at the trees.

"What did you see?" Mineera moved forward, her bright blue eyes scanning him intently. She could feel his emotions and they were raw and unchecked. He was in a very unstable frame of mind. "What did you see?" she quizzed again after he gave no response.

"I thought it was… I thought it was…" he stammered.

Jared raised his eyes as if anticipating some sort of reaction. It never came.

"Banion?" Tani placed a hand on his shoulder and turned him so they were eye to eye. Staring out through his wire-rimmed spectacles, the scholar had a concerned look on his face.

"We need to move." Banion snapped back to attention, the dazed look on his face disintegrating, leaving behind his normal, dour, serious gaze. "We need to get going. We have a long way to go."

Grabbing the sinister black case, the tribals began to lift the nuclear warhead which has become their new companion. With one tribal stationed on each side, they walked abreast, the ancient weapon between them. Banion moved out about ten paces ahead of the group. Pulling the assault rifle from his shoulder, he let it rest in his tense hands. Mineera brought up the rear, preferring to linger about five paces behind the group.

Moving through the abandoned farm, the team progressed eastward, pressing on with the goal of home in mind, enjoying a brisk but sunny day. After a few minutes of travel, they passed out of the warm field and into the dark forest beyond. As they continued into the shadows, the sun was blocked and driven away by the branches and trunks of the enormous trees. The forest had lived for hundreds and hundreds of years without human pillaging. It had grown to epic proportions, its canopy reaching into the blue sky. Staring upwards, the companions could see wisps of white clouds amidst a blue sky.

The serene setting was calming to the group as they traveled. Their journey through the Darken Realm had been fraught with peril and it was relaxing to be simply walking through their peaceful surroundings.

As the day wore on, they pressed deeper and deeper into the dense forest. In the afternoon, the companions came to an abrupt halt at a strange clearing in the middle of the woods.

Banion clenched his fist near the side of his head. Everyone in the team knew this meant they should halt. Placing the warhead on the forest floor, the tribals grabbed their weapons and skittered to Banion's side, flanking him. Holding weapons at the ready, they stared at a wondrous scene.

An enormous sinkhole surrounded an unusual tree. The ground around the perimeter had sunk and the root system of the tree was exposed at the bottom of the sinkhole. Moving forward, the team stared in awe. The enormous tree was roughly 100 feet tall, and its mighty trunk was shimmering. Light from the sun was reflecting off the wooden surface in patches of shimmering hues.

Snorting, Jared shook his head in disbelief. The entire stunned team moved forward to get a better look. Standing at the edge of the deep sinkhole, they gazed at the trunk with amazement. A light breeze overtook the forest. As it did, the branches on the strange tree began to move and sway in the wind. Light from the sun flickered on the trunk. Beams of radiant illumination bounced back. All around them, the shimmering light was reflected. The rays streaked from the tree at varying angles, nearly hypnotic as they struck the ground around it. It was as if the team was watching a host of prisms spraying light over the forest.

The sight was amazing, and the team stared in paralyzed wonder for many minutes. As they gazed at the beams of light, each of them felt a strange wave of drowsiness wash over them. Yawning, they knew that something needed to change or else they would succumb to the strange wave of dizziness overtaking their senses.

Just as the wind had picked up, it suddenly dissipated, and the soothing lightshow came to an end. Blinking, Nova 7 felt better, as if coming out of a drunken stupor. Many minutes passed before all hints of drowsiness had abated. Finally fully conscious once more, they were eager to learn more about the strange tree. Tani, always the foolish master of curiosity, was the first to suggest getting an even closer look at the strange plant.

"I'm going into the pit around the tree. Help me down?" the scholar asked his companions.

"I don't think it's a good idea, Tani," Mineera warned.

"Oh, come on. It's a tree. What's it going to do to me? Eat me?"

Jared laughed in amusement. "You never *know*."

"Oh hell, bookworm, let me help you." Grabbing Tani's hand, Banion helped the tribal into the sinkhole around the tree.

Tani tested the ground carefully, making sure it was stable before walking on his own into the pit. Stepping over the exposed roots, he moved over to the trunk. He craned his neck, pushing the spectacles up his nose and peering intently at the bark.

He could see tiny crystals embedded within the bark of the tree. Reaching out, he fidgeted with the bark. It was strangely strong, much denser than an ordinary tree's outer layer. Pulling out his knife, he jammed it into bark and broke a piece free, then eyed it closely with a smile. He returned to his friends, and Banion helped him out of the pit.

Standing around him, they stared at the bark. It shimmered in Tani's hand as he rotated it. As it caught the light, it acted like a prism, reflecting and dispersing its rays.

"Amazing," Jared declared, trying to grab the crystallized bark from his friend's hand. Scowling, Tani resisted his eager move and pulled away.

"Now, kids, there's enough bark for everyone," Banion said with a chuckle. Mineera giggled but the tribals were not amused.

"It looks like some sort of crystallized structure embedded within the wood." As he stared at the odd sinkhole around the roots of the tree, it suddenly made sense to the tribal scholar. "Look at the sinkhole," he pointed; the rest of the team followed his finger to the pit. "I bet this tree incorporates minerals from the earth into the bark. It must pull earth directly from the roots around the tree right into the trunk. The hole around the tree is where the roots have absorbed the earth itself."

The theory was compelling and the rest of the team was amazed. As they stared in wonder at the bark in Tani's hand, the wind picked up again, waving the branches once more. As the branches began to move, the sunlight began to reflect off the tree, creating a kaleidoscope of light. Shimmering beams began to pulse from the tree once more. Smiling, they stared and felt the strange lights play yet again upon their senses. Feeling docile, they all simply stared at the shimmering lights around them.

The wind stopped again and the hypnotic effects of the swirling light dissipated. Yawning, each of them shook off the drowsiness.

Tani was elated by the reaction that each of them was having to the strange tree. His quick mind had pondered another theory. "I bet it's some sort of defense mechanism; the strange lights, I mean. We're all affected by the light and it's almost hypnotic. I bet the shimmering light acts as a defense against predation. Animals are unable to feed on the tree due to the weird hypnotic lights emanating from it. The animals become drowsy and can't focus. It's an amazing adaptation."

"It's truly a wonder," Mineera agreed, smiling at the tribal. She marveled at his eager and quick mind.

"We need to move. We're burning daylight," Banion said in a gruff tone.

The team moved on from the strange tree and pressed deeper into the forest. As they did, they spotted a few more of the odd trees. They skirted around the pits and sinkholes, managing to move onto a shallow hill. Breaking cover from the forest, they crested the hill and stopped dead in their tracks. Below them, in a deep valley, an entire forest of the strange trees was spread out. As they marveled at the sight, a chill blast of wind broke over the valley.

The combined sum of the trees was amazing to behold. The shimmering light being reflected was also being split into its constituent components. Rays of brilliant blue were mixed with sullen reds. Bright splotches of yellow light shimmered amidst oranges and other hues. As the wind whipped through the forest, it looked like a rainbow of color, rapidly changing, looking like some sort of perverse optical illusion. The entire valley looked like a wave of color, ever-changing. Awestruck, the team took a break from their journey, resting on the hill above the forest. For almost an hour they rested, staring in wonder at the strange lightshow.

The Darken Realm was filled with wonders beyond compare. The members of Nova 7 had seen some of the worst things in the world. Now they were witnessing one of the most amazing wonders of nature. Even at a distance, the lightshow had filled them with drowsy bewilderment. Although they were far enough to avoid the drastic effects of the magical display, they were not totally immune. Each of them could feel the bizarre pull of the forest and each of them knew it would be certain death to pass into the forest itself. Deep down, they knew they would become so befuddled by the lightshow that they would never be able to comprehend how to escape the forest.

"What do we do now? It's a long way around the forest," Jared said, resting his head on his knees as he watched the shimmering forest.

"We can go around," Banion replied.

"No," Tani answered, analyzing the situation. "We'll wait until nightfall. We can press through the forest at night and avoid the lightshow. It will be much quicker to cross through the middle of that forest instead of going around."

"So be it." Banion respected Tani's advice. "We'll wait until nightfall."

And so the mercenary team possessing the ultimate weapon rested upon a hilltop, overlooking the forest of glass, waiting for darkness to claim the land so they could press onward, toward home.

Chapter 2
Death Drop Pass

"Are you messing with that damn acorn again?" Banion asked in an irritated tone, looking briefly away from the strange sight just ahead of them, long enough to shoot Tani a disgruntled look.

"I can't help it, it's interesting," Tani responded, holding the shimmering acorn. The tribal had grabbed it from the strange forest filled with prismatic trees. Not exactly knowing what he would do with it, Tani had held onto the acorn like a treasure. Maybe someday he would plant the acorn and watch the plant grow from a sapling into a shimmering, full-fledged tree.

"Well, put that damn thing away, I need you to take a look at something," the leader of Nova 7 responded.

Jared and Mineera were crouched beside Banion as well, but still hadn't taken a look at the next task at hand. Banion was fascinated by something up ahead of them. At the base of a wilderness trail, the same trail that the team had been following for the last week, was an ominous signpost.

A picture of a skull had been painted on the sign in white paint, above text in an ancient tongue.

"What do you need?" Tani asked with a sigh, placing the reflective acorn in his backpack.

Pointing at the signpost up ahead from the tree line, Banion motioned for Tani to take a look at it. Squinting, the tribal was unable to make out the letters. As he stood up, intending to walk down the trail to get a better look, Jared grabbed his arm and shook his head. Tani blinked a few times, befuddled.

"I don't get it," he said in a confused tone.

"The signpost has a skull on it." Mineera pointed.

Tani squinted once more and could make out the crude shape. Nodding in recognition, he held out his hand and Banion passed him his binoculars. Peering through the lenses, the tribal read the signpost written in the ancient tongue.

"It says: Beware, Death Drop Pass," he said, still scanning the sign.

"What the hell do you think it means?" Banion asked the rest of the team.

No one could readily discern the sign's meaning. Taking a brief moment to ponder the odd signpost, Mineera had a hunch. She grabbed the binoculars and panned them past the trail toward the high mountain pass just ahead of them. As she scanned the pass through the mountains, she gasped anxiously.

The entire floor of the mountain pass was pasty white. Thousands of bones, animal and human alike, were littering the ground. The layer of bones was so thick in some places that the earth below was completely obscured. In several places, the piles of bones were nearly waist-high.

Shocked by the scene, she panned the binoculars in a slow arc, looking for whatever had caused so much carnage. It took her but a brief moment to discern the danger. Resting atop the rocky spires around the mountain pass was a gangly collection of enormous birds. Nearly three feet tall, the huge fowls sat together in tight packs to ward off the intense cold. Hundreds of birds were clinging to every rocky precipice around the passageway. Their feathers were mostly black but streaks of light green adorned the wingtips. The birds had no neck at all, their heads sticking right out of their chests. The muscles bulged where the wings attached to the chest. Near these joints, no feathers grew, and the creatures' bare, gnarled skin was exposed. To round out their frightful appearance, two yellow, beady eyes looked out from each bird.

Although the birds were fairly large, they didn't look as if they could kill a full- grown human or a large animal such as an elk or deer. Baffled by the mystery, Mineera alerted the rest of Nova 7 and each of them in turn viewed the host of birds and the piles of bone beneath their rocky perches.

"I don't get it." Banion shook his head, looking at the birds from a great distance. "They're strong in number, but don't seem very big."

"The amount of bones in that pass says otherwise. They seem fairly dangerous but I can't fathom why," Jared agreed.

"What the hell do we do? This mountain range is too steep and snow packed to cross in winter. We either have to go through or go around. Banion, does the map have any other route through these mountains?" Tani asked.

"No, nothing else is on the map, but this pass is listed just as the sign says, 'Death Drop Pass.'"

"We can't risk moving on through the pass until we know the danger," Mineera stated, looking at the colony of birds perched upon the rocks. "I do feel that these birds caused the death in the mountain pass. I strongly believe that they are the cause of all the animal and human remains."

"Me too," Tani concluded. Examining the situation at hand, his mind was grinding away. "We need to perform an experiment."

"What? An experiment?" Jared asked, raising an eyebrow, looking at Tani as if he was crazy.

"Don't give me that look, Jared," Tani said, giving his friend an equally dour look in return. "I'm not crazy. We don't know what will happen if we move into the mountain pass ahead, so we need to perform an experiment to see what will happen."

"I vote you run up into the mountain pass and we all sit back here and watch," Banion snorted at the tribal. "You can give us first-hand data on what happens." He laughed dryly, but the scholar was not amused. Both Mineera and Jared snickered at the comment.

"Oh, just forget it."

"No, no," Jared countered. "We get what you're saying, but what do we do?"

Shaking his head for a brief moment, Tani pondered the situation. After a short spell of contemplation, he looked at Jared, struck by an idea. "There are lots of dead elk and deer in the mountain pass. There has to be big game here in the forest. Jared, can you track an elk, maybe a deer?"

Shrugging, Jared knew that the task would be easy. "Sure, there's still fresh snow in some places and the ground is muddy in most other places. I bet I could find an animal pretty quickly. Why?"

"Could you herd it in this direction?" Tani quizzed.

Smiling, Jared finally got the message. "Yeah, I could herd one toward that mountain pass. If you all stay back here to help, we can flush it directly where we need it to go."

"This sounds a little disturbing to me. We're going to sacrifice an animal just to see what happens? What about the animal?" Mineera asked in concern.

"Well, either we can try Tani's plan or you can come up with another course of action. I'm not too thrilled about the idea of feeding an animal to the birds, but the last thing we need is to put our lives in danger," Banion shot back.

Mineera sighed and shook her head in disgust. "When will we ever get to a point where we can stop sacrificing and killing in the name of this sick crusade?"

"We can never stop until it's finally over. We can never stop until this insane mission is completed," Jared responded, trying to speak in a calm, regretful tone to Mineera.

She appreciated his sentiment and agreed to the plan with a nod.

With that, Jared bounded off into the forest, following a fresh set of elk tracks, pressing off quickly to the northwest.

Almost an hour passed and the rest of Nova 7 was becoming a little concerned. Just before Banion was about to radio Jared, the sound of thunder erupted from the forest. An enormous herd of elk, fifty strong, burst out of the trees, driven by fear. Banion, Mineera, and Tani were stunned by the onslaught and retreated quickly, moving behind the trees for cover.

Bounding like a cat, the tribal warrior was in hot pursuit of the herd. Steering them through the forest, the youth had managed to bring not only one animal to the mountain pass but an entire herd. Deftly, he managed to direct them toward the mountain pass. When the herd broke from the forest, they halted near the edge of the pass, too uneasy to proceed. Seeing their hesitation, Jared fired his submachine gun into the air.

The sound of gunfire set off a panic within the herd. Fear-stricken, the crazed animals had only one route of escape; they charged upwards, crushing the bones of past victims. As the herd pressed deep into the mountain pass, hundreds of tiny yellow eyes suddenly became aware of the movement. With a chorus of squawking, the enormous birds stretched and spread their wings.

Nova 7 gasped as they stared at the wingspan of the birds. Although the birds themselves were only three feet tall, their wings, when fully spread, had a span of over twelve feet. They stared at the birds in awe, about to witness one of the most horrific hunting practices that evolution had ever mastered. Each of the birds in the mountain pass took flight. The entire sky seemed to darken as they began to circle the frantic elk herd below.

Running for cover, Jared sought refuge with his companions.

"Good work," Banion uttered as he stared in awe at the feeding frenzy that was about to begin.

As the birds circled, they began to fly in formation, in small groups of about a dozen. Forming hunting flocks, they looked like bomber formations. After about 30 seconds, the attack began. The groups dove down into the densely packed mountain pass, seeking to kill the frantic elk. Still frightened from the sound of Jared's gunfire, the elk herd never knew what hit them. A formation of twelve birds landed atop an enormous elk. Pressing their long talons into the flesh of the beast, the birds squawked and coordinated themselves into a straight line upon the elk's spine. Lining up one by one, they were finally in place. The elk bayed in pain and terror as the talons dug in. With a unified motion, all of the birds began to flap. In a few seconds, the enormous power of the birds was unleashed. Struggling, the elk was frantic as the birds began to lift the enormous animal off the ground. As they flapped their heavy wings, the dozen birds grasping the elk were more than powerful enough to take flight with the animal in tow.

"What the hell?" Jared gasped as several elk in the mountain pass were lifted off the ground, carried away by the sinister flocks.

Higher and higher the elk were brought into the air. Struggling, the beasts were utterly terrified. When the birds had lifted the elk about one hundred feet into the air, the lead bird grasping the elk's neck let out a shrill, piercing wail, upon which all of the birds clutching the elk, which was hovering precariously in the air, released their talons in unison. Baying in terror, the elk dropped from the sky, free-falling about 100 feet onto the rocky surface below. The impact was horrific and the elk hit the ground with a fearsome thud, killed instantly as it crashed into the jagged rocks below.

Watching in horror, Nova 7 could not turn away. Within a few seconds, the sky was raining elk, as ten more elk were lifted into the air and dropped onto the rocks below. The rest of the herd was frantic, hearing the death cries of their own kind. Driven through the pass, the herd passed out of the area quickly.

The result was a horrific scene. Eleven elk had been taken by the birds, pulled into the air and dropped to the rocks below. Their broken, lifeless bodies were covered in blood. Squawking in victory, the birds descended upon the dead elk and began to feed upon the bodies. Hundreds of birds dug their sharp beaks into the dead elk and feasted in earnest.

Mineera almost got sick to her stomach, retreating from the rest of Nova 7 and trying to find a place to throw up. Tani was clutching his face with his hands. Jared was staring with his mouth open. Banion seemed indifferent and emotionless to the carnage.

"Let's move," he ordered the rest of his stunned team. "Let's get through the pass while they're still feeding."

The rest of Nova 7, still stunned, required a couple of seconds to recover their senses. Grabbing their gear, they formed up. Tani and Jared grabbed the warhead and the team moved slowly up the slope towards the mountain pass.

The pass had become an obstacle course for the mercenary team. The dead elk were all over the area, covered by the feasting birds. As they approached, many of the birds turned to them and raised their wings in a show of dominance. Many squawked, their beaks bloody, trying to drive away the foolish humans. Skirting around the elk corpses, Nova 7 made a point not to get too close; they didn't want the birds to think that they were trying to take their prey.

Mineera was breathing heavily, trying not to look at the bloody scene. Instead she stayed right behind Banion, only an arm's length away, her eyes planted firmly on the back of his brown duster. Tani and Jared would glance at the gory landscape from time to time and then always look at each other with a look of revulsion. Banion simply focused on getting his team through the area unharmed. He was clutching his assault rifle and walked with his finger on the trigger, training the weapon on the nearest flock of birds caught up in a feeding frenzy.

"Death Drop Pass." Banion spoke in a haunted tone. "Aptly named."

"Let's make sure we never come back," Jared said.

"You got that right," Tani agreed.

Mineera nodded but did not speak; she was still queasy from witnessing the feeding frenzy and focused on her stomach and moving forward. Within a matter of minutes, Nova 7 had escaped the deadly mountain pass, pressing on quickly, trying to gain as much distance as they could from the cursed scene. The journey through the northlands was perilous but Nova 7 had succeeded once more.

Below the mountain pass, a mostly open expanse of grasslands stretched on. Pockets of forest were revealed in the open expanse, looking like islands on the sea. Taking a brief moment to view the land beyond, they all felt a sense of accomplishment. They were one step closer to home.

Chapter 3
Great Shush Valley

Small stalks of golden grass, dried in the harsh winter wind, waved in the mounting breeze. The cold air was utterly relentless, whipping across the barren, snow-covered earth. As the tireless breeze pushed across the snow, small wisps of white were driven into the air. It was wondrous to watch the tiny frozen grains shift and writhe, hissing across the snow.

For a brief moment, the tribal from Scarskin thought he was watching the desert sands, not a white, snow-filled wasteland. He was amazed by the similarities between the sand and the drifting snow. Looking away from his position, Jared could see small dunes of snow forming, the loose snow accumulating and creating enormous snow drifts. Although the wasteland from which Jared came was hell-blasted by the sun and unbearable in temperature, he would readily submit to those conditions as opposed to the frigid, ice-blasted badlands.

As he drifted from dune to dune of frozen ice and snow, his attention focused suddenly on something only a few yards away. Squinting in the bright glare of the frosty reflective snow, he caught sight of something that could not be ignored. With a playful attitude, he moved quickly, his boots crunching on the cold frozen snow.

With a smile on his face, Jared placed one foot in the snow, balancing on one leg for a brief second. Taking his left foot, he placed his heel so that it touched the toe of his right boot. Standing precariously, he peered down into the snow, then jumped out of the way. His two foot imprints end-on-end were, shockingly, the same length as an enormous track left in the snow.

Still grinning, Jared motioned to the rest of Nova 7, pointing at the imprint in the snow. An enormous footprint, 20 inches in length, was visible in the snow, next to the fresh tracks just made by the tribal warrior. Five claw marks radiated from the front of the footprint. The width of the paw print was also staggering, roughly eight inches across. Whatever had left the track was enormous; they would not want to encounter it unaware.

"I wonder what left this?" Jared said as his companions looked in dismay at the enormous footprint.

Shaking his head, Tani simply didn't want to know.

Banion immediately whirled around, checking the icy tundra for any signs of the monstrous creature. His eyes met nothing but snow-covered grasslands for at least five miles in every direction. Concerned, he said, "I'm not sure what left that track but we are totally exposed and out in the open. We have no cover and no route of escape if whatever made that track comes back."

"I sure don't want to be caught out here in the open, especially tonight. We should press on and take cover in that forest to the east." Mineera pointed at a pine forest about six miles away.

Staring at the sun, the team estimated they were only a few hours from sunset. Being caught in the open with a super-predator prowling the tundra was a real threat. As they peered back at the sun, already heading toward the western horizon, a sense of dread settled over the team. The mercenary team had just crossed a great many miles over several long days, trudging through the tundra. The exhaustion had begun to take its toll on the team members and they were all depressed by the thought of pressing on for another several hours before making camp.

Seeing the distress on everyone's face, Banion tried to give them a small boost. "It's not that far, maybe five or six miles. We can take some extra time tomorrow and rest in the camp a few extra hours if you like."

Hearing the offer relieved everyone. A break from the frantic journey home would be welcomed.

Gathering strength, they each took a shaky step forward, moving toward the woodlands ahead. The sun was at their backs as they walked, giving them warmth as they crunched across the icy snow.

Jared seemed lost in thought. He stopped for a brief moment, placing the warhead on the ground, and turned around to look at their tracks snaking across the tundra. As he looked at where they had been, a solemn look appeared on his face.

It was the first time in his life that he felt somehow older, somehow more seasoned, as if a great part of his life was over. Staring at the tracks made him think of every step they had taken, every challenge they had met, and every hardship they had overcome. Their tracks were not just impressions in the snow; they were a testament to a fantastic journey that was nearing an end. His reservations about moving on were not lost on the rest of his companions. Each of them had a strange twinge that had begun to form in their hearts after they had located and obtained the nuclear weapon. Before their success, there was always another village over the next hill and always another challenge ahead of them. After fighting so hard for so long, it was somewhat anti-climactic to finally succeed in their crusade.

Secretly, each of them yearned for the adventure, yearned to explore more of the world. Each of them had become an adventure junkie, drawn to the strife and the struggle. After experiencing so much difficulty over the vast expanse of time they had spent with each other, they hungered for more challenges. It was the success of overcoming any threat or obstacle together that filled them with a sense of exhilaration. Where most turn away and hide from strife, Nova 7 had made its mark in the world as a group that strove to do the impossible. It was this deep sense of never surrendering and never giving up that made them all feel special. Alone they were strong, but together they could hold up the very world on their shoulders. It takes a special person to search for adversity, let alone an entire group of people. Nova 7 was a legend based on fierce perseverance and reckless guile. Champions do the impossible while the meek whine about their own inhibitions.

"I'm going to miss this," Jared said with a distant look, eyeing their tracks in the snow. "I feel that part of my life is behind us and I'll never see the likes of it again. It makes me sad."

"Do you remember when we all met?" Tani reminisced with misty-eyed wonder.

"I sure do." Banion chuckled. "I was so irritated that you two little brats wanted to follow me around the damn wasteland. I felt like I was babysitting."

Jared laughed, turning to Banion. "We thought you were insane, Banion. More than once we weren't sure what to do about you."

"You're right, I am crazy," Banion said, flashing them a wicked grin. The look was so disarming, Tani and Jared both had to take a step back. "This is fun, you little runts, but we're burning daylight. If you want to ramble on about your feelings, let's do it while we move on."

Hearing his concern, they took a brief second to look once more at their tracks. With thoughts still lingering on the past, they pressed on through the tundra.

"I'll never forget each of you in the war room the day King Toil enlisted us," Mineera contributed, with a smile of her own. "When we came into the throne room, the other mercenary teams simply stared at us in disgust. It's ironic that we were viewed as the misfits and we finally succeeded where all the other teams had failed."

"Yeah, out of all the other teams, we were the only ones that made it out of the palace and out of Rasheed alive." Tani spoke softly, remembering the horrible night that had set their quest in motion.

"That should say something," Banion declared, and the rest of the team looked at him as they walked onward. "Each of us is special; each of us matters and has a purpose in the greater scheme of things. Without the skills and character each of us has, we would have never made it. There were so many times that we could have turned back, so many times we could have given up. After everything we've faced and all the hardship we've endured, we can be at peace with one another. Such friendship is rare in such a dark world. For the first time in a long time, I belong and you are all my family."

It wasn't often that Banion uttered anything but spiteful taunts and curses, but when he did step outside of his nasty demeanor, Banion meant exactly what he said, and his words were heartfelt.

"I've spent more time with you, Banion, than I've ever spent with my own father." Jared smiled.

The statement was profound and an eerie silence washed over the group. Banion absorbed the kind words and had a hard time responding. Shaking his head, he had to gain control of his emotions. He had always been part of broken families where death surrounded his existence. The only thing for which he had ever really yearned was a peaceful home. The tribal, young Jared, had looked at Banion as more than a friend; he was a father figure to the boy, a role model of sorts.

"You and Tani are the closest things that I have ever had to children. Even though you both annoy the hell out of me, I'm glad I took you two runts along with me."

In its own way, the back-handed compliment was charming. Everyone laughed at the response; it was a classic Banion comment.

"I also feel home," Mineera said, her tone light.

Tani and Jared looked at her with compassionate eyes. The traitor of the Reaper Kai was just as homeless as Banion. Cast out from her race, she lived in the middle of two colliding ideals. Viewed by most as the enemy, she had spent a considerable amount of time escaping the stigma of her past deeds and atoning for her evil actions. She would never have a home and she knew it. The close-knit team of friends were the only true connections she had.

"I'm glad you feel home." Tani's tone conveyed his empathy. "You're a good friend and a compassionate human being."

"I have a lot to atone for," she responded.

"You also have a lot to be thanked for. Don't sell yourself short, not now. You've paid for your sins tenfold," Banion added.

"I wonder why I don't ever feel that way." Mineera's voice was almost a whisper.

"The reason you have guilt is because you care. If you were heartless, you would feel nothing. Your heart has been burdened and that is a blessing. Don't ever feel that you are an outcast; you've distinguished yourself as someone who would sacrifice your very soul to do the right thing," the tribal warrior interjected. "You'll always be welcome around our campfire."

"Jared is right," Mineera said, her words heartfelt. "I will miss our journeys. I'll miss all of you when this is over and this crusade is complete."

"We still have a ways to go. I'm not sure what's over the next hill, around the bend in the road. Let's enjoy the mystery," the scholar added.

The team continued on and passed quickly across the tundra, driven by a flare in their souls, driven by hope and kinship. As they traveled, they spoke of people and places they had encountered together. They spoke of the city of Rasheed and the boat ride to Dune Station. They remembered the journey to the Concrete Barrens and its enigmatic inhabitants. They told stories of the journey northwards and the ruined military base. The crusade had been long and wrought with peril but it would always burn brightly in their souls. Although the road was coming to a close, they all had more than enough memories to keep their hearts alive and the feeling of friendship burning within them for a great many years to come.

Chapter 4
Haunted Sorrow

The tree line had been decimated. Large patches of the forest had been killed ages ago and nothing could grow in their place even after the long passage of time. Swathes and swatches of the earth were utterly lifeless. Skeletons and the remains of hapless animals were strewn about these barren graveyards, a testament to a toxic environment.

It was haunting to behold the dense forest stripped away. As Nova 7 passed through the area, most of them had a sinking suspicion what had caused the earth to be sterile and lifeless.

"Tani, what are we looking at?" Banion asked, staring at the wasted landscape around them.

"It's radioactive fallout, I'm sure of it," he responded. "See how patches of the forest are barren? After a nuclear weapon detonates, the debris from the blast is charged with radiation and the enormous dust cloud is pulled into the atmosphere. As the jet stream and wind patterns collect the radioactive debris, the air circulates the material. Eventually the toxic dust rains down and blankets the land. It takes thousands and thousands of years for the radiation to decrease. Until the fallout decays completely, the earth is contaminated and lifeless. This entire area must have had significant radioactive fallout after a nuclear blast during the apocalypse."

Jared shook his head slowly in response. Ahead of them in the forest, a thin dusting of snow was clinging to the earth. Beneath the delicate white layer, they could discern animal bones, left by hundreds of dead animals that had wandered across the barren patch of earth. The hapless victims had succumbed to the radiation and died while crossing. Their contaminated bodies eventually withered and desiccated with the passage of time. With radiation levels still high, not even bacteria or fungus could metabolize the remains. The remains looked more like mummies than skeletons, with tissue still clinging to the bones.

"We're going to make more of this?" Jared said, pointing at the creepy patch of fallout. "When that nuclear warhead we're carrying goes off, radiation is going to land somewhere and do this?"

"Yes," Tani replied immediately.

Shaking his head, he sighed and looked at the black resin case containing the nuclear warhead. For a brief moment, the team stared at the broken landscape, the results of their crusade now becoming more sickeningly apparent.

"Don't think about it," Banion warned.

"I'm trying not to," Jared responded.

As the trio conversed, none of them noticed at first that Mineera was being extremely quiet. Finally, Banion became aware of her silence and they all turned to look at her. She was standing alone a few paces back, a strange look on her face.

"Mineera?" Banion called.

Taking a brief second to collect herself, she pulled her blue robes about her shoulders as if to ward off the cold. In reality, she was trying to ward off the sounds and images surging through her mind. "I see children crying and terrified people. There is a little girl with a dirty teddy bear. It's the last possession she has left in the world. All of her toys and books are gone. Her family had to leave their home quickly and that is the only thing she has left. She's too young to understand what is happening and she thinks that her parents are punishing her since they can't give her any of her toys to play with.

"As she cries constantly, her parents are silent and keep moving forward slowly, one agonizing step at a time. There is a column of people, with scant possessions, moving through the forest, passing away from a great city." Shaking her head, trying to ward off the visions, Mineera was deeply shocked and disturbed. "We're passing down the same trail that these refugees used hundreds of years ago to escape the carnage of the nuclear war. It is a pathway of sorrow, a trail of sadness. I have a deep sense of dread that is filling my soul and it won't abate."

"It's a bad omen," Tani whispered, looking at Mineera.

"Just stop it, Tani. You're always a voice of reason. You were never superstitious. Bookworm, get it together."

"I think he's right," Jared confirmed, also feeling an eerie sensation wash over him. As the haunting feeling filled him as well, he clutched the bird totem around his neck, rubbing the worn surface with his thumb.

"We're walking the same path as refugees in ages past, refugees from the nuclear holocaust. And as we follow in their footsteps, I can hear their strife, feel their suffering. You don't find it ironic that we're carrying a weapon, the same weapon used to cause all of this death that I'm feeling? You don't feel the power of our destiny?"

As he shivered in the morning sun, the sensation began to wash over Banion as well. Staring at the worn path meandering through the forest, he focused on a fleeting emotion clawing at the edge of his consciousness. Banion tried to fight the feeling, but could not. He passed into a daydream as a whisper arose from the forest around him. With a blink, an image of a convoy of people passed into his mind. The ragged band of people was trudging onward, filled with broken hope. Whimpering erupted and he could hear something coming from the woods. Spinning around, he grabbed his revolver and eyed the trees with suspicion. As he did, a raw and powerful emotion overwhelmed his senses. A feeling of emptiness and hopelessness washed over him. The sensation was so strong, it filled him immediately with despair. Wanting to surrender, wanting to quit, he felt utterly defeated.

"We need to get the hell out of here," the leader of Nova 7 declared with fear in his voice. Banion was never rattled, never scared, but the sensations of the haunted forest path were too much to ignore, too much to handle. The other members of the team were frightened as well, but after hearing Banion's voice crack with fright, they were all ready to escape the creepy trail.

Without any hesitation, the rest of Nova 7 heeded his order with no complaints. As they passed quickly out of the area, the strange sensations began to dissipate. The whispers of the past were transient, but even as the sounds, images, and emotion disappeared, each of them remained stung and scarred psychologically. The raw power of the emotion felt in those haunted trees was too strong to simply ignore. Each of them would never forget that ugly feeling of sorrow and hopelessness.

Putting as much distance as they could between themselves and the cursed grove, the team pushed quickly into a canyon. As they traveled, the signs of radioactive fallout from ages past became even more prominent. The hillside to the north of them had large patches of earth exposed where toxic radiation was still prevalent. In the depths of the canyon, Nova 7 had to give a wide berth to similar radioactive swatches of earth, making their journey labored. With each passing moment, they began to wonder if the passageway through the canyon would become too contaminated to continue onward.

With thoughts centered on their bizarre surroundings and the restless feeling of sorrow still pressing on their consciousness, none of them were aware that they were being watched and had been for a fair length of time.

Nestled in the trees, secluded in the foliage, a beast lingered. With its enormous nose it probed the air. The smell of flesh greeted its nostrils and with a growing hunger, the beast became fascinated with the travelers. As it tracked them, sniffing the air for their trail, it drew ever closer, quietly prowling through the forest.

"What the hell is that?" Jared asked, scrunching up his nose.

"What?" Tani said in a half-hearted tone.

"That smell?"

Shaking his head, Tani indicated that he didn't smell anything.

"I don't smell anything," Mineera confirmed.

"How many times have I told you to wipe your ass, kid?" Banion chuckled.

"No, seriously, it's a faint, almost musky odor."

"Musky odor? Hey Tani, take a bath." Banion chuckled again, but his amusement was cut short. His face became serious and with a fluid movement, he brought his assault rifle to his shoulder. He whipped around in response to the sound of movement behind them. The breaking and rustling of branches echoed through the trees. An enormous form breeched the foliage and charged the team. A split second after hearing the crash of sounds behind them, Banion had already opened fire.

Thump! Thump! Thump! His assault rifle clambered with a burst of gunfire. A creature, nearly fifteen feet tall at the shoulder, reared up on its hind legs. Its body was covered with patches of brown fur, surrounding blotches of exposed, pallid white skin. It had a long snout, very similar to that of a canine. As it reared up, a strong musky smell was evident.

Banion's gunfire hit the animal in the chest with little impact. Only small wounds opened on the beast and it was readily apparent that the creature would require significant damage to vanquish.

"Take it down!" Banion screamed, retreating while firing repeated bursts of gunfire at the beast.

Seeing Banion as the biggest threat, the beast moved forward. As it got near the gunfighter, it maneuvered itself quickly, turning its backside to Banion. It lifted its tail and a stream of foul-smelling fluid erupted, spraying Banion and the trees near him. A powerful musky smell filled the air as Banion was coated in the fluid. Shouting, he rubbed his eyes. The toxic excretion was burning his eyes and he was temporarily blind.

Seeing that Banion was prone, the enormous animal whirled around and charged him. As it did, both tribals opened fire. With submachine guns humming, they pelted the animal with gunfire. Over a dozen bullets slammed into the beast's side. Halting, it turned to face the tribals, then whirled around, lifting its tail again to spray them with the foul-smelling liquid.

Tani hit the deck and Jared leapt out of the way; both of the tribals managed to avoid the toxic chemical musk.

"Our guns are ineffective," Jared shouted, pelting the animal again with a burst of gunfire.

"Jared!" Mineera yelled, moving toward the tribal. As she ran to him, a fiery spark as bright as the sun began to form in the palm of her hand. Moving quickly, the spark of light grew in size and intensity. A split second later, a searing beam erupted from her outstretched fingertips, racing through the air. With great concentration, she managed to maneuver the beam of light so that it struck the animal's face. Roaring, the beast reared up on its hind legs. As it held its paw forward to shield itself, the holy fire burned its arm instead of its face. Smoke rose as the attack singed its flesh.

"We have to disable it and get out of here," Mineera said. "It's too big to kill."

Understanding the situation fully, Jared shouldered his gun and grabbed the mighty Scar Blade from its scabbard. As he pulled it free, a dull blue glow emanated from the weapon as reflected sunlight glittered off the ancient blade. Jared rushed full speed toward the beast, which never knew what hit it, still stunned by Mineera's persistent psychic attack.

Closing the distance quickly, Jared inhaled and swung with all of his might, aiming at the creature's hind leg. Normally, with Jared's strength and extreme skill with a blade, the weapon would have sheared completely through the limb. In this case, the creature's leg was so thick that his blade was not able to fully penetrate the bone.

Roaring in pain, the creature swung its monstrous arm at the tribal. Jared deftly avoided the vicious swing, already on the move. Recoiling back, he swung again at the creature's leg, shearing into the muscle and cutting through tendons. With a roar, the beast collapsed backwards, unable to stand on its hind legs. Seeing that the beast was nearly crippled, Mineera yelled for Jared to retreat.

"Let's go!" she yelled in Jared's direction as he retreated from the beast. "Grab Banion, Tani and I will get the warhead."

As she let her burning beam drop, the creature was stunned for a brief moment. Jared bounded over to Banion and helped the cursing gunfighter to his feet. Though he was still blind, the effects of the musk were beginning to wear off. With blurry vision, he rubbed his eyes and stumbled forward with Jared's help.

Nova 7 retreated from the scene of battle with one of their own ineffective. As they tried to escape from the monster, the enraged beast got back on its feet. The enormous creature gave chase, still fairly quick though one of its hind legs was injured. Stumbling forward, it lumbered after them, screeching in anger.

"Damn it," Jared said as he looked behind them, seeing the monster give chase.

"Give me some covering fire," Tani frantically asked Jared.

Turning around, Jared took aim and fired at the monster's head. It stopped its advance as several bullets struck its face. Tani pulled a grenade free and ripped the pin out of its clip, hurling the weapon, which landed near the beast's belly. With a boom, the grenade detonated, the monster taking the heavy blast. The weapon did little overall damage but managed to injure the creature's stomach and one of its front legs.

Crashing to the ground, the beast roared and rolled around, throwing its paws around in an angry rage. Not waiting for another round with the creature, Nova 7 moved as quickly as they could through the forest, frantically trying to escape. Stunned again, the beast was even more vicious than before. It rose off the ground and charged them again, this time a little slower but still fast enough to catch up.

Banion's vision was almost back to normal. He was able to move on his own and the team picked up the pace a bit. Charging out of the tree line, they found themselves in the middle of an open area. As they stumbled out of the woods, they were unable to tell what they were looking at.

Tall pipes of iron were sticking out of the ground in the valley ahead. Each iron pipe had a slanted metal cone perched at its top. Deep holes had been dug in the earth all around the area. Although confused by their surroundings, they were sparked out of their daze by the sound of the monster crashing through the forest behind them. They moved into the clearing, now seeing smoke rising from the iron pipes.

"It's a village." Tani was the first to acknowledge the significance of the pipes erupting from the ground.

A human head popped up from one of the holes in the ground, staring suspiciously at Nova 7. The team members rushed towards the man with frantic looks. As they did, the mighty beast erupted from the woods and roared.

"Over here!" the man yelled, motioning them onward.

Even as they ran full speed, the brown-furred beast gained ground on them. Hearing it lumber toward them made each of them pick up the pace. Reaching the hole cut in the earth, Nova 7 found a slope leading down into the earth. The same man they had seen before was motioning to them at the bottom of the slope, urging them to pass through a doorway carved out of the earth. Hastily, they rushed through the doorway.

Slamming an iron door shut, the man drew a heavy bolt across the door. A split second after the door had shut, something thudded against it. The paw of the creature repeatedly hit the door, its claws screeching against the metal.

Breathing heavily, the members of Nova 7 were glad to be alive. They stared at the pale man, who smiled back at them.

"We are in your debt," Banion said in gratitude.

"It's not often that we get visitors out here, on the western edge of civilization. You owe me nothing; any enemy of the Great Shush is welcome in Red Mountain."

"Great Shush?" Tani quizzed.

"Yes, the monster that almost made a meal of you. Come with me, I will take you to the town inn." The pale man smiled.

With a sigh of relief, Nova 7 took a brief moment to collect their thoughts and catch their breath. Having passed out of the harsh wilds, they had succeeded in reaching the far western edge of civilization. It wouldn't be long before they would reach the safety of Iron Kai territory, and their quest would be completed.

Chapter 5
Red Mountain Inn

Still catching their breaths from the long run to safety, Nova 7 took a brief moment to collect themselves. Gasping, they looked at each other in disbelief.

Bam! The monster roared outside the iron door, battering it again and again. With each strike against the door, each of them jumped back a step, half expecting the savage creature to break through.

"I assure you, we are all quite safe. Our homes are engineered to keep out the Shush. We build the entrance to our homes by digging a trench that is eight feet in length. The reach of the monsters is seldom that long and most of the time, the Shush are unable to even touch the doors to our homes. You have found an especially savage Shush, one that is unusually large and lethal. I am glad you were able to seek refuge in my home." The pasty man spoke as he moved toward them. In the dim light of the subterranean home, he looked like a ghost moving through the darkness as his white skin reflected the dim light from his hearth.

"We're glad that you took pity on us and allowed us refuge. We are in your debt." Mineera bowed to the pale man.

"The Shush are no friends to my people. We live in a dangerous wilderness with dangerous animals. Any civilized people are allowed refuge against the harsh world. You are no different."

"Well, we still owe you our thanks," Banion added. Gazing around the dark house, he was growing a little anxious. He grabbed the map from his belongings and stared at it intently, finally placing his finger on the eastern edge of the map. "So where exactly are we?"

"You are in the town of Red Mountain, the western edge of the civilized northlands."

"Red Mountain?" Banion quizzed, pointing at the map. "Is this the wilderness outpost shown on this map?"

"Oh my, no. The wilderness outpost was destroyed nearly ten years ago by the Shush. Now we are the extreme fringe of the world."

"Now what do we do?" Jared asked, feeling a little odd to be standing in the middle of a stranger's house. "Do we wait for it, I mean the Shush, to go away?"

"Oh my, no." The pale man smiled and motioned the mercenary team into the next room of his house.

As the companions followed him, they were awestruck by what they saw. The adjacent room was equipped with large windows; light and people were visible through the enormous panes of glass. For a moment, they were all confused by what they saw. Drawing closer to the window, they could see an enormous underground street carved into the earth itself. Streetlights were posted in regular intervals, lit by candles. The light flooded the street and the team could see dozens of other homes lining the road, each one with a doorway leading into the wondrous byway. People were milling about in the street, talking and laughing. Children were playing, chasing a red wooden ball. The scene was serene and totally unexpected. Above ground, the town looked like a bunch of trenches with chimneys sticking out of the earth. But underground, there was a beautiful city housing thousands of prosperous people.

"Amazing," Tani said, staring out of the window, green eyes wide open, absorbing his surroundings intently.

"We live in fear of the world above, but down here, sheltered in the earth, we live happy lives. Follow me, I will take you to the town inn." Stepping forward, the pasty man opened a finely crafted wooden door, allowing the soft candlelight from the streetlights to pour into his dark home. He moved out into the street, urging Nova 7 to follow.

As the team moved into the street, patrons of the town stared intently at the newcomers. Suspicion quickly turned to warmth. Many of the townsfolk rushed to greet them, saying hello and nodding in respect. Having been in the wilds for many months, the team members were stunned by the warm reception. It took them all a brief second to collect their thoughts and remember their manners. Warmly, they returned the greetings. Feeling more at ease, they mercenary team followed their gracious host through the twisting streets of the town.

The earth hid an enormous town. With hundreds and hundreds of homes, the town spread out into the earth in many directions. Following the man through the twisting tunnels, they were all in awe, feeling as if they had passed into some ancient fairy tale. Smiling and at ease, the members of Nova 7 let out a sigh of relief. They had made it across the wilderness and risked their very lives to do so. Seeing such warmth in a joyous people was refreshing.

After traveling nearly a mile underground, the pasty man paused before an enormous den built in the earth. The front of the inn was buzzing with activity. On the front porch, two old-timers were rocking in rickety chairs, spitting chunks of tobacco into an old spattered spittoon. As the team approached, they tipped their tattered hats and smiled. Banion tipped his hat back at the two old men and felt nostalgic for his own home. The image made his heart lift and he shook his head in amazement; it was good to be back in civilized lands.

"You can find shelter, rest, and food inside. We don't get too many travelers so don't be too surprised if you are mobbed by the locals." Bowing to Nova 7, the gracious man said farewell. "I need to get back home. I was in the middle of cooking dinner. Good luck."

Waving back at him, they pushed the doors open and stepped into the lodge. They passed into the main hall, finding the room cluttered with tables and chairs. Every table was full and noisy laughter rolled out while rampant chatter rose from the patrons. As they moved inside, everyone in the inn turned to greet them. A great quiet came over the patrons as they sized up the newcomers.

"Travelers!" A man stood up from his table. He motioned to his friends, who all stood up and vacated the table. "Come over here and take a breather!"

Unable to believe the gesture, Banion's face turned bright red as the gracious townsfolk eagerly waited for them to sit.

Witnessing their good will, the team members moved over and took the seats. As the mercenary team sat down, the townsfolk didn't return to their own gossip, instead waiting anxiously for the newcomers to start a conversation.

Feeling themselves to be the center of attention, they tried not to stare back. Finally the awkward silence was broken by a bar patron.

"Where do you hail from, travelers?"

Taking a moment to consider the situation, Banion motioned for one of the tribals to respond. Tani took the lead and cleared his throat, feeling that he had to at least properly annunciate for the enthralled audience. "We have just pressed out from the western wilderness."

A shocked silence followed. After a brief moment of stillness, whispering arose around them. Finally the same boisterous man who had given his table away took the lead and addressed them once more.

"Did you say you came from the western wilderness?" he said in awe.

"Yes, we passed out of the west."

"Impossible!" a patron shouted at the back of the bar. "No one has passed out of the western reaches in all my years! Nothing exists beyond the Great Shush wastes! It is not possible that you came out of the frozen western wasteland."

"We get that a lot." Jared laughed dryly, thinking about their original trek out of the blazing western wastelands on their passage from Scarskin many moons ago. "I assure you, the passage out of the west was not pleasant. We braved many dangers to reach this town."

"How far have you come?" a woman squeaked from the back of bar.

"Hundreds of miles," Banion responded. "We made landfall on a great river that emptied into the sea."

"The sea?" a man gasped. "You've seen the ocean?"

"Yes, we pushed in from the ocean into the interior of the continent," Tani confirmed.

"You saw the great waters? You saw the ocean? What an amazing journey. What has inspired your travels?"

For a moment, the members of Nova 7 looked at each other with uneasy glances. None of them were too comfortable telling a room full of people that there was a nuclear warhead in the black case on the floor.

"We were on a scouting expedition," Banion finally conjured a lie.

Nodding, the crowd was satisfied.

"Have you any news about the war?" a man quizzed them.

"The war?" Mineera felt the hair on the back of her neck stand on end. Back to reality; the answer would not be pleasant and she knew it. Secretly she wished that the war had ended during their epic journey but she knew they would not be so lucky.

"The war against the Reaper Kai. Do you have any news?"

"No, we have been in the wilds a great many months. Any news you have is more current than our own."

"Rasheed, the Steel Crag Mining Guild, and the Mord Tech Empire have been destroyed. Last we heard, the only empire that remains is the Iron Kai. Darkness is spreading and nearly all the great houses have been swept aside."

"That is grave news indeed," Mineera responded. Instinctively, after hearing the news, everyone in Nova 7 looked at the black resin case for reassurance. Thankfully, the sinister weapon was still resting on the floor near the table. Their crusade had not been in vain; the Reaper Kai were winning the war.

Trying to change the subject, Jared looked up from the table towards the barkeep. "We've traveled many weeks and could use a good warm meal. Is there a kitchen?"

"Of course!" The barkeep moved forward with menus. Once they were placed in front of them, the team members grabbed them and got lost in their contents. The diversion was subtle but just enough to get the patrons back to their own gossip and local news. As the locals left them alone, Banion looked around the table with a dire look on his brow. Looking back once more at the nuclear warhead shrouded in the black resin case, his companions knew that the responsibility of their quest was far from over, and a drastic reality settled over them. Even after months spent in the wastelands and the wilds, the war was still raging and their purpose had never been more apparent. The Reaper Kai were on the verge of winning the war, and the hope that the warhead would not be used was a distant thought. Heroes and butchers; Nova 7 was on the verge of destiny.

As they sank into their chairs, weary exhaustion passed over them. Soon the chatter overtook them once more and the patrons began to spin tales and legends about their home in the wilderness. Listening to the tales, the team members took a brief reprieve from the enormous responsibility of their quest. With glassy eyes, Nova 7 was transported to a distant time, a time when desperate actions led the world to ruin...

Chapter 6
The Day the Sky Rained Ash

"Can't we stop?" a small girl whined, holding a tattered doll in her right hand. She was dressed in a tiny red coat with white lacy frill near the collar. As she spoke, her father did not seem to respond; he only looked at her without a single hint of color in his cheeks. The man was lost in thought, and for good reason.

"We can't stop. I am sorry, my love, but we cannot. We have many more miles to go and the daylight is beginning to wane."

"I want to go home." The little girl spoke in a resolute voice, taking care to step over a mud puddle along the trail leading into the wilderness.

"We have no home. Not anymore." Her father's tone was dire.

"Why? Why can't we go back? All of our friends stayed home. Why are we out here?"

"We are out here because I love you very much. All of us…" he motioned to the hundreds of other refugees in front and behind them on the trail. "All of us are out here because we love our families."

"I want my toys," she whined as she continued to walk, her pink pants stained in mud from the long journey.

"I'll get you new ones."

"Where's Mom?"

"Mom decided to stay in the city."

"I want to go back to her."

"No," he said, maintaining his constant motion. He didn't tell the young child that her mother was dead, disintegrated in a plume of nuclear fire. The child's mom had lived on the coast in one of the great cities, a city that had been hit by a nuclear warhead from enemies across the sea. He would never tell his child what happened to her mother.

"I want to go to her house and play. I want to watch movies with her and I want to go now!"

"I don't care what you want!" he shouted at her. The recent events had finally worn down his fortitude. He shook with rage as tears streamed down his face. Collapsing to the ground, he knelt in the mud and began to sob.

Seeing his distress, the young girl was initially taken aback by his strange behavior. But after seeing his anguish and sorrow, she grew quiet. Walking near to him, she squatted down and looked into his face. Smiling, she spoke softly. "I love you, Daddy. Don't cry."

Clutching his daughter tightly, he sobbed and held her in his arms. She was the only thing in the world that meant anything to him. All of their material possessions, money, and gadgets were all gone. Everything that had distinguished him in life from others was all gone. His splendid fishing boat and expensive clothes were now in his silent home, the home that had probably already been looted by the frenzied mobs of hungry citizens who no longer had a viable food supply. Everything the man had used to bolster his self worth after divorcing his wife three years prior was gone. He had told himself fanciful lies, that he was a success and that his possessions made him important. In reality, no amount of splendid clothes or speedboats could fill the void in his heart. Deep down, the only thing that really mattered to him was family. He had been so arrogant, so lost. In the blink of an eye, everything that made him matter was gone. The only thing that remained was his precious daughter, a child with his own blood flowing through her.

It was a hard lesson to learn. Most of the inhabitants of the great cities were convinced that help would arrive. No help arrived. As the days passed after the nuclear blasts had reduced the most prominent centers of civilization to ash-filled wastelands, the food supply ran out. Gangs of murderers and thugs hit the streets in search of sustenance. As they killed each other like wild animals, the cities turned into places of death and suffering.

Some people joined mighty war bands that raided local shops. Some of the gangs had hundreds of televisions and microwave ovens. It was comical to look at the wretched humans, clawing at each other, stealing and murdering. Once mighty, the entire race had disintegrated into savages in a matter of days. It took thousands of years to build the great empires but only a week to see it all come to an end. So vain and arrogant they were, sitting atop piles of treasure, treasure that was useless without electricity, treasure that could not feed the body or soul. And so the foolish tyrants sat upon the piles of loot like ancient dragons, amassing more useless items from a world that would never reign again. And so, like the dragons of old, they too would pass into memory.

It was so strange for the man, in the middle of the forest with his tiny daughter, to understand it all. The useless junk with which he had surrounded himself could never laugh or cry. The piles of plastic could never sing songs like his little daughter. The only thing that mattered was family. With tear-filled eyes, he stared at his child and hugged her tightly. The only thing that mattered was family. The only thing that mattered was his tiny daughter, smeared with mud, holding her tattered doll.

"I love you too. I'm sorry that I snapped at you. I'm just tired, is all. We need to get going; we still have a few more miles to go before we find shelter."

Skipping down the muddy trail, the little girl in her red coat bounced onward with a smile, hope her only ally. He stood there, motionless for a brief moment, staring at her in awe. His legacy was racing onward, down the trail towards her destiny. Looking around, the man saw others like him, with families. Hundreds of sullen refugees were passing by him with broken looks. Most stared at the ground and were unable to even speak. Others sobbed in frequent bursts of terror, brought to the brink of their sanity by memories of their lost lives.

Sighing, the man rushed off down the trail so that he could keep sight of his beloved daughter. For nearly three miles, the formation of people moved through the forest, digging a trail into the muddy earth, staining the forest with ill memories, forever cursing the place with their sorrow. The raw emotion of their plight permeated the land and stuck to it. Images of despair and memories of sorrow would forever haunt the muddy trail meandering through the forest. Part of each traveler died that day. Parts of their soul had been stripped from them, forever trapped in those haunted woods.

Passing out of the forest, the column of the lost finally reached a valley, secluded between two steep canyon walls made of rock and forested slopes. The walls of the canyon rose hundreds of feet into the air. In the heart of the valley was an open pasture, filled with horses and other animals. And in the center of the valley was an old ranch, a place that had existed for nearly a century, comprised of a dozen scattered buildings.

In old times, the canyon had once held a small town. Now, a powerful rancher had bought the entire valley and had left the ghost town intact. As the refugees poured out of the forest, they were greeted by a man in his fifties with white hair, wearing a frumpy brown cowboy hat. He had a walking stick and rested heavily upon it. As the front of the formation reached the aged man, he considered the ragged gathering, now in the hundreds. Carefully looking at them, he nodded and could not turn them away.

"Welcome to Red Mountain," he called out in a booming voice. "I don't have much, but you will all have shelter and we can share the food of this valley."

Relieved, many in the crowd began to weep. They had spent many days making their way through the heart of the wilderness and had now managed to stumble upon a secluded paradise within the forest, a refuge from the terrible war that had taken everything from them.

As the last of the people arrived from the woods, the crowd began to press on into the abandoned buildings made of smooth worn gray wood. Eagerly taking shelter, they felt that each of them had succeeded in claiming a small victory.

Their joy would be short lived.

Standing in the center of the old town, the aged rancher looked into the dark sky. A wild, powerful wind was pressing in from the western reaches of the world, the same part of the world that had been ravaged by nuclear fire. Blinking, he could barely understand what was happening. He stared in awe as the western sky grew dark. As he stood there, motionless, others looked at him and finally turned their gazes toward the sinister sky.

Gasping in terror, the horde of refugees stood transfixed, looking at the sky. An event that had never been witnessed before was unfolding. Like gray tendrils, the tortured clouds seemed to spring heavy fingers. Dust and debris from the cities, laden with radioactive ash, was being circulated by the winds. Pushed by the strong winds, the unnatural clouds heaved in the distance, overtaking the forest that the refugees had just escaped.

In that moment, dread filled them all. The heavy fingers of the clouds began to billow and arced downward from the tortured sky. Radioactive debris swirled and rained down upon the forest as if the clouds were gouging the land with their spiny fingers. Pockets of the forest were blanketed in the toxic ash from the wasted cities.

For nearly ten minutes, the crowd stared in horror at the unnatural storm overtaking the forest. Most simply did not or could not believe what they were witnessing.

"Oh my God," the owner of the ranch whispered, his face growing pale. Frantic, he surveyed all of the houses on his land and saw that many had windows that were broken and roofs with gaping holes. Looking back at the radioactive fallout raining down, he knew that he had to think quickly or hundreds would die.

Polarized by the strange events, he yelled and shouted so that all could hear his voice.

"Take refuge in here!" He pointed at the largest of all the buildings in the abandoned town. In the center of the ghost town was an enormous, splendid inn that was his primary residence. The mighty red building had been painstakingly restored and was strong against the elements. The refugees, seeing the angry clouds spewing toxic debris, did not think twice about the offer. Rushing inside, the rabble of lost people took refuge in the Red Mountain Inn.

Though protected from the normal elements of nature, the building could not withstand the radioactive storm about to overtake it. Screaming, the owner of the inn asked for help and many who were strong and willing rushed to his aid. Grabbing wooden boards and planks, the people began to cover the windows and any opening they could find. A group of men scurried to the top of the inn and began to cover the chimneys with planks of wood and sheets of plastic, sealing the building from the sinister storm of fallout about to rain down upon them.

Rushing and working to save their very lives, the refugees were able to protect the Red Mountain Inn from the harsh radioactive storm.

Some people crowded into the inn's dining hall, where two of the small windows were not covered. The horrified people stared out of the windows and watched as the land died around them.

The dense cloud of black dust overtook the land. Several low-hanging wisps of the fallout cloud landed in the valley, dragging across the ground and depositing the toxic ash as they went. Tons of radioactive debris rained down all over the area, giving a lethal dose of unseen radiation to the victims hapless enough to encounter it. The plants were immediately killed, their life-force blasted away at a molecular level. A herd of deer near the north end of canyon wall were trying to escape the strange clouds but were too slow. A tendril of dust rained down, coating the animals in the fallout. After only a few seconds of contact, the deer began to vomit and retch as the radiation dealt immense damage to their tissues. It took only ten minutes for the noble creatures to succumb to the poison. Lying down upon the ground, the entire herd died; not a single one of them was spared.

And so they sat in horror, watching the radioactive fallout scour the land, leaving pockets of poison upon the earth that would last for thousands and thousands of years. The howling winds battered the inn and the inhabitants sat in total silence, watching the world they all loved disappear forever. Each of them knew that they could never go back; each of them knew that the world would be permanently changed. As the sun set, the winds intensified. In the darkness, no one slept, not even the exhausted children. Instead, they all listened to the howling wind, filled with deadly toxic ash, pelting the landscape...

"Our people are descendants of the refugees who came to this valley nearly a thousand years ago. When the fallout clouds left, the landscape was marred with the toxins. The vegetation fell away and any animal crossing these toxic zones passed into death. Upon your travel into this valley, you could see places on the earth where nothing grows even to this day. These patches of earth will always be toxic, always deadly." The orator continued his story while staring at Nova 7. Each of them was lost in thought as they listened to the horrible story.

"The trail that passes out of the western wilderness is haunted to this day. It is known as the Trail of Sorrow. Somehow, the traumatic events of the past stained the land and that place. Only the most courageous of our people pass into those woods. I fear that place will always be haunted by the memories of that dark day so long ago.

"As we came out of hiding, we found ways to cultivate the land. We grew great pastures of wheat and hunted the animals of this valley. As time passed, we shunned the world above and sought refuge in the ground. Building burrows, we finally began to connect our homes using underground roads. After hundreds of years, we have a safe and happy society, built from the remnants and lessons we learned from the old world.

"We have vowed to never forget the past. We tell the story of when the sky rained fire so that we will never try to embrace the technologies of old, the technologies that brought the world to ruin. We tell these stories so that we will never make the same mistakes that our ancestors made. We have embraced peace and scorn warfare. We pray that neither the nuclear fire nor the great fallout clouds will be seen in our fragile world ever again."

As the man finished his tale, Nova 7 looked at each other with uneasy glances. The very weapon that had caused all the strife and suffering was resting in a black resin case next to the table. The same type of weapon that had ravaged the valley and killed millions was resting quietly on the floor. As the haunting images filled their minds, and the sinister tale still stung their ears, Nova 7 knew it was not by chance that they had come to this place, on the edge of the world. It was fortune that brought them here so that they could hear the horror and power of the weapon they now carried with them.

Fate and destiny had brought each of them to that inn so that they could witness the past. It was an omen that none of them would ever forget, an omen of future horror in which they would take part. Already bound to a new history unfolding, each member of Nova 7 prayed silently that they were doing the right and just action by delivering the weapon to the forces desperately battling tyrannical evil.

Chapter 7
Fate Evolved

A gunshot rang out. The man turned just in time to see a shadowy figure on the balcony. A burst of blood erupted from a wound in the center of his chest. He clenched his teeth, the scar on his face contorting in a twisted mass of pain. The man in bed clutched the wound and his eyes rolled back. The gun fell from his hand. The assassin on the balcony jumped into the palace garden below, hidden by the shadows of the night.

"Mineera…" the man gasped to the stunned woman standing in the doorway.

She ran to his side and pressed her hand into the warm bloody wound on his chest, tears running down her face. She was panic-stricken, and try as she might, she could not stop the flow of blood erupting from his chest.

"Don't leave…" she whimpered, and his hand clutched hers. "Damn it, don't die."

Her love was strong, but death was stronger. The man's eyes grew dark, and his hand fell from hers. He ceased to stir, and sadness welled up in her fragile soul. Mineera's grief was overwhelming as the tormented rancher died in her arms.

"Banion…" Mineera whispered in terror, cradling the lifeless body.

Within a flash, the vision changed.

Jared was standing over Banion's lifeless body with sword in hand. Crimson blood was flowing off the blade and a wicked, hateful scowl covered the tribal's twisted face. Sneering, he flexed his muscles in anger, shaking his sword as blood spewed from its serrated edge...

Sitting straight up in bed, she screamed out, "Banion!"

Frantic, she looked around the inn room and found it completely devoid of chaos and carnage. The strange dream that she had dreamt her entire life, the dream about the night Banion was attacked within the palace of Rasheed, had dissipated after the epic event. This was the first time since that intense night that the dream had come back to her. Strangely enough, in the dream, Mineera failed to save Banion from the assassin.

Still trembling and covered in sweat, she wiped the perspiration from her brow and buried her head in her hands as she brought herself under control.

It was also the first time for a long while that she had seen the vision of Jared standing over Banion's lifeless body with a bloody sword. That image had been so disconcerting to her that she had almost ended Jared's life in a fit of madness while they traveled through the Iron Gate ruins beneath the Concrete Barrens.

The mixture of both dreams had rattled Mineera to the core and she was extremely nervous about the ordeal. Trying to calm herself, she took several deep breaths.

"Mineera..." a whisper broke the darkness.

Startled by the sound, she opened her eyes and saw a point of light hovering in her inn room, right next to the door. She blinked several times, wondering if she was still dreaming.

"Mineera..." the whisper erupted once more and the tiny point of light flashed intensely.

"What do you want?" she quizzed the glowing shard of light near the door.

"Come to me," it urged her. With that, the tiny point of light passed through the solid wooden door into the hallway beyond.

Rising, she moved quickly after the strange image haunting her nighttime. Opening the door, Mineera stepped into the hallway and found everything quiet. The team had taken shelter in the underground inn for the night to get some much-needed rest.

As she stared about the hall, the tiny point of light revealed itself near the stairway. Flashing brightly, it urged her to follow.

Bounding after the tiny point of light, she never perceived someone else in the hallway. With his door cracked open, Jared was peering into the hallway, clutching the Scar Blade. He peered out the door and saw a light reflecting down the hallway. Seeing Mineera rush towards the stairs, the tribal was curious. Just a moment ago, Jared had heard Mineera screaming inside her room. The sound was so shrill and piercing, he was rocked from his own dream world.

Stumbling down the staircase in the dark, Mineera moved into the main hall of the inn. The tiny point of light zipped through the room with a rapid *zing* and passed through the main door of the inn into the underground street beyond. Keeping up the chase, she hurried onward, crashing into several tables, knocking chairs to the floor. Bursting out of the inn, Mineera found herself on a dimly lit street. The underground surroundings were stifling and only small candles hung from posts illuminated the dark passage.

Seeing the phantom light dash towards an exterior door which led outside the protection of the underground town, she rushed toward the entrance quickly. As she pulled back an enormous draw bolt, cold air streamed into the musty tunnel. Mineera charged outward into the dark night, tracking the tiny point of light as it zipped away from the open field above the town of Red Mountain. Blinking, she managed to catch sight of the tiny object disappearing into the forest a mere fifty yards away.

She kept running, passing over the iron pipes jutting out of the ground which acted as chimneys for the town below. As she moved into the forest, the darkness seemed to envelop her once more. A sickly feeling passed over her as a series of images began to play in her mind again and again. Whispers from the past began to invade her senses once more, angry and spiteful emotions driving her towards sorrow. Shaking off the eerie emotion, she caught sight of a dark shape in the trees only a few yards ahead.

Stumbling on a tree root, Mineera crashed to the ground in the darkness. She struck her head, and a jagged cut formed on her skull immediately, with a trickle of blood erupting from the wound. Dizzy, she crawled on her hands and knees through the forest toward the nearby shadowy structure.

After a few minutes of toil, still crawling on her hands and knees, she came to the foot of an ancient church, or rather the ruins of an ancient church. Blinking in the darkness, she could see the pinnacle of light inside the ruins, near a collapsed marble altar. Crawling inside, she knelt before the wondrous light. As she did, the pinnacle of light increased in size, spinning round and round. With each rotation, a bright flash of light was emitted. Soon, the spinning point of light flattened and turned into a shimmering disk. Holding her hand to shield her eyes from the light, she watched the disk spin faster and faster. A shimmering form emerged from the glowing disk, a bright outline with no real features, only a rough human shape. Seeing the familiar image, Mineera bowed in reverence to the heavenly being.

"Mineera…" it whispered.

"What is your will?" she asked respectfully, gripping her hands together and bowing again.

"It seems that the first time we met, you were also bleeding. Come forward, child."

Hearing the call of the spirit, she crawled forward, head still bleeding. As she came before the serene visage, it moved forward and placed its ethereal hand upon her forehead. As the glowing form made contact with her flesh, she felt her skin itch and then explode into a burning sensation. Praying, she let the heavenly power surge through her. Within a few seconds, the wound upon her head had closed and the pain was gone. Bowing before the spirit once more, Mineera paid tribute.

"That should sooth your pain."

"Thank you for your gracious gift. I live to serve you. Why have you come to me?"

"Your dreams are still guiding you."

"My dreams?" she asked in confusion. "What dreams?"

"The dream you had of Banion, dying in your arms."

"I don't understand. That event happened long ago."

"No. It is only a metaphor for what will happen unless you save him. He is still in danger, as is the rest of humanity. If you cannot keep him alive to fulfill his destiny, the devil will claim a victory and subjugate the land under his cruel dominion."

"What am I to do? I don't understand."

"You will understand in time. Keep Banion safe. He is still needed to save all of humanity."

"Please give me more, I need more information. Is he in danger?"

Just as she spoke, a crack erupted from behind her. Someone was lingering in the shadows behind them and had just broken a branch while moving closer.

Whirling around, Mineera looked into the darkness.

"Navezgane…" the shimmering entity whispered.

"What?"   Mineera turned to the heavenly entity. "Navezgane?"

"The tribal warrior is watching from the shadows…"

Stepping from the darkness, Jared was breathing heavily. One hand was clutching the mighty blue steel Scar Blade while his other hand rested upon the animal totem around his neck. He had a frantic look on his face, almost vengeful as he approached Mineera and the shimmering entity.

"What is this?" he asked in an irate tone, looking directly at the heavenly form near the altar.

Blinking in amazement, she looked at his face. "You can see it?"

"Yes. What the hell is going on? What is that thing and why did it say my name?" Jared rubbed the raven totem with an almost insane look in his eyes.

"Your name?"   Mineera asked, confused, looking at the shimmering entity.

"Navezgane…" it whispered again.

"Stay back!" Jared shouted, holding his sword in front of him.

"I don't understand," Mineera said in an astonished tone, rising to her feet.

The entity began to dissipate. Its form shifted slightly and began to lose shape. The dense shimmering light fragmented and came apart like a wisp of fog. In the blink of an eye, the vision was gone.

"Did Tani tell you about me?" Jared demanded with venom in his voice, rubbing the raven totem more intensely with his thumb. When Mineera was unable to respond, he jumped forward and asked her again, this time more frantic. "How do you know about Navezgane? Did Tani tell you?"

"No, I don't know what you're talking about!" She threw her hands up in the air.

"You need to leave it be. It's not real, none of it. No matter what Tani has told you, the story isn't real."

"Tani hasn't told me anything! Please just calm down."

"I can't…" But he did grow calmer, his gaze shifting off into the darkness. "Maybe I misunderstood. I'm sorry." With that, the troubled youth began to walk from the edge of the eerie ruins of the church that had been overtaken by the forest. As he sought to escape her presence, images and visions began to fill his mind.

"I don't want any part of this!" Jared looked up into the dark sky as if taunting heaven itself. The more he ran from the church, the more the visions came back to haunt him. In that moment, he remembered the sinister church built atop the mesa in the village of Song River. The entire church was a tribute to him. Inside the sanctum, pictures were scrawled on the wall, depicting Jared and deeds that he had not yet done. It had taken the youth many months to drive all of the images from his mind. In the blink of an eye, all of the feelings of doubt and hesitation came back to him in a torrent of indecision. He didn't want to believe; he simply didn't want to believe.

Frantic, he charged out of the tree line. A rage settled over him and he looked down at his chest, where the sinister burnt raven totem was still hanging. Frustrated, he took the wooden totem and threw it to the ground. As it struck the earth, the tiny eyes seemed to erupt like a volcano. Crimson light emanated from the eyes of the totem. Staring hypnotically at the strange relic, he wanted to run away and leave it on the ground. But the more he stared at it, the more he felt naked without it. It was now part of him, like his bones and blood. It was now part of him, like his sword and his nightmares.

Shaking his head in dismay, he knelt down and picked up the wooden relic. As he grasped it, a presence seemed to draw near. Feeling the soothing companionship of the long-dead shaman contained within the relic, Jared placed it around his neck once more.

For something that he hated so much, it felt so right to him, the power of the ancient raven totem filling him with warmth and sickness at the same time. He wanted to escape its power but simultaneously, it was intoxicating. Grasping the raven in the darkness, he shook his head in dismay. Even though he had attempted to disregard the powerful omens scrawled upon the walls of the church in Song River, it appeared to him that fate did not care about his needs or wants. He was a legend, some sort of savior, and his name was Navezgane, not Jared.

Dread and humility filled the tribal. As he stood motionless, he became aware that Mineera had descended from the forest and was near him. He turned to her with an apologetic look on his face. Staring at Mineera intently, he said, "I'm sorry. I have a lot on my mind."

"It's all right. I'm sorry you had to witness part of my world. I didn't want you to be frightened."

"I'm not frightened of what I saw back there, I'm frightened of myself."

Nodding, Mineera reached out and rubbed his shoulder. "Let's get indoors. I don't think this area is safe at night."

Jared nodded back, and the two companions moved off towards the inn and the underground town of Red Mountain.

While they traveled, they were both silent. Mineera was pondering the strange series of events. The spirit world chooses its champions very carefully, both good and evil. A spirit cannot make itself known unless it wants to. Looking at Jared carefully, she was suspicious of him. The heavenly creature knew of Jared and knew more about him than even Mineera did. This fact piqued her interest and she wondered what his place in the grand scheme of things was. The spirit had come looking for Mineera that night to warn her about Banion. But in a strange twist of fate, Jared was now part of the mystery as well. What was Navezgane? How did the tribal fit into the picture? And why could the tribal see the heavenly entity?

Hiding her feelings and her reservations about the boy, she observed him in hurried glances. As he walked, he was mumbling, clutching the raven totem tightly. He was lost to the totem, lost to its power. Thinking about the strange night and its events, she wondered about her dreams once more. The image of Jared standing over Banion's body with his sword stained in blood roared to the forefront once more. So many times had she seen the horrid image in her dreams. What did it all mean? Why had she seen the same thing over and over again? In the past, she had discarded this notion, feeling that evil had been sending her dreams to corrupt her and drive her from her companions. Why did these hideous nightmares urge her to kill Jared time and time again? Why did the voices that had plagued her soul while she grappled with the devil himself in the Iron Gate ruins urge her to kill Jared? Months of visions had been sent to her, tempting her to commit murder and kill the tribal warrior. She had once thought that she was paranoid about Jared, but maybe, just maybe, there was something more to it.

Hearing the warning in her heart, she decided to heed the voice from heaven. She would make sure that Banion survived to fulfill his destiny. Staring at Jared, she wondered if there would come a time when she would need to protect Banion from the tribal. Staring at the raven totem, her heart grew cold. As the night wore on, the two companions reached the safety of the town. Passing inside, they retreated back to their rooms.

The morning sun would come all too soon and it would be time once more for Nova 7 to press onward to the safety of Iron Kai territory with the holy grail of all weapons in tow. Mineera would not sleep for the rest of the night. Instead, she would ponder the mystery of Jared and Banion.

Chapter 8
Convergence of the Oracles

There was a nervous silence as all of the strangers looked uneasily at one another. With quick glances, each of the men sitting around the bonfire assessed one another with mistrust. The silence was eerie. Finally, Matthew Moralis, the Oracle of Justice, rose to his feet and cleared his throat.

Eleven pairs of eyes watched him carefully, hiding their fears deep down.

His voice cracking, the aged man in blue robes began to speak. "My name is Matthew Moralis; I am a descendant of Ceibla Moralis. I trust all of you know that name? I trust all of you know the story of Ceibla Moralis or you wouldn't be sitting here before me."

Unable to answer him, the attendants responded with complete silence. None of the men wanted to admit that they had been contacted by some sort of shimmering spirit, asked to leave their families and battle against the will of evil. It was one thing to see such an image, but to admit such a strange occurrence out loud, in front of others, was something completely different. Most of them had struggled over many months, feeling that they had gone utterly insane and that the images and dreams were nothing more than hallucinations. But to see other people afflicted with the same strange dreams was shocking on a spiritual level.

Most often, religion is something that is felt and remains locked inside one's mind and heart. To have the cover of seclusion stripped away and the faith laid bare is uncomfortable at best. Each of these men who had been brought to their current location by dreams was suffering from such thoughts, unable to comprehend that others had similar experiences. At first, the thought that others had seen the same things, dreamed the same events, seemed like an invasion of privacy on the most profound level. But, after a few moments of reflection, it was becoming refreshing to think that each of them was not alone. As Matthew Moralis stood before them, each of the men, twelve strong, reflected upon the series of events that had brought them to that meeting in the wilds of the Darken Realm.

"I know that all of you have been brought here by a higher power. I myself have dreamed of horrid battles and have been contacted by a heavenly being. I am assuming that all of you have dealt with the same issues, been driven from your homes and families to serve the spirits. Just know that here, you have a new family amongst others like you. We are all bound and tied to each other by the power of our faith and the privilege of our duty to that faith. Each of you has been chosen to be here and we cannot resist such a call. Now tell me, tell us all about your visions and dreams so that we can all seek to understand their meaning."

Sheepishly, a man rose to his feet. Still a little nervous about everything, he simply stared into the fire, trying to ignore the people around him. He took a deep breath, and words and emotions began to spill forth. "My name is Samuel, the Oracle of Saints. I don't know why I have been called. The spirit told me that I must fight but I am no soldier. I have strong faith but little courage. I'm not sure why I have been chosen."

"Oracle of Saints?" Another spoke, feeling a connection with the man. "The spirit called me the Oracle of Heaven."

"And I have been given the title Oracle of Justice," Matthew Moralis contributed with a look of recognition of his own.

"I was told to bring these." A huge man with a stocky frame moved over to his belongings. Grunting, he lifted an enormous bundle of objects covered in a cloth tarp. Returning to the bonfire, he uncovered twelve spears underneath the tarp. He grabbed one of them and showed the weapon to each of the men. Each wooden spear was nine feet in length, its tip almost resembling a harpoon. A jagged, razor-sharp tip had been forged of pure silver and shimmered brightly in the light of the bonfire. "I was told to craft these weapons. I am the Oracle of Arms. Since there are twelve of us, I assume we each need one of these."

The men nodded solemnly; the story coming together was an eerie one.

"The Oracle of Spirit." A man stood and bowed before the congregation.

"Oracle of Courage," another added.

"Oracle of Strength," yet another revealed.

As they went around the bonfire, they were also introduced to the Oracles of Miracles, Order, Valor, and Temperance. Finally, the last of them rose.

"The Oracle of Dreams," the final man said.

Sizing them up, Matthew Moralis nodded in slight recognition. "So there are twelve Oracles standing here and now we have weapons of some sort. Have you all had the dream about *her*?"

All of them nodded in agreement. The Oracle of Valor spoke to confirm these visions. "I've seen her many times in my dreams. A woman garbed in blue robes with dark skin. Her eyes are brilliant blue and she is gripped with much strife and is tormented by the will of evil itself."

"Who is she?" the Oracle of the Spirit asked in a quizzing tone.

"She is our leader, our prophet."

"Our leader? Where is she? Shouldn't she have been summoned to us so that she can lead us?"

"No." The Oracle of Saints spoke in a resolute tone. "My dreams have told me that she is currently battling her way to us."

"Battling?"

"We are at war," the Oracle of Courage contributed.

"War with whom? I am no soldier."

"War with the Reaper Kai. The actions of our ancestors have brought the world to ruin. We are all descendants of the Lost Order of Ceibla Moralis. We've been brought here to battle the Reaper Kai."

"Are the whispers and rumors of the war even true?" the Oracle of Heaven asked.

"Yes, they are very true. I just fought in a bitter campaign in the northlands. The last bastion of freedom, the mighty city of Stonen, came under Reaper Kai attack. I battled in the streets of the great city with Emperor Gunther himself. These are not mere rumors, the enemy's goal is absolute," added Matthew Moralis, the Oracle of Justice.

"So we have spears and our faith as weapons. What now? Where do we go?"

"I think I know. Well, partially," the Oracle of Dreams interjected. "I've seen a place every night, in my dreams. There is an open valley, nestled under a mountain range to the north. The entire ground is littered with the dead. A woman, our prophet I believe, garbed in flowing blue robes, is kneeling before the graves of all the fallen soldiers. Smoke is rising from the valley below where the great battle has just ended. She rises to her feet and turns to me. With a look of confusion, she stares at me in disbelief. We need to find this valley. We find this valley, we find our prophet, we find our leader."

"But where is this valley?"

"I'm not sure," the Oracle of Dreams answered.

"I might know. I'm drawn to the night sky. When I look into the dark sky, I'm always drawn to a constellation of stars, just after the sun sets. I think if we follow the stars and head in that general direction, it will mean something," the Oracle of Heaven concluded.

"Follow the stars?"

"Why not? It's no more ridiculous than what we have been experiencing over the past few months. We've been accosted by spirits and tormented by our dreams. Is it strange to follow the stars?"

"There we have it. We follow the stars and dreams to our prophet. Does anyone else have any more visions of insight to add to this quest?" Matthew Moralis asked.

"What about the creature?"

"Creature?"

"Yes, the demon," another added.

Some of the Oracles were confused, since not all of them had seen such visions or dreams.

"There is some sort of monster, born from the underworld itself. The demon is covered in faces, moving faces that are screaming."

"They are trapped souls that have been enslaved by the demon, forced inside the creature. The souls cannot rest while the demon lives and the demon feeds off their life-force, growing stronger with each soul it consumes. I have seen such visions also."

"As have I," the Oracle of Miracles confirmed.

Nodding and beginning to understand, the Oracle of Justice sighed and looked at the congregation. "We will find our leader, this prophet. We also have weapons, these spears tipped in pure silver. I'm assuming we'll use these spears to fight this creature, to fight this demon."

"We have more questions than answers at this point," one of the Oracles chuckled.

Hearing the laughter added some much-needed levity to the tense situation. Smiling, many of them broke into laughter as well. As the good feeling spread, the men looked at each other, their new family. Bound by destiny, called by the spirit world to battle, they were now fused together.

The meeting disintegrated and hunger broke over them. Settling down, they ate a meal under the stars. As the bright bonfire blazed on in the darkness, hope rose from the flames, twinkling in the shadows. With an air of good will, each of them spoke a silent prayer, a prayer that asked heaven itself for guidance to bring them all to *her*, the enigmatic woman from their dreams.

Chapter 9
Frontier Vineyards

"What the hell are you doing?" Jared asked, a look of shock on his face.

Banion had his assault rifle firmly pressed against his chest, and was moving forward slowly with a concerned look. The rest of the team was mystified by his actions and for good reason. After several weeks of travel, Nova 7 had pressed out of the wilderness and had found themselves increasingly within the confines of civilization. Sporadic farms and homesteads had been common over the last days of travel.

The team had passed into an open valley lined with withered grapevines. Hundreds of acres of grapes were currently dormant due to the cool winter conditions. Banion was leading his team through the fields with his gun at the ready.

"Is there something you know that we don't?" Tani asked, wondering if he should draw a weapon of his own.

"This is where it all began," Banion whispered.

"Where all what began?" Mineera quizzed, also confused by their leader's actions.

"The quest, the crusade that we're on."

"I don't get it."

"We've passed into the Frontier, the lands just beyond the great empires. This is the edge of the Iron Kai Empire, the land that you are standing on right now. This is where it all began, in the Frontier." Banion's trigger finger remained at the ready as he spoke.

It suddenly hit the tribals. They had been cast out of their home for the duration of twenty full moons as a rite of passage into manhood known as the Exile. When the two tribals escaped the forbidden wastelands, the first civilized town they had come upon was the hamlet of Pontiac City, a city on the edge of the world, in a part of the world known as the Frontier. Their leader was correct and finally, they understood what Banion was talking about. The mercenary team had passed into the Frontier and was now dangerously close to the war and battle lines. Nova 7 was now in harm's way, close to the conflict that had caused them to go on a journey of several thousand miles through the heart of the ruins of America.

A little misty eyed from the revelation, they were now concerned, as well. They were about to pass through the heart of the great war. Grabbing their own weapons, the tribals readied their sub-machine guns, holding them as they followed their leader through the abandoned vineyards.

War has many costs. To escape the conflict, the owners of this once-mighty vineyard had fled to safer, more remote areas, leaving behind the withered vines that had shriveled in the winter sun and harsh cold. Passing through the middle of the perfectly arranged rows, the mercenary team was ready for anything.

Mineera was the most settled of the group. Her keen sense of intuition had led her to believe that the area was free from danger. She could not perceive any hazard nor sense any ominous tidings. As a result, she calmly meandered through the vineyard, passing from row to row. Smiling, she exhaled and watched her breath crystallize in the air and jet from her mouth like a plume of fog. She shivered in the cold air, welcoming the warmth of the sun on the cloudless day.

Taking a brief moment, she stretched out her hand and grasped a withered stalk of grapes. The desiccated grapes had long since lost their precious moisture and now were nothing more than half-rotted raisins clinging precariously to the tattered vines. As she held several of the dried fruits, an eerie sensation washed over her. In that instance, she could feel the love and joy of the people who had tended to the fields in times of peace. Mineera got a very strong impression that this land was loved by many and was a source of great pride. To wander through the fields was a blessing and feeling the overwhelming sense of delight was a miracle. Soaking in the good will, she looked toward her foolish companions with a smile as they stalked about with guns at the ready. She wanted to tell them that everything was safe, but she didn't; it was more amusing to watch them stalk about like a pride of angry wolves hunting their prey. She simply stared at them and smiled. "Three Banions..." she whispered to herself.

The statement was profound. Over the long months, the crazed mercenary Banion had left a deep impression on the youths. They walked like him. They talked like him. They fought like him. As two perfect little clones of Banion himself, Jared and Tani were a testament to an odd parental relationship where Banion had taken the role of patron. The man who had lost so much had taught the two tribals so much. When they were fresh to the business, as Banion liked to call it, they were both raw and untested. Now they had a set of deadly skills and battle experience. Even though they looked like mere teenagers, they were profoundly changed, honed into fine instruments of war. Banion's ultimate legacy was the two tribals, who had learned nearly everything their mentor could teach them.

But where Banion was cruel and heartless, the tribals still had not yet experienced the true horrors of battle and war. They were armed with deadly combat experience but had yet to face death and were still untested in that regard. Mineera and Banion both had seen their share of death and carnage, an experience that had forever changed them. Banion sought to quell his demons with violence and Mineera fought her own demons with sheer grace, faith, and diplomacy. Both were opposite sides of the same coin.

Mineera's thoughts began to wander as the rest of her team moved closer to the abandoned homestead at the center of the great expanse of fields. Following Banion's hand signals, the tribals flanked the building and set up for what appeared to be some sort of ambush. As they trained their weapons on the door, Banion moved forward quickly to secure the area. Nodding at Jared, Banion signaled him to breach the door. The tribal crept forward and quietly turned the knob, freeing the mechanism from the doorframe. He motioned to Tani, who rushed inside with automatic weapon at the ready, pressing in toward the right side of the room. Jared criss-crossed behind him, securing the left side of the room. Banion closed in quickly and they went room to room, scanning the entire building within a matter of seconds.

"Clear!" Jared shouted out the front door, looking towards Mineera.

"I know," she said with a broad grin.

"You know?" Tani echoed, securing his weapon and returning to the courtyard to recover the nuclear warhead. "Why didn't you let us know the building was clear before we went in? I always get nervous when we do an entry."

"I enjoy watching all of you run about."

"Funny, real funny." Tani rolled his eyes at her.

"I have to have fun from time to time."

"Come on in, it's amazing." Jared motioned her inside.

Moving into the main entry of the house revealed a breathtaking sight. The stucco building was filled to the brim with art, ancient treasures from before the apocalypse. Towering bronze statues lined the entryway. Enormous paintings, some eight feet wide, covered the brittle, cracked walls. A sweeping spiral staircase ascended upwards into the manor. Nooks along the staircase were filled with finely crafted vases from a time and world long forgotten. Gasping, Mineera walked inside and spun around, taking in the wondrous sights. Blinking several times, she moved closer to the majority of the artwork to get a better look at it. She could barely believe that people had been that talented in the ancient times.

"Breathtaking."

"The whole house is like this." Banion moved into the entryway, his combat boots echoing on the white marble floor. "Much of the northlands were spared from the initial nuclear attack ages ago. Many examples of the ancient art world can be found in the houses of the wealthy, including this one. Some of the antiques are not just hundreds of years old but thousands of years old."

"I've never seen such things." Mineera spoke in a low tone. "The Reaper Kai never had art treasures; instead they reveled in other forms of amusement. Perversion and torture were the art forms of the Dark Order. I have never witnessed amazing portraits of sheer artistry such as this."

Though awestruck by the art, her reveling would be short lived. Cackling rose from near the spiral staircase. In addition to ascending into the top levels of the manor, the staircase also led into the basement and an enormous wine cellar. Jared and Tani both emerged with a bottle of wine in each of their hands. Smiling, they showed off their looted booty from the bowels of the manor house.

"That's stealing," Mineera protested.

"No way!" Tani was offended. "You should see the wine cellar. There are thousands of bottles of wine down there. The owners could never drink all of this. We're just helping them make room for more wine."

"Join us." Jared smiled.

Banion didn't need a second invitation. Grabbing one of Tani's bottles, he smiled back with a glimmer in his eye. He turned to Mineera, holding out his other hand. Seeing his invitation, she rolled her eyes and placed her hand in his. He pulled her forward, planting the wine bottle into her other hand.

"Maybe just one glass," she said.

"One glass?" Tani whined.

"Yeah, tonight is a celebration!" Jared laughed.

"Celebration?" she quizzed.

"Yeah, what moon is it?" Banion looked at the tribals.

"Seventeenth moon!" Tani responded quickly.

Hearing the response, she finally understood. The tribals had been exiled from their village for the duration of twenty moons. Seventeen moons had passed and only three more remained before the tribals could return home and take their place in Scarskin society. Smiling at them, she felt a sudden sadness. Twenty moons always seemed so far away. Now the end of their quest had arrived and soon the tribals would make their way back home. They had all known one another for so long, shared so many adventures, that it filled her with a sadness to think that soon their team would be broken apart and they would all go their separate ways. Thinking about such things made her feel that there was indeed something to celebrate. Smiling at them, she spoke in a triumphant tone. "Seventeen moons? We're celebrating seventeen moons and all you got was four bottles of wine? Get back down there and get some more wine! We have a party to attend!"

"That's the spirit." Jared smiled, placing his wine on the marble floor. Tani did the same and they disappeared down into the wine cellar for a few moments. Emerging from the basement once more, they were laden with several more bottles each. Laughing,

Nova 7 recovered their wine and moved to the back of the manor, where they found an enormous study with a fireplace. They lit a fire, sat on the antique furniture and broke open the bottles of wine. As they sat, the sun passed into the west and dipped below the horizon. Comfortably settled in the study, they prepared for a celebration; the seventeenth moon was about to rise.

Chapter 10
Bitter Courage

A pristine aura of light streamed into the window of the study. The full moon, bright and brilliant, bathed the two tribals in an ashen glow. Standing with smiles on their faces, they squinted in the bright light, their hearts racing. The rising of the full moon was a passage into manhood, a religious event for Tani and Jared.

The seventeenth moon had risen over the land. Only three more moons needed to pass before the tribals could return home and assume their positions as adults in Scarskin society. Each moon that had risen was a monument to their mission, a testament to courage as they lived beyond the safety of their village in a harsh world. The dawning of the seventeenth moon was a powerful omen. With only three moons left until the end of their Exile, it was a powerful moment for both of them.

Clapping from the dark end of the room, Banion lifted a half-empty bottle of wine into the air. With a sarcastic cheer, he took a swig out of the bottle. He was drunk and loved every minute of it.

"To the heroes of Scarskin," Mineera declared with a smile and tipped her wine bottle toward both of them.

"Heroes?" Banion snorted in a nasty tone. "You talking about those two little gutter rats? There's nothing heroic about them."

Although Mineera's toast was in earnest, Banion's drunken comment shattered the mood of the event. As they looked at him brooding in the darkness, Tani and Jared felt the sting of his words. Falling silent, they stood near the window, bathed in the glorious white light of the full moon. Tani, taking a small swig from his wine bottle, didn't feel like celebrating anymore.

"Oh, come on!" Banion roared.

"That wasn't very nice," Mineera said with disdain.

"I really don't care. It's a joke, you know, calling those two little runts heroes. What the hell do they know about sacrifice?" His drunken rage building, Banion lashed out.

"You're being nasty," Tani shot back.

"I'm nasty when I drink, that's why I love it so much. Booze brings out my natural inclinations."

"Natural inclinations? What, being a jackass?" Jared retorted.

"Oh! He speaks! I should have left your sorry ass back in Pontiac City."

"Just knock it off, Banion," Mineera tried to defend them.

"I don't want to. Heroes? I ask again, what the hell do they know about sacrifice? What the hell do they know about loss? Hey, kid, why do you want to be a hero anyway?"

Shaking his head, Jared was fuming. He fidgeted with the raven totem around his neck, on the verge of losing control. Suddenly, he had enough, and lashed out. "I want to be a hero to make my father proud."

"Your father?" Banion giggled. "Your father the guard? Your father who guards the elders in your village? You're trying to be a hero to make him proud?"

"Stop it." Tani spoke with venom in his tone.

"Yeah, what's wrong with that?" Jared asked.

"What's wrong with that? He doesn't even deserve to stand in your shadow. He's nothing more than a tribal guard. Tell me, kid, has he ever even killed anyone?"

"What the hell are you doing? Why does that matter?" The tribal warrior charged out of the glow of the white full moon, into the darkness and shadow of the room which concealed Banion. Nervous and agitated, he fondled the raven totem intensely.

"You're trying to make a man who's never risked anything proud. You're trying to make a man who's never known sacrifice proud of you. Has he ever even been in battle?"

"Why does that matter?"

"It matters because you have been in battle. How many people have you killed on our little adventure? You want to make someone who's never risked a damn thing proud. It's sad, you know."

"Just shut up."

"No." Banion rose to his feet, charging towards the tribal. Standing toe to toe with him, he glowered, exhaling the stench of wine into his face. "You want to be a hero?"

"Just stop it." Jared looked away.

"You know what a hero is?" Banion yelled at him, throwing his wine bottle to the floor.

"Just stop it."

"I'm a hero." Banion laughed dryly, eyes flashing with hate. "You want to be a hero, look at me!" Grabbing Jared, he shoved him hard.

Instinctively, Jared's hand dropped to the hilt of his sword. As she watched the event unfold, a chill ran down Mineera's spine. What she was witnessing rang out in her mind. It was strangely familiar. Running to them, she watched in horror, almost unable to act. Was this it? Was this the dark dream she had seen? A drunken brawl that could end in tragedy?

"Look at me," Banion coaxed Jared. The tribal locked eyes with Banion. Banion's soul was so devoid of love and life that Jared was frightened. The rancher was nothing more than a wild animal masquerading as a human dressed in a brown duster. "Why the hell would you want to be like me?"

The question almost brought tears to Jared's eyes. Looking at the older man, he felt totally vulnerable, totally defenseless before the raw emotion in Banion's eyes.

"Jared, a hero is someone who's lost so much that nothing can fill the void but brutality. You know why I fight like a wild animal? I fight because I've lost everything. Everything that I've ever loved has been crushed, murdered by an enemy with no remorse. Why do you want to be like me, kid?"

"You fight with such passion. I've never known anyone so dedicated to a cause as you. When I see you fight, it inspires me. I want so bad to be like you, it's scary. I want to feel that passion, that fire. I know it sounds crazy but I envy you." Jared's tone was heartfelt. "I'm proud of you, Banion. In the end, it's not my father that I want to be proud of me. In the end, I want you to be proud of me."

"You can never be like me. I don't ever want you to be like me. Jared, the reason I care about you all so much is that you are nothing like me. I have so much hate inside of me, I don't even understand why it hasn't consumed and destroyed me." Shaking his head, he grasped Jared's shoulders and looked into his eyes. "A hero is someone who has lost so much that nothing else matters but vengeance and hate. In order to be a hero, you must experience loss, true loss, somebody you love so much that you can't live without them. Once that happens to you, it changes you, warps you. Something inside of you snaps when someone that you love is taken from you. The rage builds like a thunderstorm in your heart. I fight with rage, not passion. I fight because I hate and want to destroy and punish. I don't ever want you to experience that fate, Jared. I don't want you to be like me."

"All I've ever wanted to be since we met is you. I see such strength in you. I wish you could see how much you mean to me. You've taught me so much, about myself more than anything. Seeing your life and hearing your voice is an inspiration to me. I know you think that's foolish, but I don't. You have a lot to be proud of," Jared said, looking directly at Banion.

"Promise me something, Jared." Banion grasped the tribal's shoulders firmly.

"What?"

"I see so much of myself in you that it scares me. Don't let it consume you. Don't ever let it consume you like it did me. Don't ever let the rage overtake you," Banion said, his voice quiet yet intense.

Without speaking, Jared nodded back, his eyes filled with tears. Overtaken with emotion, Banion moved forward and hugged Jared. The move was so unexpected, Jared almost retreated. Never before had Banion shown such sentiment. Perplexed for a moment, it took Jared a brief moment to respond. Finally, he returned the gesture and hugged him back. Releasing him, Banion smiled at Jared. He slapped the tribal on the shoulder, then moved away from him and recovered his fallen bottle of wine.

"I'm sorry I ruined the party. It's something that I seem to excel at, dumping lemons onto the birthday cake." Laughing at himself, Banion was truly apologetic to his companions.

Stunned by the raw emotion, Tani and Mineera watched the event completely dumbfounded. They stared at each other in amazement, neither of them saying a word.

Grasping the wine bottle, Banion held it in the direction of the tribals. "You're both courageous, and I'm happy to say that you are not heroes. To Jared and Tani, may they find peace."

"To Jared and Tani," Mineera toasted them.

The tension had eased and the companions felt relieved. Living such a fraught life in such dark times was taxing even to the most seasoned and hardened. As the glowing light of the full moon streamed into the study within the manor house, the companions rested near the fire and quenched their thirst, drinking their fill of wine. During their reprieve, they spent time simply laughing and remembering the long journey that had brought them to that very spot. It would be a night that each of them would remember for the rest of their lives.

Chapter 11
Blockade

As their leader shook his head in disgust, the rest of Nova 7 could tell he was dismayed with the situation. Down below in the valley, along the main highway, was a ramshackle barricade constructed of burned-out vehicles and other metallic debris. Over 50 Biogtech troops and at least five Reaper Kai priests were lingering near the barricade. With a sigh, Banion turned to the rest of his team, throwing the binoculars to Jared.

Jared confirmed the dire circumstances. The barricade was meant to stop any travel down the dirt highway that led into the heart of the Iron Kai Empire. Nova 7 was less than 30 miles away from the capital city of Stonen but there were sizable enemy forces barring their passage into the safe zone. If they could not breach the Reaper Kai defenses, they could not deliver the nuclear warhead to Emperor Gunther.

"Can we go around?" Tani suggested. "There's a heavy enemy presence on the road, but maybe we could sneak around the perimeter and head into the woods."

"No go." Jared motioned to Tani. Handing his brother from Scarskin the binoculars, he pointed to the tree line around the barricade. "There are troops dug into the tree line as far as I can see. Trying to breach the perimeter on foot would be suicide."

"Even under cover of darkness, it would not be advised," Mineera warned. "Most Reaper Kai war parties this large would have a psychic tracker and they would be on to us before we even hit the perimeter."

"The entire defense is set up to repel an assault by infantry. There are defensive bunkers dotting the entire area. I agree with Jared, an assault on foot would be suicide," Banion concluded.

"But then what do we do, Banion?"

"I'm not sure."

Pondering the difficult task at hand, the team reflected on the situation. Finally, Tani broke the silence.

"There are more troops dug into the woods than on the road. Could we bash through the defenses along the road?" he asked with a glimmer in his eye.

"What do you mean?"

"Oh, I don't know. Maybe bash our way through the barricade and keep going. That way, all of the troops in the forest and surrounding area would be useless and too slow to react. By the time they figured out what happened, we would be long gone."

"This is the last challenge in our way. If we can get through this enemy perimeter, it should be a straight shot to the capital. If we can't get through, the enemy would claim the nuclear warhead and have one hell of a prize. We risk the entire war on this single maneuver, you realize," Mineera added.

"That's why we have to cut through them quickly and escape just as quick. I agree with Tani, we need speed and should think about bashing through that barricade using a vehicle," Jared said, crouching on the ridgeline above the intimidating amount of enemy forces in the valley below.

"It would take a big rig, some sort of semi truck to batter through that barricade. If we fail and wreck, the enemy will be all over us in a few seconds and it'll be over," Banion contributed, grabbing the binoculars back from Tani and viewing the scene below once more.

"Hey, what about that abandoned gas station we passed yesterday morning?" Jared asked. "There was a big rig truck in the parking lot and several torn-up cars. I bet we could get at least the truck to work."

"It's too much risk. If the truck fails to breach the barricade, we hand over the nuclear warhead to the enemy."

"Not if we're in two separate vehicles. Maybe use the truck to hit the barricade. If the truck stalls out, the warhead will be in the other vehicle and we can keep it out of the enemy's hands," Tani strategized.

"I like your thinking, but who's going to be the bait in the lead truck?" Jared asked with an almost comical smile.

"I'll do it." Banion's tone was resolute.

"Absolutely not!" Mineera protested. Suddenly, she thought about the vision of the angel that had come to her in the ruined church. The angel had told her that Banion was too important to lose. In addition to the heavenly warning, Mineera had deep emotions centered on Banion and the thought of losing him to this wild plan was too much to bear. "There has to be another way."

"Another way?" the leader of Nova 7 repeated in an angry tone. "You see all those enemy forces down there? The Reaper Kai are reinforcing the entire area for an invasion. We're running out of time. We need to break through those lines and get this warhead to the Iron Kai as soon as possible. We don't have the luxury of waiting. And what is it to you anyway if I want to drive the truck? I haven't had a mother in a damn long time and I sure as hell don't need one now. I'll drive the truck."

Shaking her head, Mineera became angry. "Fine, then I am going with you. Jared and Tani can drive the backup vehicle with the nuclear warhead."

Staring at each other in disbelief, Tani and Jared had a bad feeling about the entire situation. The thought that Mineera and Banion could both be killed, leaving the tribals to fend for themselves on the last leg of the mission, sent a shiver of panic through them. For the first time in a long time, the concept of finishing the mission alone was becoming a credible reality.

"I'm not sure I like this plan anymore," Tani whined.

"Yeah, this sounds like a bad idea," Jared agreed.

"We don't have any other options. Breaking through the barricade on the highway is our best shot. It will be tricky and it's extremely dangerous, but it is our only option at this point. We could spend weeks trying to break through. Each day we spend this close to the enemy lines is giving the Reaper Kai additional chances to capture us. The fate of the Darken Realm is hanging on our ability to reach Stonen with the nuclear warhead. We don't win a prize if we get killed and the enemy gets the warhead. Time is not on our side and we need to make a decisive action to ensure our victory," Banion reasoned, trying to overcome the tribals' fear.

"I don't like this plan either, but we need to get away from enemy forces as soon as possible. The psychic abilities of the Reaper Kai are potent and we risk it all tarrying near their defenses. All it takes is an attuned tracker to ruin this entire mission. I wish there was another way but there isn't. We need to do this," Mineera concluded.

"Fine." Tani sighed and nodded his head in agreement. Jared nodded in reluctant approval as well.

"So there you have it. Our plan is to hijack a truck big enough to bash through that barricade and another vehicle that the tribals will drive carrying the warhead. Everyone got it?"

The tribals meekly agreed.

"And one other thing, you two little gutter rats. You've got to promise Mineera and me something." Banion looked at the tribals with a serious gaze. "If we get into trouble, you have to push on. The fate of the Darken Realm is too important to risk on your emotions. You two got that?"

They could not agree, and simply stared at him in disbelief. Seeing their reservations, he moved forward quickly and grabbed each of them by the shoulder. Like an eagle's talons, his hands dug into their flesh. The youths squirmed in his iron-like grip, staring at him with full attention.

"This mission is too important for you to risk the fate of the Darken Realm on your emotions. Mineera and I will be in the lead truck. If anything happens, you have to promise me to keep going and deliver the warhead to Emperor Gunther."

"I can't do that." Tani shook his head.

"We finish this together," Jared added.

Banion gripped them even more tightly, the pressure of his fingers intense. Gasping in pain, they looked into his fierce eyes. "Promise me!"

"Okay, okay!" Tani whined. "We promise to keep going."

Jared did not respond. Banion pulled him aside and looked at him with a stern gaze. "You understand the importance of this? If you don't break through, hundreds of thousands of people could die at the hands of the Reaper Kai forces. This is probably the most important thing that you will ever have to do. Can you promise me to keep going and finish this mission, no matter what?"

Sheepishly, the tribal warrior could not even look him in the eye. "Yeah, Banion, I promise to keep going and deliver the warhead, no matter what happens."

Staring him down, the leader of Nova 7 could tell that his admission was only halfhearted. For another moment, Banion glowered at the tribal. "Don't let the Reaper Kai do to another family what they did to mine. You got that, kid? Don't you dare let them cause any more suffering."

Understanding the gravity of the situation, Jared nodded in agreement. "You can count on me."

"Good," Banion responded, quickly stepping away from the tribal. Moving to the center of his team, he looked at each of them in turn. "Let's get out of here. I don't want to hang around here any longer, it's too dangerous. We have some walking to do to get back to that abandoned gas station we passed yesterday."

Agreeing with their leader, Nova 7 set out to enact their desperate plan to break through the Reaper Kai battle lines. The fate of all had never been in greater danger. After traveling thousands of miles, their entire mission would hinge upon one last wild act. If Nova 7 could not break through the Reaper Kai battle lines, the nuclear warhead would be useless. If they failed outright and were killed, the warhead could fall into the hands of the enemy and would seal the fate of the entire Darken Realm, handing over the entire continent to the forces of evil. With only the last few steps of their journey ahead, Nova 7 had never been in greater peril. Hiding their fears, each of them dredged hidden courage from the depths of their souls, preparing to do the impossible once more.

Chapter 12
Road to Ruin

Grinding his teeth, Banion looked over at his passenger. Mineera had a wild look in her eyes and gazed back with an uncomfortable stare. Rubbing her hands together in sheer anxiety, she said a quick prayer and let out a loud sigh.

"You ready for this?" she asked Banion.

He looked back and pulled away his black cowboy hat so that he could see better. "Hell, no, I'm not ready."

"We don't have a good chance, do we?" she asked.

"Nope," he answered immediately. "It's all about the tribals. We're the bait. I just hope they manage to punch through."

As he pressed down on the gas, the stacks on the back of the big rig sprung to life, and with a loud gurgle, emitted a foul black stream of exhaust into the air. Banion jammed down on the clutch, shifting the truck into its lowest gear. The semi slowly lurched forward with a roll of its wheels, gradually picking up speed as Banion ground away at the gearbox.

As the lumbering truck accelerated, a rusted-out muscle car roared by it. Tani waved as they sped past, peeling out along the right side of the truck. They laughed as the back end of the car whipped back and forth. Jared was hanging out the window, yelling at Banion and Mineera.

"Damn it!" Banion yelled into his radio. "Knock it off."

Tani made a rude gesture at Banion with his left hand, then whipped the car around the front of the truck, passing to the left then cutting back on the gas. The muscle car came alongside the big rig as it picked up speed.

Thundering down the road, the truck was cruising along the dirt highway, causing an enormous cloud of dust to rise into the sky. Banion slammed down the clutch, shifting the rig into the highest gear. Black smoke belched from the stacks and the engine whined as the diesel fuel powered the corroded motor.

Ahead of the charging vehicles, only a few miles down the road, was the barricade created by the Reaper Kai army. Staring at the plume of dust and dirt behind the truck, Banion knew that the enemy would have a few minutes' warning before they reached the blockade. Cursing, he propped his assault rifle on his lap with the barrel of the weapon hanging out the window. He grabbed the radio to speak to the tribals in their own vehicle, the one holding the weapon of the ancients.

"One minute until contact. Back off and let us crash through the barricade ahead. After we punch through, hit it and get the hell out of here."

"We got ya," Jared replied, readying his sub-machine gun. Pulling the slide back, he chambered a round and then clicked off the safety on the weapon. Jittery, he exhaled a full breath and prepared himself for the coming conflict.

"Thirty seconds!" Banion yelled into the radio.

As they crossed over a hill, the barricade came into view. The enemy was stunned. Seeing the truck roar over the hill at full speed sent the defenders into a frenzy. Reaper Kai priests ran to view the charging big rig, immediately barking out orders, while Biogtech soldiers slowly responded to the menace charging down the road. A split second before Banion struck the barricade with the semi truck, the Biogtechs took hasty aim and opened fire.

Automatic weapons fire erupted, pelting the truck. The windshield was struck several times and the bullets roared through the cabin with frightening speed. Flecks of glass sprayed all over Mineera and Banion. They crouched to avoid the gunfire as more bullets shredded the vehicle.

Holding the tempo of the attack, Banion never faltered. Calm and collected, he peered over the dashboard and steered the truck toward the right side of the barricade, then gritted his teeth, bracing himself for the collision. Smashing into the barricade, the truck held fast and an enormous amount of debris was thrown into the air. The sound of strained metal resounded with a deafening screech as the truck punched through.

The front of the truck vaulted several feet into the air, clearing the barricade and propelling twisted metal in front of the charging truck. As the vehicle crashed down onto the ground, Banion vaulted forward, striking his face on the steering wheel. He was left reeling from the blow, a stream of blood pouring out of his nose. Shaking off the trauma, he let it bleed as he punched the gas. The rig tore forward, with much of the barricade wedged underneath it. Dragging the debris slowed the truck considerably.

The priests shouted out to their robotic minions, ordering them to continue the attack. As they sprayed the back of the truck with bullets, Mineera was more than ready. Having calmed herself after the first hail of gunfire, the psychic had already channeled energy around Banion and herself, erecting a barrier of white light. The shield managed to save them from certain death. The bullets from the enemy troops rammed through the metal frame and panels on the big rig, penetrating the cabin, but Mineera's psychic barrier held fast, completely protecting them from harm.

The glow from the truck could not be ignored. Many of the Reaper Kai priests witnessed the display of psychic power and were immediately drawn to the cabin of the truck. Seeing Mineera sent them into a frenzy. She had once been a high-ranking member of the Dark Order, known to most, and had betrayed them long ago. Seeing her sent a shiver of fear into the Reaper Kai priests. Many knew that she had joined the legendary mercenary team Nova 7, which had struck out into the wastelands to recover a nuclear warhead to use against the Reaper Kai. Her emergence back to civilization, especially so close to the capital city of Stonen, was clearly gravely significant. Speculation rose to epic proportion in the span of a few seconds. They *knew* that Nova 7 had succeeded in their mission to become a nuclear power.

Having cleared the barricade, the tribals roared through the wreckage, close on the heels of Banion and Mineera. Roaring away from the scene of combat, they were ill prepared for what lay beyond the barricade.

As he careened over another hill, Banion almost jack-knifed the semi trying to avoid the menace in the roadway ahead of them. An enormous encampment of literally hundreds of Biogtechs and

Reaper Kai priests was spread across the road. Lurching strongly to the right, the semi truck hurtled off the roadway into the field beside it. Banion crashed straight through the encampment. Roaring through several tents, he killed a half dozen Reaper Kai, smashing into them as they lingered completely unaware inside. A grisly splash of blood splattered the linen tents as battered bodies were flung high into the air.

Not letting off the gas, Banion spouted a litany of curses as Mineera hung on for dear life. He pulled hard to the left using all his strength, steering the truck back onto the highway. From its position several feet below the edge of the road, the truck launched a few feet into the air before landing back onto the dirt highway.

Having nearly collided with Banion as he veered off the road, the tribals bumped along, the right wheels of their car drawing precariously close to the edge of the raised road.

"Holy shit!" Jared yelled as the car pitched to the right, hitting his head on the door frame. Tani, who was driving the car, was also stunned and gripped the wheel with white knuckles.

"Hold on!" Tani yelled and pulled hard to the left. Just a split second after they had gotten the vehicle under control, Banion's big rig veered towards them, still reeling wildly from launching back onto the highway.

Slamming on the brakes, Tani almost rear-ended the truck. He skidded across the dirt road, steering the car with deft agility to maintain control. Sweat was pouring down his face as he finally managed to stabilize the vehicle.

Wide eyed, he glanced at Jared, and just in time. Seeing several Biogtechs out the right side of the car taking aim, he yelled out a warning at Jared. Without even thinking, Jared ducked down. A spray of bullets roared through the car. Seeing them smash through the glass was frightening enough, but Tani himself took a bullet in his right arm. The bullet rammed through his flesh and a spray of blood spouted free as the round exited his limb. The bullet hole torn in his right forearm began to bleed heavily. Gritting his teeth, Tani removed his right hand from the wheel, flexing it in pain.

After hearing Tani scream, Jared blinked several times, still stunned by the gunfire. Seeing the wound sent him into action. Pulling his belt off, Jared wrapped it around Tani's upper arm, fashioning a makeshift tourniquet. Tani yelled in pain as Jared applied pressure, fighting to keep the car under control. Blinking with tears in his eyes, the tribal scholar kept up his speed and managed to escape the remaining gunfire.

As Tani and Jared fought to escape, Mineera and Banion were not so lucky. Dozens of Biogtech soldiers were on the attack. Several dozen sub-machine gun rounds tore at the truck with devastating results. Although Mineera protected both herself and Banion with her psychic powers, the truck was damaged heavily. Several bullets had pierced the rear tires while another had clipped the fuel line. Another series of shots had hit the front of the rig, piercing the radiator. A haze of steam was already leaking from the bullet holes.

Knowing that their ordeal was about to get extremely dangerous, Banion didn't even flinch. He held the gas pedal down, pushing what was left of his truck down the highway. With each passing second, the truck lost power and slowly began to grind to a halt. Jared and Tani watched in horror as their teammates began to slow down.

Distracted by Banion and Mineera, Tani was ill prepared for another unexpected attack. Roaring down the road, an enemy light-armor vehicle came directly at them. With a Biogtech gunner manning a heavy machine gun atop the vehicle, the situation was about to turn desperate. Opening fire, the machine gun launched a barrage at Tani and Jared. As they attempted to steer out of harm's way, the hot lead slammed into the dirt road, creating tiny clouds of dust where the bullets hit.

"Get the hell out of here!" Banion yelled into the radio. "Keep going and don't stop, there are too many enemy troops here!"

"We can stop and get you!" Jared yelled back into the radio.

"No way in hell, kid. There are too many troops and with that armor on us, we don't stand a chance. Get the cargo out of here and get to Stonen."

"I'm not leaving you!" Jared yelled.

"You don't have a choice, kid. Don't let it end like this. Don't let us lose at the very end. Everything we've fought for has to be for something! Get the cargo to Stonen, stop the Reaper Kai."

"Damn it, no!" Jared shouted back.

"Do it!" Banion replied, radio crackling.

"We have to do it." Tani's voice was frantic.

"Stop the car!" Jared yelled at his friend.

"You know damn well that I can't. We can't risk it."

"Stop the car!" Jared grabbed the wheel, trying to take control of the car.

"Get out of here!" Banion yelled into the radio and the tribals could hear the desperation in his voice.

Releasing the wheel, Jared punched the dashboard with his fists. The impact was so fierce, the skin on his knuckles split. He let out an angry roar. Without saying another word, Tani and Jared obeyed Banion's order. They couldn't even look at each other. Heeding their leader's words, they punched the gas and escaped the battlefield, leaving their companions' failing truck lingering further and further behind.

In a clearing just seven miles beyond the barricade, Banion's truck ground to a halt with a trail of steam flowing from the cracked radiator. With a dire look in his eyes, Banion looked at Mineera. Reaching out to her, he grabbed her hand and spoke in earnest. "I'm so sorry."

Looking back, she exhibited no fear; instead, she had an almost feral, animalistic look in her eyes. Squeezing his hand with her own, she replied, "We're not dead yet." She pushed the door open, jumping down onto the ground outside the big rig. With a calm tremor, power began to fill her. As she extended her hand, a white hot ray of burning light tore forward from her outstretched fingertips. The armored vehicle that had tried to kill Jared and Tani reached the scene and was ill prepared for Mineera's attack. Her holy fire, as bright as the sun, slammed into the vehicle and utterly incinerated it. The blast was so intense, the fuel tank detonated, shattering the vehicle into a smoldering mass of burning fuel.

Seeing her stand against insurmountable odds, Banion readied his assault rifle and prepared for the worst. In the distance, the Reaper Kai camp they had just breached was buzzing with activity. Hundreds of Biogtech soldiers had been ordered to advance upon the failed vehicle. As the agents of the Reaper Kai sought to slaughter Banion and Mineera, gunfire broke over the scene, pinning the remnants of Nova 7 near the wreckage of their truck. Unable to flee, Banion and Mineera prepared to face an entire enemy army, totally alone.

Chapter 13
Vulture One-Four

The radio crackled to life in the Truce Hall. One of the radio operators stood up and cranked up the volume on his radio receiver, resulting in an instant reaction to the transmission in the room around him.

"Targets have breached the perimeter on Highway 17 and are en route to Stonen. Immediate support requested on position. Mineera of Nova 7 was seen in the target vehicle and is at coordinates 164.87.36. The target vehicle has been disabled and units on site are requesting fire support," the raspy voice of a Reaper Kai priest sounded from the radio.

Captain Maddock rushed over immediately and cranked up the volume further on the transmitter. The entire room fell silent as they heard the words *Mineera* and *Nova 7* uttered on an enemy transmission.

"Gunther!" Maddock yelled, but the Emperor of the Iron Kai was already on his way. Charging across the room, he almost stumbled over the wiring draped across the floor. Stunned, he looked frantically at the radio receiver that had been monitoring local enemy radio transmissions.

"I repeat, send all combat units to coordinates 164.87.36. The target is Mineera," the raspy voice broke the silence once more.

"Barricade six-one, orders received. Eight squads of Biogtech soldiers en route to target crash site," a different voice responded.

"Northern support camp orders received. Biogtech assault rigs en route to target crash site," a third priest spoke over the radio.

The room was dead silent. Everyone knew of Mineera, the legendary Reaper Kai diplomat who had betrayed her entire race to transmit critical war information to the city- state of Rasheed just prior to the beginning of the war. Wide-eyed wonder was reflected in every face, including Gunther's. The radio transmission also mentioned Nova 7 and this further piqued everyone's interest. It was a totally impossible mission, scouring the ruins of the old world for an intact nuclear weapon. It just didn't make sense that the legendary mercenary team that had dropped off the grid over a year ago had miraculously reappeared less than thirty miles from the capital city of Stonen. Hope seemed to spring from this intriguing fact.

Gunther blinked in wonder as the impossible was suddenly made real. In that instant, he knew without a shadow of a doubt that Nova 7 had succeeded in their mission and were trying to bring the weapon of the ancients to the city of Stonen. He slammed his hand down on the table near the radio. The technicians and military personnel were stunned by his violent gesture, but were even more stunned by the dramatic development.

Grabbing the technician by the shoulder, Gunther spoke in a direct commanding tone. "What's the range on this receiver?"

"Not far, only about 45 miles," the technician responded.

"Where the hell are those coordinates?" Gunther boomed, and the room was set in motion. Several technicians pored over maps. Within seconds, a technician rushed to him and slammed the map down on the table, pointing excitedly. The location was a mere 23 miles from Stonen.

"Hell, we can almost see them from here." Gunther's tone was frantic. "We need to get them the hell out of there." Shoving the radio technician out of the chair, he sat down before the radio equipment, fiddling with the instruments for a second and changing the transmission frequency. "Vulture One-Four, this is Overlord. Vulture One-Four, do you copy?"

"This is Vulture One-Four; acknowledged, Overlord, go ahead," the radio crackled back.

"Vulture One-Four, your orders are to extract any mercenary or civilian personnel at coordinates 164.87.36. Bring as many gunships as you have ready to fly and drop combat personnel all over the landing zone. The coordinates are a crash site and there is a heavy Reaper Kai presence en route to the landing zone. Overlord over."

"Vulture One-Four; acknowledged, Overlord. Twelve gunships are fueled and ready for battle. Combat loading will commence immediately, Overlord. Twelve squads of shock troops will deploy and secure the landing zone. Vulture One-Four over."

"Vulture One-Four, be advised. Possible hazardous cargo is at the landing zone and must be recovered at all cost. I repeat, any cargo at the landing zone and all personnel at the landing zone must be extracted. Overlord out."

"Vulture One-Four two minutes from take-off. Orders acknowledged, Overlord. Vulture One-Four out."

Breathing heavily, Gunther turned away from the radio transmitter and looked at Maddock with a solemn gaze. Rising to his feet, he stared at his trusted captain with an uneasy look. Mad Dog Maddock returned the gaze and spoke to him in a whisper. "Is this real? Is it really Nova 7?"

"I don't know." Gunther exhaled loudly.

A roar erupted from the mountainside. The enormous underground airstrip sprang to life. Steel doors opened on the rock face and the humming of powerful engines resounded. Rushing out of the hidden airfield came twelve Iron Kai gunships loaded with seasoned infantry, roaring off towards the west.

Gunther and the rest of his staff stared at the gunships heading off into battle. Closing his eyes, the Emperor of the Iron Kai said a silent prayer. When he opened his eyes, he stared at his military advisors. Everyone in the room was on their feet and completely silent. Their faces ashen white, all present knew that the next few minutes would determine their fate. If it really was Nova 7 on the fringe of Stonen with an intact nuclear warhead, the war against the Reaper Kai would soon be over and the Iron Kai would be victorious. If it really was Nova 7 with an intact nuclear warhead and the Reaper Kai recovered the weapon, the Iron Kai were doomed.

*   *   *

"I can't do this!" Tani yelled in a frantic tone. He slammed on the brakes of the muscle car, which skidded to a halt on the dirt highway. As tears welled up in his eyes, he was shaking in horror.

Jared was silent and had his head buried in his hands. Looking up from them, he stared at Tani with a wild look in his eyes. He turned to the back seat of the car and stared at the black resin case holding the nuclear warhead, the salvation of all, resting in that sinister black case. Cursing, Jared wanting nothing to do with the nefarious weapon, a weapon they had risked their lives to obtain, a weapon that had caused the tribals to make the horrible choice to abandon their friends in the most desperate of times.

"I can't do this either," Jared said, and tears filled his eyes as well. "We can't abandon them. I don't give a damn what Banion says. I can't let them die! To hell with the warhead. We need to go back!"

Tani was pasty white. The loss of blood from the gunshot wound to his right arm had taken its toll on him. He, too, looked in the back seat at the nuclear warhead. Shaking his head, he wished that they had never found it. "What do we do with it? We can't just leave it at the side of the road."

"We don't have any time. We have to go back now but we can't leave it here. We have to take a chance and go back for Banion and Mineera and hope like hell we don't get killed in the process and the Reaper Kai get the warhead."

"You know what you're saying, don't you? If we go back and get killed, the war is over and the Iron Kai will be annihilated and hundreds of thousands of people will die."

"I know what I'm saying. If we fail, a lot of people are going to die. But we can't just leave a nuclear warhead in the bushes at the side of the road. We need to go back and get Banion and Mineera out of there. Are you with me?" Jared's tone was solemn.

"Yeah, I'm with you," Tani said, sighing in frustration. "This had better work, because if it doesn't, Banion is going to kill us."

"I'm not sure that we can even get back to them in time. There's a good chance they're both dead already."

"Don't say that!" Tani whined.

"I'm sorry," Jared responded. "I'm losing my mind!"

"Me too," Tani said, grasping the steering wheel with both hands.

Spinning the wheel, the tribal scholar punched the gas. The muscle car roared to life and its back end whipped around, sending a plume of dirt into the air. Tani brought the vehicle under control and turned toward the scene of conflict from which they had just escaped. Rushing down the roadway, the tribals knew what must be done. Ignoring duty and common sense, the reckless youths followed their hearts and charged headlong into the fray in a desperate attempt to save their friends from certain death.

Chapter 14
Desperate Times

Smoke was rising into the air near the crash site. Speeding to the aid of their companions, Jared and Tani were ill prepared for what they were about to encounter. Only a mile out from the ruins of the big rig, a host of Biogtech soldiers had closed in on the highway. Several dozen squads under the control of no less than 20 Reaper Kai priests were drawing dangerously close to the scene. As the tribals came near, several of the squads nearest to the road opened fire.

Veering strongly to the right, Tani punched off the edge of the road, steering the car through the open field just north of the dirt highway. His actions, though quick, were not quick enough. A shower of bullets rammed into the car, puncturing the fuel lines heading into the engine. As he tried to retain control, the vehicle spurted fuel into the engine compartment and began to lose power. Tani knew that they had crossed a terrible line. Their vehicle was losing power and there was a good chance that they would not even reach the crash site.

Cursing, Tani felt very foolish. The tribals were risking the lives of hundreds of thousands and now they hadn't even made it past the advancing Reaper Kai forces. Gritting his teeth, Tani kept going, bumping along the field next to the road. In their current position, they were safe for now, but the advancing forces would soon be at their heels.

Another battle line had formed a crescent pattern around the big rig. Mineera and Banion were both pinned in the wreckage, fighting a desperate battle. As they had already been cut off from escaping on foot, the battle was reaching a crucial stage. Bursts of gunfire were keeping advancing Biogtechs at bay while Mineera continually hurled beams of holy fire at the battle lines. Due to their position in the open, fleeing would mean a certain death. Seeing their companions under enemy fire, Tani steered the failing vehicle close to the big rig.

As they bumped along the field, the car came under enemy fire immediately, and the tribals instinctively ducked down. Their luck protected them as several bullets ripped through the car, narrowly missing them. Grinding to a halt only a few yards from the truck, the car would move no further, and now all of Nova 7 and the nuclear warhead were in the center of a hornets' nest. To their west, forces advanced along the road. To the southeast, close to 300 Biogtechs were closing in.

"Damn it!" Banion roared at them as the tribals exited the vehicle. "If we get out of this alive, I'm going to kill both of you! I can't believe you had open road and came back! What the hell were you thinking?"

"We couldn't leave you!" Jared yelled while crouching behind the big rig.

"It was stupid, kid, real stupid. We're pinned down and enemy troops are swarming us! What the hell are we going to do now?"

"I don't know." Tani shook his head. Running over to the car, he pulled the warhead out of the back seat and positioned it behind the big rig. With the heavy amount of fire they were taking, it would only be a matter of time before the warhead got hit by gunfire. The thought of a nuclear warhead getting pierced by a bullet was not a savory one. "We couldn't leave you here. Just deal with it."

"Get down!" Mineera screamed.

Several thumps sounded in the distance. Reaper Kai forces had set up mortar positions and immediately launched a host of mortar rounds. Whistling through the air, the deadly projectiles began to rain down on their position. Nova 7 hit the deck and braced for impact. Three mortar shells exploded around the perimeter of the crash site. Rocked by the explosions, each of them was jolted with a fresh shot of adrenaline. Although the first set of mortar rounds missed their mark, the enemy troops would continue the barrage, keeping them pinned down as the infantry advanced closer and closer on their position.

"Hit 'em!" Banion yelled and trained his weapon on two squads of Biogtechs that had drawn dangerously close to their position.   The tribals responded to his orders and took aim, shouldering their sub-machine guns.   Firing bursts, the three mercenaries felled several of the Biogtechs immediately.   Splashes of hydraulic fluid sprayed into the air as they collapsed, giggling as they bled out.   Nova 7's aim was true and they managed to gun down several more before the enemy even had a chance to respond. The return fire was too hasty to be effective and did not even come close to hitting any of the team members.

Mineera was aiding the cause.   As she extended her hand, a searing beam of white light shot forth.   Sweeping back and forth, she cut through the Biogtechs, melting them and incinerating them in wide swaths.   Their defense was effective but the continual flow of enemy troops was getting hard to handle.   Each wave was drawing closer and closer.   It was just a matter of time before they were overrun.

Thump.   Thump. Thump.   The mortar positions opened up once more and the shells came whistling down upon them.   One shell hit the tribals' car, detonating and sending a deadly spray of shrapnel into the team.   Jared took a wedge of metal in his back, the heated shard lodging in his shoulder blade.   The rest of the team was only stunned for a brief second.

A lance of fire rocked across the battlefield.   As it did, a frosty wisp of rising wind erupted around Jared.   A psychic attack had been aimed at the team.   With only a split second to respond, Jared positioned himself between the rest of the team and the attacking force.   The raven totem held strong as the ancient magic protected the tribal.   Although the lance of psychic fire hit Jared dead-on, the sinister attack was dissipated by the ancient raven totem.

Jared immediately responded to the attack and took aim. The Reaper Kai that had just attacked them took two bullets in the chest, and fell to the ground, mortally wounded.

Thump. Thump. Thump.   Three more mortar rounds burst around them.   A crackle of dirty energy raced across the battlefield as another psychic took aim. Bullets ricocheted off the metal vehicles around them. The situation had turned dire for Nova 7. They were completely pinned and hundreds of troops were nearing the crash site. If something didn't happen soon, they would perish and the Reaper Kai would claim the ultimate prize.

Cackling, a squad of Biogtechs neared the perimeter of the crash site. Crawling over the vehicles, they were only a few yards away. Banion fired at the troops as they clambered over the wreckage. Jared dropped his gun and drew the Scar Blade. Rushing forward, he began to slaughter the mechanical troops with a fury of well placed attacks. Limbs were severed and some were cut completely in half as the tribal let his battle prowess overwhelm his senses. Brown fluid erupted from the machines as they were butchered.

As he killed the remnants of the squad, another was about to overrun their perimeter. Tani was on the scene and was lobbing hand grenades into their midst. The well placed explosives had devastating results, killing most of the squad. Mineera backed him up by incinerating the survivors with holy fire.

Thump. Thump. Thump. The mortar rounds crashed in again. This time, they were dangerously close, so close that Mineera was caught by the shockwave of one blast. Thrown off her feet, she crashed against the car and her limp body collapsed to the ground. Unconscious, she was out of commission with a nasty head wound.

"Mineera!" Tani yelled and came to her side. He tried to stir her, but she would not respond.

"Get back here! Leave her!" Banion yelled as he slammed a fresh magazine into his assault rifle.

"I'm out of grenades," Tani yelled.

Jared did not respond; he was caught in the midst of his own struggle. Several more Biogtechs had breached their perimeter and he was cutting them apart with his ancient blue steel sword. Everywhere around them, bullets whistled past, coming dangerously close to killing them. With only three members still functioning, Nova 7 was only minutes away from being killed.

Just as things seemed totally hopeless, the sound of air support stunned Nova 7.

Coming in fast and low over the battle, a formation of green helicopters roared into the fray. Not sure what to think at first, the entire team hit the deck, wondering if they were enemy support. Much to their surprise, the helicopters were friendly. Heavy machine guns opened fire on the Reaper Kai forces as the gunships made their initial pass over the crash site.

Raising his fist in the air, Banion cheered them as they passed over. The initial attack from the helicopters had driven back the Biogtechs nearest to the crash site. Passing around to the north, several of the helicopters hovered in the air about 300 yards north of the wreckage. Ropes dropped down from their sides and seasoned Iron Kai infantry rappelled out of the gunships. With six squads of support troops on the deck, Banion knew that they had a fighting chance to escape the nightmare they were now living.

As the closest gunships unloaded, the other six helicopters were strafing the enemy troops. After they had driven back the hostile forces, more ropes fell and additional infantry rappelled into the harsh battle.

Thump. Thump. Thump. The ceaseless mortar fire careened into the crash site. Several Iron Kai troops took the brunt of the Reaper Kai attacks and were blown to bits. Screams echoed as the soldiers took refuge in the crash site.

"Damn good to see you," Banion greeted them as they took up defensive positions in the wreckage.

"I'm Lieutenant Hayes. We have direct orders to extract you and your entire team. We also have orders to recover any cargo you may have. Do you have any cargo?" the Iron Kai officer inquired as a tremendous boom rocked the landscape. Artillery fire sounded in the distance.

"There are four of us. One is down." Banion pointed at Mineera, and a field medic ran to her side and began to stabilize her bleeding by bandaging her head. "We also have this!" Banion pointed at the black resin case holding the nuclear warhead.

"What the hell is it?" Hayes asked.

"It's a nuclear warhead," Banion shouted into the chaos.

"Say again." Hayes was stunned, staring at the case as all color drained from his face.

"It's a functional nuclear warhead."

"Holy shit." Hayes' voice was awed and jittery. Grabbing his radio, he frantically spoke into it. "Overlord, this is Alpha One-Six. The crash site is secure but we're taking heavy fire. Enemy artillery has opened fire on our position and we have over 300 enemy troops inbound. Precious cargo is at the crash site. Requesting heavy armor support and additional infantry at our position. Alpha One-Six over."

"Alpha One-Six, this is Overlord. Green light on heavy armor to your position. Estimating four minutes on armor support. We dispatched armor to your position after the birds were in the air. APCs are en route to crash site with additional infantry. Evacuate all mercenary personnel and the cargo immediately. Get those gunships on the deck and get them the hell out of there, Alpha One-Six. Overlord over," Gunther responded to the radio transmission from the Truce Hall, 23 miles away from the battle.

Just as Gunther finished speaking, enemy artillery shells rained down, exploding all over the area. Several of the infantrymen were killed instantly and many were wounded. The situation was getting more and more intense. The Reaper Kai were throwing everything they had in the area at their opponents, as were the Iron Kai.

"Negative, Overlord. The landing zone is not secure. Enemy mortar positions and artillery are pounding the hell out of us. Requesting extraction two clicks to the north. We need to escape on foot to the secondary landing zone. Alpha One-Six over," Hayes yelled into the radio.

"Green light to extraction. Pull four squads out with the cargo and mercenary personnel by chopper. Overlord out."

"Nova 7, we're leaving," Hayes yelled at them. He fired out a quick round of orders, and four squads efficiently formed up around him. Grabbing all of their gear, the soldiers then grabbed Mineera and prepared to escape the crash site. "Let's get the hell out of here!"

The other eight squads rose and aimed heavy fire on the advancing Biogtech army. As they fired and fought the legions of evil, Hayes, with four squads of infantry, protected Nova 7 and the precious cargo and pushed north away from the crash site.

As they rushed to the landing zone, Iron Kai armor raced into the fields. Taking up positions, they opened fire, pounding the

Biogtech forces with artillery shells. The amount of fire put on the Reaper Kai forces was substantial enough for Nova 7 and Hayes to escape with the nuclear warhead.

Safe and secure within an Iron Kai helicopter, Nova 7 and the nuclear warhead rose into the air. Viewing the battlefield below, each of them was thankful to be alive. They rushed away from the scene of conflict, their mission finally over. Nova 7 had succeeded. Finding the nuclear warhead had not been enough; finally, they had succeeded in returning to Iron Kai territory with the weapon intact. Exhausted from the ordeal and worried about Mineera, the team members were silent and unable to comprehend what they had accomplished.

The helicopter raced home, back to the city of Stonen. With the precious cargo at hand, the war against the Reaper Kai was about to take a dramatic turn.

Chapter 15
Unlikely Victors

The sound was nothing more than a collage of noises. Rising gradually in both pitch and intensity, it just didn't resonate properly. Feeling almost nauseous, Mineera tried in vain to breach the darkness that had overtaken her. As the sounds became clearer, she could perceive a terrible throbbing pain in her temples. With a conscious push, she opened her eyes. At first, the light was horrific, a blinding wash of blazing pain. Struggling, Mineera blinked several times as the sounds and images finally came into focus.

The first image that came into her mind was a man. Focusing on his voice, she could hear him speaking to her, but it took a few seconds for her mind to catch up. Her gaze traced his features, revealing a man who had seen too much worry for his days. She focused on his mouth, which was speaking to her, framed by a fiery orange beard, and watched the fragile cracks in his skin, small wrinkles taking shape. Gazing upward, she finally looked into his eyes. As she did, Mineera perceived a heavy heart, one that had seen and experienced untold atrocities. Finally, his words echoed in her mind.

"I believe that this is the first time in a very long time that a Reaper Kai has been sent to the infirmary instead of the gallows." Gunther spoke with an almost playful air. Although much worry had taxed his soul, in that very moment he felt liberated, as if the weight of the world had been lifted off his shoulders.

"I am no Reaper Kai," Mineera responded, staring up at him with her bright blue eyes. "Not any more."

"Indeed," Gunther boomed back, gently rubbing her hand. As he consoled her, she became suddenly aware of her companions. She looked past his shoulder, and the fierce soul of Banion O'Neil came into focus. When Mineera smiled, the mercenary leader of Nova 7 smiled back at her. Taking off his black cowboy hat, he knelt close to her bed and reached out his hand. Gently pushing away her long flowing hair, he caressed her cheek gently.

"It's all fine now. Don't worry about a thing," he said, with a sincere sense of peace in his eyes. Seeing his gentle demeanor was somehow haunting to her. For as long as she had known him, he had been on a mission of vengeance, with nothing but anger and despair in his heart. Stretching out her intuition revealed the anger was still there, but it had been calmed, soothed for the time being. Experiencing his soul and emotion made her feel that everything truly would be all right.

"Did we do it? Did we make it?" she quizzed him with a gentle smile.

"Yes, we finally made it." Jared appeared near the other side of the bed. The tribal, although still in his teens, seemed more like someone in the middle of his life. His face radiated a deep sense of pride and accomplishment. She reached out and grabbed his hand with a smile.

Tani appeared near the foot of the bed, rubbing his right arm continually, fidgeting with a fresh bandage that had been placed over the gunshot wound he had sustained during the harrowing battle to reach the city of Stonen. Smiling at her, his bright green eyes were filled with wonder, not fear; hope had replaced doubt. "It's good to see you," he smiled, his tone heartfelt.

"Tani." She smiled back and found herself overwhelmed by her emotions. After months and months of strife and hardship, Nova 7 had finally succeeded in their mission, bringing the most horrible of weapons to the Iron Kai Empire. In that moment, she remembered the long road that had brought them to this very point. Seeing each of them alive filled her with a joy she had never known. Breaking down, she wept openly.

Witnessing her emotion filled her companions with a sense of nostalgia and joy as well. Tani also began to weep, moving over and kneeling down next to her, grabbing her hand with a smile. Jared's lower lip trembled but he maintained control. Banion was stoic as ever, but even a man perpetually gripped with anger was filled with joy in that moment.

"You have all done a great service, not only for us, but for all other nations that have fallen under the tyrannical will of the Reaper Kai. Your deeds of daring and courage will be remembered for generations to come." Gunther's voice was heartfelt. "I won't detain you further. I will find you all later. Until then, share all the hospitality of this palace." With that, Emperor Gunther moved away from Nova 7. Just before he left the room, he halted for a brief moment, lingering in the doorway. After some consideration, he turned back and looked at each of them in turn. Even though he never said a single word, the look he gave them said it all. With a glance, he said *thank you* once more.

Finally, the mercenary team that had done the impossible was all alone in the infirmary.

"Now that we made it, I'm going to kill both of you," Banion said while staring down the tribals. "You should have never risked the lives of so many for us. I told you to push on, no matter what happened to us. You shouldn't have come back for us."

"We just couldn't do it, Banion. We just couldn't leave you both to die out there alone." Jared spoke while looking at Banion without fear. "After everything that we've done together and everything we've experienced, we just couldn't let you die out there. In the end, I would rather die than live my life as a coward and know that I failed the people that mattered most to me in life."

"You would have done the same in our shoes," Tani said. "It wasn't a hard choice. We would have gladly sacrificed ourselves for both of you. I couldn't have lived out the rest of my life knowing that I failed you."

Banion did not respond; instead, he simply looked away, caught up in the emotion of it all. The broken man, Banion, had lost his soul long ago, and the courage of the two tribals was almost incomprehensible to him. They would have sacrificed themselves to save Banion and Mineera and they would have done so willingly.

"I'm glad everything worked out. I am happy that we all made it out alive," Mineera said with a smile.

Banion was still pensive. Finally, he looked at Jared and Tani. They could tell that he was fighting back tears. An eerie silence filled the room as they stared at him. Banion exhaled a lungful of air, his eyes growing soft as he smiled at the tribals. "I give you my thanks. Thanks for coming back for us. I don't deserve such kindness but I do appreciate it."

"Don't deserve it?" Tani shook his head in disbelief. "You are truly one of the most selfless people I know. You've sacrificed and lost everything you've ever loved in this world to secure freedom against evil. You deserve the gratitude of all, not just us."

"You taught me what a real hero is, Banion, someone who knows true loss and suffering but keeps going. I never understood why you fought with such passion until recently. A hero is someone who feels such emptiness and loss that they will never surrender and never yield until justice is served. You are a true hero, someone who's risked it all for the sake of doing the right thing. You have led us, inspired us. You deserve everything, Banion; don't ever tell yourself otherwise." Jared smiled as he spoke.

"All that I am, I learned through suffering. All that I am is due to strife and agony. Anguish was my teacher." Banion shook his head in despair.

"All that you are is from suffering but you never let it rule you. Of all the people I know, you were dealt the worst hand in life, but you managed to survive and persevere. Your standing here before us now as a great leader is a testament to your strength, not weakness. You managed to maintain your humanity no matter what was done to you. You kept on the right path where lesser men would have failed, consumed by the darkness of their own blind, vengeful obsessions. Don't ever thank us for what we've sacrificed for you. We've lost nothing compared to you. We all owe you our deepest thanks and sincere admiration. Don't ever think that you don't deserve it," Mineera concluded, and the two tribals smiled at him, each patting him on the shoulder.

Looking away from them, he wanted to flee their kindness. Having suffered so greatly, Banion truly felt that he did not deserve their compassion. It was a tough place for him emotionally. For so long he had defined himself as a mercenary for hire on a quest of retribution. Now that their mission had succeeded, he had a difficult time trying to redefine himself. The raw emotion that he felt was out of place. He felt naked in this new, foreign world. In that moment, he knew that he simply didn't fit anymore. His entire personality and soul were no longer meant for such a world. Hiding his emotions, he sought to change the subject, shifting the topic away from himself.

"When the sun next rises, the world we be a much different place due to our actions. The Reaper Kai will know terror and will be put to dust. You have all done a great service. Thanks for believing in me, thanks for coming with me and bleeding with me," the leader of Nova 7 declared, looking each of them in the eye in turn. They responded to his sentiment and nodded in acknowledgement.

A true feeling of victory washed over them. Basking in the strange sensation, they reflected on the crusade. The glow of success was hanging over them, an almost euphoric sensation of completing the ultimate goal. With so much doubt hovering over each of them during the mission, it seemed almost miraculous that all of them had made it out alive and had survived the epic journey through the ruins of America. It hadn't been a simple task to hold together and reach that point. It hasn't been easy to endure the physical hardships and rough environmental conditions they had to face. It wasn't painless to weather the difficult emotional hardships they had encountered. All in all, the crusade had pushed each of them to their limits physically and mentally.

As they contemplated the journey, each of them felt a sorrow wash over them. Even though they were successful, it was the end of an age for each of them. It was the end of a bizarre rush of events that they knew would never come again. Bound by friendship through hardship, they were now a family. It filled all of them with a sense of sadness that the mission was finally over. No longer would they wonder what was over the next hill and beyond the horizon. No longer did their minds have to imagine hidden terrors lurking around the next bend in the road. It was certain that now that the mission was over, they would soon part company and live out the rest of their lives.

With seventeen full moons having risen for the tribals, they would soon have to leave for the return expedition back to their village of Scarskin somewhere in the great wastelands. Mineera was without a home and would undoubtedly have to find a place for herself in a new world freshly ravaged by warfare. And finally Banion, a man who had lost it all, a man kept alive only by a sense of vengeance, would have to contemplate his existence. With his family dead and gone and his oath of revenge fulfilled, what would be his place? What road would Banion have to walk?

All of these factors would weigh heavily on each of them. But even though they would be left with an empty place in their hearts, the journey itself would never be forgotten. When they first met, all of them had hidden fears and insecurities. Over the course of the quest, all of them had battled fierce inner demons and had triumphed over self doubt to achieve incomprehensible results. The lessons they had learned about themselves and humanity would always live in their hearts. Through strife and doubt was born strength. Through suffering they found friendship and the bond of family. Through the death of their enemies they found love for one another.

In the end, their beliefs and hearts had been sculpted by anguish, but it did not leave them as lifeless husks filled with terror. Instead, this torture had pushed them to evolve into a heightened state where fierce moral convictions had formed, as opposed to seething hatred.

Living through such events can turn the most hardened into lost souls filled with self pity. Nova 7 had held onto a belief in one another in order to cope with and understand this terror. Through their friendship and fierce loyalty to each other, a much different set of emotions was chiseled into them. Courage, honor, valor, love, sacrifice, honesty, and trust were forever etched inside their souls. The journey had tested them and had nearly killed all of them, but instead of descending into madness, they persevered and survived, becoming stronger.

The essence of the sorrow that all of them felt was based upon this idea. They had never known who they really were until they were tested under the most horrific conditions. The sorrow they felt was due to the fact that each member of Nova 7 had learned their true place in the world and discovered their own personality through one another. It was as if they all had gone through a second childhood, being tested at the highest levels. Losing each other was like losing that second childhood. The lessons learned were burned into them, but it was sad to think that the companions would soon have to part ways, and there was a good chance that they would never see each other again.

As they laughed and talked, all of Nova 7 felt the same emotions. They never spoke about such sentiment; they didn't have to. Each of them felt the same way and knew the sadness of leaving was weighing heavy on all of them. Focusing on the best of times, they recounted daring deeds and acts of selfless courage. Ignoring the inevitable parting of ways, they skirted the intense emotion and talked of the good times. In the end, victory had never tasted sweeter nor more bitter.

Chapter 16
History of the Dark Order

The main hallways within the palace of Stonen were quiet. All of the military personnel were inside the Truce Hall, making preparations for the nuclear launch that would occur just after sunrise the next morning. As the Iron Kai military prepared the warhead, the rest of the city was in complete silence. For the citizens, it was just another day. The city's civilian population was still recuperating from the vicious Reaper Kai attack, and the general sentiment was somewhat somber.

The members of Nova 7 were keeping close to Mineera, who was still recovering from her wounds. They tended to her needs late into the night. Finally, totally exhausted from her ordeal, she fell asleep and the rest of the team tried to do the same. With the great crusade finally at an end, the only thing on their minds was the next morning, a time when the sky would rain fire once more as a plume of nuclear energy would be unleashed against the Reaper Kai capital of Detro Tech City.

Banion couldn't sleep a wink, but that was normal. Jared was tossing and turning endlessly in his bed. As the tribal warrior thought about the next day, he continually fondled the mystical raven totem around his neck. Tani was even more agitated and couldn't even get himself to lie down in the bed. Though they all suffered anxiety in different ways, the reason was the same. Nova 7 had found a nuclear weapon and had returned that weapon to the Iron Kai Empire with the intent of eradicating an entire race. Even though the Reaper Kai were evil to the core and would never relent or yield, it was still a heavy emotional burden to think that one was directly tied to the genocide of an entire race by use of a nuclear weapon.

On many occasions, they had each thought about the consequences of their actions, but they always seemed to defer the emotions for a later time. The time to defer was over and the time to deal with such emotions was now. As their conscience wore at their senses, each of them wondered if it could have been different. Was there some way to avoid the outcome of the war? Was there any possibility for a peaceful solution?

Time and time again they tried to imagine that it could have been different. Time and time again they tried to forget the horrendous images burned into their memories. Banion had lost his mother, uncle, and wife to the Reaper Kai. His stance on the matter was resolved quickly and he knew that there was no other way. Jared changed his mind back and forth several times but finally his thoughts continually settled on the images and events of the night Rasheed fell to the Reaper Kai. Jared concluded that such reckless aggression and needless slaughter demanded harsh retribution. The thought of genocide was on his mind but in the end, he felt strongly that the use of the warhead on the Reaper Kai was the only solution.

Tani, on the other hand, seemed to have the hardest time with the issue facing them. He was stricken with fear about the entire situation and felt that his actions had directly led to the success of the mission. If it were not for Tani, the warhead would never have been liberated from its highly protected vault. This fact made the tribal feel directly responsible for the events unfolding. He was certain that his actions would lead to the deaths of several hundred thousand Reaper Kai. All of Nova 7's actions would ultimately lead to the destruction of an entire race. This overwhelming raw emotion led to a deep sense of dread that had crept into his soul and would not abate. To say that Tani was rocked with guilt was an understatement.

Still too restless to even lie down, he stood up and exited the palace infirmary. He wanted to escape his emotions but his emotions followed him. Sighing, he shook his head and looked around the hallways of the great palace of Stonen. His surroundings were strangely quiet, almost a little too quiet considering what the next day would bring to the world. It almost made him want to laugh, seeing the deep solitude and loneliness of the palace. For a split second, it almost felt like the night before Rasheed was attacked by the Reaper Kai. Shirking the odd feeling, he decided to allow himself to get lost and explore the palace.

Passing down the main hall, he spun around on more than one occasion, feeling almost as if someone or something was watching him from the darkness. He shook off the creepy feeling and wandered the halls, passing from room to room until he was totally lost and unable to find his way back to the infirmary. Despite his disorientation, he found he simply didn't care. There was no sense of time for Tani as he wandered and contemplated the events that had taken him, so long ago, from the tribal village of Scarskin to a place where he was right smack in the middle of a military strike that would reduce a city to a rising plume of radioactive ash.

As he was passing down a great hallway, a strange smell greeted his nose. It was so stunning to him, he thought he was hallucinating. The smell of Tani's old room back in Scarskin seemed to waft through his nostrils. Blinking several times, he looked around and began to sniff the air. He followed the weak scent, finding himself before a darkened archway that led into a shadowy series of rooms beyond. Breathing in quickly, he knew the smell was unmistakable. The smell of old, worn books filled his nose. Smiling, he knew that a library was just beyond the archway.

Elated by his discovery, his mind drifted away from the thought of mass genocide and he rushed inside, truly excited. Hungering to explore the library, the young scholar was shocked when he ran into someone within the dark chamber.

A strong man with a fiery red beard had materialized in Tani's path. Harmlessly bouncing off the man, Tani fell backwards and hit the stone floor.

Emperor Gunther was somewhat startled to find the tribal wandering around the imperial palace. Seeing him land hard on his rump, Gunther stretched out his hand to help him to his feet. Stunned, Tani felt the fire rise in his cheeks. He had only met the emperor earlier that day and felt suddenly that he was intruding upon the library and the emperor's personal space.

Looking at Gunther remorsefully, Tani tried to apologize for the intrusion. "I'm so sorry, I didn't see you in here and I'll get out of your way." Turning away, Tani tried to remove himself from the room.

"Hold on a second," Gunther boomed in a powerful voice which was so stern and commanding, Tani felt weak before him and halted dead in his tracks. Turning around, the tribal scholar had a sheepish look on his face, sensing that he was about to be reprimanded. "You are Tani, correct? A member of Nova 7? We met earlier today?"

"Yeah, I'm terribly sorry to intrude in here. I smelled books and thought I would have a look."

"You smelled books?" Gunther chuckled, his expression amused. He stared at the tribal, sizing him up. Finally his gaze settled on Tani's wire-rim glasses. "I would assume that you are the scholar that I've heard so much about, a demolitions expert and intellectual of the ancient world?"

"Yeah, that's me," Tani said, his cheeks still flushed.

"Well, if you're looking for books, you've come to the right place." Motioning him inside, Gunther urged Tani to enter. "Come on in and take a look. We have a wonderful collection."

"I should really get going." Tani's tone was meek.

"Get in here and have a look." Gunther spoke with a light grumble in his voice.

Nodding, Tani did not want to disobey his host.

The southern wall of the library featured a sprawling window overlooking the great lake below. An enormous table constructed of dark wood stood near the window, and upon it was a finely crafted lamp with a stained glass lampshade, lit with electric bulbs. A huge book was open on the table, filled with strange pictures and diagrams, as well as a considerable amount of fine text.

Seeing his interest in the book, Gunther suddenly became uncomfortable and closed it. Smiling, Tani viewed the book with odd recognition. "I've seen that book before."

"I don't think so," Gunther said. "This is an extremely rare book."

"No, really, I've seen that same book before."

"I doubt it. There are only two in existence, this being the first and the other is in…"

Tani interrupted. "The other is in the great library in Rasheed."

Stunned, Gunther smiled at the tribal. "You have got to be kidding me. You've seen *The History of the Dark Order*? No one but the ruling family had seen it, I thought."

"I haven't seen it directly. The librarian read to us from the book, giving us a brief summary of Reaper Kai history," Tani responded.

Intrigued by Tani's intellect and powers of observation, Gunther pulled out a chair and motioned to the tribal. The scholar sat down, looking at the book with hungry eyes. Seeing his interest, Gunther sat in the chair next to him. He opened the ancient tome, but seemed hesitant to show it to Tani. Finally, the tribal's curious eyes urged Gunther to share the wicked tome.

"There are only two copies of this book in existence. The two copies were originally in this library. When King Toil wed Asagara, the murderous Reaper Kai priestess, I sent the second copy to him as a wedding gift. This gesture was officially considered as an insult by Rasheed at first, and I was scorned as a troublemaker. But after King Toil learned more about his new bride, it was quite apparent that he regarded the gift as a blessing. After his wife was killed in Dune Station by your friend Banion O'Neil, King Toil severed all ties to the Reaper Kai Empire and conspired with me in secret, forging an alliance between our two nations. The book apparently survived, as you encountered it in the great library of Rasheed."

As Gunther spoke, Tani was enthralled. Not wanting to interrupt, he watched closely as Gunther began to flip the pages, revealing demonic images and mystic symbols.

"Over 700 years ago, Emperor Reginald Dauer ordered a history of the Dark Order to be written. Mind you, this was over 200 years prior to the first insurrection that plunged our empire into a 300-year civil war. Dauer was a visionary for our people and had extensive knowledge that a secret society had formed and was practicing some form of devil worship. This secret society was said to have members that could summon spirits from hell itself. Others claimed that they could manipulate objects by thought alone. There was also evidence that some were able to coerce and 'possess' others through meditation. As rumors of this secret society grew, Emperor Dauer watched them very carefully and had even sent spies to try to infiltrate this cabal. His mission was a success and he started to compile information about their strange powers and their sinister rituals."

Still enthralled, Tani urged Gunther to continue.

"His spies had uncovered that the secret society was arranging all of the marriages between their followers. The high priests were trying to breed society members to create enhanced abilities. The priests felt that through selective breeding and absolute control over mating through arranged marriage, they could create an entire race of people that had these supernatural abilities. The initial matings did prove fruitful, as many of the offspring were born with psychic abilities. This enhanced psychic ability gave the secret society power. They used this power to influence businesses at first and finally they began to infiltrate the government and military. After several generations of arranged marriages, they shifted to a more intricate plan of selective reproduction."

Gunther flipped the page, revealing a grotesque picture of some sort of perverse mating ritual where red-robed priests were impregnating captives shackled to a wall. Gasping, Tani was shocked by such perversion.

"This was the first time that breeding rituals had been observed. The priests began buying slaves from the less civilized regions of the Darken Realm. The slaves were used to accelerate the breeding process. If a child did not display psychic abilities by age eight, that child was sacrificed. Killing off any child without psychic ability purified their race. As a result of this mating ritual, there was not a single adult who didn't have psychic powers."

"That is totally obscene," Tani said in a harsh tone, absolutely shocked.

"That's not the half of it. After gaining substantial power, and with the majority of their order possessing psychic abilities, all of the spies that had been infiltrating the order for several generations were put to death. The last information that was uncovered dealt with ancient texts from before the apocalypse. As the story goes, the Dark Order had procured writings from nearly 4,000 years before the apocalypse. The priests were translating the demonic writings and supposedly had stumbled upon a ritual of binding, a ritual that was reputed to bind demonic entities to the living.

"It was during this time that a great plague broke over the empire. Thousands and thousands died. Members rumored to be part of the Dark Order were unaffected by this strange plague. Centuries of mistrust boiled over and the Great Purges were initiated by the emperor, who blamed the Dark Order for the plague gripping his empire. Bloody witch hunts began and many priests and innocent people alike were slaughtered. The rising tensions gave birth to an open civil war. The Dark Order rose from the shadows with considerable might and sought to overthrow the empire. It was in these times that the Reaper Kai were born and separated from the Iron Kai Empire.

"The next 300 years saw bloodshed unmatched. During this time, the Iron Kai fought openly with the Reaper Kai and the results were devastating. More people in our empire died in the last years of the civil war than exist throughout the entire empire today. Our population was so horribly decimated that even now we still do not have the population that we did one hundred years ago. We believed that the Dark Order had been destroyed during the final days of the civil war, but we were horribly wrong."

"I've heard this part of the story from the librarian in Rasheed. The Reaper Kai were thought to be annihilated, but they had retreated into the wilds of the Darken Realm instead, growing strong in the solitude," Tani contributed.

"You are correct." Gunther nodded at Tani. "During their disappearance, they mastered ancient technologies, uncovering a robotic production site in the ruins of an ancient city. When they brought this technology back to life, the Biogtechs were born, machines that followed their demonic masters without question. Unlocking further ancient technology, the Splicers, mechanical parasites that disable a human host and take it over, were then unleashed, thus giving the Reaper Kai additional slaves."

"We encountered this technology; the Splicer is a true horror of the technological world," Tani said. Nodding in agreement, Gunther continued the story.

"Also in this time, the priests continued their research of the ancient demonic texts. The ritual of binding that I spoke of before had been mastered. The Reaper Kai watched the stars and communed with demons, searching for a sign. As the story goes, a child was born from the Reaper Kai with exceptional powers, a child that was able to commune directly with demons by allowing them to enter his body. This child was so strong and filled with hate that even though the demons freely entered his body, he was able to control the spirits within him.

"Knowing that this child was their dark messiah, the Reaper Kai order performed the ritual of binding, sacrificing this child while performing the ancient incantations. This resulted in dozens of demonic spirits being bound into the dead corpse of the child. What they didn't expect was that the soul of this child never left. The child awoke, a lifeless husk filled with demonic forces within. This child, although his body was no longer alive, fed off the evil energy and grew into a frail, withered form. This priest came to power over the Dark Order and is known as Father Vertigo."

"Vertigo!" Tani spoke in an excited tone. "The priest that Banion and Jared killed in the battle of Rasheed?"

"Supposedly killed," Gunther concluded in a grim tone. "We have intelligence from Rasheed after the fall of the city that Vertigo survived and is still 'alive'."

"Supposedly killed?"

"Father Vertigo is extremely powerful. Legends say that he has walked this earth for the last 200 years or more."

"So where is he now?" Tani quizzed.

"We don't know. We suspect that he is in Detro Tech City, the capital of the Reaper Kai Empire. When we detonate the nuclear warhead in their city tomorrow, I hope that he is finally put to rest and is killed for all time."

"I never realized the extent of the evil that has consumed your empire for the last 700 years." Tani spoke with a melancholy look on his face.

"You look disheartened."

"I am. I've spent the last hours thinking that what we have done by finding the nuclear warhead was completely wrong. I felt guilt for being part of an act of genocide, but I never really understood what was at stake. I had no idea that the Reaper Kai had caused so much suffering, especially over the last 300 years."

"Our estimates and casualty reports from the 300-year civil war to today show that roughly a half a million people have died as a result of the Dark Order. Think about your home, master Tani; how many people live in your village?"

The horror suddenly overtook him. "Our village has about twenty, maybe twenty five thousand people. To imagine that five hundred thousand people have died as a result of the Reaper Kai is unthinkable."

"I know. That is why we must do what must be done. I don't like the thought of using a nuclear warhead, but the world cannot exist if the Reaper Kai are allowed to survive. We must purge them once and for all from this earth; drive them to the grave forever. Do you know how many sleepless nights I have had, listening to the radios in the Truce Hall, listening to my people die and suffer on the battlefield? The sound of their voices and seeing them die in battle is something that has been burned into my soul. I simply cannot let another generation suffer the wrath of the Dark Order. I cannot do it. Even though using the power of the ancients is horrific, it is a risk and sacrifice that I'm willing to make."

"I was foolish to think that our crusade was heartless," Tani said solemnly.

"There's nothing foolish about wanting peace in this world. Never think that questioning genocide is an act of weakness. I don't want to do what must be done tomorrow, but I have to, so that my people and the future people of the Darken Realm can live peaceful, productive lives without the taint of evil gripping them. I'm sorry that you had to be part of this, Tani. I'm sorry that you had to bear this burden and stain upon your soul. If we had other options, I would welcome them."

"I never thought that I would be here, having to wrestle with such a dilemma. I was naïve when I left home, thinking about adventure. Sure, we've seen the world and traveled across this continent many times, but the things that I've seen and felt scare me. I know how you feel. When Rasheed fell, we were there. I can never forget when we escaped onto the ship in the harbor. So few escaped onto the boats, and as we pulled away from the harbor, I can remember hearing the screams and seeing the terror on the faces of those who were left behind. In that moment, I felt lucky to be alive but also guilty. I felt that I didn't deserve to be saved and almost wished that I would have died that night. After everything that we've done, only now do I understand why I was saved, why all of Nova 7 was saved. If it weren't for us, the war would be very different," Tani concluded.

Gunther nodded, a somber look gracing his face. "I have never admitted this to anyone, not even my most trusted officers. We are on the verge of ruin, this empire. The enemy is much stronger than I'd ever imagined. It was blind fortune that we survived the invasion and managed to repel the Reaper Kai forces. Your success is more important than you think. If it weren't for your actions and the actions of Nova 7, this empire would fall. It's not a matter of if but when. The reason that you survived was to save us all. Don't ever think that you don't matter. You were spared that night so that you could save us all from tyranny. Don't feel guilt for living that night, feel proud that you've honored their deaths by bringing justice to their killers. You are a savior, not a monster, and don't ever think otherwise. These are tough times and you were strong enough to do what must be done. I will always value what you've done, and will do whatever I can to help you and the rest of Nova 7 for the rest of my days on this earth."

Gunther smiled at the tribal with a heavy heart. Reaching out, he patted him on the shoulder. He turned to look out the window of the library, where the darkness clung to the land. There was a smile on his face as he looked into the darkness of the night. Instead of despair, his expression was one of hope.

Tani looked out the window as well. He understood in that moment what Gunther was thinking. Even though the land was bathed in darkness, the morning light would soon burst over the horizon and drive away the shadow; when the sun rose, the taint of the Dark Order would also be driven away. Hope was on the horizon and an end to suffering, an end to tyranny, was close at hand.

Chapter 17
Liberation

An ominous darkness clung to the tower. Even though the morning sun shone brightly upon it, the light did not seem to penetrate the unnatural gloom. Slowly ascending the stairs into the tower, Marion Toil gripped her hands together tightly. She had been summoned by Father Vertigo himself and was not anticipating this audience. Getting herself under control, Marion focused on her secret thoughts. She knew she had to hide certain truths from the lord of evil or she herself would be in mortal danger.

Concealing these truths deep down within her twisted soul, she put up a barrier of thorns around her mind, filling herself with feelings of cruelty and malice. Letting this angry hunger take over, she allowed the haunting rage to envelop her as it had on so many other occasions. But where in the past she had let these destructive feelings rule and guide her actions, today this set of emotions was used to obfuscate and hide her true thoughts.

Step by agonizing step Marion ascended the tower. The closer she got to the top, the more the air seemed to chill and almost buzz with evil energy. To stand in the presence of Vertigo, an entity that had walked the earth for hundreds of years and was totally ruled by the demons held within the husk that was his body, was truly unnerving. Looking down at the stairs, she determined to try not to look at him directly, for if she did, he might be able to tell her true intentions, intentions that could lead the Reaper Kai order to ruin.

A harsh smell greeted her nose. Looking up from the steps, she spotted a sinister creature garbed in red robes gibbering at her, speaking the language of darkness. The Goat Minion snarled at her approach even though she had been summoned to the chamber. She stared the beast in the eye; it did not relent, nor did she. For a brief moment, they maintained eye contact and there was a sense that combat was about to erupt between the two. Finally, after several strained, tense moments, the Goat Minion bleated at her, stomping its right hoofed foot against the stone landing several times. Unintimidated, Marion passed beyond the foul creature and pressed on into the tower room. Averting her gaze from the figure before her, she dropped her eyes to the floor once more.

"You sent for me, master." She spoke in a coy tone.

"We received a radio transmission from a blockade within the Iron Kai Empire, a mere 30 miles from the city of Stonen. Apparently, two vehicles punched through the barricade and ultimately escaped with the help of Iron Kai gunships. The lead vehicle was driven by a man matching the description of Banion O'Neil, accompanied by Mineera of Gogoli, our old diplomat, who betrayed us. It appears that Nova 7 has breached the perimeter and escaped into Iron Kai custody." Vertigo was greatly angered by the news. As he spoke, his strange voice boomed from his frail frame with supernatural splendor. The more agitated he became, the more the light seemed to fade and wither around him. Marion felt as if she were witnessing a solar eclipse; she shifted uneasily as the room became unnaturally dark, so dark that she could barely see Vertigo's pasty white face leering at her in the shadows.

"That is grave news indeed." Marion's tone was submissive.

"Grave news?" Vertigo boomed once more. As he did, a specter of blue light erupted from his body, a ghostly form that swirled around him for a few seconds before disappearing back inside him. "Nova 7's mission was to obtain a nuclear warhead. After many months of not being able to find them, they show up on the doorstep of the Iron Kai, over 2,000 miles from their last known position. I have sought the council of great spirits but cannot divine if Nova 7 was successful in its mission. As a result, I have no idea if they have discovered a nuclear warhead. It is possible that Nova 7 has succeeded in their mission, and the Iron Kai are now in possession of a nuclear warhead!"

Blinking several times, Marion was stunned. Could it be true? Was it possible that the team had truly done the impossible and now the most powerful weapon that the ancients had ever created was in the hands of the enemy? Although shocked by this revelation, deep down her heart was lifted; the end of the Dark Order, the end of her agony, could be drawing near. Most of the Reaper Kai would fear such news, but Marion remained dispassionate, not wanting to allow Vertigo to read her true intentions, intentions that had already led her to betray the Reaper Kai and allow a known enemy scout, Globulus, to escape unharmed.

"That is not possible," Marion declared, continuing the ruse. "It cannot be true that Nova 7 has uncovered a nuclear warhead. No such weaponry still exists."

"Not possible? Our Reaper Kai expedition sent to kill Nova 7 and recover the warhead has not made contact with us in over five months. Somehow, Nova 7 eluded our forces and managed to escape unharmed, and now it is possible that they have the prize of all prizes. And I am certain that a nuclear launch will be close at hand. I have communed with the spirits and they have revealed nothing to me. I have no idea what the target of the warhead will be! Your foul sibling from childhood, Globulus, has escaped with knowledge that I still draw breath and that I am here in Rasheed. I sent your mercenary assassin Guillotine to track and kill him, but as of yet, I've heard nothing from him, as well. Have you any news from Guillotine?"

The question spiked a sense of fear in her. Marion herself had slaughtered Guillotine by allowing her spiders to feast on his warm flesh in an attempt to atone for her sins, and enabled Globulus to escape with information about the Biogtech production facility in Metalweaver Flats and that Father Vertigo was still alive and in the city of Rasheed. Marion's intent was to put things right, in her own sick way. She had betrayed Vertigo and the entire Reaper Kai order. Knowing that Vertigo was extremely attuned to emotions, Marion was certain that her soul had crossed a terrible line.

As she stood in the darkness, he could feel her fear; sense the dread rising in her heart. He stepped forward into the gloom, the outline of his ashen face revealed in the flickering candlelight. His forked beard came into view, quivering like a tuning fork set in motion. Staring at her, he almost appeared to be sniffing the air to catch the scent of her fear.

"What's this?" he crooned and his black pupils settled upon her. "Let me into your black heart."

A sickening feeling washed over her; the soul of Vertigo himself had stretched forward and touched her, invading her senses and mind. Struggling, she knew that she only had a few seconds to throw up a defense against his dark magic. Immediately shifting her thoughts, she focused on memories, harsh memories of Vertigo and everything vile and cruel that he had ever done to her.

Thinking of past events, she remembered the countless times that she had been tortured for failing him. As she raised these memories to the surface, she could still feel the agents of darkness batter and beat her. Straining, she sensed the scent of her own blood waft through her nostrils as she thought of the torture she had endured. She focused on the hate she felt for him, the feeling of loathing that coursed through her. It was all his fault, the suffering she had endured, both physically and spiritually. A surge of anger rocked her. In that moment, her entire soul was polarized and this emotion began to take shape in her mind. She hated Vertigo with all of her being and allowed this feeling to take over. Quivering, she gritted her teeth while staring at him. She wanted nothing more than to see him suffer as she had. She wanted him to feel pain, the same pain that she had felt in extreme torture. Giving in to the hate, she knew that it would be her only way to survive his soul digging around inside of her mind.

The sensation of hate was so pure, so strong; Vertigo could feel nothing else in her. He had suspicions about her, but he could not sense any deception in her due to the loathing anger she had towards him. It was strange that this emotion of hate could prevent him from seeing that she had betrayed him and the entire Reaper Kai order. As she maintained this strong aura around her, Vertigo retreated, unable to read her.

"I'm glad you hate me." He spoke in a dark tone. "I know that I am a powerful leader and have influence over you, since you loathe and want to kill me. It is a great thing to be the focus of such anger. You honor me with your rage. I've always said that your hate will make you strong."

"You have no idea how strong I am." She smiled in the darkness of the room. In that moment, she was something worse than Vertigo, something totally consumed with bitterness. Smiling at him, she knew that her betrayal would eventually lead to his demise. She had crossed a terrible line again, this time selling out her evil cohorts to find peace and atonement with Globulus. Globulus would escape into the northlands and would reveal that the primary production facility was not Detro Tech City but rather Metalweaver Flats. This revelation would lead to an offensive strike against the facility and could lead to the destruction of the Reaper Kai war machine, which could ultimately lead to the destruction of Vertigo himself. "My hate has made me very strong, Vertigo. Through your dark vision, I now know my place in this world. I know my destiny. Thank you for your tutelage; it was not wasted, my lord. In time I will pay you homage for your teachings." Bowing before him, she had a sinister look on her face.

"Since we have not heard from your assassin Guillotine, we have no idea if Globulus has made contact with the Iron Kai. If he has, there is a good chance that the nuclear warhead will be directed at me, here in Rasheed," Vertigo speculated.

"What is your will, my master?" Marion asked.

"We are evacuating Rasheed and will move our operations to Metalweaver Flats. I cannot risk being the focus of such an attack. But we must make haste. If Nova 7 reached Stonen last night, there is a good chance that the warhead will be fired as soon as possible. We are leaving this city immediately."

"But what of Detro Tech City, my lord? The Iron Kai will surely target our capital city if they do not target Rasheed."

"I have just sent word to our people in the city. I have ordered them to fight to the death and keep as many enemy troops as possible pinned, so that if a warhead does hit, we take as many Iron Kai troops out of action as possible."

"That is insane!" Marion was shocked by his logic.

"Insane?" he boomed. "There is no other option. If we retreat from the city, the Iron Kai will slaughter our people as they flee. If we retreat, the Iron Kai will take control of our production facilities. We cannot afford to escape. Our only option is to stand and fight, no matter what the cost. If the enemy has a warhead, the Reaper Kai in Detro Tech City already have a death sentence on their heads. This way, we can kill as many of the enemy troops as possible before the warhead hits. I want to cause maximum damage to the enemy; nothing else matters."

Such reckless ambition was chilling. Vertigo knew that his people were doomed and instead of trying to save them, he ordered them to fight to the death and accept their fate, being incinerated in a plume of nuclear fire. In a world of madness, such actions were the norm, not the exception.

"Your will be done, my lord. We will abandon Rasheed and travel to Metalweaver Flats."

"Excellent. Ensure that we leave within the hour," Vertigo rasped.

Marion bowed before the lord of evil and quickly exited the tower. Rushing down the stairs to make ready to escape Rasheed, she had a secret wish inside her heart. Deep down, Marion hoped that Globulus had made it to the safety of the Iron Kai territory. If he had, there was a good chance that the target of the nuclear warhead would be the real threat to peace, the secret element of the Reaper Kai war machine. Marion hoped deep down that the target of the nuclear attack would be Metalweaver Flats and secretly wished that she would be there when the warhead came down; she wished in the core of her soul that she would be burned out of existence in a flash blazing radiant energy, finally free from the sorrow in her heart.

Chapter 18
Full Retreat

The assault was relentless. Just before dawn, nearly 20,000 Biogtech soldiers, led by a staggering 10,000 Reaper Kai priests, focused on punching through the heavily fortified Iron Kai battle lines within the besieged metropolis of Detro Tech City, along the waterfront and center of the city. The number of casualties on both sides was mounting quickly and there was real doubt if the battle line could be held at all. Field Marshal Mills, leader of the Iron Kai Forces in the Reaper Kai capital, watched in horror as the enemy forces attacked ceaselessly. Although Mills had nearly 70,000 troops, the attack he faced was fierce and deadly.

"Field Marshal Mills!" a radio burst out in the command center within the heart of the Reaper Kai capital.

"This is Mills," he said into the radio, wiping the sweat from his brow. From his vantage point in the abandoned office building, he could see additional troops pouring from the heart of the Reaper Kai capital.

"This is Captain Gray. We are being overrun on the water front. Requesting immediate air support. Gray over."

"Negative, Gray. Air support from Stonen has been grounded by the emperor himself. You need to hold that position. Mills out."

"We're getting slaughtered out here!"

"The entire Reaper Kai army has mobilized. All of our positions are under heavy attack. You must hold. We do not have any additional reinforcements to allocate."

"Damn it! Orders confirmed. We will hold. Gray out."

Just after Gray had confirmed his orders, the radio crackled to life again, this time from another officer pinned down near the center of the city.

"This is Lieutenant Dawson. I'm requesting immediate artillery support on position 10.12.342. We're being attacked by a heavy amount of Biogtech troops. Dawson over."

"Negative, Dawson. Artillery support is already being allocated to another position. You'll have to hold until we get the other location under control. Mills over."

The radio was silent for a brief second, and that eerie silence spoke volumes. The Iron Kai army had been laying siege to Detro Tech City for over a year, and the entire military in this region was on the verge of breaking down both physically and psychologically. The eerie silence was a testament to despair and Mills knew it.

"Acknowledged, HQ. Dawson out."

Slamming down the transmitter, Mills, too, was on the verge of falling apart. The enemy had never pulled all of its troops out for a full attack. All along the battle lines, the nearly 70,000 Iron Kai troops were being assaulted by tens of thousands of Biogtech troops and Reaper Kai alike. Some portions of the city were even reporting that unseasoned Reaper Kai children, only ten years of age, were involved in the battle. Thankfully for the Iron Kai troops, these children were too inexperienced with their psychic abilities to pose a real threat. But looking at the situation, Mills wondered if he could hold the battle lines and repel this full-scale attack. It seemed to him that every Reaper Kai in the city had been mobilized to attack his troops. Little did Mills know that he was absolutely correct; Father Vertigo had made a direct order for every Reaper Kai in the city to counter-attack the Iron Kai.

Mills himself was on the verge of giving up. His eyes quickly darted back and forth as he watched the enemy surge toward his own troops.

The fighting was extremely deadly and it had been estimated that the Iron Kai had lost over 10,000 troops since dawn. The enemy had taken similar losses, fighting like frenzied ants without any regard for their own safety. Mills watched this reckless assault with grim fascination. He witnessed hosts of priests charge machine-gun positions with psychic fire racing through the air, as well as other deadly demonic attacks. He stared in awe as dozens of priests were shredded by machine-gun fire. Normally, the psychic warriors were extremely effective, with one priest able to eradicate an entire squad of Iron Kai. But today, they were not under any restraint and there was no strategy at all to their actions; they simply continued to charge and die by the hundreds.

Seeing this behavior made Mills feel very uncomfortable. It just didn't make any sense. Over the last year, they had been playing a very careful game of attack and counter-attack with the enemy, and every move was cautious on the part of both armies. What Mills was witnessing in the Reaper Kai looked like pure desperation. As he shook his head in awe, his suspicions were about to be answered. The radio sprung to life once more.

"Field Marshal Mills," the radio crackled. For a brief moment, he did not respond, could not respond. Dreamily he looked at the radio and the words coming from it seemed to linger in his mind without comprehension.

"Field Marshal Mills," the radio crackled again.

Fighting with himself, he finally grabbed the radio and spoke into it. "This is Mills."

"I need you to authorize a defense action order. This is Emperor Gunther."

Stunned, Mills blinked several times. A defense action order was one of the most profound orders that could be issued in the Iron Kai military. Receiving a defense action order always meant something extremely critical. During the entire course of the war, Gunther had only issued one other defense action order— the declaration of war against the Reaper Kai.

"This is Mills, I'm waiting to authenticate your order." Mill snapped his fingers, and in response, an aide grabbed a lock box and quickly opened it, revealing a small book filled with codes and ciphers.

"The authentication code is echo alpha charlie nine one six bravo two five tango." Gunther spoke in a very calm voice.

Scanning the cipher book for the authentication code, Field Marshal Mills' aide nodded his head and confirmed that the defense action order was correct.

"Defense action authentication code has been authorized, Emperor Gunther. I am awaiting your orders," Mills said, a lump forming in his throat.

"I'm issuing a full retreat order for all of our forces and troops engaged within Detro Tech City. You have two hours to pull everyone out. Leave all artillery and heavy equipment. You are to proceed to no less than eighteen miles away from the city. I will issue a second order exactly two hours from now. You need to respond immediately to this second order."

Mills' heart was pounding and confusion enveloped him. "Say again? Full retreat?"

"That is confirmed," Gunther replied in a confident tone.

The confusion turned to rage. "We've fought and died over the last year to take this city. Do you know how many lives we've lost trying to take the ground that we've captured? If we retreat, all of   our   gains   are   for   naught."

"Are your forces under heavy attack right now?" Gunther quizzed him.

"Yes," Mills shot back.

"Are they fighting without any regard for their own safety? Are the enemy troops fighting out of desperation?" the emperor quizzed him again.

"Yes..." Mills' mind began to spin. He was stunned that Gunther was so clued in to the battle from such a distance.

"The package has been delivered and the enemy knows it. You have your orders, Field Marshal Mills," Gunther boomed into the radio.

Finally, Mills understood. The nuclear warhead had been recovered and was nearing launch. Looking at his watch, he marked the time and sprung into action. Motioning to all of his radio operators, he instructed them to execute a full retreat. Stunned, they waited a few seconds, unable to comprehend. Finally he blurted out that an inbound nuclear warhead was on its way. After hearing the news, the radios sprung to life. Within a few seconds, the order for a full retreat hit the airwaves.

The panic that ensued was horrendous. Having been under heavy siege for several hours, most of the troops felt that the city was being overrun. Fear took over and it didn't take long for their morale to buckle after hearing the order for a full retreat. Abandoning their posts and positions, the very same fortifications that it had taken them over a year to secure, sacrificing countless lives in the process, the Iron Kai army fled the city.

As the Iron Kai troops fled, a deeper sense of dread washed over the Reaper Kai. Both armies knew that the end was near. Having been ordered to engage the Iron Kai and kill as many as possible, the agents of evil gave chase, trying to maximize the slaughter in one last desperate act…

*   *   *

After forming a perimeter roughly 20 miles away from the city, the Iron Kai troops were gunning down any Reaper Kai that had given chase. Having taken refuge in a forest, the Iron Kai troops were killing anything that tried to escape Detro Tech City. The fields between the edge of the city and the forest protecting the Iron Kai troops were bloodied as thousands of Reaper Kai were slaughtered while trying to flee the doomed metropolis. With only ten minutes until the deadline, Field Marshal Mills had ordered his troops to dig in and take up defensive positions from the impending nuclear blast. As the troops outside the Reaper Kai capital braced for the attack, there was an ominous silence amongst the inhabitants of the Truce Hall.

The radios were pouring out panic as most of the Iron Kai troops managed to escape the city. Gunther stood over by the great windows of the Truce Hall, looking down at the great lake below. A heavy sense of dread had invaded his senses. The nuclear warhead was only a few minutes away from launch. All of his trusted military advisors as well as the members of Nova 7 watched him with silent gazes, waiting for him to say something. Collecting his thoughts, he turned from the window and faced his advisors.

"I have lived as emperor since I was a young child. In that time, I have had the opportunity to serve with the finest men and to serve the greatest empire in the entire Darken Realm. In that great number of years, I have borne witness to countless deeds of daring and courage as our soldiers have defended this empire from the Dark Order. In that time I have also witnessed countless acts of murder and slaughter wrought by the enemy that have stained this world for countless generations.

"It is difficult to weigh human life. I have struggled with this decision since the start of this war. I have struggled to see if an act of genocide could ever be construed as conscionable. I have concluded that no act of genocide is proper, no act of genocide is conscionable."

As he paused, those assembled in the room were confused. Had Gunther had second thoughts about using the nuclear warhead? Tensions had risen significantly. The emperor had just ordered a full retreat of all Iron Kai forces from Detro Tech City. If he had second thoughts about the use of the nuclear warhead, the Reaper Kai would certainly win the war.

Witnessing the panic on their faces, he did not respond to their frenzied looks. Instead, he maintained complete control and began to speak once more.

"No act of genocide is ever conscionable. For centuries, we have tried to form a peaceful existence between our empire and the Reaper Kai. In all of that time, not one diplomatic order has been honored by the Dark Order, not one promise kept. Every time we strive for peace, we are brought slaughter. No act of genocide is ever conscionable but we are not allowed the luxuries of conscience. We are not allowed a peaceful outlet to this war.

"The goals of this war are absolute. Either the Iron Kai or the Reaper Kai will win this battle and the loser will be put to death. We cannot allow the Reaper Kai to survive, nor can they allow us to live. The civil war that erupted hundreds of years ago is still a bitter beacon to both empires. It has come down to this and there is no other option in my opinion. No act of genocide is conscionable, but we must do this to survive. We will use the nuclear weapon on the enemy. We will then commit to purging and killing all remaining Reaper Kai that walk the earth. Our goal is now absolute: not one Reaper Kai will be allowed to live after this day."

Pausing once more, Gunther saw significant duress on the faces of his men. It was indeed a tough decision and burden to bear. Despite their deep concern, everyone in the room knew that it must be done. Everyone knew that countless diplomatic actions had resulted in nothing more than death and deceit.

"This is the darkest day in my life and in the history of this empire. If there is any other option, please let me know. If there is any other way, let me know now so that we can avoid this atrocity." Gunther's appeal to his officers was heartfelt as he begged for another option.

A brief silence fell over the room. Gunther looked at each officer in turn. Each of them looked back and nodded in agreement to his decision. Gunther then turned to Nova 7. Banion was the first and he nodded his head immediately; after having lost his entire family, foster family, and beloved wife to the Dark Order, there were no more doubts in his mind. Next Gunther looked at Jared, who reluctantly nodded in agreement. Mineera was next. Having been part of the Reaper Kai, she knew better than anyone in the room what they were capable of. If the Dark Order was not destroyed, Mineera knew that there would be endless darkness and suffering brought upon the world. Considering the alternative of demonic rule, Mineera nodded her head in agreement to using the warhead.

Finally, Gunther looked at Tani. They had spent the last evening poring over history books, and the tribal was extremely reluctant to use the warhead, feeling directly responsible for the deaths of a hundred thousand Reaper Kai. Having wrestled with the question for a long time, Tani remembered all of the horrible things that he had seen and endured on their travels. In that moment, his thoughts returned to the dock in Rasheed, and to the thousands of terrified citizens growing distant as the boat that the team had used to escape pushed out into the ocean. The screams that he had heard on that night were still in his mind, stinging at his sanity. Blinking through the memory, the tribal scholar knew that such hate could not be allowed to survive. With a determined nod, Tani gave his consent to the nuclear attack.

The decision was unanimous; not one person in the Truce Hall disagreed with the resolution to fire the warhead. Seeing this unity, Gunther moved over to the technician, turned his gaze to him, and asked, "What do I need to do?"

"Everything is ready for launch; all you have to do is lift this cover and press the button." The technician rose from his chair, allowing Gunther to sit at the launch controls.

Gunther lifted the cover, his finger quivering over the button. In that moment, he was rocked with extreme duress. He shook all over and tears began to run down his face. Shaking his head, he wished that there was another way; he wished that there was another alternative. He closed his eyes and took a deep breath. With a whisper, he uttered words meant only for his own ears. "I hate myself for what must be done. I hate this world for what must be done." Opening his eyes, Gunther pushed the button.

A resounding boom filled the space of the hall. The missile rose off the ground, propelled into the sky. As it rose in height, it began to arc, angling towards the Reaper Kai capital. Cutting efficiently through the air, the missile carrying the nuclear warhead hurled toward its target. Everyone in the Truce Hall ran to the window, looking off into the distance where the blast would occur. As the warhead flew toward its target, toward its destiny, Gunther grabbed the radio transmitter.

"Field Marshal Mills, three minutes until impact. Get all of your troops down and protected. Order them not to look at the blast. May our ancestors be with all of you. Gunther out."

Walking over to the Truce Hall windows, Gunther stared out, as did the other onlookers. An event that very few in the history of the world had ever witnessed and lived to tell the tale was about to take place. The most powerful weapon that mankind had ever created was about to be unleashed once more.

Chapter 19
The Day the Sky Rained Fire

There was a chill riding the morning wind. Cold air driven from the northlands had bathed the landscape with a fresh layer of frost. The forest and its surroundings were glistening in the sunlight as icy crystals clung to the landscape. The entire world appeared to be covered in a pristine, white blanket.

Beyond the forest, open fields stretched on toward a concrete metropolis. Littering the earth between the mighty city and the forest were frozen bodies, thousands of them, dressed in crimson robes, lying on the frost-covered stalks of golden grass. Streaks of blood had frozen in the frosty conditions, a grisly testament to hate. The dead were a silent display of failed hope. Intending to flee the doomed city, they had been cut down by gunfire as they fled.

Although the grasslands littered with the dead were a testament to anger and to the bitter finality of war, they were but a taste of the horror about to be unleashed.

Riding the cold winds of the northlands, a fearful messiah of change was hurtling toward the doomed city. A weapon made of anger, forged of ancient iron and failed dreams, the instrument of death was held aloft in the sky with a trail of burnt propellant, which served as the only evidence that it was truly in the world. As it traveled, tiny gears on the wings of the missile carefully adjusted with the intent of precisely targeting the city below. Electronics hummed and whistled inside the device as it came closer and closer to its destination.

Whirring, sensors inside the weapon clicked on as it neared its final descent. Created ten centuries ago, it still worked wonderfully, being the culmination of a hundred years of advanced engineering. So much time and love had gone into a device which had but one single purpose: to destroy. In a dark world, the weapon was a message, the only voice that evil would have no choice but to hear. Nearing its destiny, the mechanical weapon began to calibrate its altitude over the target. The tiny wings made a few final adjustments and the missile began its final sequence. A host of microchips sprung to life only a few seconds before its glorious death.

The time had come. The message was clear. Death was near at hand. A half mile above the target, the iron messiah, the weapon harvested from the ruins of America, was ready to sing its own praises and destroy the utopia of the devil himself. The nuclear weapon was a prophet of sorrow, a device that craved suffering and murder.

The home of the Dark Order braced for the weapon of the ancients. The weapon hummed as everything reached a state of perfection, each parameter precisely defined and fully aligned.

A bang tore the air over the Reaper Kai capital. A small explosion erupted from the warhead as the nuclear material was driven together to form an energetic mass of death. A split second later, the weapon roared to life.

A blinding flash of energy erupted as a shockwave of fire more intense than the sun exploded. The force of the blast roared toward the doomed city below. Intense energy and blinding light raced downwards. As the explosion struck the buildings, matter was torn asunder, blasted apart on a molecular level. The heat was so intense; concrete melted and turned to blistering vapor. Steel melted and disintegrated. Wood turned to smoke. Flesh turned to steaming vapor. As the sphere of energy engulfed the city and its inhabitants below, screams faded into the roar of radiant heat. The concussion and force of the blast vaporized the entire core of the city, driving down into the earth itself. As the earth took the brunt of the blast, the very shelf of the planet groaned as tremors rocked the landscape, setting off a series of earthquakes radiating from the epicenter of the blast.

From the radioactive crater, the blast wave reflected back into the air, sending a secondary shockwave of fire into the city. A roaring halo of energy erupted from the core of the crater, splintering outward, consuming everything in its path. The burning shockwave disintegrated the heart of an evil empire. The production facilities, monasteries of the devil, the cursed breeding pits, and homes of the Dark Order were all reduced to ash and fire. Grinding onward, the hungry flames raced down the streets, incinerating the demonic Reaper Kai in a blinding blaze.

As the force of the blast finally subsided, a vacuum formed at the center of the city where the blast had begun. Racing backwards, the air was pulled into the center of the radioactive crater. The force of the winds was so intense that tons and tons of debris and ash were sucked into a vortex of rising wind. Inhaling the radioactive dirt and fragments of matter, a superheated rising thermal of air grabbed a torrent of filth and levitated it high into the air.

It was a terrifying event to behold. The pristine layer of frost on the ground that had been gleaming white only a minute ago grew dull as all the light in the world seemed to disappear. An enormous cloud of debris was being pulled into the air. For many minutes the hungry vortex sucked the radioactive ash from the nuclear blast. As the ash rose thousands upon thousands of feet into the air, the sun, the very bringer of life to the world, seemed like a dim nightlight, drowned out by the rising plume of death. The towering mushroom cloud of ash erupted in the air, turning the day into a dim sunset. In the dingy grime of dust, large fragments of flaming, smoking debris began to rain down all over the area. Smaller fires erupted all around the blast crater as the flames consumed more of the city, causing more smoke to rise into the air.

For many tense moments, the rising plume of radioactive ash rose higher and higher into the air. The blast was so powerful that a plume of radioactive sludge towered nearly 40,000 feet in the air, taller than the highest mountain on earth, higher than any bird could fly. There was no natural wonder comparable to the devastating raw power that had just been unleashed.

As the weapon of all weapons decapitated the Reaper Kai Empire, the soldiers who had laid siege to the city for over a year cowered in the dim light. A chill ran down their spines as tendrils of debris began to rain down around them. Radioactive fallout, deadly dust charged with lethal radiation, began to collapse down from the black clouds. Fleeing in terror, the soldiers wished that such an event had never occurred.

While the Iron Kai army fled the field of battle, other onlookers stared on in horror. Hundreds of miles around, people had felt the blast and rushed to see the monstrous mushroom cloud rising into the air. In that moment, they knew that the Dark Order had been dealt a mortal wound and even though they hated the Reaper Kai, they hated even more that such reckless power had to be unleashed in the name of salvation.

In the Iron Kai capital city of Stonen, a group of leaders and heroes watched the blast from afar. Everyone in the mighty Truce Hall clambered around the windows, staring toward the Reaper Kai Empire in the distance in silent horror as the mushroom cloud drifted into the atmosphere. Although they believed that the war was over and that they were safe, each of them felt that a dire and horrible line had been crossed. There were no cheers of happiness, no boasts or war cries. Instead, everyone who had witnessed the event felt a somber wash of reality strike them. Not one person uttered a single word. Most could barely watch the spectacle unfold. After seeing the mushroom cloud rise into the air, most retreated from the windows, unable to watch any more.

The world had been betrayed once more that day. The callous power unleashed was a testament to a failed race of people whose ideals had led them to believe that power, true power, was born from technology and the need to destroy. In that moment, hundreds of thousands of people in the Darken Realm looked into the sky and knew that true power was not forged from uncontrollable weapons. Although the end of the Dark Order was apparent, with the dead turned to ash and drifting through the sky, it was a hollow and shallow victory.

Victory is a foolish ideal. Honor is a lost cause. Power is a ruthless savior. In a world filled with such death, there is no victory, honor, or power. Dreams are burned to ash, tyrants are made kings, and all are made to suffer. War has many consequences but only the foolish fail to see that violence always ends in ruin. Humanity is made up of nothing more than petty fools. As long as humanity exists, there will be fools. As long as humanity exists, there will be war. As long as there is war, the great circle of hate will exist and all are made to suffer.

Chapter 20
Retaliation

The setting sun had never looked so sweet. It was three days after the end of the war. News had spread quickly that the Reaper Kai had been utterly crushed. Their capital, Detro Tech City, had been reduced to ash and rubble by a nuclear assault. The survivors of the attack staggered from the ruins and sought to escape. Emperor Gunther, who had ordered the complete eradication of the Dark Order, had other plans for these survivors. Nearly 10,000 Reaper Kai who had survived the nuclear attack were killed in small skirmishes as they tried to flee from the toxic rubble.

On the edge of the Frontier in the northlands, a victory celebration was in full swing. The small town of Meeker's Grove was holding a banquet to honor the accomplishments of the gallant Iron Kai army.

As the sun pushed towards the western horizon, music erupted from the center of town. Jugglers, singers, dancers, and other entertainers were adding to the festive mood. Enormous wooden tables had been set up near the center of town and thousands of inhabitants patiently waited in lines to get their share of the feast. Troughs of bread were spread out near gigantic serving trays covered in finely roasted meats. Beer was plentiful and many of the townsfolk were already close to becoming utterly intoxicated.

The tempo of the celebration was festive. Laughing broke out among the assembled townspeople as the thought of war grew distant. The mayor of the small town ascended a podium and gave a victory speech. It was somewhat comical to many of the onlookers as the mayor embellished the town's role in the war. In reality, Meeker's Grove had supplied food to the Iron Kai Empire and nothing more, but the drunk mayor made it sound as if the small town had won the war.

While they reveled in their happiness, darkness overtook the land once more, plunging the world into shadow. As the celebration reached untold levels of joyous festivity, something ominous waited in the darkness.

Outside the town, near the outskirts, lingered a hidden terror. An army of Biogtechs 10,000 strong, led by 2,000 Reaper Kai battle priests, made ready to assault the township.

Hissing in the language of the devil himself, the lord of darkness, Father Vertigo, had taken to the field himself to deliver a potent message to the people of the Darken Realm.

"As foretold by our forefathers, we now stand on the field, ready to kill and slaughter all those feeble patrons of the light. We are beyond any sense of humanity. We stand as a beacon, a living embodiment of evil. We stand to serve our masters in hell with zealous intensity. It is your birthright to kill. It is your birthright to rule. As the enemy had laid waste to our brethren, we shall do the same and put to dust all those who would dare oppose us," Vertigo boomed in the darkness. He was seated atop a frail- looking horse with gleaming yellow eyes. Even though he was small in stature, Vertigo emitted a roaring oration to his troops. "We have suffered a great disgrace! The Iron Kai have killed most of our glorious race. It is your duty to avenge their deaths. It is your duty to send a message. Let your rage guide you. Let this disgrace lead you to do unspeakable acts. I want you to remove all shackles of morality. Do not have any remorse for the anger you feel. Take your rage out on the helpless. Do not feel guilt for killing them, setting them free from their failed beliefs. Teach them in their final moments that pain is the only outcome of their wretched lives."

His words had worked the Reaper Kai into a frenzy. Feeling a bloodlust wash over them, they hungered for the kill, licked their lips in anticipation of mass murder. "Go forth, my minions! Revel in the slaughter of innocence! Leave none standing. Leave none breathing. Kill everyone you meet, kill everyone you see. Make them suffer!"

A booming series of drums broke across the landscape. Howling in the darkness, the Reaper Kai priests were driven into an insane bloodlust. Screaming in rage, they drew weapons and braced themselves for the slaughter.

Marching from the darkness, the horde of Biogtechs hit the edge of the town with frightening results. Many of the townsfolk were drunk or well on the way to inebriation and were caught totally off guard. The rabble of robotic soldiers breached the perimeter and opened fire, cackling in the darkness. The laughter was shocking to hear, rising in intensity as the mindless robots began to kill and slaughter. Surging through the streets, wave after wave of mechanical soldiers stood twelve abreast, bearing automatic weapons. As they fired upon the banquet attendants, the results were staggering. They mowed down the people, leaving none unscathed. People of all ages were put to death without hesitation.

The attack was so surprising that panic rocked the townsfolk. There was not a single person who tried to resist the armies of darkness. Fleeing into the night, the shocked people were ill prepared for what lay beyond the buildings and protection of the town. Many rushed out of the town into the lush fields beyond. What they found was inescapable death. Chanting erupted in the darkness. Reaper Kai psychic warriors were channeling demonic energy. As they targeted the panicked citizens, screams sliced through the darkness. A light show of vibrant psychic attacks illuminated the night as hundreds were killed within a few minutes. Green streaks of light arced across the grasslands. Lances of fire erupted from the priests' fingertips. Purple wisps of demonic magic lingered and crept across the ground, seeking victims. Letting out bloodcurdling war cries, the priests hacked and bludgeoned the citizens, killing many in fierce close combat. The bodies and corpses mounted, and nothing could stop the Reaper Kai.

The town was absolutely surrounded. Those who remained near the buildings sought refuge within the houses and shops, barring the doors in a feeble attempt to resist the attack. Sinister to the end, the Reaper Kai forces didn't waste any time trying to break down the doors. Instead, they used flamethrowers to light the buildings on fire. The terrified townsfolk began to scream in agony as they were burned alive. Those who escaped by crashing through windows or running into the street were cut down by gunfire, shot by a barrage of bullets as they tried to flee.

Feeding their sadistic urges, the priests enjoyed the reckless slaughter, laughing and boasting as they butchered hapless victims. Father Vertigo further fanned the flames of savagery by praising his subjects, calling them saviors and heroes of the Dark Order. Hearing his praise, they embraced the cruelest parts of their natures. The slaughter became a testament to intense malice. Many of those trapped were tortured and mutilated as Vertigo watched with proud eyes, egging his minions on to perform even more inhuman acts of hatred.

The vicious attack was truly unnerving. In less than thirty minutes, over 2,000 people were murdered. Not a single citizen of Meeker's Grove survived the attack. There was not a single person left standing to tell the tale, just as Vertigo wanted. Smiling in the darkness, he could feel evil power coursing through him. He had committed a massacre but still wanted to kill more. His hunger would never be satisfied until all enemies were slaughtered and the Reaper Kai controlled the entire continent.

As Vertigo ordered his soldiers out of the burning town, the army set its sights on further atrocity. The Reaper Kai forces marched onward and by the time the sun rose over the Darken Realm, three more towns were laid to waste and over 8,000 people left dead in their wake.

The message of the Dark Order was clear; no other race would be allowed to live. There would be no mercy; there would be no salvation from the army marching across the Darken Realm. Although the Reaper Kai had been dealt a powerful blow, having lost their capital city, they were by no means defeated. Their primary production facility in Metalweaver Flats was churning out hundreds of Biogtech soldiers a day. The nuclear attack on the Reaper Kai was dire, but Vertigo had more than enough forces to put an end to the Iron Kai. With rage and a sense of vengeance guiding the remaining Reaper Kai priests, they were more savage and more dangerous than ever before.

Town after town would fall; city after city would be put to dust. The onslaught of death was so intense, it would take weeks for the Iron Kai to even discover that the Reaper Kai were still a threat. Vertigo's plan was to kill as many enemies as possible before they were discovered. The march across the Darken Realm would leave a bloody swath of death that would exceed the casualties seen during the entire first half of the war, a war that many thought was over.

Chapter 21
Recon

For more than a week, the entire Darken Realm had been celebrating the destruction of the Reaper Kai, save one empire: the Iron Kai. Gunther, much to the dismay of his people, failed to recognize that the end of the war had truly come. After a battle against the Reaper Kai Empire which had lasted for hundreds of years, he was skeptical that one military action would be potent enough to put the final nail in the coffin of the Dark Order.

His somber demeanor had filtered down through the ranks and the entire empire was pensive. His thoughts dwelt primarily on the multiple attacks that had been perpetrated by the Reaper Kai while their capital, Detro Tech City, was fully blockaded. Most of his military advisors felt that the Reaper Kai were secretly transporting troops through their battle lines, but Gunther thought otherwise. Deep down he had felt for a long time that there was a secondary, secret production site employed by the enemy.

Looking out the windows of the Truce Hall, Gunther stared at the lake below. A choking fog had settled over the lake and he was unable to see past the shoreline. The white mist at which he stared mirrored his senses and his thoughts. He knew that there was something he was missing, but it was just outside his field of vision. What was he missing? What secrets did the enemy still hold? Had he been made a fool this whole time? Much indecision and mystery clouded his mind, just like the fog clouding the lake below. His emotions were an exact mirror image of his surroundings. If only he could clear the fog in his mind, he might be able to understand the enemy better. Shaking his head in dismay, he wished that the sun, with its radiant light, would burn away the mist in his mind and allow his soul a reprieve from the unknown. With a sigh, he knew that the fog was still clinging to the world as it was clinging to his fragile senses. Moving away from the windows, he walked over to the communications area.

It was still early morning and most of the technicians were sleeping. Gunther had given most of them several days off after they had worked roughly eighteen-hour days for the last year. With the enemy on the run, he felt he could afford them that small luxury.

Staring at a pasty-eyed technician who was rubbing his eyes, Gunther watched him yawn deeply, still intently listening to radio communications throughout the empire. When he tapped him on the shoulder, the technician came to attention and crisply saluted Gunther, removing his headset quickly so that he could listen to his words.

"Any word from the reconnaissance teams?" Gunther asked with a distant look in his eye.

His technicians had grown weary of the question. Before the nuclear attack on Detro Tech City, Gunther had ordered seven reconnaissance teams to scour the Darken Realm for any possible secondary Biogtech production sites. They had been deployed months ago and as of yet, despite direct orders to make reports every three days by radio, none of the recon teams had reported back in over a month. In terms of military recon teams, not hearing back for a week was understandable, but not hearing from a recon team in a month usually meant that the entire team had been killed. With all of the recon teams most likely dead, Gunther was charging ahead blindly, leading an empire by sailing into a thick bank of fog like a captain on the ocean.

"I'm sorry to report, sir, that none of the recon teams have checked in yet. I will report any news of the recon teams immediately to you." The technician was courteous as he spoke, even though he had grown tired of the question. Gunther would typically ask at least ten times a day since the nuclear destruction of the enemy capital.

"I'm tired of waiting. Get Captain Maddock up here," Gunther ordered the technician. "I want him to put together fresh recon teams and get out there immediately. The last thing we need is another ambush."

"Ambush?" the technician echoed in a tone of disbelief. "The enemy is finished, my lord. Their capital has been reduced to ash and radioactive rubble."

Gunther shot the technician a dirty look. "I don't remember asking you for your opinion. Get Maddock up here."

"That won't be necessary, Gunther." Mad Dog Maddock, the emperor's trusted captain, pushed into the Truce Hall with a look of urgency on his face. "I have news for you."

Approaching Maddock briskly, Gunther could tell that something serious had occurred. "Your timing is perfect. I was just about to have you send out fresh recon teams."

"That won't be necessary, either. I was hoping that you would have some time for an audience with two visitors?" Maddock's tone was tense. "I think you'll find their story most interesting."

"Visitors?" Gunther asked, raising his eyebrows.

"Globulus of Rasheed and his mercenary companion seek an urgent audience with you."

"Globulus? King Toil's old bodyguard and war master?" Gunther quizzed. He had met the hippo hybrid many years ago on a diplomatic mission to Rasheed. A gigantic hippo covered in heavy scars was hard to forget.

"The same, my lord. He and his companion have urgent news about the Reaper Kai."

"Send them in, Maddock."

Maddock left the Truce Hall and returned a split second later. Striding into the Truce Hall in his wake was an enormous beastly creature. Standing so tall that he had to duck down to enter the room, Globulus was a monument to physical intimidation. Hundreds of pounds of solid muscle surrounded a frame of solid bone. His coppery brown skin was covered in scars where bullets had dug into his flesh or where other combat weapons had slashed him in the past. His eyes were fierce but gentle and he focused on Gunther with a look of relief.

His companion was a small woman. Dressed in combat fatigues, she was a comical sight. Such a petite woman looked out of place in combat attire. Her black hair was cut short, just below the ears. She walked with a light gait, soft and silent. Her face was delicate but a look of exhaustion covered it. The two companions had traveled a great many weeks with little rest, pressing on quickly to deliver dire news to the Iron Kai Empire.

"This is, of course, Globulus of Rasheed." Maddock gestured toward the beastly hippo warrior. "His companion is Carla Reins, one of the best mercenary snipers in all the Darken Realm, I am told."

Gunther regarded each of them with a polite nod of his head. Anxious to hear their news, his words were direct. "You both have my attention."

Collecting his thoughts, Globulus took a brief moment to formulate the information into a cohesive set of phrases instead of a panicked cry for help. "After our demolitions strike on the Gold Road, we set out to return to the Iron Kai Empire to aid further in commando attacks against the enemy. Our journey took us into the north western wastelands, roughly in between Rasheed and Rust Spire. We were a great many miles away from civilization when we came across something curious, something that turned our hearts to ice."

Taking a brief reprieve to take a breath, Globulus paused in his storytelling. Gunther felt a lump begin to form in his stomach. Tension was visibly present on his face and he knew that it was going to be a rough day. "What did you find?" he quizzed them.

Carla picked up the story at this point. Her voice chirped and chattered on quickly at breakneck speed. "There was a patch of earth disturbed by the passing of many troops, soldiers on the march. We investigated and found that the tracks were those of Biogtech soldiers, thousands of Biogtech soldiers."

"Biogtechs? Out in the wasteland northwest of Rasheed? There's nothing out there but one or two ramshackle towns. Why would there be thousands of Biogtechs in the middle of the wasteland?" Gunther was skeptical, but deep down he knew that this was it, the recon intelligence that the Iron Kai so desperately needed.

"We followed the tracks deep into the wasteland, seeking their origin. We passed into a town that had been sacked by the enemy. A Goat Minion attacked us that night as we slept in the ghost town."

"I don't like where this is going. A Goat Minion was in the ghost town? They don't usually wander outside of Reaper Kai-controlled territory; usually they're found near large bases or fortifications," Gunther added.

"You are correct." Carla's tone grew serious and she slowed her speech due to the serious nature of the topic. "Globulus was severely wounded by the encounter with the Goat Minion. We slowly pushed onward, moving to follow the trail of the Biogtech army. We managed to find ourselves in a heavily patrolled area. Reaper Kai tracker teams were swarming the desert and foothills. I had been there before and there'd been nothing but cacti and bare earth. But with the heavy Reaper Kai presence, we knew that whatever they were guarding was worth the risk. Passing over a ridgeline, we found ourselves above Metalweaver Flats."

The knot in Gunther's stomach had grown and pushed into his throat. Though barely able to talk, his eyes were wide as he listened to the chilling story unfold. He nodded for them to continue, not wanting to interrupt.

"We sat on the ridgeline above the valley and found excavation equipment tirelessly working to uncover a massive production facility, created by the ancients. In this valley, we saw hundreds of Biogtechs emerging from a production building. In that short span of time, we could literally watch them march out of the production buildings. I would say that they are producing a Biogtech soldier roughly every fifteen minutes."

"A Biogtech every fifteen minutes? A Biogtech soldier every fifteen minutes is 100 a day, roughly 3,000 a month!" The world seemed to shatter. The mystery of the Biogtech assaults on Rasheed, the Steel Crag Mining Guild, the Mord Tech Empire and even the Iron Kai finally made sense. The primary production facility was not in Detro Tech City, but rather in Metalweaver Flats. The numbers of troops being created was staggering. Shaking his head in disbelief, Gunther almost felt his knees buckle as his vision seemed to dull. Feeling as if he was about to faint, he was not receiving the news well. Anger exploded from him as months of frustration spilled over.

"We just used a nuclear warhead on their capital city, a city that we were slowly beginning to take with our army! Now I find out that their primary production site is in Metalweaver Flats! It took a miracle to locate that nuclear warhead and we wasted it! With the enemy making 3,000 troops a month, there could be tens of thousands of Biogtechs already out there!" Gunther boomed, his face bright red.

"That's not all, Gunther," Globulus said in a somber tone.

"Out with it then!" Gunther bellowed, irritated beyond belief.

"Father Vertigo still lives. He was alive in the city of Rasheed when last we were there."

"Rasheed?" Gunther was confused. "We have intelligence from multiple sources indicating that Vertigo was killed by Banion O'Neil and the local militia the night Rasheed fell."

"I was there the night Banion killed Vertigo. But when I was captured, I was taken to Rasheed. Vertigo still lives."

The situation was downright desperate. With the lord of the Reaper Kai still alive and the primary Biogtech production site fully operational, the Dark Order was still an enormous threat to the Darken Realm.

"I felt that we had cut the head off the snake." Gunther shook his head in dismay. "The entire war, they've made fools of us. I always felt there was a secondary production site but I never fathomed that it was churning out so many Biogtechs. If we don't act immediately and knock out that production facility, we are doomed."

"What are we going to do, Gunther?" Maddock asked with concern.

"We're going to invade Metalweaver Flats. Summon the war council; we cannot waste a single minute. Get Field Marshal Mills and Field Marshal Graves on the horn. We're mobilizing our entire army and everything we have to take out that production facility. Contact what is left of the Rasheed army, the Steel Crag Mining Guild militia, the Mord Tech infantry, and Globulus' tribe. Get every soldier you can and get them ready to march."

Maddock rushed over to the radio station and began to mobilize the Iron Kai Empire.

"What about us?" Globulus quizzed him.

"You? You and your little sniper friend are coming with us," Gunther boomed. "I want you to lead us directly to this production facility. I will not risk getting lost in the wasteland with our army."

"We'll take our leave then; it seems you have your hands full," Carla said, nodding to Gunther respectfully.

"One more thing." Gunther's tone was heavy. "Talk with Nova 7. They're still here in Stonen, taking a much-needed break. They are the best mercenary team in the entire Darken Realm and I have a sinking suspicion that we'll need their help again on this one."

"It's been a long time since I've seen them. We'll talk with Banion and Nova 7," Globulus concluded with a nod.

"Thank you for what you've done. Without your intelligence on Metalweaver Flats, I fear we would have been overrun by the enemy and not even known what was happening. You both have done a great service to the Iron Kai Empire."

"We were happy to serve."

The two companions exited the Truce Hall. As they moved down the hallway of the palace, technicians and military advisors who had been summoned to the Truce Hall were already rushing down the corridor, ready to make war once more.

The situation had never been more desperate. The Reaper Kai had been dealt a horrible blow but they were by no means defeated. War was brewing and the location of the final battle between the Iron Kai and the Reaper Kai was now known. If the Iron Kai failed to destroy the production facility in Metalweaver Flats, the Reaper Kai would slowly erode their defenses and overwhelm the Darken Realm with a never-ending tide of robotic soldiers.

As the mystery of the enemy unfolded, the fog on the lake began to burn away. Just as the haze of darkness had that had muddled Gunther's thoughts for many months finally lifted, the radiant sun burned through the fog. The mystery was gone, the indecision had left. Warm light lit the Truce Hall as the military advisors prepared to make war. Staring out at the fog being driven away by the sun, Gunther viewed the event as an omen. His heart surged and he was resolved yet again to see his people through this dark time. Hope was rekindled in his heart as, once more, this great leader set out to do the impossible.

Chapter 22
Reunion

"I would suggest you stop looking at him. You're only agitating him further," Mineera said, sighing and shaking her head. Looking directly at Jared, who had three beers in his stomach already, Mineera was trying to coax the tribal out of a fistfight.

Nova 7 had taken a much-needed rest after making it back to the Iron Kai Empire. They had been spending several days in the local pubs and bars. Growing bolder, the team decided to frequent a local military bar, one filled almost exclusively with Iron Kai soldiers.

"I want to piss him off," Jared said in a loud tone. People seated around the mercenary team stared in disgust. Nova 7 were clearly outsiders. Dressed in dirty clothes, the mercenary team smelled like they just had crawled out of the local sewer. The arrogant teenager boasting loudly was driving a spike of anger into the local patrons.

For military personnel, there was always a fight, always a need to be the biggest and baddest in the room. This situation was no different. A solider with a crew cut had been loudly mocking the mercenary team, laughing and jeering in their general direction. Banion simply ignored the fool; he knew better than to feed into his delusions. Tani retreated back from the situation, feeling a little intimidated and not wanting to draw attention to the team in such a hostile environment. Mineera also sat calmly, not even giving the soldier the time of day.

Jared, on the other hand, having drunk several beers, felt that he should give the soldier a piece of his mind. Staring at him, Jared began to laugh and point at the soldier, trying to push him over the edge.

"Where did you crawl out from, you little rat?" the soldier asked, standing up and extending his hands in an aggressive display. "You want to get your ass kicked, little kid?"

Smiling, Jared stood up and shouted back, "You're the one who's going to get his ass kicked if you don't shut your damn mouth. You want some? Come and get some!"

Angered, the soldier pushed through the crowded bar. Hurling his hands forward, he tried to grab Jared. However, the clumsy soldier was too slow and never knew what hit him. The drunk tribal was still more than a match for him. Ducking, Jared lunged forward and moved past the soldier. Trying to elbow him, the soldier swung his right arm around. Jared scrambled aside, grabbed his arm and spun it downward. Not wanting his arm to break outright, the soldier yielded to the attack, driven to his knees. Stunned by the savage counterattack from the teenage tribal, the soldier hesitated a split second, and that was all Jared needed. Closing his fist, Jared swung and smashed the soldier's nose, crushing it with a crunching thud. The attack was so quick and brutal that the soldier was almost knocked out. Continuing the assault, Jared punched him several more times, cracking a tooth and splitting his brow open. The dizzy soldier crashed to the floor. Unable to rise from the flurry of attacks, he simply covered his face in a crude attempt to shield himself.

Jared was out of control. Jumping on top of the soldier, he began to pummel him, striking him again and again. The rage that was inside of him was building like a volcano. Tender wounds that had cut his soul had begun to fester. Somehow, he was splintering, on the verge of madness, and the rage he was displaying was a tell-tale sign that he had a wounded heart and his spirit was stained.

"Jared!" Mineera yelled out as she watched him lose control.

"Hey, knock it off!" Tani whined.

Even Banion was stunned by the crazed act. It reminded him of so many other occasions when the tribal's rage seemed to take control of him. In that moment, Banion felt pity, not for the soldier being beaten senseless, but for Jared. Watching the tribal brutalize the soldier reminded Banion of himself, a shattered soul that cared about nothing but getting even. In that moment, he pitied Jared even more than himself. *"What have I done?"* Banion whispered to himself as he watched the disturbing events unfold. He felt guilty. When he had met the tribal, Jared had been arrogant but timid. If he could go back, Banion would have liked to make things different; he wished he could have spared the tribal's soul from the tumultuous events that they'd all had to endure.

Jared was lost in the zone, lost in a haze of rage. As he punched again and again, the soldier's face was beginning to look like hamburger. The tribal couldn't stop and to watch his behavior was truly frightening. Just when things were looking dire, someone moved in from behind the tribal.

Without warning, Jared was pulled off the soldier. Squirming, he was surprised to find that whatever had a grip of him was strong enough to completely lift him off the ground. He dangled in the air, cursing and shaking violently, trying to escape the iron hold. As he shouted wildly, the rest of Nova 7 was stunned to see what was gripping Jared.

It took a brief second for anyone to recognize the strange figure in the crowded bar. Standing tall and holding Jared like a child would hold a doll, the beastly creature was not human. Blinking in amazement, Banion was the first to make the connection.

"Globulus?" he asked with a smile, standing up and staring in awe.

Turning to view his captor, Jared cursed at the hippo hybrid restraining him.

"I think you need to calm down, little one," Globulus grumbled. "I'm not above crushing you to red paste." Throwing him down on the floor, Globulus turned around and spoke to several horrified soldiers who had watched the event unfold, ordering them, "Get your friend out of here and clean him up. And just so we're all clear, I suggest that you don't give Nova 7 any more crap. They saved all of our asses and they deserve your respect!"

The soldiers were stunned. Staring in disbelief, they viewed the mercenary team with bewildered glances. "Nova 7?" one patron echoed as if he was dreaming.

"That's right," Globulus snarled again.

Finally realizing that the team was Nova 7, everyone in the bar was more than happy to give them wide berth. The stories and legends about the team had reached the northlands. Suddenly, the atmosphere in the bar went from hostile to frightened. Not wanting any possible conflicts, no one in the bar would even look in their direction. This apprehension finally allowed Nova 7 a reprieve.

Globulus stared at Jared, wordlessly making the point that he needed to calm down and to get his act together. Jared acknowledged the silent message and sat down at the table quietly once more. Taking a brief moment, the hippo hybrid scanned the table. One after the other, he gazed at each member of Nova 7.

"It's good to see you again," he said to all of them. "It's also good to see that you all made it back alive."

Banion replied with a broad grin, "You seem surprised."

Globulus laughed, exposing his enormous tusk-like teeth. "Yes, I am surprised. The road that you've traveled must not have been easy."

"You're not kidding," Tani said, happy to see Globulus once more.

"Come on over here." Globulus motioned to a petite woman with short black hair near the bar.

Approaching quickly, Carla eyed the companions seated at the table with a look of amazement. "Nova 7, I presume?"

"This is Banion O'Neil, the gunfighter from Dune Station I've told you about." Globulus gestured at the leader of Nova 7.

"No further introduction is needed. I thought you were a myth, a story told to scare little children. Your reputation has preceded you." She gave him a nod of respect, unable to see his eyes, hidden in the darkness beneath the brim of his hat. He nodded back and did not speak to her.

"These are Jared and Tani from the tribal village of Scarskin, a village *somewhere* in the wastelands. And that blue-robed vision of evil in the corner over there is the Reaper Kai diplomat that I busted out of Darkpine Prison just before the war broke out." Globulus smiled at Mineera as he spoke about her.

"You're always so charming," Mineera countered with a similar smile.

Staring uneasily at the people around the table, Carla suddenly felt very small. Their reputations had preceded all of them. Tani was rumored to be the best demolitions expert in the wasteland and a brilliant scholar. Jared was whispered to be a sinister Reaper Kai witch-hunter, rumored to have killed many Reaper Kai single handedly and able to withstand their demonic attacks unscathed. Rounding out the team was Mineera, the legendary Reaper Kai diplomat who had betrayed the Dark Order in a wild attempt to aid the kingdom of Rasheed prior to the outbreak of the war.

To say that she was in the presence of greatness was an understatement. The members of Nova 7 were talented and extremely dangerous. She felt a little uncomfortable around such people. The usually cheerful chatter that distinguished her grew silent. She simply stared at them in soundless awe.

"It's good to see you again, Globulus, and it's nice to meet you, Carla." Mineera smiled and pulled back her blue hood so that it exposed her face. Her stunning blue eyes set atop the backdrop of her dark skin were a dramatic sight. "What brings you to Jared's drunken brawl?"

"Hey!" Jared grumbled.

"Not a word, kid. You almost killed that soldier." Banion shot him a dirty look.

"He was asking for it," Jared shot back.

"But you were looking for it," Tani added.

"Fine!" The tribal warrior brooded and sat back in his chair, staring at Carla and Globulus.

"So what the hell are you doing here in Stonen?" Banion quizzed his enormous friend.

"The war." Carla spoke in a dull tone, almost inaudible.

"The war?" Tani repeated, confused. "The war is over."

Mineera had a somber look and was pensive. Seeing her dismay, Tani looked at Carla, then at Globulus.

"It's over, right?" Tani felt horror creep into his soul.

Banion looked at Tani and shook his head in disagreement. "I was afraid of this."

"You can't be serious?" Tani felt violated on an emotional level. "After everything we've done, everything that we've fought for, the war has to be over!"

"Not here, bookworm." Banion tried to coax Tani into silence.

Many of the bar patrons had overheard part of the conversation and an eerie silence was beginning to fill the room. With quick glances, the soldiers in the room were trying to spy on the mercenary team. Globulus looked at Banion, who then looked at Tani. With a silent motion, Banion told the tribal scholar to shut his mouth. Disturbed by the topic of conversation, Tani wanted to keep talking but he had enough sense to keep his mouth shut, for the time being.

A tense quiet filled the room as the members of the legendary mercenary team shot each other quick glances. Trying to break the tension, Globulus changed the topic.

"The beer is looking a little pathetic at this table. Barkeep!" Globulus boomed.

Rushing over, a man with a bright red face looked at the hippo hybrid uneasily. "Yes?"

"Get a fresh round for everyone here."

"Yes, right away."

Tapping his enormous finger on the table, Globulus passed the time by staring around the room at the rest of the silent patrons. He felt that if he shot enough of them dirty looks, they would eventually stop trying to eavesdrop on them. Finally, the barkeep rushed over and put a fresh round of beer on the table. As Globulus grabbed the beer mug, it looked like a thimble in his hand. Raising the mug, he tilted it toward Banion.

"To Nova 7! Their daring deeds and endless courage have forever changed the world," Globulus boomed.

Many of the bar patrons tipped their mugs in their direction and cheered the team.

As they drank down their beer, Globulus looked directly at Banion, who looked back with a calm look on his face. They both knew what was going to happen; the team would be called on once more to defend the world against the Reaper Kai.

Tani watched the two uneasily. Between them lay some hidden truth too horrifying to know but too chilling to ignore. A knot formed once again in Tani's stomach.

The friends toasted again and again. In that moment, they were home, in the presence of good company, remembering the past they had shared. They spoke of the prison break in which Globulus had saved Mineera. They remembered how Banion met the tribals. They spoke of the battle of Rasheed and the flight from the harbor. They reminisced about the siege of Rust Spire. They spoke of the vicious Guillotine and how Jared had saved slaves from a convoy of enemy trucks. They remembered the Concrete Barrens and the cruel Lavosi.   They recounted how Carla saved Globulus from the dungeons of Rasheed. They spoke of the military base and the sinister sentinel that protected the nuclear warhead. As the liquor flowed and the stories were spun, each of them smiled.   Such kinship was rare and each of them felt that they were indeed part of something greater than themselves.

As the day wore on, the tales of daring seemed to dissipate. The tales of bloodshed and suffering were replaced by tales of hope. In the end, the conversation turned to loved ones long gone and loved ones far away from the stench of death and war. In the end, it was all about home and family. It was all about kinship and bonds of friendship.

Chapter 23
Fractured

Tani was suspicious. In the darkness of the room, he heard a door shut in the hallway. Unable to sleep, he crept to the door of his room. When he pressed his ear to the door, he could hear voices in the hallway. Cracking the door open, he peered out and saw Banion with all of his gear in hand, conversing with someone.

Opening the door fully, Tani could see Globulus standing in the hallway. As the door opened, the conversation between Globulus and Banion ended immediately. An uneasy silence erupted between the trio as they exchanged terse glances.

"What's going on?" Tani asked, looking at Banion's gear with suspicion. He was carrying his backpack and all of his weapons.

Banion did not respond, unable to even look at Tani. Tani blinked several times until finally, it hit him. "Where are you going?" the tribal scholar asked in alarm.

Globulus let out a sigh and stared at Banion. "You didn't tell them?"

"Nope," Banion said succinctly. Ignoring Tani, he took several steps down the hallway.

Before he had taken more than two steps, Tani cried out in a frantic tone, "Banion, what's going on? Where the hell are you going?"

"I'm leaving." Banion's tone was direct.

"What?" Tani whined with a bewildered look on his face.

"Take care of Jared for me, bookworm." As Banion moved down the hallway again, Tani had to sprint toward him. Grabbing him by the shoulder, he forced Banion to turn around and face him.

"Look at me." Tani spoke with tension filling him.

Banion averted his gaze, hiding his eyes under the brim of his cowboy hat. His inability to look the tribal scholar in the eye further put Tani on edge.

"Why won't you look at me?"

"Just let it be, Tani," Banion grumbled. "I need to get out of here and you sure as hell aren't making this easy on me."

"What's going on?" A familiar voice sounded down the hallway. Jared had poked his head out the door after hearing Tani shouting. The concerned tribal warrior was watching the scene unfold with a look of shock.

"Banion?" Mineera's voice rang out as she opened the door to her own room. A feeling of panic was coursing through her as she sensed the raw emotions in the hallway. Feeling that Banion was trying to escape, she rushed out to confront him as well.

"Great!" Banion mumbled while shaking his head in disgust. "The gang is all here. Thanks, bookworm!"

"Globulus, what's going on?" Tani turned his attention to the hippo hybrid.

Shaking his head, Globulus folded his arms across his chest in a defiant gesture. "This isn't about me, Tani, ask Banion about it."

"Ask Banion about what?" Jared asked, stepping up to confront Banion.

"The war, I would guess," Mineera added, and she was right.

Unable to look any of them in the eye, Banion dropped his head and looked directly at the floor. "I'm leaving."

"I don't understand." Mineera suddenly felt betrayed. After everything they had all been through together, Banion was going to sneak out in the middle of the night and disappear from their lives. Deep down, she felt stung in the heart, feeling that she really meant nothing to him. "You were going to sneak out in the middle of the night without telling us?"

"Yeah, what are you doing with all your gear?" Jared also felt betrayed. To him, Banion was like a father figure. Blinking furiously, he clenched his jaw and shot him a dirty look.

Banion ignored the cold stare and stood in the center of the hall with his head drooping. As he tried to collect his thoughts, he was torn apart inside, ripped to shreds by raw emotion. Shaking his head, he licked his lips and then chewed on his upper lip for a brief second. Biting hard, he almost drew blood, but the splash of pain jolted him out of his melancholy.

"I'm leaving you all because I care about you. I'm leaving because I can't stand to see any of you get hurt."

"I don't understand," Tani said, a soft look illuminating his features. He was fighting back the tears and felt foolish at the thought of weeping.

"The war is not over." Banion's words were like frost on a summer day, evoking an instant hostility in Jared and Tani.

"What do you mean the war isn't over? We brought the warhead and they used it. What else needs to happen?" Jared roared.

"The enemy is wounded but not defeated. The primary production facility was left unscathed. Reaper Kai forces are massing in the desert and are forging more Biogtechs." Banion spoke with a somber look in his eyes.

"After everything we've done, everything we've risked, it wasn't enough?" Tani felt the tears well up in his eyes. The toll the quest had taken on him had forever scarred him, forever turned part of his soul into a lifeless husk. He shook in disbelief, unable to comprehend the implications of Banion's words.

"No, Tani, it wasn't enough," Banion concluded.

"So what's going on then?" Jared asked.

"I'm leaving to finish the job."

"Finish the job?" Mineera stared in disbelief. "What is wrong with you? Who do you think you are? You think that you can take on the Reaper Kai Empire by yourself?"

"It's my burden and my burden alone. I will not risk your lives anymore. I cannot risk it. I just can't do it. This is my decision and my decision alone. I'm leaving you to aid the Iron Kai in ending this mess once and for all."

"How noble!" Jared growled at him. "You were going to abandon us after everything that we've done together? We bled together, heart and soul, Banion. We share a bond that means more than family."

"That's why I need you all to get away from this mess while you still can. I made horrible choices in the past and sucked all of you into my twisted crusade of vengeance. You've paid the price for my arrogance. I can't take any more from you. I've already taken too much."

"It's not up to you decide what we are willing to risk." Mineera spoke in a commanding tone. "If you value us, if you value what we have together, then you'll level with us and talk to us. What have you gotten yourself into, Banion? What's going on?"

A silence broke over the hallway once more. The companions stared at their leader in utter disbelief. Blinking, his eyes shifted back and forth, looking at each of them with frantic gazes. His heart began to bang in his chest. The stress was almost too much for him to bear.

"The Iron Kai have mobilized their army. Emperor Gunther has asked me to put a team of soldiers together to perform some sort of covert strike on the enemy production facility," Banion finally revealed the truth to his companions.

"Covert strike?" Jared quizzed.

"You have a team, Banion. Here we are." Tani spoke with hope in his eyes.

"I can't do it to you. I care too much about each of you to put you in danger ever again," Banion almost shouted at them, agitated and frantic.

"It's not your choice, Banion, it's ours," Mineera declared as she stepped forward. Gripping his shoulder, she reassured him. "I'm volunteering to serve once more. I would never think of abandoning you and I know you would never abandon us."

"I'm in also." Jared nodded his head fiercely at Mineera's proposal.

"Me too!" Tani said, the tears receding back into his eyes.

"There's a good chance that none of us will ever come out of that Reaper Kai production facility. It's more dangerous than anything we have ever encountered."

"It doesn't matter," Tani said, solemn.

"It should. It's not just a simple matter of storming the facility." Banion motioned to the hippo hybrid. "Intelligence from Globulus indicates that Vertigo is very much alive. It seems the lord of the Reaper Kai is stronger than anyone has ever imagined, able to survive death itself. If we go into this facility, we might face the most evil, most demonic leader of the Reaper Kai Empire. It's not a mercy mission; it is a dangerous attack that will most likely kill us all."

"I cannot in good conscience allow you to risk your life alone. Just as we mean the world to you, you are in our hearts. You're part of each of us. You're part of this family." Mineera's tone was heartfelt.

Nodding, Banion looked up and smiled at each of them. "I care about each of you more than you could ever know. Before I met you all, I was reckless and consumed with hate. In my life, I've lost everyone I have ever loved. I vowed long ago to never allow myself to love again or let anyone into my world, and I let myself forget what I truly want out of life. In our journeys and travels, each of you has taught me compassion. I'm not the same person that started this crusade long ago. I've grown and learned to cherish hope and the sense of family that each of you has given me. I know that I can't make this choice for you, but I wish you would reconsider. If you truly value me, don't go with me, let me go alone. I don't want to risk any of your lives."

A silence came over Nova 7 once more. Each of them had tears in their eyes. As they stared at each other, a strange sensation washed over them. The greatest mercenary team in the history of the Darken Realm was fractured, torn apart not by dissention but by compassion. It was a tense, emotional time for each of them. They valued one another so much that the sense of danger Banion had conveyed made the decision easier. Instead of fearing the coming darkness, they were inspired by one another, feeling a deep sense of family and commitment to one another. Banion's attempt to drive them away was futile. The more dangerous the mission, the more each of them knew that they had to do it together. They each knew that the only way they could make it was together.

None of them spoke and they didn't need to. The team shattered and broke apart. Jared, Tani, and Mineera left the hallway and disappeared into the darkness of their rooms. For a moment Banion stood and watched in silent trepidation. His heart was screaming. His mind was wishing that each of them would not return. But one by one, each of them emerged from their rooms, tattered backpacks in hand.

And so it was that Nova 7, broken apart by the threat of death, had come together to triumph over darkness. Standing in the hallway, Nova 7 was united and the message was clear: they would stand together once more. Fighting back the tears in his eyes, Banion had never felt better. He was home again, in the company of friends and the only people that he loved in the entire world.

Chapter 24
Battle Plans

The members of Nova 7 were anxious and for good reason. The entire Iron Kai army had mobilized and was now within striking distance of Metalweaver Flats, the final Reaper Kai stronghold that remained in all the Darken Realm. Emperor Gunther was overseeing the operation personally and was at the camp near the edge of the desert. The final battle was about to be waged and the victor would emerge as the ruler of the Darken Realm.

It was just after sunset. Gunther stood outside a large tent in the center of camp. Holding a mug of ale in his hand, he watched the light begin to dim. He took a deep breath and exhaled, letting the moment resonate in his mind. Calmly he thought about the task at hand. Taking a sip of his ale, he let the tasty brew roll down his tongue to the back of his mouth, enjoying the dull burn as the alcohol moved towards his stomach.

"The choices we make can re-forge the world, or bring it to ruin..." he whispered with a dim smile. Steadying himself, he mentally reviewed the meeting, slowly thinking about each point and how to perfectly convey his message. Feeling the chill air in the desert, he took another swig of his ale. A light warm buzz began to fill his being. Nodding to himself, Gunther knew that he was ready to address the crowd that had amassed inside the tent. Setting his ale down on the sand, he promised the mug that he would return. He saluted the ale with a smile, then pulled aside the flap at the back of the giant tent.

Pushing inside, he could see that there were close to 100 people in the tent. A motley assortment of battle-hardened military officers was staring with anxious glances as he entered. Steadying himself, Gunther moved to the front of the audience without a hint of fear. Everyone's gaze was on him as he walked and he knew it. With a serious look on his face, he turned to address the crowd.

"Good evening." His voice was almost deafening. As he looked around the tent, many saluted him and many others gave him reassuring nods of approval. "Let's get to it."

Gunther motioned to a screen, and a projector began to display an image of the surrounding terrain. Walking to the display, he inspected the diagram closely before he spoke, knowing full well that clarity was his ally and ambiguity was deadly.

"Our reconnaissance teams have finished a thorough evaluation of the fortified Reaper Kai installation. We are 37 miles away from the objective. We're located here, about a half day's journey from an abandoned town." Everyone watched carefully as he pointed at the screen, trying to fully absorb the information. "We have just over 30,000 infantry and 20 light artillery weapons. Our armored division was unable to approach this area due to the deep desert sand. Unfortunately for this assault, we will not have tank support. Our helicopters will be able to support our ground troops for limited attacks but our fuel is scarce and needs to be brought in to continue the attack.

"Reaper Kai forces in the region have retreated from the neighboring areas. Over the past weeks, the Reaper Kai army has been slaughtering the local population and capturing slaves. Our estimates indicate that cleansing operations carried out by the enemy have led to roughly 50,000 casualties of innocent townsfolk over the past two weeks. We have also identified that the Reaper Kai have spliced upwards of 20,000 slaves, who are now totally obedient to the implants attached to their skulls and spinal cords. These slaves will fight for the Reaper Kai and in addition, roughly 40,000 Biogtech troops are defending the desert leading to Metalweaver Flats."

A roar of whispers broke through the audience as the number of enemy forces was revealed. With 40,000 Biogtechs and 20,000 spliced slaves, the Iron Kai army was outnumbered.

"How many Reaper Kai priests are estimated to be in the valley?" Field Marshal Mills asked in ominous tone. The entire room fell silent and listened intently.

"We estimate roughly 2,000 Reaper Kai priests are defending the installation in addition to the other enemy forces."

"Two thousand?" an officer repeated in a concerned tone.

"Two thousand seasoned priests; we believe that they are all war priests, ready for battle, unlike many of those encountered during the siege of Detro Tech City. They will be extremely tough and are extremely dangerous."

"What about enemy armor support?" Mills asked once more.

"Our intelligence indicates that the Reaper Kai also have several hundred Biogtech assault rigs identical to those encountered during the invasion of the Mord Tech Empire. Without our tank support, we're also in great danger from these assault rigs."

"It seems we have too little here to make this attack possible." Field Marshal Mills' tone was aggressive.

"Not entirely true. The remains of the Rasheed and Steel Crag Mining Guild militias have rallied to our flag and have volunteered to aid in the attack. We also have the support of what remains of the Mord Tech army. Several clans and smaller provinces have also sent limited support. An important ally from the southern reaches of the Darken Realm, the Crushing-Fist Tribe, has sent nearly 1,000 hippo warriors. With all of the additional support, we're looking at an additional 8,000 ground troops, bringing our total to 38,000, a sizeable army that matches the might of the enemy." Gunther spoke with a confident tone.

Some of the panic about being overwhelmed had dissipated, but the sizes of both armies being led to battle were roughly comparable. There was very little advantage on either side and many felt that the battle could go either way. And with every resource enlisted in the coming battle on both sides, the entire fate of the Darken Realm would rest on this one battle, winner takes all. There was absolutely no room for error on Gunther's part or the Reaper Kai would be victorious.

Knowing that their fate and the fate of the entire Darken Realm rested in Gunther's hands made many in the crowd very uncomfortable. Everyone watched him carefully, looking for any sign of weakness. Thankfully they could find none; Gunther was extremely confident and rational about the entire operation.

"After careful analysis of the installation in Metalweaver Flats, we found a significant flaw in the enemy's defenses. Our technicians, using thermal imaging of the enemy installation, have uncovered that there is a tremendous heat source located in one of the buildings. We know that the building contains enormous super-computers. These super-computers must be controlling and coordinating the vast number of spliced slaves. Each spliced slave has a small computer integrated into their nervous system. The amount of programming and computer power needed to coordinate tens of thousands of slaves must be enormous. We're certain that the heat source in this building is the Splicer relay, the supercomputer that controls all of the spliced slaves. The Splicer relay is in turn attached to an enormous transmitter that sends the communication signal to a satellite built by the ancients that is still operational and still in orbit. The signal is then relayed to each independent Splicer, which in turn controls the respective hosts. If we knock out of the Splicer relay, all of the spliced slaves will no longer be under the control of the Reaper Kai. With the amount of enemy forces reduced by 20,000 and all of the slaves free, our forces will have a significant advantage."

Gunther's words left the room stunned. Their leader had taken a grim situation and had arrived at a solution, and a realistic one at that. If the Splicer relay was knocked out of commission, the Iron Kai would have a sizable advantage. The entire battle and its outcome thus rested upon this one single act.

"So we shell the building housing the Splicer relay with artillery and the enemy loses 20,000 troops?" an officer asked.

"Not quite that easy. The enemy has fortified the entire valley. We don't have a long enough range on our artillery to take out this building. In order to get close enough to use our artillery, we have to wipe out all of the enemy forces dug into the area," Gunther responded.

"Take several of our helicopter gunships and destroy the satellite transmission equipment on top of the building then," another officer suggested.

"Not possible. There are anti-aircraft guns close to the center of the installation. We wouldn't be able to get close enough to use the helicopters on the Splicer relay itself," Gunther countered.

"But how are we going to take out the Splicer relay?" someone quizzed Gunther from the back of the tent.

"Good question." Gunther motioned to Captain Maddock near the back of the crowd. Maddock nodded back and walked to the front of the tent. Looking at all of the assembled soldiers and officers, he addressed them confidently.

"We have selected seven strike teams to undertake this mission. The plan is to drop each team behind enemy lines near the ridgeline behind Metalweaver Flats, outside the range of the anti-aircraft guns. The mercenary teams are to then infiltrate the facility and knock out the Splicer relay using explosives. The entire mission will hinge on one of the teams knocking out the relay. As a diversion, we'll attack the Reaper Kai forces in the valley to keep them on their toes just prior to inserting the mercenary teams behind enemy lines to take out the Splicer relay. With all of the chaos we'll cause by a full scale assault, the strike teams should be able to reach their objective," Maddock concluded.

"These strike teams are Iron Kai special forces?"

"Six of the teams have been selected from Iron Kai special forces. The last team, lucky number seven, is the mercenary team that recovered the nuclear warhead deployed on Detro Tech City. The last team that will be going into the Reaper Kai installation is Nova 7," Gunther said, and a chill rolled down his spine as he did so.

A strange quiet came over the officers as they heard the identity of the last team. The legendary mercenary team that had recovered the nuclear warhead was mythical. Glorious tales of daring and courage were synonymous with the name Nova 7. Each member of the team was potent and legendary in their own right but together they were something entirely different. Together they were a finely oiled machine, an instrument of death and destruction able to succeed at any task, no matter what danger faced them. Hearing that the illustrious mercenary team was heading into the installation to take out the Splicer relay gave everyone hearing the plan a strange sense of hope. Suddenly the doubt began to lift. Suddenly, the fear of failure was gone. The impossible would be made possible. Nova 7 would bring about a miracle once more.

"There will be secondary briefings with your commanding officers detailing the specific tasks of your troops." Gunther looked out into the sea of officers and smiled. A gentle feeling filled him as he saw his men ready to make war once more. His heart was soaring and it felt wonderful. There was no fear of the coming conflict. Gunther had resolved to fight with all his might and to never surrender to the enemy. Feeling hope fill him, he let the sensation overwhelm him. Taking in a fresh lungful of air, he inhaled with the intent of telling his men what he really thought of them.

"For the first time in my life, I have no fear. I have no fear because as I look out into this sea of faces, all I have is hope. I have unwavering hope in my heart since I have the privilege of serving with the finest army in all the land." Gunther's voice was booming and filled with joy as he addressed his officers. "You are embarking on the most monumental siege of all time. In our history, there has never been a battle of this magnitude. You are embarking on a journey into the history books. When the dust settles and the bullets cease to roar, the cries of your dying enemies will be replaced with cheers of victory. When the trials of war are conquered, our empire will be standing and the Reaper Kai will be crushed underfoot once and for all. Do not fear the coming conflict; embrace the hardships and endure. Embrace the victory that we will taste as the enemy is trampled underfoot. I vow that we will be victorious. I pledge to never surrender, never to lose hope. I vow to serve this land and this army with every drop of blood in my veins. Here's to you, my noble officers!" With a firm, energetic gesture, Gunther saluted all of his officers.

Seeing his display, all of them began to cheer. War chants and battle cries erupted. Saluting him back, they were all ready to carry out his orders. The gears of war began to grind again. Feverously, the officers set out to get everything ready for the coming battle. Time was running out and as the clock ticked, the seconds were passing quickly. Soon, it would be time for a final battle. Soon it would be time for the final conflict to erupt between bitter enemies. A blood feud that had been raging for hundreds of years was about to play out. It was almost time for the final battle between the gallant Iron Kai and the demonic Reaper Kai.

Chapter 25
The Night Before

Banion was covered in sweat. He had been in the fields the entire day, laboring to fix the barbed-wire fence that kept the cattle in the northern pasture. The day had been sweltering and the rancher was totally exhausted, dehydrated beyond belief. As he directed his mighty black steed towards the center of Birthrock, he blinked several times and looked around. His mind told him that something was out of place. Shaking off the strange sense of dread filling him, he pulled back on the reins and his horse came to an abrupt stop.

Jumping down from the mighty horse, he tethered the beast to the railing. He tipped back his hat, letting the sweat roll down his brow. Wiping the perspiration away, he felt happy inside. The surroundings were those of his former home. Rushing up the stairs, he stood on the porch of his house. Excitedly, he twisted the doorknob and pushed on inside, finding himself engulfed in the sound of music. Even measures and rhythms emanated from a piano near the wall.

A slender woman with long flowing black hair was seated at the piano. She wore a white dress and was intently pressing on the white ivory keys. As she depressed each key, a melodious tone erupted from the musical instrument.

Banion stopped dead in his tracks. The woman seated at the piano was his beloved wife Lily. For a moment, he stood there, with a lump in his throat. The emotion began to tear at his soul. With a whisper, he spoke her name in amazement. "Lily?"

The woman seated at the piano did not respond. Instead she continued to play the instrument and the tempo of the music increased dramatically. As she banged away feverishly at the keyboard, the music was almost frantic.

"Lily-" Banion called loudly to the woman seated at the piano. His tone was harsh and almost abrasive. As he cried out to her, she stopped playing immediately, the last note resonating as a dull twang within the wooden instrument. She had responded to his shout but did not turn around. Stunned by her behavior, he called out again.

"Lily, it's me," he said, tears stinging his eyes. The emotion was overpowering him.

She did not respond. Instead she lowered her head and seemed to be examining the keys on the piano.

"Why won't you talk to me?" he asked, the rhythm of his words broken.

Gripping her fists together, she shook her head as if in sadness. She stood up from the piano and left the room without turning towards him, leaving Banion with a stinging sense of rejection.

Rushing after her, Banion followed his wife into their kitchen. "Are you ashamed of me?" he asked, feeling guilt wash over him.

She simply stood in the kitchen with her back to him. Still silent, she did not respond.

"Are you ashamed of me? Is that why you won't look at me? Are you ashamed of what I've done? Are you ashamed of what I've become?" Banion persisted, desperate to get his beloved wife to communicate with him.

It didn't matter what he said; she simply stood in the kitchen with her back to him, eerily silent.

"I miss you so bad. Every night I think about you. Every night I wish that things could have been different. I should have been there for you, in those final moments of your life. I would give anything to go back. I would do anything to change things. I wish I would have been there that day so long ago. I failed you and I am so sorry. Please, just look at me. Please look into my eyes. I love you so much."

She would not respond to his words. The more she kept silent, the more frantic Banion became.

"Please don't be ashamed of me." His tone was heartfelt.

As he spoke, she began to walk out the back door of their house. He ran after her, charging out the doorway. As he exited the building, Lily was nowhere to be seen. Frantically he spun around, scanning the area for her. Out of the corner of his eye, he saw the flash of her white dress disappear beyond a corner. Running after her, he came around the side of the building and found nothing; his beloved Lily was nowhere to be seen.

A brisk wind broke over the land. The chilling blast struck his sweaty skin, making him shiver. As the wind assaulted him, a whisper erupted from the wind with the sound of Lily's voice. "Come home to me…"

Shouting, Banion sat straight up in his cot. Looking around, he found that his silver long-barreled revolver was clutched in his shaking hand. The hammer had been pulled back on the weapon and his finger was resting on the trigger of the gun. Seeing that he had almost fired the gun in his sleep, Banion felt deeply sobered. He knew that he was beginning to lose his grip on reality and was glad that no one had startled him during the dream, for if they had, he would probably have shot them with his revolver.

Easing the hammer down on his revolver with his thumb, he shook his head in disgust. He stared at the gun in his hand with a grim look in his eye. The weapon was a symbol for Banion. It symbolized his emergence into a world of violence. The first time he had taken a life, he had done so with that weapon. As he held it in his hands, the metal was cool to the touch.

Sighing, he thought about that frightful day when his uncle Frank had been gruesomely beaten to death by Asagara Toil. He could still remember that flash of anger that erupted in his soul as he saw Frank die upon the stage, and the sinister Reaper Kai priestess laughing at his lifeless body. He remembering jumping down and clutching the weapon in his quivering hand. Taking aim, he had fired but one single shot, a shot that elevated him into a world of violence. At the age of fifteen, Banion had killed for the first time and he did it out of pure rage. Clutching the silver revolver now, he felt very sad as he thought about the strange vision that he had just seen in his dreams.

His beloved Lily would not even look at him. Feeling ashamed, he stared at the cold steel revolver in his hand. Shaking his head in disgust, he knew that it had to end. He couldn't live his life as a never-ending killing spree.

"I will set things right, Lily. Mark my words, I will set things right. I will make you proud," he said aloud, trying to fight back the tears.

With a sigh, he stood up from his cot and grabbed his black cowboy hat. Placing it on his head, he began to scan the darkness around him. Nova 7 was taking a vital rest before tomorrow. The team had agreed to take on the most dangerous of all missions, jumping into the lion's mouth and infiltrating the Reaper Kai production facility in Metalweaver Flats.

The night was cloying, and Banion began to walk toward a linen tent near the edge of the military encampment. In the distance, he could see a familiar glow. Walking toward the tent, he could see young Tani seated behind his laptop computer, banging away at the keys with a quizzical look on his face.

"What are you still doing up, bookworm?"

Peering over the rim of his glasses, Tani's inquisitive green eyes looked directly at Banion. "The technicians loaded several programs onto my laptop. They can hack into security systems if I attach this remote cable to the access panel. I've never used the software before, so I want to be absolutely sure I know what to do if we encounter security doors within the Reaper Kai facility."

"Sounds exciting." Banion chuckled.

"You have no idea." Tani smiled back. "What are you still doing up?"

"Couldn't sleep."

"Couldn't sleep?" Tani laughed. "I don't think I've ever seen you sleep more than twenty minutes at a time. Is something bothering you?"

Usually Banion would ignore such questions but on this occasion, he looked at Tani and nodded, blurting out an ominous question. "Are you ashamed of me, Tani?"

Tani was flabbergasted. "What?" he asked in alarm.

"Are you ashamed of me?"

"No!" Tani raised his eyebrows emphatically as he spoke. "Why would you ever think that?"

"It's nothing," Banion said with a sigh, thinking once more about his dream. "I just don't want anyone to be ashamed of me."

Feeling suddenly sad, Tani looked at Banion and closed the screen on his laptop, giving his friend his full attention. Looking down at his battered hands, Tani rubbed the stumps where his fingers had been blown off long ago in an accident with homemade dynamite. Not knowing what to say, he didn't think; he simply opened his mouth, unsure what was going to happen.

"When I first met you, Banion, I honestly thought you were the most insane person that I had ever met. Now that I think about it, you're still the most insane person I've ever met." Tani laughed and Banion began to chuckle.

Staring at each other, they took a few seconds to compose themselves.

"Thanks a lot, bookworm."

"No, really, Banion. I've never met a person who has lived a more tortured life. You've lost everything you've ever loved. Despite all of the anger inside of you, I value knowing you. Even though you scare the hell out of me, I know that you're the most courageous friend I could ever have. During our travels, you've taught me so much, not only about the world but mostly about myself. Every time I've faced a tough decision during this journey, you've helped me through it. When it seems so dark that there is no hope, there you are, charging onward like a crazed rhino, bashing through the opposition. You're a role model to me in every way. I could never be ashamed of you, Banion."

"You're too kind, Tani," Banion said with a sigh.

"Did you have a bad dream?" Tani finally figured out the source of Banion's strife.

"Yeah." Placing his hand into a pocket in his duster, Banion retrieved a gold wedding band, looking at it in the dim light. Tani examined the ring silently. "I had a dream about Lily again."

Tani remained silent, knowing full well that Banion's dead wife was a very touchy subject.

"I got so scared in the dream and it felt so real. I kept crying out to her but she wouldn't talk to me, she wouldn't even look at me. I felt so ashamed, so ashamed of everything that I've done. I just got rattled is all. Sorry for all the weirdness, Tani." Banion said, returning his wedding band back into the pocket inside his duster. "Have you seen Jared anywhere?"

"I saw him about an hour ago up on the rocks above the camp. He was doing his exercises."

"Thanks, Tani, thanks for everything." Banion's tone was appreciative.

"You're welcome, Banion, any time," Tani responded with a smile.

Slinking off into the darkness, Banion found himself on a dimly lit trail snaking out of the enormous military encampment. Ascending the trail in the dim moonlight, he could hear someone breathing heavily. As he rounded a boulder at the top of a small ridge, Banion could see Jared holding his sword in the air, slashing at unknown foes.

Watching him for a brief second, Banion marveled at his dedication to mastery of the sword. Night after night, the tribal would exercise and perfect his use of the weapon. It was amazing to watch Jared. Each slash and swing looked like an extension of his body. Each move was precise and powerful. Inhaling, he drew the blade back. Exhaling, he swung at an imaginary foe with a vicious slash. It was expertise at its finest, with his body perfectly toned and his reflexes wickedly dangerous.

Sensing that he was not alone, Jared whirled around and caught sight of Banion in the darkness.

"You scared the crap out me," Jared exclaimed, grabbing a rag and wiping the sweat off his brow. Hoisting his canteen, he took a swig of water and approached Banion. "What are you doing out here?"

"I wanted to give you something," Banion said, stepping forward.

A little stunned, Jared eyed him suspiciously. "Are you drunk?"

"Just a little bit." Banion smiled. He extended his hand, holding his uncle's revolver. Motioning, he tried to give it Jared.

The tribal looked at him oddly, unable to accept the gift. "I don't get it."

"Take it," Banion coaxed him.

"Why?"

"I want you to have it."

"But it's your uncle's. I know it means a lot to you."

"It would mean a lot to me if you had it. I'm done with it."

"Done with it?" Jared stared at him in incomprehension.

"After tomorrow, I'm done with all of this. I'm done with all the violence and bloodshed. After tomorrow, I'm going home, back to Birthrock. I'm going to start over again, raise cattle and put this all behind me."

"Raise cattle?" Jared almost started laughing.

"What's so funny? I was a good rancher."

"I just can't see it. What did you do if you couldn't herd an animal into a pasture, shoot it?" Jared laughed.

Banion grumbled a bit. The tribal was having fun at his expense and he knew it.

"Seriously, Jared, take the gun. I want you to have it," he repeated, handing it to the tribal once more. Jared still resisted, eyeing him uneasily. "It's too dangerous for me to have it anymore."

"But why me?" he quizzed.

"You know I never had kids. You and Tani are the closest things that I have to kids. You're my family. I want someone to take it and pass it on. You know, give it to your son someday."

"My son? I'm barely grown myself." Jared smiled at Banion.

"Then maybe I should club the hell out of you with it instead," he said in a nasty tone, offended that his friend would not accept the gift. "Just forget it."

"Stop." Jared shook his head. "I was just messing around. I would be happy to take your uncle's revolver; or rather, I would be honored. I know how much it means to you; that's why I'm so hesitant to take it. It's just strange, is all."

"What's so strange?"

"Well, you know, it's the last thing you have to remember your uncle by, and I know you cared for him very much. I just want you to be sure. It's a big deal to give it up."

"I know." Banion looked at the weapon, a sense of nostalgia washing over him. "I just can't live like this anymore. I can't explain it to you, Jared. That gun is a symbol; it's a symbol of me, the true me and everything that I've lost. In a sense, all of my anger and rage is in that weapon. It symbolizes the moment that I crossed a terrible line. Although I value it as my most prized possession, I know that something inside of me has snapped. I just can't do it anymore. I hope you can understand."

"It would be an honor to have it, Banion. I will give it to my son someday, but I'm not sure I can tell him where it came from."

"Why not?"

"He would have nightmares the rest of his life if I told him about you. Hell, I have nightmares sometimes just thinking about you." Jared chuckled.

Smiling back, Banion extended his hand again and this time Jared grabbed the weapon. As he did, the tribal marveled at how heavy it really was and how cold the metal was to touch. Holding it, he spun it around and looked it over.

"I forgot how heavy it is." Jared smiled. "I'll keep it safe, Banion."

"I'm sorry, kid." Banion spoke in a heartfelt tone.

"Sorry for what?"

"You know, sorry for everything. I should have never brought you two little runts with me. You both would have been better off without all of this insanity."

For a brief second, Jared reflected on the comment. Shaking his head, he disagreed with Banion. "I've thought about that a lot, Banion—if we had never met, and if Tani and I had never gone with you. It's been rough on all of us but in the end, I would never change a single thing. When I left Scarskin so long ago, I was so proud and felt that I could take on the world. I was never more wrong. In seeing the things that I've seen since knowing you, I found that I was naïve and headstrong. I know I'm arrogant, but at least I can honestly say that I've finally seen my share of this world. I've learned more about myself in the months of traveling across the continent than I've learned the rest of my entire life. If I would have never known you, Banion, I would have never known myself, my true self. Don't ever say you're sorry for giving me the greatest gift in my life—being able to understand myself."

Smiling, Banion reached out his hand and roughed up Jared's hair like a person would roughly pet a homeless dog, with a comical air. As he tussled his hair, he looked at Jared's ponytail in disgust.

"You know that you've always looked ridiculous with that ponytail?" Banion jabbed playfully at the youth.

"Yeah, yeah. Laugh it up, cow puncher."

Laughing, Banion made a move to head back to camp. "Get some sleep, kid; we need to be at our best tomorrow."

"You too," Jared shot back.

"I already slept my twenty minutes tonight." Waving, Banion turned away and began to head town the trail that led into the heart of camp.

As he walked away, Jared stood in the dim light of the moon. Staring in awe, he held Banion's revolver, marveling at the gift with a smile. It was truly a wonderful present, and Jared cherished and treasured the weapon. Placing it into his belt, he liked the feel of it now that it was in his possession. As he savored the gift of such a wonderful legacy, he watched Banion disappear into the darkness of the night.

Grabbing his gear, Jared moved away from the trail and spread out his sleeping mat. Lying down on the cold ground, he stared up into the night sky, tracing the form of the moon with his finger. Jared thought about his life, reminiscing about his home for the first time in a long while. Staring up at the moon, he wondered if his family at home was looking into the sky and thinking of him. He wondered what had happened over the many months since his and Tani's departure from Scarskin.

In the cold night, one hand closed around the strange raven totem around his neck, a symbol of power. While he fidgeted with the ancient relic, his other hand clutched Banion's gun. A strange sensation filled him as he clutched the two items. Each was a symbol of power; each was a symbol of strife and violence. As he clutched the items, his mind began to scatter. Growing drowsy, the warrior from Scarskin fell into a troubled sleep, one filled with dark dreams of violent conquest.

As he thrashed about in his sleep, tormented by the dream world, his hands never dropped the raven totem or Banion's revolver. It was a dark omen of dire events to come.

Chapter 26
Bitter Enemies

Tension was flourishing. Every soldier within the Iron Kai camp was filled with anxiety. Being able to discern a person's thoughts was a potent ability, but it could be downright crippling to perceive the combined thoughts of thousands of people.

Mineera was like a caged animal. She was nervous and tense. The thoughts of an army were forced into her mind by means of her keen psychic abilities. Although she wanted nothing more than to hide from these emotions, she could not. Driven away from the camp, Mineera was walking through the darkness of the night trying to exile the voices from her mind. As she fled, a lonely wanderer caught sight of her and moved to intercept her. Mineera was completely unaware that someone was stalking her in the darkness.

Moving away from the edge of the enormous encampment, she sought to quell the troubled voices invading her being. As she began to distance herself from the camp, the emotions of the army began to dissipate. The further she walked, the less the voices in her mind rattled her soul.

When she had fled far enough away, she was suddenly aware of a presence. Blinking, she felt keenly nervous. She whirled around to find a form standing behind her in the darkness. Reeling back in surprise, she nearly stumbled. The shadowy form extended its hands in a gesture of peace, attempting to make her feel more at ease.

"Be still, it's me." Banion stepped forward with a smile on his face. "I startled you, didn't I?"

Nodding emphatically, Mineera let out a sigh of relief. "Yes, you did."

"You seemed frantic so I decided to see if you were doing well. You just seemed a little out of sorts back there in the camp."

"Sometimes it's just too much, feeling the emotions of others. Tonight I'm having a hard time severing the connection between myself and them. There's a lot of tension and anxiety in the camp. Most of the soldiers feel that tomorrow will be the last battle and the winner will take all. After gauging the situation myself, I think they're correct. I don't think one of the factions will be left standing after this battle. Either the Iron Kai or the Reaper Kai will survive, but not both."

"I'm having a hard time myself," Banion admitted. "For me, tomorrow will be the end of an age."

"Walk with me then. The desert is quiet tonight," she coaxed him. Normally, he would have denied her request but that night he was seeking companionship. He nodded in agreement, and the two of them left the edge of the camp, passing beyond the sentries.

"Are you frightened about tomorrow?" Banion asked her as they walked.

Thinking about his question for a moment, she hesitated in her response. "Yes, I am. I don't fear the battle or our mission, but I'm still frightened. I'm fearful of being homeless, truly homeless. I have no doubt that we will be victorious but when we do win, the Reaper Kai will finally be destroyed. In a sense, I'm scared since I will be alone in this world, the last of my race. Although I know that the Dark Order cannot be left alive, I still feel that I will never have a place again in this world, no home to go back to. It's a strange thought, but as long as the Reaper Kai survive, I feel that somehow I have a home. I feel that once the Reaper Kai are destroyed, I'll have no home or place in this world."

"That's not so strange." Banion spoke in a somber tone. "I feel the same way. My entire life has been defined by the Reaper Kai. Every part of my life has been affected in a horrible manner by the Dark Order. I feel that once the Reaper Kai are destroyed, I'll have no purpose left in this world. I feel that my entire life has been defined by a bloody sense of vengeance. But once they are gone, who am I supposed to be? What road can I possibly walk after my entire life has been spent trying to destroy them? I feel thankful that we stand on the doorstep to victory but also feel a sense of sadness. I feel empty and I don't know what road I can possibly walk. You and I are in the same predicament. We've both been defined by the Reaper Kai and without them, who are we?"

Mineera listened to his wisdom and found it made perfect sense. There was dread in trying to define oneself after a lifetime of memories. "You and I are more similar than I once believed."

"Yes, we are." He turned to her, looking at her face in the darkness of the night. He looked into her eyes and she looked back. "Both of us were born from different worlds but were forced to walk the same path, a pair of lost souls without a home. When I first met you, I wanted nothing more than to end your life. Now, I see you as a potent champion of change in this world. It's strange to me that the bitterest of enemies could have learned to set aside their differences and accept one another."

She looked back and felt the sorrow in her heart lift. The man standing before her had haunted her dreams for Mineera's entire life. Every night, she would dream of him, seeing visions of Banion. He was part of her in a sense, bound to her by fate and destiny. She looked at him with a smile, and he returned her gaze, bowing his head gently in a gesture of respect.

"I wish it didn't have to end. I'll miss you and the tribals. I wish that we were still in the wilds of the Darken Realm. I wish that we still had open road ahead of us. I'll miss all of our adventures together. I wish that this was not the end of our journey." She began to tremble and for good reason. After the battle was over, and if Nova 7 survived, the team would split and would each go their separate ways, forced to live new lives after the shadow of darkness had been lifted.

What would this new life be? How would each of them find their place in the world?

"I wish it didn't have to end either," Banion said, misty-eyed. "I've just found a new family with Nova 7. It will be hard for me to give it up. I would do anything for you all. I would give anything for the people of this family."

"You've given enough," she stated firmly.

"I can never feel that way." He smiled. "I don't ever feel that I've given enough."

"Why not?"

"Because of everything that was given to me by this team. I was broken and shattered, a lost soul with no direction that craved nothing but death. I wanted to deal out justice and make others suffer. I wanted to punish everyone around me for what I was feeling. I was in a dark place, a pit with no hope of escape. Every member of Nova 7 threw a rope down to me. You helped me climb out of the pit of despair and learn not to hate. You taught me that it's acceptable to feel alive. It's been a tough road for me to come back from the edge of the pit, but I'll never forget the kindness and charity that this team has given me."

"You're too kind," Mineera said. "Even if we threw you a rope, you still had to climb up it. You were the one who had to struggle every step of the way. You give us too much credit."

"No, I don't," he protested. "You helped me most of all. Your actions defined you as a kind and just leader. No matter how dire and desperate the circumstances, you always challenged me to do the right thing. I cannot ever forget that. We were once bitter enemies but in the end, you taught me the most."

"I think we both learned a lot from each other. You taught me about sacrifice, giving everything for something greater than yourself. I've never met anyone who has lost so much and was able to give up the hate and anger like you have. You should be proud of what you are, of what you've become," she concluded.

"I'm gonna miss you when this is all over," Banion said, taking a step toward her. She looked at him with slight confusion. Awkwardly, he stretched out his arms. Mineera eyed him, not knowing what to expect. Taking another step forward, he drew close to her, then wrapped his arms around her, pulling her close for a hug. The sentiment was so startling, Mineera didn't know what to do. It took her a brief second to respond. Then, returning the affection, she placed her arms around his back and embraced him firmly.

In that moment, they held each other. In that moment, they both had a home. There was no sense of loneliness or abandonment. There was no sense of bitterness for what the world had done to them. They both felt alive and happy to be in the presence of such a strong friendship.

"I need to get going." Banion retreated away from her quickly. "The sun will be up soon and I need to check my gear and clean my assault rifle."

Just as abruptly as their moment of connection had started, Banion had drawn away from her again, putting up the usual formidable shields around his soul. His demeanor changed immediately and he seemed sterile and somewhat lifeless once more. Such emotion was inside of him but was rarely displayed. Retreating back to his comfort zone, the staunchly tough Banion was back to normal.

"Thanks," she said and grasped his hand in both of hers.

Withdrawing his hand, he turned away from her and moved back toward the camp in the darkness of the night. He moved a few steps and stopped suddenly. Turning around, Banion looked directly at her in the dim light. He tipped his hat to her and smiled. "See you in the morning."

With that, he turned away from her and moved into the darkness. Seeing him disappear into the blackness of the night made her feel suddenly sad. He was a radiant soul but in the end, he had been stained and tormented. In his passing, he had merged with the dark shadows around him. Such imagery stunned her and in that moment she finally understood him all too well.

Even though he was out of sight, she waved to him in the darkness. Standing alone, she took a brief moment to close her eyes. She breathed softly, thinking about the events that had brought her to that very place, alone in the desert at night, pondering her existence. Calming herself, she found a brief moment of solace, the last moment of solace that she would have for a very long time to come.

Chapter 27
The Minute Before the Darkest Hour

The morning sun had just risen over the eastern edge of the desert. As the glorious light drove away the blackness of the night, a mighty army stirred. The people of the Darken Realm had united under a single banner in an attempt to finally put to rest the atrocities committed by the Dark Order. Their goal was absolute; the complete genocide of the Reaper Kai race had been ordered by Gunther, and his gallant soldiers took up the call without question. After enduring years of desperate fighting and witnessing brutal acts of savagery, there was not a single soldier who had survived without emotional scars.

Soldiers from all nations had answered the call to battle. Troops from the kingdom of Rasheed had enlisted in the cause, wanting nothing more than to drive a dagger into the heart of the Reaper Kai Empire. Valiant soldiers from the Steel Crag Mining guild had answered the call with bitterness biting at their senses. The mighty Crushing-Fist Tribe, a powerful army of hybrid hippo warriors from the marshes to the south, took to the field of battle in defense of the kingdom of Rasheed. From the northlands came mixed units hailing from the Frontier territories, the first region to come under fire at the beginning of the war. And finally, the Mord Tech Empire had sent every able-bodied soldier to fight. Standing tall and proud, the Mord Tech army was equipped with an assortment of chemical implants to be used in the coming conflict.

The amount of troops taking to the field of battle was enormous. Under the banner of the Iron Kai, over 40,000 troops had been mobilized to battle over 65,000 Reaper Kai troops. The battlefield was a slender section of desert stretching in a northwesterly direction, lined on both sides by sheer canyon walls. The objective was to assault the main forces while commando teams infiltrated the enemy fortification in an attempt to destroy the Splicer relay, the electronic supercomputer network that controlled the 20,000 spliced slaves under the control of the Reaper Kai. The plan was to destroy the relay and thus drastically diminish the fighting capacity of the Dark Order. If the plan was executed properly, the spliced slaves would be free of Reaper Kai control, giving the Iron Kai army a sizeable advantage over their dark brethren.

The fate of the Darken Realm rested on this single military struggle. If the Iron Kai could not take the production facility in Metalweaver Flats, they were doomed due to the high-scale efficiency of the facility. If the Iron Kai could not win the battle, they would be overwhelmed by a never-ending host of Biogtech soldiers. In the entire war, a more crucial battle had never been waged.

Reflecting upon the enormity of the situation, Gunther took a moment to think about his life and the arduous task ahead of him.

Mounting a black steed, Gunther took a deep breath and prepared himself. The emperor had decided to address the formations in person, riding to the head of the combat divisions to rally his troops for the impending battle. He was nervous and for good reason. If Gunther failed, it would be his direct actions that would lead to the demise of the entire Darken Realm. He knew that not a single mistake could be made in such a crucial battle.

He took a brief moment to collect his thoughts and rally himself, letting his reflections on the war overtake him. He thought about all of the horrible things that he had experienced during the struggle against the Reaper Kai. As he focused on these thoughts, he was overwhelmed with a deep sense of rage that stemmed from all of the injustices that had to be endured. It didn't take long for his blood to start pumping through his veins. He wanted to win; deep down in his heart, he wanted to win more than anything. Yielding to his enraged emotions, he knew that he was ready to make war. Gunther kicked his horse hard in the sides. The noble animal neighed and reared up, slamming its hooves down on the desert sand with a loud thump. As it shook its head in anger, Gunther led his mount out of the encampment, with all eyes firmly fixed upon him.

The generals and other high-ranking officers came to his side, reining their own horses beside their leader. As they rode in formation, Gunther kicked his horse again so it bolted toward the battle lines. This gesture was mimicked by his officers, and the command group charged in quickly to address the troops. This bold and aggressive action by the command group set the stage for the battle to come. Seeing their leaders charging to the battle formations sent an instant wave of hope through the soldiers. Cheering, they roared and watched Gunther move in front of the formation.

The front ranks of the army were now viewing their gallant leader with pride. Once more, Gunther kicked his horse, which reared up again, neighing in anger. As it slammed its hooves down on the sand again, another wave of cheers crested through the army. Gunther wanted his troops aggressive and ready to kill, not meek and submissive.

As they cheered him, the army began to chant his name over and over again. Gunther grew stern, his posture suddenly rigid. Raising his right hand, he crisply saluted all of the soldiers before him. They saluted him back with more wild applause. Allowing them to feel the fire and adrenaline hit their blood, Gunther permitted his troops to cheer for a moment.

The army was so enormous, only a small portion of them could actually see or hear Gunther, but it didn't matter. The front ranks were utterly enamored with their leader and their cheers and war chants were strong enough to polarize the entire army. Like a wave, the chants and cheers passed into the back ranks of the army until every soldier, some 40,000 in all, was yelling in defiance of the Reaper Kai.

Finally, Gunther raised his hands and the entire army fell silent.

With voice booming, he addressed the great army. "Today is the greatest honor of my life. I have been given the opportunity to lead the most gallant and courageous army in the history of the Darken Realm."

A cheer rose and rippled throughout the entire army. The back portion had no idea why they were even applauding, but hope is infectious.

"We have been served slaughter and reckless outrage by the Reaper Kai Empire. There is not a single person in this army who has not suffered or bled due to the reckless acts of the enemy. Not a single soldier who is standing before me has been spared from the darkness. I want you all to realize that the suffering and bloodshed ends once and for all this day! We will march across the desert and take what is ours! We will crush the enemy underfoot and finally remove the stench of evil that has infested our lands for centuries. Do not fear the battle before us; embrace the courage within your hearts. Feel the outrage that you have suffered. Let that outrage guide you. Make the enemy suffer for your losses. March into the desert before us and eradicate them all. Never surrender, never lose hope! Death to the Reaper Kai!"

The booming war chants were deafening. Mirroring their zeal and luster, Gunther chanted the same war cries, making a fist with his right hand and holding it in the air above his head. The chants died down as the assembled forces stared at Gunther with pride and respect. A silence came over the army as he gazed at the troops spread out before him. His voice boomed out once more.

"Soldiers! Stand at attention!"

They immediately responded to his order. The command trickled through the ranks with frightening speed. He had complete control and was stunned to see such discipline, especially from an army with so many different factions. Extending his hand, he issued the first battle command.

"Soldiers, full advance! Give them hell!" Gunther shouted.

With that, the Iron Kai combined forces marched out into the fray, charging the heavily defended expanse known as Metalweaver Flats. As they advanced on the enemy position, the sounds of demonic trumpets roared and the boom of distant artillery fire rattled their bones. The first shots of the final showdown with the Reaper Kai Empire had just been fired, and the bloodiest battle to be fought in a thousand years erupted.

Chapter 28
The Battle of Metalweaver Flats

A whistle cut through the air. With a loud thud, an artillery shell slammed into the desert sand. A split second later, a deafening boom resounded as a shockwave of shrapnel was sent into the massed soldiers. Screams rose as their bodies were pierced by the white hot metal. One soldier held his bleeding stomach, crashing to the ground. Another near the impact crater clutched his shoulder where his forearm had been sheared off at the elbow by the blast. Many others were mangled beyond recognition and their lifeless bodies were sprawled around the smoking crater.

Confronted with the horrors of battle, Carla Reins was utterly terrified by the bloody images and inhuman screams.

"I can't do this!" she cried out, grabbing the belt of the mighty mutant hybrid in front of her. Globulus did not falter and continued to press onward.

"There's no retreat. We'll never have another chance at this. If we don't stop the enemy in this battle, the Darken Realm is doomed!" he yelled.

"I'm scared." Her voice was raw.

"We all are. Don't let it get the better of you."

"This is too much; we need to get the hell out of here. I can't do this!"

"You have to. We have no choice at this point. You will fight or you'll die." Globulus spoke in a gruff tone. As he did, several squads of massed Biogtech soldiers shambled over a nearby sand dune. Their white pasty bodies almost made them glow in the bright burning sunlight. Seeing the mindless robots readying for an attack, Globulus ordered a preemptive strike, screaming to his hippo brothers.

"Crushing Fist to arms!" he yelled. "Open fire!"

The mighty hippo warriors were enormous. Each was wielding a heavy machine gun and brought considerable force to the battlefield. Bellowing out war cries, the warrior hippos at the front ranks of the army opened fire, sending a heavy barrage of machine gun rounds into the approaching Biogtech soldiers. The bullets were so strong, they literally cut the robotic soldiers in half. A brief second after the attack, several dozen Biogtechs were shredded into puddles of hydraulic fluid and twitching robotic body parts.

Carla and Globulus fought side by side. Sweeping his machine gun back and forth, he fired short bursts, killing Biogtechs in a sinister display of raw power. Carla was crouched behind her companion, rifle at her shoulder. Firing well placed shots, she gunned down the opposition while trembling and cowering from time to time as screams and explosions rocked the battlefield.

The surge of enemy troops was in earnest. Hundreds of Biogtech soldiers kept coming. Within seconds, the entire ridgeline was covered with the robotic troops. Grasping submachine guns, they opened fire slowly at first. The trickle of bullets turned into a torrent as they continued to crest the ridge line.

The Biogtech counterattack was intense. Hundreds and hundreds of bullets were fired at the hippo warriors. Although most hippo warriors were resistant to gunfire in general, the amount of bullets striking them could not be ignored. Many of the warriors in the front ranks were raked with dozens of bullets. Staggering, several of the gallant hybrids were severely wounded. As they crashed to the ground, both sides of the bloody exchange began to take on casualties.

"Fight on!" Globulus yelled and his own kind listened to his orders without a hint of fear.

The Biogtechs were outmatched. Within a few minutes of heated battle, close to 200 Biogtechs had been destroyed and the hippo warriors had only lost a handful of soldiers. Roaring out war chants, they continued to push on. The hippo war band had been stationed on the left flank of the canyon walls. Proceeding undaunted, they were pressing on quickly into enemy territory, much quicker than their allies toward the middle of the canyon, who were being barraged repeatedly by artillery shells. To the hippos' right flank, the remaining Rasheed militia troops that had survived the war thus far were more than happy to charge forward with their hippo allies.

The attack and charge of the hippo warriors gave the Iron Kai army a serious advantage. Taking up elevated positions along the edge of canyon, the hippo war band spread out and began to pummel the Reaper Kai forces with heavy machine-gun fire. The Biogtech troops were so thick that the hippo warriors didn't even have to aim. The gunfire cut into the flank of the Reaper Kai army with devastating results. The amount of casualties began to cut deep into the enemy. As the Reaper Kai flank began to buckle, their command responded immediately.

Seeing the hippos cleaving through the army, the Reaper Kai general, Brother Deathmoon, ordered a full attack on the ridgeline. Immediately, the artillery crews targeting the hippo warriors dug in on the side of the ¢anyon. Within a few minutes, the whistle and booms of artillery filled the air.

"Take cover!" Globulus yelled, grabbing the stunned Carla and throwing her to the ground. As they hid beyond the rocks, the shells came down and exploded in the midst of their war band. Screams echoed as many hippos were mortally wounded. The artillery attack stunned the Crushing-Fist clan. Hiding, they were unprepared for the next attack.

Lumbering from the massed troops in the burning sands, assault rigs, enormous Biogtechs, moved to engage the hippo warriors. Using the artillery barrage to move in for the kill, the black Biogtech assault rigs managed to make it halfway up the hillside before the hippo army caught sight of them. Not wanting to kill their own, the Reaper Kai artillery attack stopped a split second before the assault rigs reached the perimeter of the hippo army.

Screams broke the air as the sound of cannon rounds thumped and popped. The assault rigs were heavily armed and their shoulder-mounted cannons were deadly to the hippos. Many were killed outright, unable to even respond to the threat. After taking a fair amount of casualties, the hippo army finally counterattacked, focusing their heavy machine guns on the giant death machines; however, their attack had little effect. The heavy machine-gun rounds were mostly deflected by the high-tech black armor plating on the Biogtechs. Some bullets still managed to pierce the armor, and several of the assault rigs began to stumble.

Feeling nearly helpless as his soldiers' weapons proved ineffective, Globulus ordered a charge. The noble hippo warriors immediately responded and drew hand weapons. Most of the hybrids clutched sledge hammers in each hand. Cursing the robotic soldiers, they rushed forward, many being cut down by the harsh and deadly cannon fire.

The assault rigs were ill prepared to battle in close combat with the enormous hippo warriors. The battle line of the Crushing Fist hit the assault rigs like a tidal wave. Knocking the death machines to the ground, the hippo warriors began to pound on the Biogtechs. Unable to fight back while on the ground, the machines were pounded to death. Cracks and crashes were ripping the air as hippos yelled and crushed the robots, battering the black armor into broken fragments. The attack was so intense that the entire detachment of assault rigs was engaged in bloody close combat. It didn't take long for the hippo warriors to crush and dismember the robotic soldiers. The left flank of the attack had been secured once more and the Iron Kai once again had a sizeable advantage.

*   *   *

Having dug in, the Iron Kai soldiers had ground to a halt in the center of the valley. Their ranks had taken the brunt of enemy artillery blasts. Hundreds of soldiers were scattered across the bloody sand dunes. Using the blast craters as crude bunkers, pockets of Iron Kai held off a torrent of enemy troops in enormous numbers. The blast craters were becoming littered with the bodies of dead Biogtechs, which began to mount in huge piles around the craters. The valiant Iron Kai soldiers were holding their own and many parts of the army were advancing around the densely packed center of the battle.

A strange gibbering broke the battle lines. Ordering a charge, the Reaper Kai had a plan of their own. Ranks of bloodthirsty Goat Minions, savage slaves of hell itself, pushed their way through the Biogtech troops. Launching into the void, they rushed across the earth, scrambling over the corpses of the dead.

Baying fiercely, with madness guiding them, they hurled themselves into the fray without any regard for their own safety. Only a few were felled by gunfire before they reached the impact craters defended by the Iron Kai soldiers.

Ill prepared for the attack, the terrified soldiers knew that death was near. The craters became a place of great suffering, echoing with raging screams. Stabbing and slashing, the Goat Minions battered the hapless soldiers, butchering them into piles of dismembered body parts and bloody pools of battered corpses. The attack was so ferocious that every impact crater was overrun. The crater floors were littered with screaming soldiers, there bodies being mutilated as they tried to desperately crawl from their blood-filled tombs. The enemy was insatiable. Within the span of ten minutes, hundreds of Iron Kai had been slaughtered.

As a gap opened in the middle of the battlefield, demonic trumpets sounded. Scrambling forward, Biogtech soldiers began to overtake the impact craters, using them as defensive positions of their own. A fierce fire fight erupted as hand grenades and mortar exchanges intensified the bloody conflict.

And so the battle buckled backwards and forwards, the Reaper Kai surging ahead and then driven back by the Iron Kai troops. The dance of death was costly and the center of the conflict was rife with death. Mounting piles of the dead mixed with the cries of the wounded turned the surreal epic battle into a pure vision of hell.

Hope was replaced with sheer terror. Unable to function in the thick chaos, many soldiers simply wished for death, unable to comprehend that such terrible visions could be endured. Hearing the screams and smelling the blood of their countrymen sent panic into many of them. The battle was so thick, so intense—there was no escape. Once the soldiers were thrown into the middle of the conflict, the gears of war ground away, consuming everything in sight. Those who entered the center of the conflict were given a death sentence where one's life was measured in minutes, not years; longevity was momentary.

As the ebb and flow of battle surged back and forth, a gallant push led by Iron Kai forces finally secured the blast craters, creating a refuge once more, a place to defend and hold. As the battle raged on, the Iron Kai managed to gain the upper hand at the center of the conflict.

With the Crushing Fist and Rasheed forces holding the left flank and the Iron Kai taking ground at the middle of the conflict, the focus of the struggle suddenly shifted to the right flank, where Mord Tech and Steel Crag militia were fighting a desperate struggle of their own.

*   *   *

Lances of fire were streaking across the battlefield. War priests, garbed in blood- red robes, were fiercely attacking the right flank of the conflict. Hiding behind an endless horde of Biogtechs, the Reaper Kai priests were hurling potent psychic attacks into the Mord Tech soldiers who were trying to take a boulder field.

With fighting conducted from boulder to boulder, the battleground was a strange maze. Hiding amongst the rock formations, the concealed Reaper Kai were praying to demons for power. A small band of Reaper Kai, extremely potent in battle, had already killed hundreds of Mord Tech soldiers. From time to time, soldiers would simply collapse onto the ground, gripped by convulsions and seizures as psychic attacks burst their internal organs and punctured blood vessels in their brains. It was a battle of deception and vicious cruelty.

The Biogtech soldiers marched endlessly through the maze of rocks. Stalwart and strong, the Mord Techs led the assault as their allies from the Steel Crag Mining guild protected the flank of the formation trying to take the boulder field.

Unable to push on, the Biogtechs were gunned down or chopped to pieces by the soldiers. The Mord Tech soldiers, relying on a host of drug implants, were able to take severe punishment as well as unleashing a myriad of potent hand-to-hand combat attacks. Even as many Mord Techs were damaged and mortally wounded, they would rise again as the chemical cocktails racing through their arteries replenished and restored them from the verge of death.

Having fought an awkward stalemate, the Mord Techs had resolved to finally push forward under the direction of their courageous leader, Grand Marshal Deetric. The Mord Tech troops activated their drug implants, and were soon overtaken by a battle rage.   Receiving the order for a full advance, the soldiers rushed through the maze of rocks, dodging gunfire and charging the hidden Reaper Kai priests. The attack was sudden and brazen.

Unable to rely on the seclusion of their hiding spots, many of the red-robed Reaper Kai were stunned to find the Mord Techs charging through the fray, bayonets and knives at the ready. The attack was well placed and planned and could not have come at a better time. With the left flank and the center of the battle secure, the Steel Crag militia was unchallenged and descended quickly onto the boulder field. Caught between the two sharp edges of a pair of scissors closing, the Reaper Kai forces were cut off from their main force.   Being hit head-on and flanked at the same time was a shocking reality.

Closing on the boulder fields, the Steel Crag soldiers cut down hundreds of Biogtechs and managed to take up solid firing positions just as the enraged Mord Techs surged through, sweeping into the boulder field like a horde of crazed killing machines. As they engaged the Reaper Kai priests at close range, the members of the Dark Order were flooded and overwhelmed by the Mord Tech onslaught.   Chanting war cries and feeling the battle-enhancing drugs sting at their brains, the Mord Techs never faltered.   A massacre ensued as nearly 50 Reaper Kai priests were butchered and slaughtered. Any priests who fled came into the gun sights of the Steel Crag militia, who gunned them down as they fled. There was no escape; the Reaper Kai priests were completely cut off. It took only a few minutes for the boulder field to be taken by the Mord Tech troops and the Steel Crag militia.

With the center of the battle under control, the Mord Tech army was able to push quickly along the right edge of the canyon. With a rapid surge, they managed to flank the Reaper Kai army. On the left flank, the hippo warriors of the Crushing Fist, supported by the Rasheed soldiers, were pummeling the forces of darkness. In the center, Iron Kai forces had made substantial attacks and were actually pushing the enemy back.

Each portion of the offensive was making solid gains and the Reaper Kai forces were beginning to crumble.   On the ridgeline above the battlefield, Gunther nodded his head in satisfaction. The enemy was fully engaged and he knew the time had come. He nodded to his trusted captain, who picked up the signal immediately.

Maddock moved away from the scene to assemble the commando teams that were ready to attack the Metalweaver Flats facility itself. It was time for the seven commando teams to strike at the heart of the manufacturing facility. The goal was to knock out the Splicer relay and free all of the enslaved soldiers and civilians, numbering 20,000. If these slaves were liberated, it would be the final nail in the coffin and the Reaper Kai would be destroyed.

As Maddock rushed to assemble the commando teams, Nova 7 prepared for one final mission, a mission that would take them into the heart of darkness itself. It was time for the team to make one final stand against the Reaper Kai order and bring the forces of darkness to their knees once and for all. It was time for Nova 7 to deliver a killing blow to the enemy or die in the process. Never had it been more dangerous, never had the stakes been higher. The freedom of the Darken Realm once again rested in the hands of Nova 7.

Chapter 29
Dark Miracle

The victim ceased to struggle. As blood poured from the slave's open wounds, the body went limp, passing into death. Tossing the corpse into an enormous pile of bodies, the Goat Minion removed the final victim from Father Vertigo's sacrificial altar.

The floor was coated in blood and littered with the remains of 100 innocent captives, now lifeless. In the center of the room was an enormous basin made of black marble and filled with human blood from the scattered bodies. Standing above the basin was Father Vertigo, hands and forearms drenched in gore.

In one hand he held a twisted black steel blade, while in the other was a smoking caldron that expelled a noxious fume into the air. Chanting above the basin of blood, Vertigo was in the final phases of a dark ritual, a bloodletting verse that had been unraveled from demonic knowledge put to paper thousands and thousands of years ago.

"Come all my children. View the splendor of darkness!" Vertigo yelled and plunged the twisted steel dagger into the basin of blood. As he did, the blood trembled. Murky black shapes began to form within the basin. Smiling, he knew that the dark miracle was almost complete.

Hearing the words of Vertigo, all creatures foul and dark drew near the lord of evil. Kneeling on the bloody floor before their dark master, the Goat Minions paid homage to him. A coven of Goat Minions and Reaper Kai priests formed at the perimeter of the room. Holding their hands toward Vertigo, they began to pray to the demonic forces. Each of the chanting dark priests lent his power to Vertigo.

Holding his hands outstretched, he could feel the power of his coven course through his frail body. The psychic energy from his servants was being channeled into his body with frightening results. Blue ghostly forms began to emerge around him. Screams of the dead and damned roared to life. Staring around the room, Vertigo's rotten black eyes scanned his coven.

Screaming, he urged them for more power, more hatred.

"I need more!" he wailed. "Cater to your darkest dreams! Feel your souls blacken with despair and hatred. Feel greed and lust fuel your hearts. Focus on all of the pleasure you have wrought in the service of evil. Focus on letting the animal within you feed your soul!"

The Goat Minions and Reaper Kai priests followed his orders and thought of selfish carnal pleasure. They focused on greed and reckless ambition. They allowed themselves to be fully consumed with evil teachings. As they focused on such dark thoughts, Vertigo was infused with further power.

His body was surrounded in a swirling blue maelstrom of light. Wisps of dark spirits circled his body, howling in anger. Ghostly forms appeared in the room, floating around Father Vertigo as if waiting for something, something vile. Wracked with supernatural power, he lifted off the ground, floating in the air. As he rose higher and higher, the energy increased with each passing second. The chanting mounted to fervent levels as the coven of darkness thanked the demons in hell for blessing them with such malign power.

"In times of war, in times of great suffering, great power can be summoned!" Vertigo held his hands outstretched as he levitated off the ground. As he spoke, one of the blue demonic entities rushed inside his open mouth, infusing him with further power. Shaking, his frail form convulsed and twitched as additional spirits entered his body, further powering him. He kept the demonic entities within his body in check, seeking to unleash the raw power building inside of him.

"It is our right as children of darkness to ask our masters for infernal power. I knowingly ask our dark masters this day to aid in our effort against those that oppose our will. We have cherished the rights of evil and have been dutiful in our pledge to uphold the laws of suffering and indulgence. In this dark ritual, we pledge ourselves once more to the shadow!" Vertigo yelled, and the coven bowed before him, placing their foreheads on the bloodstained floor.

Chanting and dark prayers erupted in the language of evil. The chanting rose in tempo as all of the minions of darkness opened the palms of their hands and directed their psychic abilities into Father Vertigo. Wracked with an additional burst of demonic energy, he shook uncontrollably.

Uttering thanks to hell itself, Vertigo whispered the final verses in the ritual. As he uttered the final word, he floated down toward the basin of blood that was now turbulent. He plunged his hands into the basin, finally completing the ritual.

An eerie quiet fell over the room as the ritual ended. Staring in anticipation, the twisted priests and Goat Minions were ready to watch a miracle unfold, a dark and terrible manifestation of demonic power on earth.

The basin of blood trembled violently, emitting shockwaves of power. Jets of blood sprayed from within. Black nodules, clumped together, were expelled from the sinister basin and landed all over the fresh corpses that had been sacrificed to perform the ritual. Within a few seconds, all of the blood in basin had been expelled onto the piles of corpses.

Staring in horror, the coven watched the black clumps begin to move. A crackling sound erupted as the tiny black spheres broke open. Small forms, budding insects and maggots, emerged from the black nodules. With frightening speed, the tiny insects began to devour the corpses, feeding on the dead flesh. Within moments, the insects swarm had encased the dead bodies. Enormous cockroaches chewed into the corpses, their wings flapping as they devoured the dead. A swarm of locusts erupted from another pile of remains. The locusts emitted an enormous clatter as they feasted on the dead, filling the room with shrill chirping noises. Finally, a buzzing rose from the far corner of the room as an enormous swarm of flies set to devour the other pile of bodies.

As the swarms of insects devoured the dead, the next generation was already gestating, as fresh eggs broke open and the insect larva burrowed into the corpses. The brevity of the insects' gestation period was staggering. Entire generations formed within a matter of seconds. Where at first there were only a few writhing insects upon the corpses of the dead, now an entire living carpet was hungrily devouring and reproducing at a phenomenal rate.

Confused and alarmed, the coven backed away as the sound of the feeding became deafening. The hungry flies, cockroaches, and locusts all chewed away, creating a sickening clatter. Fear overtook many of the coven members and they fled the scene, unable to further witness the horror that had been unleashed by Father Vertigo's infernal miracle.

Within a few minutes, the insect swarm had taken flight. Thousands upon thousands of the locusts were flying around the room in dense masses. The flies were so thick that those in the room could not see much further than a few feet. Cockroach colonies covered the walls, so numerous that they were several layers thick and the walls beneath were totally obscured.

The scene was completely unnerving. As the piles of bodies were stripped to the bone, many of the insects sought fresh flesh. Alighting on the priests, the insects started to bite. The Reaper Kai yelled and fled as the insects tried to devour them. Rushing from the chamber, many fell to the ground. They landed with a sickening crunch, crushing many of the insects covering the floor. The terrified Goat Minions charged over fallen Reaper Kai, trampling several and wounding many. The wounded lay upon the ground of the chamber, unable to escape. Descending immediately upon them, the swarm of insects began to devour the living. Their screams were short lived. The swarm immediately coated them in a living mass of hunger. Much as they flailed around, it was in vain. The mass of insects needed to feed, and feed they did. All those that failed to escape the chamber were consumed, their flesh utterly stripped to bare bones within minutes.

In all the chaos, only one remained devoid of all emotion. Father Vertigo stood completely still in the center of the room. As he extended his hands, the ravenous brood of insects seemed to listen to his will. When he shifted his hands, the swarms responded and followed his commands. Elated by such raw power, he sought to put an end to the war once and for all.

His ritual chamber opened to the sky. Above him, two steel doors had been retracted. Staring upwards, Father Vertigo raised his hands in the air. As he did, the ravenous swarm of cockroaches, flies, and locusts took flight and surged out of the room.

The day was turned to night. Rising out of the chamber, the enormous swarm of death was so thick that the sun could not penetrate it. Buzzing and screeching, it swirled around in the air, circling the building first and finally spreading out over the entire production facility. The swarm was so enormous, it sounded like thunder.

"Feed well, my children!" Vertigo yelled. "There is so much warm flesh for you to consume!"

Smiling in glee, Father Vertigo flexed his hands, ordering the horde of insects to do his bidding. The swarm responded, granting him complete control. Retreating to his bone-encrusted throne, Vertigo sat down and began to meditate. Focusing on controlling the swarm, he willed them to travel into the desert. The swarm heeded his commands, and obediently raced off. With hunger and reproduction its only instincts, the swarm was a perfect weapon. Ordering the insects to do his will, Father Vertigo commanded them to descend upon the Iron Kai army and feed upon them.

The tide of battle was about to shift once more and the Reaper Kai now had a sizeable advantage. The doom of the Darken Realm was drawing near.

Chapter 30
Into the Den of Evil

In the command post, all seven of the strike teams listened intently to the mission objectives one last time. Gunther was standing before them, presenting the teams with a layout of the Reaper Kai production facility. There were seven flagged buildings listed on the map, one of which, according to Gunther, contained the Splicer relay. However, Gunther didn't tell the strike teams that he knew exactly which building hid the Splicer relay. The lucky team to be sent to the correct building was Nova 7.

"Everyone prepare to move out," Gunther boomed. "The enemy is fully engaged and this is a prime opportunity to strike. Mount up troops and give them hell!"

Grabbing their gear, the six Iron Kai commando teams left the tent and headed off to the helicopters poised to take them beyond the ridgeline, away from the hazardous range of anti-aircraft weapons. The teams were then to rappel down into the facility to search their target building for the Splicer relay. As the teams left the tent, Tani grabbed his gear and moved off toward the exit.

Suddenly the young scholar stopped dead in his tracks. None of the other members of Nova 7 were following him. Surprised, he gazed at them in incomprehension. "Come on, we need to go."

Banion simply stared at him uneasily. Looking at the rest of his team members, Tani was confused and moved back to address them. "Aren't we going?"

"Yes, but we have a few minutes," Banion responded.

"I don't get it," Tani shot back.

Not wanting to answer him, the rest of his teammates were silent. Finally, Gunther, sensing that the scholar had not been fully informed, moved forward to speak with him.

"The Splicer relay is located in the target building that has been assigned to Nova 7," he said, hoping the tribal would understand his meaning.

"I don't get it. You told the rest of the teams to search these other buildings. Why would you do that if you knew where the target building is?"

"The other teams are acting as decoys." Gunther's tone was solemn.

Tani blinked in confusion. "You mean the other teams are bait? You had no intention of them taking out the Splicer relay?"

"Listen, Tani, in desperate times you have to make difficult decisions. I felt that it was in the best interest of this operation to send the most skilled team after the primary target."

"But all those men are going to die!" Tani finally understood.

"Yes, I'm sending them to their deaths so that Nova 7 has the best shot possible at completing the objective."

"I don't want any part of this," Tani protested, while the rest of his team was sullen and silent, not wanting to get involved.

"You don't have a choice," Gunther shot back.

"Yes, I do, I can walk away right now."

"You can, but you won't. We need you and you know it. We can't do this without you."

"But this isn't fair! All of those soldiers are going to die to protect us! It's not fair!"

"War isn't fair. You do what you need to do to win. Sometimes there have to be sacrifices to complete your objectives. I know it seems deceptive, but this is the only shot we have. The other six teams are going to hit the facility a few minutes before you do to cause utter chaos so you can complete your mission. They are all soldiers and they know the price of failure," Gunther explained, trying to calm the tribal scholar.

"But why us?"

"You are the best of the best, the team that brought the nuclear age back to the world. I wouldn't risk the lives of my men if you weren't the best of the best. This is about survival of the fittest. If we don't win this battle, we lose the war. Much must be risked and I made a decision to do so."

Tani fell silent and shook his head. Staring at the rest of his team, he suddenly felt guilty. So many good men would lose their lives just so Nova 7 would have a single chance. Sighing, he bowed his head in dismay. As he did, the sound of the helicopters taking off brought his attention to the soldiers who were about to lose their lives. In the end, they were decoys, nothing more. He shook his head in disbelief as he turned to the rest of his teammates, who had known the entire time.

"Why didn't you tell me?" he quizzed them.

"If you would have known, it wouldn't have changed anything. We have the same objective either way," Banion responded.

"We were having a hard enough time dealing with it. We wanted to spare you the guilt," Jared contributed.

"You should have told me," Tani exclaimed, feeling somewhat betrayed.

"It was a decision we made to keep you focused. The last thing we wanted is for you to be out of sorts," Mineera agreed with her companions.

"I value you and this team, Tani," Gunther added, trying to pull him out of his malaise. "Focus on your mission and worry about this later. You have a job to do and everyone is counting on you. I want you to stand tall and push this aside for the time being. Can you do that?"

"Yes," Tani responded immediately. "I'll stay focused."

"Good." Gunther looked at his watch. "You're up in thirty seconds. Grab your gear and get ready to move out."

Nodding, Tani prepared his gear once more and the entire team moved outside the command tent. Captain Maddock motioned Nova 7 to a nearby helicopter, and the mercenary team prepared to take off. As Maddock signaled the pilot, the engines surged and the rotors sprung to life. It took but a few seconds for the helicopter to reach full power. As it rose into the sky, Tani looked down and saw Gunther staring back at him. For a second their eyes locked. Saluting Tani, Gunther stood tall and proud, urging the youth to have no fear. Tani understood the gesture and responded. Raising his hand, he returned Gunther's salute.

"Ten minutes to the drop zone. We're putting you a few clicks outside the others' landing zone. Get your weapons ready and prepare yourselves. You're about to enter the den of the lion itself. You're about to enter the heart of darkness and one of the most fortified positions in the entire Darken Realm." Mad Dog Maddock spoke with an almost evil glimmer in his eyes.

Checking his weapons, Jared chambered the first bullet from his submachine gun's magazine. His hand brushed across his neck and grabbed the raven totem. Kissing it, he let the ancient relic return to its place around his neck. The strange totem was emitting a fierce chill as if anticipating the coming battle. Moving his hand down to his waist, he pulled the Scar Blade free and saw its metallic blue glimmer. On the other side of his waist, he caught sight of Banion's silver revolver tucked into its holster. Smiling, he brushed his hand across the cold steel of the weapon, then closed his eyes, satisfied, and prepared for the coming battle.

Tani fidgeted with his gun, checking the chamber several times. Seeing a bullet resting inside gave him only mild comfort. Tugging on his bandolier, he ensured that all of his grenades and demolitions charges were intact and accessible. Checking his backpack, he ensured that his laptop computer was ready. Momentarily content, he began to drum his stumpy fingers on his knee nervously.

Banion had a blank expression on his face. He clutched his assault rifle loosely in his left hand while his right hand groped around inside his brown duster. His fingers dipped inside a pocket, and he fidgeted with a metallic object within. Moving the tip of his finger around, he traced the form of his wedding band. Silently, he thought about his wife, who had died so long ago. With misty eyes, Banion whispered so that only he could hear the sound of his voice. "I will make you proud, Lily. I *will* make you proud of me once more." With a sigh, his right hand left his pocket and he looked out the open door on the side of helicopter.

Mineera was resting with her hands folded. She had her head down and was praying. As she made ready for the coming conflict, she focused on not allowing fear to creep into her heart. She had a premonition that the building that contained the Splicer relay was in fact the same building where Father Vertigo resided. Knowing that a confrontation with the lord of darkness could ultimately lead to all of their deaths, she prayed to be given the strength to resist and triumph over such evil. Satisfied, she opened her eyes and stared at the rest of her companions.

For a brief moment, there was peace. In that moment, Nova 7 looked at one another. Such kinship was legendary. Smiling, each of them encouraged the others without saying a word. Their final moment of camaraderie was cut violently short.

"What the hell is that?" the helicopter pilot blurted out in distress.

Maddock ran to the front of the chopper and looked out. Many miles before them, the six gunships carrying the other commando teams were racing across the desert. Just ahead of them, it appeared as if the entire day turned to night. A black, dense cloud was rushing across the desert towards the battle lines of the war below. Blinking several times, Maddock was unable to tell what he was looking at. The black cloud seemed to move with a supernatural perceptive ability and from his distant location, he could not make a solid decision on the matter. The six gunships continued on course and the black cloud seemed to lunge suddenly toward them.

Like a living tendril, part of the infernal insect swarm summoned by Father Vertigo shot directly at the gunships. The pilots took evasive action, managing to steer clear of the insect swarm—all save one. Helicopter 3 was caught in the mass of swarming insects on the move. The swarm slammed into the gunship like a black arm extending, with frightening results. The insects splattered against the windshield, instantly covering the entire front window with a layer so thick that the pilot could no longer see. As the pilot desperately tried to remain in control, the intake on the helicopter engine was flooded with the surge of insects. Sucking in thousands of locusts, cockroaches, and flies, the engine whined and began to shudder.

Screaming, the terrified passengers tried to remove the insects now consuming them. The pilot, unable to see to steer, was losing control quickly. It took but a few seconds more for the final intake on the main rotor to seize, completely jammed with crushed insect parts. Spinning round and round, the out-of-control helicopter could no longer be kept in the air. Hurling towards the ground, it pitched suddenly to the right, throwing several members of the commando team out to their deaths.

It took but a few seconds for the helicopter to slam into the floor of the desert, exploding into flaming rubble and killing everyone on board.

The other five helicopters managed to escape the strange swarm of bugs. Continuing its flight, the helicopter carrying Nova 7 raced forward toward the insect swarm at a staggering speed.

"Get us the hell out of here!" Maddock yelled at the pilot.

Panicked, he jerked the control stick hard to the left. Lurching sharply, Nova 7 hung on for dear life. They grabbed onto anything they could and braced themselves as the helicopter pilot tried to maneuver around the swarm.

Many of the insects slammed into the helicopter but the pilot managed to avoid the main part of the black cloud. The insects crusted up the windshield as he struggled to keep control. Although he was scared half to death, the pilot's quick thinking saved the helicopter from certain doom. When he gained control, the helicopter once again pushed on toward the mountain range behind Metalweaver Flats.

As the helicopter steadied, each member of Nova 7 looked down into the desert below. Commando team 3 had been completely annihilated, killed in a fiery crash. Seeing such a vision was sobering for the team. The mission was not going to be easy to complete and had already claimed the lives of nine valiant Iron Kai soldiers.

They looked at one another once more, but this time, there were no smiles; instead, each member of Nova 7 had a look of dread in their eyes. As fear began to creep into each of them, Maddock yelled, "Five minutes to the landing zone. Get ready."

Steadying themselves, each of them prepared for the task at hand: assaulting the heavily fortified Reaper Kai facility known as Metalweaver Flats.

Chapter 31
Hell on Earth

The crosshairs of the weapon settled on the chest of a red-robed priest. Breathing softly, Carla let the weapon rest against her shoulder. She held her breath for a brief second, then placed her finger on the trigger. With a slight tug, the high-caliber sniper rifle discharged, recoiling immediately. Carla watched her mark; it was a direct hit. The bullet slammed into the Reaper Kai, lifting him off his feet and throwing him to the desert sand. Without twitching even once, the priest passed into death.

As the rest of the enemy squad scrambled for cover, she took aim and gunned down another Reaper Kai within seconds, striking this one in the neck with the sniper rifle, pitching him forward like a rag doll.

As she focused on the immediate threat facing her, something ominous disturbed Carla's concentration. A great shadow suddenly plunged the desert into darkness. The change in lighting was so severe, she felt as if the sun had been consumed. Trying to focus on slaying yet another Reaper Kai at long range, Carla was caught off guard.

In the distance, a low rumble greeted her ears. Finally letting her next target drop out of the gun scope, she looked up and saw Globulus with a deep look of dread on his face. The mighty hippo warrior was trembling. He took a few steps back as if horrified by what he was witnessing. Looking at his face, Carla followed his gaze upward into the darkening sky.

In the distance, it looked as if a blanket of darkness was surging forward across the desert. Carla straightened slowly, staring as she witnessed the most terrifying vision of her entire life. A formless cloud of black death was surging from the sky, changing form erratically as it charged toward the Iron Kai army. The low rumble was growing in intensity. As the swarm charged over the dunes, the sound intensified into a low, ominous humming.

"What is that?" Carla gasped. All of the valiant hippo warriors around her were unable to even respond.

"I have no idea," Globulus said, trembling at the bizarre sight.

Panic broke over the entire army as the blackness of the coming swarm drove away the very sun itself. In a matter of moments, it seemed as if they were all standing in a world bathed in a premature sunset.

The low hum turned into a clatter of buzzing as the dark cloud descended upon the army. Screams, shrill wails of fright, erupted across the entire army as the cloud of ravenous insects crashed into them. As they were engulfed by the swarm, panic drove a wedge of fear into the Iron Kai army.

Immediately, the insects focused on the wounded. Thick swarms of cockroaches began to chew and tenderize their flesh. Locusts driven by intangible hunger nibbled on the bloody troops. Flies ripe with an insatiable appetite landed and began to deposit eggs to fuel the next generation. Maggots immediately hatched and began to feed on the dead and dying.

Screams of agony erupted as the soldiers were consumed, their very flesh stripped from their bones while they were still alive. Their tortured cries echoed amidst the intense buzzing whirl of the swarm. The scenes of fellow soldiers completely covered head to toe in a writhing carpet of hungry insects were too much to bear. Terror was the only companion of many soldiers as they sought to flee the bloody sights and sounds. Collapsing, the entire front ranks of the Iron Kai army buckled and began to retreat. As they did, the mindless Biogtechs laughed in glee, firing their guns into the fleeing soldiers. The carnage wrought by the attack was horrendous. Within a few minutes, hundreds and hundreds of Iron Kai lost their lives, their bodies falling to the ground and instantly devoured by the ravenous horde of insects. Bloody bones, stripped of all flesh, were readily apparent all over the battlefield, silent testament to the demonic power of Father Vertigo.

As more and more soldiers died, additional insect offspring were generated and the swarm began to grow quickly as additional cockroaches, locusts, and flies sprang to life from the corpses of the fallen.

"We need to get out of here!" Carla screamed in terror. As she did, a Rasheed soldier collapsed to the ground, completely covered in a living layer of ravenous insects. The sound of their mandibles cutting his flesh to pieces was nearly drowned out by the sound of his screaming. His open mouth was filled with the hungry insects, chewing on his exposed flesh as his scream was ultimately drowned out. Seconds later, the bones of his torn form were exposed as the swarm consumed what was left of him.

Staggering backwards, Carla was filled with a terror that she had never known before. Just then, an artillery shell landed and detonated in the midst of the soldiers huddling nearby. The blast was devastating, killing several of the hippo warriors. Immediately, their remains were beset upon by the ravenous horde. Carla shook her head, unable to comprehend the horrors of battle. The sights and sounds of death were all around, urging her to flee.

As a wave of panic roared through the ranks of the hippo tribe, Globulus, witnessing the chaos and bloodshed, fell to his knees and shook his head, letting out a whimper of defeat. Pounding his fists against the sand, he watched the hungry insects skittering across his thick hide, trying to bite and chew upon his flesh. With twisted fascination, Globulus watched the horrific events unfold around him.

Many of his countrymen began to flee the battlefield. Blinking in confusion, his mind was filled with images from his past, images of war and of everything that he had lost.

The gentle face of King Toil raced through his mind. He could still see the soft lines of his wrinkled smile. He could still hear the murmur of his gentle voice. When Globulus was young, King Toil had been his foster father, a kind and giving mentor who had taught him the ways of the world. As images of King Toil raced through his terrified psyche, he felt more at peace.

Suddenly, the images shifted to a darker time, a time when deception was ruling the land. The night that King Toil died flashed into his mind with resolute clarity. In that moment, the king's assassination played out once more in his consciousness. Globulus could still hear the ring of gunfire split the air with a deafening crack. He could still remember seeing the king clutch his chest as a fountain of blood erupted where the bullet had struck him. He could still remember the spike of hate and anger that coursed through him as he witnessed his foster father die.

Next a wave of guilt rocked him. The sounds of screaming citizens rang out in his mind. In that instant, his memories had transported Globulus back to the night when Rasheed fell to the Reaper Kai. He could remember watching the innocent civilians plead for mercy as he stood atop the deck of a boat that was pressing out of the harbor. He could still remember the panicked looks on the faces of all those who were left behind. He could still remember his guilt for surviving, after fleeing from the terrible battle. In that moment, he wished that he would have stayed and fought even though it would have meant his death.

He shook his head in dismay as another series of images filled his mind. This time, they were of his father, his real father.

Dredging up painful memories, Globulus thought about his life. When he was but a small child, he was sent to live in Rasheed as a debt of service to the kind King Toil. For sparing the Crushing-Fist clan the ravages of famine, King Toil asked for only one thing: to be given the strongest child from their tribe to be raised as his own and serve as King Toil's war master. Globulus was the child chosen to receive this high honor, forced to leave his real family and expected to grow up in the world of humans, far away from his own kind.

Globulus remembered how throughout his entire life, he had always resented his father for sending him away, exiling him to Rasheed. Deep down he had always wondered why he had been cast out, why he was chosen. It took a lifetime of pain and agonizing self doubt before Globulus gathered up enough courage to travel home and confront his father.

When Globulus finally met his real father, there was something more powerful at work than selfish hate. When he finally looked upon his father, all of the pain was wiped clean, cleansed and flushed away by tears of joy and happiness. His father welcomed him back with open arms and Globulus felt so thrilled to finally be home again, his real home. But where happiness prevailed, it was to be short lived.

Globulus' noble father ordered his son to flee with what remained of a broken army during the siege of Rust Spire. Obeying his duty to his tribe and people, Globulus left his father's side and retreated with all that remained of the shattered army. It was a terrible blow to his psyche, being forced to flee again in the most desperate of times. Globulus' father did not survive the battle but gave the defenders of Rust Spire enough time to retreat and live to fight another day.

In Globulus' opinion, the loss of King Toil and Chief Stoneskin represented a failure to answer the call to duty. So many times was he forced to retreat. So many times was Globulus forced to run and then later feel the guilt of cowardice sting at his heart.

As his tribe died around him amidst the sound of explosions and screams, he blinked and began to feel a spike of rage tug at his mind. Watching his army flee filled him with sorrow. He looked around him, tears streaming down his face. Pounding the sand with his enormous fists, he let the feeling overtake his senses. "Never again!" he screamed in the chaos of the battle. "I am not running this time, do you hear me?" he screamed again as if trying to contact the dead spirits of King Toil and Chief Stoneskin. The feeling of rage coursed through him and he knew what must be done.

So many times had he fled, but on this day, he would not. So many times did he have to walk the road where he was spared and so many good people lost their lives, but on this day, it would not happen again. A feral rage exploded from his soul and he grabbed his weapons. Rising to his feet, he looked around at the battle unfolding around him and knew that the enemy must be punished for their past transgressions.

"Do not flee!" Globulus screamed to his brethren. Many were already charging away. In the midst of the deafening buzzing, they stopped in their tracks and viewed their leader with hesitation.

"Globulus! We are being overrun!" Carla screamed at him.

"I am not running! I can't do it anymore, I just can't do it," he shouted at her.

"We don't have a choice!"

"I am not a coward!" Globulus boomed back.

"This isn't about being a coward!"

"Yes it is!" He began to yell so that others around him could hear his voice. "I would rather die than live my life as a coward! The enemy has taken much from us, but they will not take any more! To arms, my brethren! This day we stand and fight in the loving memory of our beloved Chief Stoneskin and the compassionate King Toil! To hell with the enemy! Raise your weapons in defiance and crush the enemy under foot! Fight with me!" Aiming his weapon, Globulus opened fire. Machine gun fire raced into rank after rank of advancing Biogtech soldiers. His weapon tore through them, felling many.

Though most could not hear his courageous vow and speech, many witnessed his act of courage. Globulus stood by himself at the forefront of the battle lines, putting himself in harm's way to battle the enemy with every ounce of strength and courage in him. This powerful defiance of the enemy even in the face of such insurmountable odds was truly awe-inspiring. Even if he stood alone against the entire Reaper Kai army, Globulus would never retreat, never flee. This display of courage and heroism sparked a chain reaction in the fleeing army of noble hippo warriors.

Seeing their leader face off against an entire army polarized the troops around him. Screaming battle cries, they took arms and charged to his side, firing bursts of machine gun fire into the ranks of advancing enemy soldiers. As more and more moved to support him, the fear was replaced with outrage. More and more hippo warriors saw their brethren retaking the field of battle. Like a chain reaction, the hope of slaughtering the enemy was infectious. Due to Globulus' defiant stand against the enemy, his entire tribe was rallied from despair. Taking to the field of combat once more, they stood united.

As the insect swarm ravaged the battlefield, artillery rounds chewed into the earth killing at will while massive explosions rocked the battlefield. Gunfire sounded like thunder as hundreds of bullets were exchanged every second between the mighty armies. The screams of the dying clashed with the war cries emitted by those gripped by incomprehensible acts of courage. Never had such a battle been fought under such horrendous conditions. The death tolls were staggering on both sides of the conflict.

Although the army of hippo warriors led by Globulus on the left flank was standing firm and actually advancing on enemy positions, the rest of the army was not faring so well.

The battle had become a disaster within a few short minutes. Ranks of Biogtech soldiers were on full advance and the Iron Kai army had been cut into several large pieces. Many pockets of the valiant Iron Kai army were now surrounded, trying desperately to cut a swath through the endless ranks of Biogtech soldiers in order to regain a solid battle line.

But as they fought on, the insects descended and fed without recourse. No longer were the bodies of the dead numerous enough to satiate the wild hunger of the swarm. The living were now becoming targets for the sinister insect swarm. Screaming, many soldiers swatted at themselves, trying to crush or drive away the biting bugs chewing into their flesh. As they tried to battle the swarm, bullets tore into their ranks, felling and killing many. The more that fell, the more the swarm grew in size and intensity.

The right flank had retreated back to the boulder field, taking up defensive positions against the advancing Biogtech throng. The Mord Tech soldiers were rattled but managed to hold their ground within the boulder field. After having sustained heavy casualties, it was a miracle that they had not been overrun. Their stalwart attitude, driven by immense hatred of the Reaper Kai, had given them the strength and will to survive against terrible odds. The majority of the Steel Crag militia had been annihilated, taking the brunt of the enemy counterattack. Nearly 1,000 soldiers had been slaughtered during the Reaper Kai offensive to retake the desert valley.

The enemy attack was in earnest. Under the horrendous battle conditions, the Reaper Kai had a sizeable advantage and were capitalizing on killing. Burning through rank after rank of valiant soldiers, they seemed unstoppable. The once-equal battle forces were now tipping the scales of victory in favor of the forces of evil. Time was running out for the Iron Kai and their allies. If something drastic was not done quickly, the battle would be lost and tens of thousands of soldiers would be slain, their bodies used as fuel to power the demonic swarm of insects ravaging the battlefield.

With such heavy losses, it would be impossible for the Iron Kai to survive without additional help. With the 20,000 spliced slaves whom the Reaper Kai had under their control, the Iron Kai were heavily outnumbered. If those same slaves were to be liberated and free will returned to them, the battle would shift in favor of the Iron Kai. Once free, the slaves would turn on their hated masters. Once freed, the spliced slaves would fight for the Iron Kai and the Reaper Kai would be doomed. The entire battle depended on freeing the spliced slaves from their servitude to the Dark Order. They needed a miracle; they needed an insane wild card to be thrown into the game of war that they were playing. They needed lucky number seven once more.

It was a time for heroes. It was a time for destiny. Fate was calling and Nova 7 was ready to answer the call. With the battle going ill, it was up to the valiant band of mercenaries to rescue the army from certain death. The fate of the Darken Realm was in the hands of Banion, Mineera, Jared, and Tani. If Nova 7 could not destroy the Splicer relay, the Iron Kai army was doomed.

Chapter 32
Entry Team Seven

The helicopter began to descend. Dropping in altitude, it landed atop a flat, open grassy meadow. Exchanging quick glances, the members of Nova 7 gave one another nods of encouragement. Each of them took a deep breath.

They jumped out of the helicopter, landing in the sea of green grass which was waving in the intense turbulence of the spinning rotor. With weapons ready, they looked back at the helicopter as it rose into the air, turning quickly to the southwest and moving away at a rapid pace. Within seconds, the helicopter was gone and the members of Nova 7 were alone on the ridgeline.

The meadow would have been serene in normal circumstances but on that day, it was a source of mystery. The high grass could be concealing lurking foes, waiting to pounce upon them. Holding their weapons at the ready, they spread out and slowly made their way across the pristine field of grass.

As they passed beyond the meadow, a boulder field came into view. Holding his hand in the air, Banion gestured for his team to stop advancing. The rest of the team took up a position behind a nearby rock formation, pausing to listen to him.

"This is it. We are now in harm's way. Keep your eyes open and stay sharp. I want to try and slip into the base undetected. If you see hostile forces and we can sneak past them, I want you to do so. Brute force will get us killed under these circumstances. If you have no other option and must engage, do so and don't think twice about it. Hesitation will also get us killed." Banion spoke in a near-whisper.

The other members of Nova 7 nodded back, understanding what must be done.

Taking a brief second to look at them, Banion had a smile on his face. "I have never been more proud of anyone than I am of all of you today. We have been given one of the greatest honors possible by being given this dangerous mission. I know we won't fail. I have the uttermost faith in all of you."

Nodding back, the rest of Nova 7 appreciated the sentiment and some of their anxiety retreated. A stern look covered Banion's face and everyone knew that it was time to be completely serious. "Let's do it."

Pressing his assault rifle to his chest, he readied the weapon in a firing position. The tribals did the same with their submachine guns and Mineera focused and reiterated a prayer in her mind to calm her nerves. Banion moved into the boulder field, motioning to the tribals. They acknowledged his hand signals and fanned out, each one of them taking a flank.

The warm sun mixed with the chilling wind on the ridgeline and clawed at their senses as they explored the boulder field. The wind whipping through the rocks intermittently emitted a whistling noise that set them on edge. Like deft cats, each of them prowled silently across the area. With short bursts of speed, they rushed around the edge of the boulders, training their weapons in the direction they traveled. They were perfectly in tune with one another. Each of them knew the position of the others and they worked not as individuals but rather as one single organism. The creature known as Nova 7 had many dangerous appendages and each appendage worked in perfect concert with all of the others.

Passing through the boulder field, they quickly made it to the ridgeline only a few miles behind the enemy stronghold, then halted, scanning the complex below. The other mercenary teams that had survived the desert crossing had already hit the perimeter of the enemy base. Using binoculars, Nova 7 viewed the other teams as they slowly advanced through the military base undetected. Gunther had been correct; with all the chaos caused by the battle, most of the Reaper Kai were focusing on the fighting, not the threat of enemy commando teams penetrating their perimeter.

"They're moving inside right now," Banion whispered to his companions. "We need to press on quickly."

Securing a rope, they rappelled down the rock face and found themselves directly behind the Reaper Kai base in Metalweaver Flats. Preparing for the final assault, they moved quickly across another boulder field, concealing their movements as they rapidly advanced on the enemy fortification.

Nova 7 was nearing the perimeter of the installation when all hell broke loose. The sound of gunfire erupted near the center of the facility. Several of the commando teams had made contact with enemy forces. The element of surprise had ended. Rushing to the corner of the furthest building in the complex, Nova 7 had just made it to the outskirts of the base when sirens broke the air. It was official; the Reaper Kai had been alerted to the presence of enemy forces within the compound.

"Damn it!" Banion said harshly as he looked around the edge of the building. Already, Reaper Kai priests were swarming with squads of Biogtechs toward the center of the complex. Banion estimated the enemy forces were a mere 40 yards away.

"Now what?" Tani asked, training his gun on the Biogtechs.

"We wait," Banion shot back in a dark tone.

"We wait?" Jared repeated, confused. "The other commando teams are going to be overrun."

"I know," Banion replied. "They'll give us the diversion we need, just like Gunther said. The enemy will attack the other entry teams, and we'll let them."

Mineera assessed the situation with growing dread. The sound of screaming echoed in the distance as more gunfire erupted. The Reaper Kai and Biogtechs were rushing to the scene. Listening to the intense battle unfold, Banion waited patiently for the opportune moment to move.

As the battle in the center of the facility reached its utmost intensity, Banion ordered them inside. Rushing through the center of the buildings, they took care to move quickly, away from any windows.

As they rushed past doors, a shot of adrenaline hit their systems. Each door they passed could be an invitation to disaster. Would more enemy troops suddenly rush out? Would the enemy see them as they pressed deeper into the base? These and many more questions plagued their senses as they sought to breach the building holding the Splicer relay.

"Open fire!" a man yelled in the distance. One of the Iron Kai commando teams had taken up a position atop one of the buildings and was now firing on enemy forces engaged below them. The hum of automatic weapons heightened as they slammed the Reaper Kai forces with hot lead.

Banion assessed the unfolding situation with deep appreciation. The ruckus caused by the other teams was so distracting, it allowed Nova 7 to reach their target building with ease.

Just outside the door, Banion moved up a metal staircase, alert and ready to engage at any moment. Hesitantly, his hand reached forward to grab the doorknob. Shaking a bit, he nodded to Jared and Tani, who made ready to charge into the building. Jared flung the door open, and was the first to go through it, charging to the right with weapon ready. Tani crossed behind him and charged to the left, securing the other flank. Banion was the next to cross the threshold. Mineera took up the rear and moved in behind them.

The interior of the building was dimly lit and a great amount of noise overwhelmed their sense of hearing. They blinked frantically, waiting for their eyes to adjust. The room in which they were standing was enormous, larger than most warehouses. At the center of the room, large conveyor belts were whirring away, squeaky wheels rotating as robotic raw materials were transported. Beyond the conveyors were sets of robotic arms, tirelessly positioning the materials to build new Biogtech soldiers. At one station, arms were being attached to the torsos. At another, the heads were being welded onto the bodies. Each section of the production facility generated a fierce amount of noise. Each of the team members was essentially deaf, unable to hear even their own footsteps in the harsh noise.

The room was almost completely devoid of sentient life. On the far end of the conveyor, two Reaper Kai priests were pointing at different parts of the conveyor line as a third fixed one of the machines. The priests were positioned near the stairwell leading upwards into the building, barring their passage further into the installation.

Banion quickly scanned the rest of the room and found it empty. Looking at the three Reaper Kai and hearing all of the noise gave him an idea. Motioning to each tribal in turn, he gave them an order to take aim at a different target. They acknowledged his command and crept forward, concealing themselves under or behind the equipment. As they got into firing position, one of the priests began to scan the room with a look of concern. Due to all the sound in the production area, none of them heard the sirens outside or the fierce battle raging. The Reaper Kai seemed suddenly concerned but it was too late. Banion motioned to his companions, and the attack was on. Firing their weapons, all of them struck true and the three Reaper Kai priests were pelted with a precise burst of gunfire. Killed instantly, they crumpled to the ground, the gunfire muted by the intense noise in the room.

Rushing forward, the team met up at the staircase. As they reached it, Mineera grabbed her chest as if having a heart attack. She gasped several times and her eyes rolled back and forth in trepidation.

"What is it?" Banion asked urgently.

She shook her head, a look of terror sharpening her features. Looking at him with an ominous gaze, she whispered, "Vertigo. I can feel his presence. He's here, in this building, somewhere above us."

"Vertigo?" Jared said in alarm, his thoughts returning to that fateful night in the Rasheed palace where the tribal first encountered the lord of evil.

"Yes, I'm sure of it, he is here," Mineera responded.

As she spoke of Vertigo, an intense chill began to erupt from the totem around Jared's neck. Staring down at it, he knew that they needed to move. An intense evil was drawing near and the totem around his neck was vibrating violently.

"We need to move!" Jared spoke in a frantic tone. "Something wicked is drawing near."

When they looked up at the staircase, they found it bathed in an icy blackness. From time to time, a dingy bulb would flicker in the dark passage ahead of them. With their stomachs lurching in fear, they eyed the staircase with mounting dread. Each of them was anxious thinking of what lay beyond. In the end, they knew they would have to face Vertigo. It wasn't mere coincidence that the lord of the Reaper Kai was barring their passage; it was fate.

Shakily, Banion placed his boot on the first step. His footfall echoed in his mind with a thud. Taking a deep breath, he moved up the staircase and the rest of the team followed, ready for anything.

Destiny was calling. With labored steps, they hesitantly moved onto the second floor of the production facility. It was a time for courage; it was a time for strength; it was a time for heroes.

Chapter 33
A True Hero

"Get down!" Banion yelled.

A host of Biogtech soldiers, three squads at least, were advancing down the hallway. Jared and Tani hit the deck a split second before the automatic weapons fire roared to life. They ducked as the gunfire ripped through the walls and glass windows, blowing free fragments of glass and flecks of wood. The tribals were huddling behind a metal desk. As they watched in horror, several bullets tore clean through the desk, leaving jagged holes only a few inches from where they were concealed.

Nova 7 was pinned down in a series of offices and had been under fire for several minutes. Enemy reinforcements had been sent to their position and the situation was growing grimmer and more desperate by the minute.

"Return fire!" Banion yelled and stepped out into the hallway. Leveling his mighty assault rifle, he opened fire, spraying the advancing Biogtech assault team. His shots were well placed and he blasted two Biogtech soldiers. Staggering, they collapsed, but their mindless brethren continued to advance, cackling as their empty red eyes scanned for more targets.

Jared and Tani crouched and brought their own weapons to bear. Shooting out of the shattered windows, they sprayed the soldiers with a burst of gunfire. Jared eliminated two Biogtechs while Tani managed to kill one on his own. Though slow, the Biogtechs still had the advantage due to their sheer numbers.

The Biogtechs took aim once more and fired a hail of lead at Nova 7. Retreating further into the room, the tribals took up defensive positions and hit the deck as the submachine gun fire rattled through the office once more. Computer equipment was blasted to bits as sparks of electricity popped in the air. Wiring and fragments of electrical boards rained down, but the tribals were unharmed. As they squinted in the harsh gunfire, they caught sight of a flash of movement in the room. A blue flurry of cloth flew by as they saw Mineera charge past them with her hand thrown forward in front of her. A glowing barrier of white energy surrounded her as she charged.

Seeing her advance, the Biogtechs trained their weapons upon her form and fired full auto. Confident, she maintained her concentration. The bullets rammed into the barrier of psychic energy surrounding her, generating bright flashes, and were stopped completely. Ricocheting off the mystical barrier, the spent bullets rained down with a clatter onto the floor.

Without warning, Mineera threw her other hand forward. A searing beam of holy light, potent as the sun itself, roared forward from her outstretched fingertips. Like a superheated sword, the beam rammed into the Biogtech war party and cut it to pieces. Having mastered her psychic abilities, Mineera was able to maintain the shield around herself and attack the Biogtech war party simultaneously. Such power was unsettling to behold. The war party was completely outmatched.

Maintaining her supreme concentration, she swept the burning beam of holy fire back and forth, melting and incinerating the Biogtech soldiers. The attack was extreme enough to completely obliterate the Biogtechs. Within a few seconds, the entire Biogtech war party had been destroyed, utterly disintegrated by Mineera's fierce psychic attack.

The last of the foes had been laid to rest but it had come at an extreme cost. Mineera had expelled a substantial amount of spiritual energy. As she staggered down the hallway, bright blotches of light filled her vision. Her breathing heavy, she almost passed out from the ordeal.

Seeing her in distress, Banion ran to her side and steadied her. Smiling at him, she gripped him tightly and looked up into his eyes.

"Thanks." She spoke in a labored tone, still gasping for breath.

"Thank you," he rattled back at her. "Things were getting tough there for a second."

Their minor reprieve from combat was short lived. A door opened at the end of the hallway. Red-robed forms, four in total, emerged. For a brief moment, the cloaked figures simply held their ground, inspecting the remains of the dead Biogtechs. A split second later, they looked at Banion and Mineera in the hallway. As the four threw back their hoods, Banion and Mineera stared in horror. Sinister black fur was bristling as their beady, hate-filled eyes stared at them. Sniffing the air, their pink snouts sought out their scent. Bleating in anger, the Goat Minions drew weapons from their cloaks and charged.

"Najaszim!" Mineera gasped in terror, and for good reason. The Goat Minions of the Reaper Kai order were the most foul and loathsome creatures imaginable. "Run!" Mineera shouted to Banion, who was still steadying her.

Stumbling backwards, he pulled her still-weak body with him. They moved into the office where Jared and Tani were, and Banion slammed the feeble wooden door. Moving a desk in front of the door, he quickly sought to defend their position. A second later, the Goat Minions rammed into the door at full speed. The force was so severe, the desk moved back a few inches and the doorframe was broken. A black hairy hand emerged through the void, fumbling for anything it could grab. Banion kicked the wooden door shut and held his foot against it. Placing the barrel of his assault rifle against the door, he opened fire, spraying the Goat Minion behind the door at point blank range. He fired repeatedly and the sinister creature took a full seven rounds before it began to falter. A bloody spray erupted as the creature's body was torn to shreds.

As one of the Goat Minions died against the door, the other three were beginning to climb through the windows that had been shot out during the last exchange. Tani leapt to his feet immediately. Training his submachine gun, he fired on the nearest Goat Minion climbing through the window. He had solid aim, and pelted the agent of darkness repeatedly with gunfire. Even though he had struck it many times, it still continued to advance, bleating and gibbering in a demonic language. Wanting to kill the creature quickly, he moved over only a few feet from it and took aim at its head. Firing a burst, Tani shot the Goat Minion several times in the face. It died immediately, its body slumping over in the window sill.

By the time the first two Goat Minions expired, the other two had managed to breach the defenses of the office. Two sinister Najaszim eyed Jared with a look of hatred. As they rushed toward him, Jared had only a few seconds to react. Grasping his submachine gun in his left hand, he opened fire while his right hand closed around the hilt of the Scar Blade. Pelting the first Goat Minion with a few hasty shots was a miracle; it slowed the creature enough for him to draw his sword.

Screaming, the unwounded Goat Minion swung a hatchet right at Jared's neck. The deft and agile tribal rolled onto a desk to avoid being decapitated. On his back, Jared dropped the gun and plunged the blue-tinted Scar Blade into the stomach of the creature. It roared in pain but continued to attack. Reeling back, it swung the hatchet at Jared's face, bringing the weapon down with great force. Letting go of his sword, he flung both of his hands forward and caught the arm of the savage Goat Minion swinging at him. The attack was so strong, Jared could not stop it outright, only deflect it. The blade of the hatchet rammed into the desk only a few inches away from his ear. Wrenching his head to the right to avoid the blow, he was momentarily stunned, and that was all the Goat Minion needed to place him in mortal peril. The furry hands of the Goat Minion closed around Jared's neck.

Gasping, he tried to fight off the creature throttling him to death. Fumbling in his belt, Jared's hand closed around Banion's silver revolver. He pulled it free, jammed the weapon into the ribcage of the Goat Minion and pulled the trigger as fast as he could. The high caliper weapon discharged several times and the bullets shredded the Goat Minion's internal organs. It took three bullets from the mighty revolver to finally drive the creature back. Crumpling to the ground, it died instantly.

Still gasping for breath, Jared never imagined that the last of the four Goat Minions, the same one that he had already shot several times with his submachine gun, was almost upon him.

Still on his back, he heard the scream of the final Goat Minion a split second before he was attacked. Rolling off the desk, he hit the floor and rolled several feet to avoid the impending attack. The move could not have come at a better time. The final Goat Minion slammed and slashed a long knife at Jared several times as he rolled. Each attack barely missed the tribal.

A flash of white light lit the room. Mineera blasted the Goat Minion in the face with a searing blast of holy flame. The attack blinded the creature long enough for Tani and Banion to respond. Closing in on the creature, they took aim and both fired on it. Rocked with gunfire, it staggered back and forth as multiple bullets tore its flesh. Finally, it collapsed to the ground and died.

Rushing to Jared, the rest of Nova 7 helped him to his feet. Jared rushed to recover the gore-stained Scar Blade, holding the blood-soaked weapon in the air with a hazy look in his eye. As Mineera looked at him, a strange feeling coursed through her. Looking at her surroundings, she was having a premonition; a vision from her dreams was coming to life. A scream rose in her heart. She had seen this vision before.

"We need to get out of here now!" she yelled.

The rest of the team was shocked by her frantic tone, and panic set in. They all knew Mineera would never act this way unless she was immensely troubled. Charging over to the door, they quickly moved the desk and charged into the hallway beyond. Moving past the dead Biogtechs, they came to a metal door, the same door from which the Goat Minions had emerged.

"This is it," Banion said intently. "This doorway leads to the top level of this building and the Splicer relay."

The door was sealed electronically with a keypad. Banion slammed his fist into it, but it would not budge; an electronic lock secured it firmly. "Damn it, bookworm, get this door open quick or we're all dead."

Frantic, Tani ran to the door and looked at the keypad. "I can do this. I just need some time."

"We don't have any time," Banion yelled. "Get that door open now! More reinforcements are probably on the way!"

Fumbling, Tani's stumpy hands unscrewed the face plate on the keypad. As he did, a cackle erupted from the far end of the hall. Another squad of Biogtech soldiers had entered the hallway.

"Jared!" Banion shouted.

The tribal spun around and dropped to one knee. Taking aim, he opened fire a second after Banion. Their bullets raced down the hallway and slammed into the first Biogtechs breaching the hallway. Collapsing, they fell in the doorway, hydraulic fluid draining from their bodies.

"Mineera, I need your help," Tani said urgently.

Coming to his side, she looked at him in confusion.

"I need you to hold these wires in place." Pointing, the tribal gave her two wires to press against electronic leads in the locking mechanism. Opening his laptop, he jammed the other end of the cables into the ports on his computer. He then initiated the hacking software in his computer. Engaging, the hacking software began to decode the lock. Both Mineera and Tani were now totally engrossed in getting the door open and were not paying any attention to the battle unfolding behind them.

"Loading!" Jared yelled as he fumbled with his gun. There was no more ammunition left in his weapon.

Banion tried to hold the door as best he could but there were just too many Biogtechs surging through the opening. Firing short bursts, he tried to keep the flood in check.

"Damn it!" Jared cussed as he dropped the fresh clip on the floor. Fumbling for it, he never saw the end of his life approaching. Three Biogtechs stumbled through the doorway. As they raised their weapons, Banion screamed. He took aim, his assault rifle quivering in his hand, but his gun jammed as he pulled the trigger. Staring at the three Biogtechs taking aim at Jared made Banion's heart run cold.

Blinking, he stared at Jared in horror. The Biogtechs were only a second away from killing him. In that moment, everything inside of Banion screamed. He loved Jared as a son. A frantic pulse of anger rolled through him. A flash of his mother, his uncle Frank, and his beloved life Lily rushed through his mind. He could still see their forms torn and killed by reckless hate. Outrage filled him; there was no way in hell that he would lose Jared like he'd lost all the others in his life. His mind screamed as he shook his head in determination. "Not again!" he yelled and hurtled towards Jared. As he did, the Biogtechs opened fire.

Time stood still. Rushing toward him, Banion moved in front of Jared, shielding him with his own body. The bullets tore forward. Shoving Jared backwards, Banion saved him from certain death. A split second later, he felt several stings of pain strike his body.

Lurching forward, the bullets tore Banion's body. Blood erupted with a spray as he collapsed onto the cold steel floor. Despite having been shot several times, Banion tried to recover and slumped up against the wall. Fumbling with his assault rifle, he managed to unjam the wedged shell casing. His torn body was bleeding profusely but it didn't matter, it simply didn't matter to him. The only thing Banion cared about was saving his companions.

Firing back, he killed two of the Biogtechs. The final Biogtech returned fire and struck Banion twice more, the bullets ramming into his chest.

"No!" Jared screamed. Finally, his weapon was reloaded. Returning fire, he managed to kill the final Biogtech.

Just then, Tani, who had not witnessed the horrendous events unfolding behind Mineera and himself, yelled out in excitement. The electronic door opened, allowing them to pass inside.

Falling onto his back, Banion could feel the warmth go out of his body. Warm blood was seeping from multiple wounds on his chest and legs. His vision began to grow dim. In the haze, he had a vague impression of his companions crouched over him, their hands fumbling around on his chest.

His head rolled to the right and he stared down the hallway. In the distance he saw a woman garbed in white. As he blinked, the woman grew closer and closer every second. Finally she was standing only a few feet away from him. Her back was turned to him but she was very familiar.

"Lily?" Banion gasped, staring at his wife. "Lily, is that you?" he mumbled as his companions desperately tried to save his life.

She would not turn to look at him; instead, she remained with her back to him.

Sadness overtook his senses as his body bled to death. His vision was growing ever more blurry and he could no longer hear his companions speaking to him. Staring at her, tears filled his eyes. "I'm so sorry," he whispered. "I'm so sorry for what I've done. I'm so ashamed of what I've done."

As he spoke, the vision of his wife trembled. She turned to face him, tears streaming down her face. "I'm not ashamed of you," Lily whispered to him. "I could never be ashamed of you. I love you so much."

"Why wouldn't you look at me before?" he whispered at her ghost. "Why wouldn't you look at me any of those other times I saw you?"

"It wasn't time for us to be together again." She smiled at him. "Banion, come home to me," she whispered.

"Lily!" he whispered.

Pushing the tribals' hands away from his chest, Banion's bloody hand reached into his duster. Fumbling for a second, his fingers closed around a cold metal object in his pocket. As he pulled it free, his companions could see his gold wedding band.

Gathering what was left of his strength, Banion looked at the ghost of his beloved Lily beside him. She crouched before him with a smile, stretching out her hand toward him. With a gasp, Banion placed his wedding band on his finger. As he did, Lily whispered once more to him, "Come home to me." She reached out and touched him, grasping his hand.

Smiling up at her, Banion let out one final gasp. His body grew limp and the fire went out of his eyes. Passing into death, Banion finally made his way home, back to a home of happiness, back home to a place beyond death and suffering. In the end, his soul had made it back to the loving arms of his wife.

His companions were in shock. The courageous Banion O'Neil was gone, having sacrificed his own life to save Jared. The disbelief was shattered by the sound of more Biogtech soldiers. Dragging Banion's body beyond the doorway, Tani closed the electronic bulkhead a few seconds before another host of Biogtech soldiers arrived.

In the stunned silence of the dark room, Jared, Tani and Mineera crouched before his body, each of them placing a hand upon him. In their hearts they could not comprehend that Banion O'Neil was dead.

Chapter 34
Birth of a Hero

Gasping in fear, Mineera stepped back from the horrid scene. Her mind could not comprehend the grisly image before her. Shaking her head back and forth, the psychic maiden fought to control herself. Grief and frustration coursed through her, mingling together. A rage, a hate-filled pressure, was building up inside of her.

Jared, his sword stained in blood, turned around. At his feet were the remains of Banion. His eyes were filled with hate and he gazed at Mineera in disgust. The strange totem around his neck was glowing intensely, its red eyes hungering for more blood, more suffering.

When Mineera tried to run, her legs would not move. The tribal youth moved toward her, hate burning in his eyes. When she tried to yell, her voice would not sound. The youth moved ever closer, gore-stained blade in hand.

"Damn it, Mineera!" Jared screamed, his cheeks flushed red. There was a crazed look in his eyes.

Mineera stared at Jared dreamily. Her subconscious was screaming that something was wrong. "Jared?" she asked in a confused tone. The hotheaded youth had Banion's revolver in one hand and the mighty Scar Blade in the other.

"Wake up!" Jared shouted angrily. "Snap out of it. We have a job to do."

Mineera looked around and found her surroundings unusual. Old, corroded metal walls and steel girders rose around them. She spun around and caught sight of Tani sitting on the floor, leaning against the wall, a look of shock on his face.

"He's gone!" Jared said in a matter-of-fact tone. "There isn't a damn thing we can do about it now. We need to get moving."

"This isn't real!" Mineera said in a triumphant tone. "This is a dream, I've seen this all before! This is a dream!"

"It's not a damn dream!" Jared shouted, grabbing her shoulders and shaking her fiercely. She remained in a daze, her mind feverishly trying to comprehend what was happening.

"This is not real!" Mineera wailed, grabbing her face in her hands. "Banion cannot die! The spirit told me that I needed to protect Banion so that he could fulfill his destiny and bring the world from darkness. This can't be real!"

"We need to get the hell out of here." Tani spoke in a daze, gripping his hands tightly, staring at Banion's lifeless body. "He was our strongest. If Banion is dead, we have no hope, no chance of completing this mission. It's over."

Jared stood beside Banion. Looking down, he couldn't believe that their leader was really gone. Kneeling before him, Jared grabbed Banion's shoulder and jostled him, hoping desperately that he would respond to his touch. But to no avail; Banion did not stir. Shaking uncontrollably, Jared felt a spike of anger rock his being. An image of Banion's face filled his mind. He could hear Banion's stern words flood through his being. *"A hero is someone who has lost so much that nothing else matters but vengeance and hate. In order to be a hero, you must experience loss, true loss, somebody you love so much that you cannot live without. Once that happens to you, it changes you, warps you. Something inside of you snaps when someone that you love is taken from you. The rage builds like a thunderstorm in your heart. I fight with rage, not passion. I fight because I hate and want to destroy and punish. I don't ever want you to experience that fate, Jared. I don't want you to be like me."*

Seeing Banion's face in his mind and hearing his voice made Jared's skin prickle. His blood was pumping as he stared at Banion's body. Rage, a simmering hatred, began to form in his soul. Bitterness flooded Jared as he stared at Banion. Frustration took over. Dropping his weapons, he clutched Banion's lifeless hand in his own.

Jared would never hear Banion's voice or know his wisdom ever again. He had been taken from him. Flashes of memory filled him and with each passing second, the anger in his heart grew stronger. The totem around his neck flashed violently as the rage overwhelmed his senses. Forming a fist, Jared pounded the cold steel floor, thumping it with his knuckles until blood erupted from the shredded skin.

As his body shook, the sadness in his heart turned to cold fury. Hope was lost. The world was only filled with death. Rage exploded through Jared. Anger took him. He began to rise from beside Banion's body, darkness racing through his soul. When he rose to his feet, Jared was no longer the man he was; he was a specter of death, a man lost to the shadow, a man destined for vengeance.

"Stop your whining!" Jared shouted at Tani, who was whimpering on the floor. "Shut your damn mouth and get to your feet. We have a job to do!"

Tani blinked through the haze of his own misery and stared at Jared uneasily. His friend was shaking in rage, holding his blood-soaked blade and, in his violent trembling, flinging drops of blood from its tip. With sick fascination, Tani simply stared at Jared, paralyzed by shattered hope.

"It's over, Jared. We can't hope to win without Banion."

When Jared rushed forward, Tani cowered back, feeling as if he was about to be struck. Seeing Jared's charge, Mineera intercepted him and held him back. "Just stop it!" she yelled at him.

"Get on your feet!" Jared screamed in rage at Tani. "Don't you dare quit on me now! We have a job to do! I want satisfaction!"

"Satisfaction?" Mineera looked into his eyes. "What you want is death!"

"I want death!" Jared confirmed. "And nothing is going to stop me! Banion was taken from us and his death needs to be avenged."

"It's over." Tani spoke in a calm tone. "Let's get out of here."

"So this is it? This is how we honor his memory? We honor Banion's death by failing? I will not fail him!" Jared shouted.

"What do you propose?" Mineera was angry. "What are we going to do? Father Vertigo is very near. What are we supposed to do? Fight him without Banion?"

"We'll do whatever it takes to honor Banion, Mineera. If it means our very lives, we will honor him. Stand with me, right now, right here. The enemy has taken much and I won't budge another inch. Stand with me, right here, right now!"

Mineera simply looked at him in disbelief. She felt for a brief moment as if she were looking into Banion's harsh, hate-filled eyes. In reality, Jared had become Banion, reduced to a shattered soul by the loss of Banion. In a strange sense, his mentor's death had polarized the youth into something completely frightening, a strong warrior with the skills and now the rage to take the mission to the bitter end.

Mineera looked over at Tani, who was still in shock, mumbling to himself and rubbing his hands tightly. Seeing his duress, she moved over to Tani. As she drew near, he looked up at her through his wire-rim spectacles. She crouched and looked into his eyes, forming a spiritual connection with him.

"I'm so scared, Mineera. I'm so damned scared," Tani whispered to her.

"Jared is right. We need to keep going," she coaxed him.

"I know." Tani shook his head in despair. "I know we need to finish this."

Standing up from the floor, Tani wiped his nose and cleared the tears from his eyes. Nodding at Jared, he came forward. The trio stood and gained strength from one another.

"The time to mourn Banion is not now. We need to focus on our duty and our mission or else a lot of people are going to die. If we don't finish this mission, the entire Darken Realm will be overrun. Stay focused and push onward. If we face Vertigo, I'll deal with him." Jared's tone was dangerous.

Looking at him in doubt, Mineera tried to speak but Jared cut her off.

"I'll deal with him!" he confirmed again with a flash of darkness in his eyes.

Nodding back, Mineera shot Tani a look of concern that was instantly mirrored back by the tribal scholar.

A tense moment of silence ensued. Each of them turned to view Banion's lifeless body. As they did, each of them fought back tears. Paying him one final moment of respect, Mineera whispered to him, "I will be back, I promise you, Banion. I'll come back for you."

Taking one final look at their valiant leader, they forced the sadness from their souls and sought to endure. The passage ahead of them ended in a metal staircase that ascended upward into the darkness. Taking a confident step forward, Jared let the rage in his heart guide his actions. With each step, he became more enraged, more filled with hate.

The tribal from the wastelands of the Darken Realm had made not only a physical journey but an emotional one. The timid boy from Scarskin had transformed into something sinister. This metamorphosis had been guided not by knowledge and understanding but rather by hate. Even though Banion had left the world of the living, part of his soul remained and it had been infused into Jared. The sheer anger and bloodlust Banion experienced for the Reaper Kai had now been transferred into Jared.

A hero is someone who fights with true passion due to the inescapable feeling of loss. A hero fights to prevent atrocity and to quench a lust for vengeance. Banion died that day, but something else was born from his sacrifice. Jared had become Banion, a reckless hero who would charge ahead no matter the cost to himself.

Chapter 35
The Hero Navezgane

Charging up the metal staircase, the tribal warrior was oddly silent, his movements both aggressive and cat-like. In one hand he held the gore-stained Scar Blade and in the other, Banion's long-barreled silver revolver. A look of pure hate was on his face and his muscles were tense, full of anger, waiting to unleash brutal attacks on anything that got in his way.

He was too quick for Tani and Mineera to follow properly. With rage guiding him, Jared charged headlong into the fray and before his companions even knew what was happening, violent slaughter was unleashed.

Clearing the staircase, Jared saw four Reaper Kai priests. They were stunned to see the tribal warrior and hesitated a brief moment, half expecting Jared to do the same. Quite to the contrary, Jared never faltered. Rushing forward, he rested his sword on his shoulder, preparing for the kill.

Before the priests could react, Jared was upon them. Screaming a war cry, Jared launched into the air, propelling himself into their midst and swinging with all of his might. The Scar Blade swept around in a wide arc. As it smashed into the neck of one priest, a spray of blood erupted and followed the arc of the blade as it spun around him. A second priest was unlucky as well and the blade crashed into his chest. The priest crumpled backwards, and Jared leapt into the air once more. His left hand spun around and the barrel of Banion's revolver took hasty aim, sending a bullet into the second priest and shattering his skull.

Landing behind the stunned priests, Jared crouched and whirled around with his blade at leg level. With devastating precision, the Scar Blade struck the knee of the third priest. As it sheared completely through, the severed limb fell away while the Reaper Kai screamed in agony.

Finally able to concentrate, the remaining unwounded priest uttered a hasty dark prayer and began to focus his psychic powers on Jared. A bright flash of light erupted from the Reaper Kai's fingertips. A crackling sphere of superheated energy roared toward the tribal warrior. With a dry laugh, Jared simply smiled as a blast of chilled air rolled around him. The raven totem around his neck vibrated violently as the frigid air enveloped him in a rising vortex. The bright sphere of destructive energy that had been intended to kill Jared rammed into the rising cone of cold air erupting from the raven totem. The attack was stopped, utterly dissipated by the powerful relic.

Shocked by his dark spell's lack of effect, the Reaper Kai took a step backwards. With a look of darkness in his eyes, Jared ran forward and threw the gore-stained blade forward. Desperately, the Reaper Kai flung his hands in the air in a crude and feeble attempt to protect himself. However, the tribal's attack could not be turned away. The tip of the Scar Blade rammed deep between the bones in the Reaper Kai's ribcage, causing him to gasp in pain. The mighty sword had punctured his heart, mortally wounding him. Falling backwards, the Reaper Kai died instantly. Jared pulled the blade from his flesh as he watched the priest utter his last breath.

A flash of madness was on his face. He wanted more. Looking around, he saw the last of the Reaper Kai trying to crawl away from the scene, his leg sheared off at the knee. Staring at him, Jared let the rage flood his senses. Walking calmly up behind him, he rammed the tip of his sword into his back. Screaming, the priest slunk away from his blade. Not satisfied, Jared stabbed him again.

"Jared, stop!" Tani cried in alarm as he rushed forward, horrified by the scene unfolding before him.

Shaking his head, Jared wanted more suffering. He drew back his blade, about to stab the surviving priest once more. Preempting the insanity, Tani leveled his submachine gun on the wounded priest and fired at him several times, killing him instantly.

Robbed of his vengeance, Jared dropped his weapons and shoved Tani roughly, so hard that the tribal scholar stumbled and fell backwards. He landed hard, his wire-rim glasses falling off his face and dropping to the floor. A look of shock covered Tani's face and his eyes were glazed with tears. He was stunned and hurt by his friend's forceful reaction.

"Stop it now!" Mineera yelled and grabbed the tribal. Spinning around, Jared flung her away, propelling her backwards as well. Though he stood amidst the dead, it wasn't enough for him, not in the least. Grabbing his weapons, he charged off down the hallway, looking for more victims.

Staring at each other, Mineera and Tani were filled with fear. Banion was dead and Jared had completely lost his mind. The tribal had turned into a killing machine and nothing could satiate his hunger. Hastily rising to their feet, they charged on after him.

They lost sight of him for a few seconds. In the time it took for them to reach him, more screams of agony erupted. Rounding the corner, Tani and Mineera almost stumbled over the corpses of two more Reaper Kai, horribly mangled and dismembered by the wild fury of the tribal warrior.

It was a nightmare watching him kill without mercy. Both of them felt their skin crawl as he surged onward, constantly pushing forward and slaughtering anything in his path.

The hallway ended at an enormous set of steel doors. Intricate pictures were etched into the steel, depicting strange creatures and some sort of demonic ritual taking place. Stopping before the enormous doors, Jared paused his wild advance. He stood completely still as if trying to sense what lay beyond. As he stood there, transfixed, a brisk chill surrounded the youth. The raven totem around his neck burned brightly, its sinister red eyes hungering for the demonic energy that lay in wait beyond the door. Jared was hungry for death and craved more enemies. The totem around his neck craved dark power and was starved for demonic energy. The potent symbiosis between Jared and the totem was about to be realized. Both needed and fed off the other.

Placing his hand on the door, Jared closed his eyes and breathed in heavily. The raven totem around his neck hummed violently as a potent blast of frosty air surrounded him. He exhaled, his breath visible in the chill air. Whatever lay beyond the door was darkness itself, the most potent of evil.

"This is it." Jared spoke in a calm tone. "It all ends here."

Tani and Mineera simply stared at him in horror. Their beloved friend and companion was gone. What remained was a twisted semblance of a person, a tortured soul that had been utterly corrupted by rage. Looking at each of them, he said quietly, "Stay behind me. I will end this."

Pushing the door open, the trio moved into the throne room of Father Vertigo. They found Vertigo standing before his throne forged of human bone. A dispassionate look covered his face as the team moved into the room. His arms folded behind his back, it was very evident that the lord of darkness was not concerned with their arrival. As the team stood before the avatar of evil, all creatures loathsome and vile came to the aid of Vertigo.

Slinking from the darkness, a host of Goat Minions, savage beasts of hate, flanked the dark lord. Gibbering, the host of creatures bayed and bleated, taunting the trio with demonic fury.

"Hail all ye fools who simply come before me to die. What savage impertinence and reckless guile brings the ragtag Nova 7 into my clutches? Is it pride or stupidity that drives you? What makes you think a pitiful band of mercenaries can stand before the coming darkness?" Vertigo's frail form was filled with a haunting rage as he spoke.

"It's over," Jared declared, staring at Vertigo with unwavering hatred. "I am ending you this day."

"Indeed. You are that brat from the palace of Rasheed, aren't you? That fool who desecrated my presence? Your blade bit my flesh; I will not forget such sacrilege. You are correct, it's over. I will first crush your will and then wither your body. I will capture your friends and I will make you watch as I peel the flesh from their bones."

"Shut your mouth!" Jared yelled.

Chuckling, Vertigo taunted him further. "Such anger. Tell me, boy, where is your hero? Where is Banion? Did he perish? Did he finally get what he deserved in this life? A coward's death? A failed oath of vengeance? Tell me, boy, how does it feel to have your role model rotting in the building below us? After I am finished with you, I will take his body and cut it into pieces. I will send what remains to the farthest reaches of the Darken Realm. You, just like your precious Banion, have failed. Prepare to die here in this place, for you will have no salvation!" Vertigo stared at Jared, howling hate- filled words at the youth and further enraging him.

Beyond the entryway, a steel staircase ascended upwards into the darkness. A sign on the wall read "Communications Relay." Looking at the staircase, Jared knew what must be done. Motioning to his companions quickly, he spoke in a mere whisper.

"Get up there and destroy that relay. I'll hold them off," Jared ordered Tani and Mineera.

"What?" Tani screeched. "No way!"

"Go!" Jared shouted at them. There was a staunch confidence in his voice. "I can kill them all. Don't worry, I can do this."

Vertigo saw them conversing and knew what was happening. His pasty white finger emerged from his black robes to point in their direction. "Kill them!" he shouted.

As he looked at Jared, tears erupted in Tani's eyes. He felt that it would be the last time he would ever see him. Hesitating only momentarily, Jared shouted again at both of them. "Get up there and end this. Destroy that relay and end this war! I can do this!"

His confidence was unwavering. Frazzled and at the end of their ropes, Tani and Mineera were not in an emotional position to argue. Understanding their duty to the war effort, and not just to Jared, they looked at him one last time and charged up the staircase to destroy the Splicer relay.

As they rushed upwards, the sound of battle erupted in the throne room. Jared, completely alone, was facing an entire host of savage Goat Minions and Father Vertigo. It was a time for desperate deeds of daring, and the fate of the entire Darken Realm now hung in the balance. It was up to Mineera and Tani to finish the mission. Nova 7 was falling apart and the life of each of them was in grave danger. If Mineera and Tani could not knock out the Splicer relay, the war would be lost and the Reaper Kai would claim the entire continent, plunging the land into never-ending darkness.

Chapter 36
Battle of Betrayers

Rushing upwards into the darkness, Mineera and Tani were hurriedly pushing into the shadows of the upper floor of the building. As they passed beyond a narrow opening, the two companions found themselves on a narrow catwalk some two stories above the factory floor below. The machines whirred busily as the production facility continued to manufacture additional Biogtech soldiers.

As their attention turned from the factory floor to the catwalk, it was readily apparent that *something* lingered ahead of them, standing on the far end of the catwalk and protected by the shadows.

Tani and Mineera experienced a frantic fear building inside of them as the shadows at the far end of the catwalk began to shift. Small forms skittered along the catwalk and clung to the railings. At first they were unable to tell what the strange forms were, but eventually it became shockingly apparent that a host of spiders were making their way towards them.

Holding her hand forward, Mineera spoke a silent prayer and a shimmering sphere of light formed around her hand. When she flexed her fingers, the searing beam of radiant light shot forward, slamming into the horde of spiders, burning them to death. It took but a few moments for Mineera to dispatch them all.

A cruel, sadistic feminine laugh erupted from the far side of the catwalk. The shadows shifted once more. Stepping from the darkness was a woman clothed in blood- red robes. Her hood was covering her face but enough of it was revealed for Tani and Mineera to recognize her.

Marion Toil, the Great Betrayer, clapped her hands together and giggled once more. Halting their advance, Mineera pushed Tani behind her. Toil was a formidable psychic warrior and Mineera wanted to make sure that Tani was safe.

"So this is how my life will finally end!" Toil spoke in an excited tone. "Do you know how long I prayed for this day to come? Do you know how long I have suffered to reach this day?"

"Let us pass." Mineera's tone was dry.

"Let you pass?" Toil giggled. "Of course I will let you pass, but first you must pay a toll to reach your goal." Marion Toil advanced upon them without a hint of fear in her eyes. She smiled the entire time and held her hands out in an act of submission.

Her bold advance was disconcerting and Mineera and Tani both took a step back. Moving to the center of the catwalk, Toil knelt down before them and smiled in glee. She pulled away her robes so that her neck was completely exposed and tapped a pulsing vein in her neck, motioning to the companions. "I will let you pass, but first you must do me a favor!"

"What do you want, witch?" Mineera asked harshly.

"Witch?" Toil laughed dryly. "You dare call me a witch? Are we so different, you and I? Both of us have betrayed our empires to seek a higher power. You rose from the pits of hell to embrace the light and I shunned justice to favor darkness. We are both outcasts without home or country. We are both betrayers of our own kind. We are no different, you and I. Only the color of our cloth and shade of our souls set us apart."

"We are completely different. I did not have the luxury of a normal upbringing. I was raised in the Dark Order, told from day one that evil is the only option. I was tutored and twisted my entire life to do the will of evil. In the end, I shunned the Reaper Kai to find my true place," Mineera concluded, bold and confident.

"Your true place?" Toil giggled again. "You think that I had a normal upbringing? How dare you!" she shouted. "Do you know what it's like to grow up in a world in which you're number two? Always in the shadow of your father? I never had a luxurious childhood. I was always tempted and taunted by what I should be, by what I could be! The Queen of Rasheed! You were the blessed one, Mineera. You were brought up in an environment that teaches the true order of humanity."

"Reckless death and demonic pleasures are not the natural way of things."

"I understand that all too well now, here at the end of the road. I understand that what I did to my father, my people, was wrong. But I cannot change what I've done. That is why you will help me with my burden, my sickness."

"I don't understand." Mineera's eyes were haunted as she spoke.

Pulling back her robes again, Toil revealed her ghastly white neck. The blood was pumping and she tapped the vein on her neck again. As she did, a sick feeling filled Mineera. Shaking her head, Mineera acknowledged what Toil wanted, while refusing to take any part of it.

"Your toll for passing this bridge is to end my life! Kill me and end my suffering! I cannot live with the pain and guilt inside my heart," Toil pleaded with Mineera.

Shaking her head again, Mineera knew she could not murder Marion Toil. "I can't do it!"

"You must!" Marion screamed. "End my suffering!"

"I've changed, it isn't right!" Mineera pleaded with her.

"Do it!" Toil was in an enraged state.

"I can't do this!"

"You will do this or you will die!" Toil dropped her hands to her side, gathering her concentration and stretching outwards with her feelings. Drawing upon psychic energy, Toil began to pray to the demonic powers. She focused on Tani, forcing her thoughts into the tribal. Tani staggered backwards a step, feeling faint and dizzy.

"What are you doing?" Mineera shouted in alarm, seeing Tani grow paler by the second.

"Kill me or the tribal dies. I know why you're here. If the tribal dies, you won't be able to shut down the Splicer relay on your own. Make a choice, Mineera: end my life or the boy dies!"

"I can't do this!" Mineera countered.

Tani fell to his knees and began to gag. Holding his throat, he could barely breathe. After a few more seconds of gagging, he fell to the floor and began to convulse upon the catwalk.

Mineera's heart froze as she saw the tribal being tortured by Marion Toil's psychic powers. Feeling scared, Mineera knew that it was up to her. She pulled the knife from her belt and looked at its jagged blade, her hand trembling the entire time. As tears formed in her eyes, Mineera knew that she had to make a tough choice. Either Marion Toil would die or Tani would die. Edging forward, she shook the entire time, thinking of the horrible act she would have to perform in order to save her friend.

Seeing Mineera advance upon her filled Toil with great joy. Smiling, she flexed her fingers again and again. Each time she flexed her fingers, Tani was rocked with another set of tremors as he seized uncontrollably.

Standing before the hated betrayer of Rasheed, Mineera quivered and stared at the knife in her hand. A gagging sound rose from behind her. Tani was being killed by Marion. As she observed the situation unfold, a strange thought entered her mind; maybe, just maybe, there was another way.

Seeing the change in Mineera's demeanor put Toil on edge. Blinking several times, she was ill prepared for what was about to happen. Instead of ending her life, Mineera reared back and swung her right leg with all the strength she could muster. The tip of her boot came forward with tremendous force and slammed into Toil's jaw. Snapping backwards, Toil's head took the brunt of the impact. She crashed to the catwalk floor and was knocked senseless. As Marion fell unconscious, the psychic control she had over Tani dissipated immediately and he stopped convulsing.

Rushing to his side, Mineera crouched before him and clutched his sweaty hand. Shaky and gasping for breath, Tani rose to his feet with Mineera's help. With labored steps, they both moved across the catwalk. Slowly they made their way ever closer to their goal of knocking out the Splicer relay.

As they neared the fallen Toil, she began to stir. Quickly she sat up and stared in hatred at Mineera. Wiping the blood from her chin where Mineera had kicked her, Toil was furious. "You shouldn't have done that! I would have let you pass if only you would have ended my suffering! Now I'm going to kill you both!"

As she flexed her hand forward in their direction, a shockwave of psychic energy roared forth. Mineera, being a psychic herself, was immune, but Tani was flung into the air and hurled against the back wall of the room. As his body slammed into the steel wall, he crumpled downwards and landed on the catwalk. He did not stir.

Mineera drew her knife, for her powers would not help her in this struggle. Psychics could not use their powers against one another due to the substantial mental endurance housed within them. Leaping off the floor of the catwalk, Toil took to her feet and pulled her robes aside, revealing a steel club. She tugged the weapon free, her eyes burning with hatred as she smiled and taunted Mineera. "I'm going to kill you and after I do, I'm going to bash the tribal's skull to pieces!"

Staying calm, Mineera prepared to fight Toil in close combat. With a roar, Toil screamed and rushed forward. She was on the attack and swung at Mineera's head. Mineera took a step backwards to avoid being killed by the vicious assault. Lost in rage, Toil screamed again, swinging downward in an arc towards Mineera. This time, Mineera was unable to escape the attack as the steel club smashed into her leg at the knee. Gasping in pain, she fell forward, still managing to swing her blade forward and clip Toil's arm, tearing a gash in it.

"You shouldn't have done that, either!"

Retreating, Toil wiped the blood from her arm and shot Mineera a hate-filled look. Mineera was still down, her leg left horribly wounded by the attack. The situation was dire. Tani was still unconscious and Mineera was barely able to fight. With malice burning in her eyes, Marion Toil, the Great Betrayer, set her sights on killing Mineera. Letting out a scream of rage, the sinister Reaper Kai priestess charged, her steel club raised above her head.

Mineera saw Toil charge her and felt hope begin to fade within her. Saying a silent prayer, Mineera prepared to meet her maker.

Chapter 37
Destiny

A vision of Banion crashing to the floor, bleeding, flashed in Jared's mind. Jared flexed his hand and gripped the Scar Blade tightly. A spike of anger rocked him. Another flash of memory lit his mind. He could see the peaceful Banion laughing with his hat tipped downward, grasping a silver flask filled with whiskey. As the memories erupted in his mind, Jared was suddenly aware that he was not alone.

Looking down, he could see the throat of a creature grasped in his left hand. The Goat Minion was struggling under his strength, gagging and coughing as its eyes bulged out of its head. As he choked the creature to death, Jared had a dispassionate look on his face. He viewed the killing as a necessary evil, something that was normal and to which he was fully accustomed.

Though the creature clawed at him, Jared failed to feel any pain. He squeezed his left hand tighter, causing the Goat Minion to begin gurgling and emitting a horrid cry of anguish. A snap of anger coursed through Jared as an image of Banion's lifeless body flooded his mind. Looking down at the creature, Jared raised the Scar Blade, resting it on his right shoulder and clutching the filthy, gore-stained blade with his right hand. With a quick motion, he stood up and simultaneously grasped the sword with both hands. He brought the weapon down, impaling the bloody blade into the prone Goat Minion, still gasping for breath. The ancient sword split the monster in two, killing it instantly.

Resting his foot against the dead creature, Jared pulled while using his leg to push at the corpse. The Scar Blade slid free and Jared stood in the middle of the room triumphant. All around the tribal warrior was a horrid scene. The floor and walls were spattered in blood. Severed limbs and lifeless bodies surrounded the youth. Eight savage Goat Minions had been slaughtered and utterly mangled by Jared's fierce combat prowess. Standing amidst the dead, the youth had a deranged look upon his face. His forearms were smeared with blood, his posture tense. The hungry raven totem hanging around his neck emitted a swirling flow of cold air around him. Staring at the lifeless bodies surrounding him, Jared craved more violence.

Scanning the room, the tribal's gaze finally fell upon the lord of evil, Father Vertigo. In that moment, their eyes locked. The tribal's harsh stare met the rotten black globes of the dark priest. For a brief moment they pondered one another, searching for weakness. The exercise was utterly futile. Both of the combatants in the staring contest were utterly devoid of fear. Instead, an intense malice for the other simmered in their eyes. A loathing hatred for one another burned in their hearts.

"They're all gone," Jared taunted the aged priest. "All of your minions have been put to death and we are at last alone together."

"Foolish boy!" roared Vertigo. "Do you actually believe a brat from the wastelands, mere tribal trash, can withstand my might? I have lived for centuries, communing with demons, harvesting their infernal power. You are nothing to me, nothing more than a stain upon the floor beneath my boot. You will need more than luck to survive my wrath."

"If you surrender, I promise to end your life… somewhat quickly." Jared leered at Vertigo, utterly arrogant and headstrong.

"You worthless little wretch! You dare threaten me?" Vertigo hissed. He stared at the youth with rage building inside his husk of a body. A scream of anger erupted from him as his frail body coursed with raw energy. As he yelled, the totem around Jared's neck burned brightly, the red eyes of the raven lighting the room. "I shall enjoy killing you."

A calm came over the dark priest. Focusing his immense powers, he began to channel demonic energy through his frail frame.

A swirling maelstrom of blue light erupted from his sinister form. The burst of energy was so intense that Vertigo rose from the floor, his frail body taken into the air by the demonic magic. Levitating above the ground, he stared with pure hatred at the simple boy from the wastelands. Whispers filled the room and the very light was pushed aside, utterly consumed by the darkness of Father Vertigo. As he held his arms above his head, a sphere of crackling black energy emerged between his hands. The sphere grew in size quickly, seeming to suck all light in the room into its form. With a quick move, Vertigo released the swirling sphere of dark energy, hurling it at Jared.

Seeing the sphere rush towards him, Jared held his ground. He exhaled, releasing a visible trail of ice as his breath froze in the air, the totem around his neck already responding to the wicked attack. As the sphere raced forward, there was no fear in the tribal. Bracing himself, he stood stalwart against the psychic attack. The burning black sphere struck the tribal in the chest. As it did, the raven totem erupted in its own brand of dark magic. A cyclone of piercing chill swirled out, absorbing the demonic attack. The vortex of chilled air pulled at the sphere, luring it into the burning red eyes of the totem. A mere second passed, and the normally devastating psychic attack was absorbed by the totem, leaving Jared unharmed.

Stepping forward, he brushed a layer of ice off his right forearm. The tiny crystals rained down on the floor with a frozen clatter. Completely unscathed by the attack, Jared felt even more powerful. He stood before the dark lord exhibiting no fear whatsoever.

Stunned by the lack of effect his powerful attack had achieved, Vertigo eyed the youth with suspicion. A strange feeling formed in his stomach, a feeling that the dark father had never felt. For the first time in his life, there was doubt. Staring in disbelief, Vertigo pondered the strange impotence of his sinister assault. As the doubt built, it gave birth to hesitation. The hesitation turned into something to which Vertigo was not accustomed. In that very moment, a shiver ran down his spine. For the first time in his life, the dark priest felt fear.

"What is it that you crave, boy?" Vertigo hissed at him. "What is it that drives you?"

Blinking, Jared was caught off guard. Instead of further violence, Vertigo chose to speak to him. Hesitating, his mind shifted, and that was all Vertigo needed. Even though the raven totem housed considerable power, it could not push away Vertigo's invasive thoughts and prying soul. Sensing weakness in the youth, he sought to exploit it.

Vertigo picked up a sense of inadequacy as he focused on the boy. There was weakness beneath all of the arrogance. There was a feeling of doubt, the same feeling that was filling his own thoughts. Prying further, he knew that the boy craved combat, the thrill of battle and the taste for the kill. Now understanding his hidden desires, he sought to corrupt and coerce Jared.

"I can give you what you want, Jared," he coaxed him. "I know what drives you. Is it so bad to crave what you do?"

Jared felt something strange at the edge of his senses, a perverted presence clawing at the doors to his mind. The raven totem around his neck vibrated violently but a haze seemed to be taking him to a dark place. Listening to the soothing words of Vertigo, Jared felt at peace and wanted to hear more. "What do I crave?" he asked in a drowsy tone.

"I can see your secret desire. I know that you hunger for battle. I can see that every chance you have to fight, you do so willingly and enjoy it."

"I do enjoy it," Jared said in a dull tone, lowering the Scar Blade as he did. "But…"

Sensing his thoughts, Vertigo smiled and knew his soul and dark desires. "But… but you feel hollow inside, as if you need something more when all of your enemies are slain?"

"Yes…" Jared confirmed. The tip of the Scar Blade was now resting on the floor and the boy's tense, aggressive stance had been replaced by a lax, almost drowsy demeanor.

"I know what you really want, boy: death without end, enemies without end. Battles to last forever, new challenges and new enemies to slaughter. Is that what you really want, boy?" Vertigo smiled and took a step forward, submerging his hand into his robe. He pulled a dagger free, its blade coated with a sticky black liquid, deadly poisonous.

Unable to answer, Jared's mind was screaming. He could see the dark lord advancing upon him. A drop of the black poison streamed off the tip of the dagger, slowly turning into a strand, which fell like molasses from the weapon. He wanted to act but he could not. The voice in his mind was so strong and so soothing, he could not react.

"I can give you what you really want. I can give you endless enemies and glorious battles. The Reaper Kai still have many enemies; much of this world still needs cleansing. You could cleanse the weak for me…" Vertigo smiled. Stepping forward again, the aged priest looked like a cat stalking its prey, slowly inching forward so the mouse would not run outright, beguiling its victim with its penetrating stare.

Shaking, Jared's right hand tried to react. His body could not move; he could only stare in terror as the dark priest advanced upon him. Vertigo was coming nearer and nearer, drawing terribly close. Not knowing what to do, Jared's mind began to spin. Was this it? Was this the end? Killed by the lord of the Reaper Kai?

As his mind began to wander, Vertigo's control waned a bit, and Jared had a split second to react. His left hand closed around the raven totem hanging from his neck, which instantly emitted a harsh blast of cold air. As it touched his flesh, the artifact was able to cleanse his spirit of the dark tendril of energy driven into his mind by Vertigo. The chill wind was strong enough to repel Vertigo's invasive thoughts. His control over the youth began to crumble swiftly and he fought desperately to maintain his hold.

His efforts were to no avail; Jared had regained his composure. Standing only a few feet away from the boy, Vertigo knew that he had to act quickly. Rushing forward, he tried to impale the tribal with the poison-coated dagger. However, the sluggish malaise that had gripped Jared was now gone. Seeing the blade rush toward his chest, the tribal spun to the side, avoiding the attack. As he did, Jared swung and exhaled, throwing his weight into a counterattack. The blood-smeared Scar Blade spun and struck bone, cleaving through Vertigo's arm. The dagger and arm crashed to the floor, failing to harm him.

Unable to stop the assault, he knew that this might be his only chance to slay the wicked priest. Hacking away feverously, Jared slashed multiple times, wounding his opponent severely. Black sprays of blood erupted from the wounds. Crashing down,

Vertigo gasped and his black, rotten eyes rolled back and forth. Pain filled him as he stared in disbelief.

"You really are a fool. You can never defeat what is immortal. Kill me now and I will be remade. My servants will repair this battered body. You can never win. I will outlast you and outlive you. I am eternal!" he shouted in defiance as trickles of black ooze rolled down his chin.

Jared took a step forward, causing the raven totem around his neck to gyrate uncontrollably. Stopping, the tribal looked at the relic. As he took another step forward, the totem grew more aggressive, and a hum began to pierce the air. The gleaming red eyes were like searchlights, their beams focusing on Vertigo as he lay prone on the floor.

Jared understood his destiny all too well. An image of the village of Song River filled his mind. In that church atop the mesa, crude pictures were scrawled on the wall, many of them depicting Jared and many others depicting Father Vertigo. Suddenly, it all made sense. Closing his eyes, he could hear the inhabitants of the village chanting over and over again: "Navezgane... Navezgane... Navezgane."

"Do you hear me, boy? You cannot prevail against what is eternal!"

"I hear you. But I want you to know that it's all over."

"Fool!" Vertigo began to curse at Jared.

Jared took another step forward. The raven totem was now hovering in the air around his neck, craving more evil energy to satiate its hunger. In that moment, Vertigo looked up and his eyes locked with that of the strange relic. As he stared into the fierce red eyes of the wooden idol, a deep terror washed over Vertigo. It made sense. The relic craved and fed on evil energy. It could absorb all things evil. Blinking in fright, Vertigo began to tremble. Jared moved forward another step, and a frosty vortex of air circulated around the totem. Like icy fingers, wisps of frost began to migrate toward the dark priest. Feeling the cold bite his body, a wail of anger rose from him. Several of the demons in his body were screaming out in terror, feeling the strange pull and hunger of the idol.

"Please don't!" Vertigo pleaded.

His cry for mercy was in vain. Thinking back to Banion, the tribal smiled and drew the Scar Blade over his head, preparing for the killing blow. He could see Banion's eyes in his mind, hear his voice, and knew his spirit. Looking down at Vertigo before him, Jared knew what must be done.

"For Banion," Jared declared, holding the weapon above his head. He hesitated a brief moment, the blade tensely shaking in his nervous hands. Then, with a strong, unwavering strike, Jared brought the weapon downward, aiming for the dark priest's neck. His blade was true and the Scar Blade sheared off the head of Father Vertigo, decapitating him.

The lifeless body of Father Vertigo crashed to the floor. As it did, the host of demons housed inside his body began to flee. The room was filled with haunting wails as dozens of evil spirits erupted from the corpse. Jared had seen this sight before, during the fall of Rasheed, when Vertigo had been slain in battle. However, this time, the blue demons that erupted from Vertigo's body were not allowed to leave. As they tried to escape Vertigo's dead body, the raven totem fought back, hungry and needing to feed on evil energy. The icy wisps of frost shot outward quickly, wrapping around the eerie blue ghosts. Many tendrils of frost shot forth from the raven totem, which was vibrating so violently that it caused a piercing noise to rip through the air.

The twine that secured the raven totem to Jared's neck disintegrated. As he stepped back, the raven totem was hovering in the air above Vertigo's body. The icy tendrils grappling with the evil spirits were growing stronger, engulfing the demonic entities with potent ancient magic. One by one, the blue ghosts were sucked out of the corpse and pulled into the totem. Each spirit that was consumed made the totem hunger for even more demonic power. The icy tendrils began to glow with radiant light, consuming the evil spirits with rabid intensity. The burning light was so powerful that Jared had to shield his eyes.

The raven totem's feeding frenzy reached a deafening pinnacle as a small explosion erupted. Thrown backwards, Jared hit the floor hard and was dazed for a few seconds. When he recovered, he sat up just in time to see the raven totem floating above a pile of smoldering ash. The last of the demons housed inside Father

Vertigo disappeared into the ancient relic, all of the evil now fully consumed.

With a final bright flash, the totem fell to the ground, landing in what remained of Father Vertigo.

Momentarily stunned by the latest events, Jared recovered and rushed to the scene. A smoking pile of ashes lay in the center of the room. In the middle of the smoldering ash was a familiar form. The raven totem, an icon of ancient power, was half buried in the pile of ash. Its worn wooden form was utterly silent.

Looking down at the relic, Jared crouched and recovered it. It felt cold as ice when he picked it up. As he gazed around the room, an eerie sight filled the tribal's vision.

On the floor, only a few inches away from him, was Vertigo's head, still intact after the totem's feeding frenzy. The black rotten globes that were the dark priest's eyes were staring directly at Jared. As he looked back, an eerie feeling came over the youth. Retreating from the lifeless head, Jared knew that it was finally over. Father Vertigo had been killed and would not be returning. The demonic entities that had fueled his body had been consumed by the raven totem and would never return to the smoldering ash that was once Vertigo's body.

The immortal lord Vertigo was gone, slain by Jared of Scarskin. As Jared pondered the battle with strained disbelief, urgency began to tug at his senses. Although the lord of the Reaper Kai had been slain, the war was still raging and the mission's objective had yet to be completed. Looking at the staircase leading upward, Jared rushed to help his companions knock out the Splicer relay and put an end to the war once and for all.

Chapter 38
Full Circle

Marion Toil charged the downed Mineera, as Mineera tried desperately to avoid the attack, slinking backwards on her injured leg. Her situation was grim. Screaming in rage, Toil brought the steel club down on Mineera. Mineera defended herself, flinging her arms upwards to block the attack. The club rammed into her forearm forcefully, thudding as it hit her bones.

Wincing in pain, Mineera tried to rise to her feet. Her knee had been brutally bashed and it was a tough struggle against the witch. Shaking, still reeling in pain, Mineera grabbed the steel club in Toil's hand. Wrestling over the weapon, the two combatants eyed each other with disdain.

"So this is how it's finally going to end for you. Where is your God now? Tell me, fool, where is your God now?" Toil sneered at Mineera, still struggling.

"I cannot believe that after everything we've been through, this is how it's going to end. I still have faith," Mineera replied in a dignified tone, still wincing in pain but far from giving up.

"Faith? Where did your faith get you? Your beloved Banion is dead and soon you shall be as well. Your faith is pointless. The only true power is aggression."

"Then why did you repent? Why did you find horror in what you have done if faith is pointless? You regret what you did to your father and the kingdom of Rasheed. Stop this pointless violence. We both know that you regret your actions. Stop this insanity!" Mineera pleaded with her.

"Shut your mouth!" Toil screamed in rage. With a forceful kick, she brought her knee upwards, striking Mineera in the stomach. Shrinking backwards, weak from the fight and unable to breathe, Mineera collapsed. Toil was on her immediately. She struck Mineera again, the club battering her exposed back and hurting her ribs.

Swinging around, Mineera grabbed Toil's leg and pulled with all of her might. Toil was off balance and fell to the catwalk. Scrambling forward, Mineera grappled with the sinister Reaper Kai priestess over the club, fighting for control. Punching repeatedly, Mineera slammed her fist into Toil's jaw, trying to knock her senseless. With each blow that landed, Toil grew more hateful, more enraged. Fighting like a wild animal, she tore at Mineera, clawing at her face and trying to bite her.

Sinking her teeth into Mineera's hand, Toil viscously bit her. The savage attack broke the skin and a trickle of blood was smeared across her lips. Shrinking back, Mineera was losing ground fast. Toil seized the opportunity and surged forward, grabbing her head. She slammed it down onto the metal catwalk, trying to kill Mineera by shattering her skull. Dizzy from the attack, Mineera was defenseless. Toil grabbed her by the throat, beginning to punch her face over and over again. After a few seconds Mineera was totally limp, bashed and bruised by her opponent's savage fury.

Panting like a dog, Toil rose to her feet and grabbed the steel club. Breathing heavily for a few seconds, she tried to regain her composure. Mineera was not in a condition to fight. Savoring her victory, Toil sneered at Mineera. She clutched the steel club in her shaky hands, preparing to move in for the kill.

Barely able to move after being horribly beaten, Mineera was still dizzy and on the verge of unconsciousness. Feeling that the end was near, she said a silent prayer, moving her lips so that only she herself could hear the words.

This only incensed Toil further. Scorning such prayer, she began to laugh. "You think that will save you?"

Nodding back in defiance, Mineera replied, "Yes."

The smile disappeared from Toil's lips. A rage began to overtake her. "All I wanted is for my suffering to end. All I asked of you was to kill me to end the despair in my heart. You could have avoided all of this!" Marion Toil screamed. Raising the club above her head, she prepared to strike the final blow and kill Mineera.

The sound of muted footsteps echoed behind them. Mineera blinked through the haze as a shadowy form bounded down the catwalk, closing on the frightful scene. Every muscle in her body tensed. Marion screamed, the weapon quivering in the air above Mineera's head. As she breathed in, steeling herself to deliver the death blow, a thud rocked her. A sword, a gore-stained blade, was embedded in her chest. Marion gasped, the steel club falling from her hand.

Staring in sick fascination, she looked down and saw a blue steel blade poking out from her chest. A trickle of blood collected on the weapon's blade. Drooling to the floor, a bloody spray hit the catwalk. She blinked several times as a jagged pain emanated from the wound. Grasping her shoulder, Jared forced the witch to her knees, then moved her forward to pull the weapon free. As he did, the trickles of blood surged to a flowing stream of gore. Clutching her chest, Marion Toil gasped in pain once more.

"Impossible…" she stuttered in disbelief. "Vertigo is dead?"

"Vertigo is dead," Jared confirmed, moving over to Mineera. Crouching down, he helped her sit up. Still dizzy from the attack and wounds she had suffered at the hands of Toil, Mineera gripped Jared firmly and acknowledged that she would be fine. "Vertigo is dead and he will not be returning," Jared spoke again, touching the wooden raven talisman around his neck.

The look of pain turned to a wicked smile. Tears filled Toil's eyes as she was rocked with emotion. Deep down, Marion was glad that Vertigo was dead. The tears turned to a sob as she broke down and cried. Growing weaker by the second, Marion Toil gasped for breath. She reached out to grab Jared's arm. With heartfelt appreciation, she smiled at him. The darkness in her eyes was gone. The wickedness had left her spirit. Seconds from death, Marion gripped Jared even tighter. "Thank you…" she gasped as a trickle of blood rolled out of her mouth. "Thank you for setting me free. Thank you for freeing me from the shackles of my own existence. Thank you for bringing me death."

Her eyes rolled back into her head as the room began to spin. Gasping once more, she spoke in a mere whisper. "Tell Globulus… tell Globulus that I am so sorry." She gagged as the fire left her body. Growing cold, she whispered once more, "Tell Globulus that I love him very much. Tell him that I love him."

As she spoke her last words, Marion Toil, the Great Betrayer, passed into death. Jared and Mineera stared for a brief moment and then looked at each other. Both were speechless and overwhelmed both emotionally and physically. Such death and suffering bore a heavy toll upon the soul. Unable to even think, the two companions lingered for a moment, lost in thought, gripped by sorrow.

As the tension began to abate once more, Jared and Mineera knew that duty was still calling. Outside the factory, they could hear the continuous sound of artillery booming. Knowing full well that the war was far from over, they sought to end it once and for all. The Splicer relay was just beyond the door at the end of the catwalk.

Mineera was out of commission, still horribly wounded from the attacks she had suffered. Motioning to Jared, she spoke softly. "Go get Tani. I'll be all right. Go get Tani and end this."

Jared nodded, his expression solemn. Rushing over to Tani, he found him looking around with a dazed look on his face. The tribal scholar was vaguely aware of his surroundings and his conscious mind was finally beginning to awaken. Jared helped him sit up. Tani smiled as he saw Jared's face looking back at him.

"I never thought I would see you again," Tani said with tears in his eyes.

"It's almost over." Jared's tone was confident. "Stay alert and help me. I can't knock out the Splicer relay alone. I need your help."

Grabbing Jared, Tani hugged him and slapped him on the back. Jared simply looked back without responding. He pulled Tani to his feet and the two of them staggered down the catwalk, past Mineera and into the control room which contained the Splicer relay. As they reached the entry to the relay room, Tani and Jared turned back to look at Mineera. She was sitting up against the railing, exhausted and in extreme pain. Nodding confidently at them, she motioned them onward. "End this. Don't worry about me. Keep going and end this war, end all of this suffering."

Nodding back, the tribals from Scarskin pressed on alone. The fate of the Darken Realm now rested in the hands of two youths, two mere children who were forced to grow up in a dark world. Destiny was calling. Jared and Tani moved forward to meet it.

Chapter 39
The Last Stand

Emperor Gunther was standing his ground. The entire Iron Kai army had sustained enormous casualties and was rife with fear. Watching them buckle and fall back, he knew he had to do something quickly. Having just reached the battlefield, Gunther had mere moments to save his entire army from utter ruin.

As he advanced on his frightened horse, the faces of those whose morale had been utterly shattered were revealed to him as they rushed away from the scene of battle. Gunther charged past them on his mighty horse, uttering boisterous war cries and cheering all the way.

As the broken soldiers saw their valiant leader rushing to the front of the battle, they stopped dead in their tracks and stared in wonder. Their leader, their glorious leader, had not distanced himself from them. Gunther was willing to die and bleed for his soldiers. This mighty man was no coward; instead, he was a model for all, a reckless hero who would risk it all for his own men.

As Gunther charged onward, the sickly swarm of insects that had been plaguing the army suddenly ceased to stir. The millions of cockroaches, locusts, and flies that had been on a rabid feeding frenzy began to fly erratically. Suddenly, without warning, the insect swarm collapsed from the sky, falling to the ground. Twitching, the swarm abruptly passed into death.

A strange ceasefire broke through the battlefield as the insect swarm died. It was a powerful moment in the battle. Instead of being utterly overwhelmed and seemingly helpless, the Iron Kai army once again had a fighting chance. The Reaper Kai forces retreated into ominous silence as well, and for good reason. The sudden death of the insect swarm meant only one thing: Father Vertigo had been slain and his sinister dark magic had been foiled and confounded. Without his nefarious spells, the insect swarm could not be sustained.

And so the two great armies collected in the center of the valley while an eerie silence gripped the landscape. Standing atop mounds of dead bodies, the two combating forces prepared for the final conflict, the final stage in the battle where only one army would leave the battlefield.

With the death of Vertigo and the insect swarm, the Reaper Kai lost their edge. Knowing full well that the two armies were relatively balanced, the remainder of the Reaper Kai command ordered a sinister attack. The 20,000 spliced slaves were ordered to the front of the army. The plan was simple: overwhelm what remained of the Iron Kai army with the slaves and then sweep in and clean up what was left after the assault.

The two great armies in Metalweaver Flats began to assemble for the final showdown. Gunther charged through the entire army, yelling out battle cries and rallying his troops. With each boisterous shout, his army responded, echoing his war cries. Like a ripple of hope, these battle cries surged through the ranks, inspiring the broken soldiers to fight on. The shapeless army began to form ranks, valiant soldiers answering the call for one final stand against the army of the devil.

Having reached the front of the army, Gunther pulled back the reins on his horse. Bucking backwards, the horse reared up on its hind legs, letting out a shrill and piercing scream and flailing its front legs aggressively. Seeing such rash action rekindled the fire in the hearts of all those who witnessed the act. Gunther was out in the open, completely defenseless and completely without fear. There was no hint of terror in their mighty emperor. He was a true leader, someone not afraid to get his hands dirty and risk his own life to reach the objective. Gunther did not place his own safety above that of his men. Seeing his rash actions made his troops feel truly needed.

Its morale now bolstered, the Iron Kai army prepared to make war and finish the job.

But as the valiant forces of the Iron Kai readied themselves, evil was plotting their demise once more. Twenty thousand spliced slaves, mindless victims of the Reaper Kai, massed and advanced upon the Iron Kai battle lines. Like a shapeless mass, the horde of spliced slaves shambled onward. Clutching hand weapons, they topped a sand dune and began to descend. With each step they took, Gunther shouted and chanted, racing back and forth in front of his army, preparing them for the worst.

"Today is the end! We stand on the threshold of victory! History will remember our deeds this day! A tyrannical army, a legion of evil that has plagued the world since the fall of man, will be put to rest, utterly crushed before our might. It is our destiny as sovereign people to resist the will of evil. It is our destiny to free ourselves from the taint of darkness. Today, all people of the Darken Realm stand united as a single army with one intent: freedom," Gunther boomed, and a fire was lit in the hearts and souls of all who witnessed him speaking with such conviction.

"I have never been more proud than I am today. As I look out, I view a sea of courageous faces. I see a group of people dedicated and willing to risk their very lives to put an end to the Dark Order. I am proud to be one of you. I am proud to fight with you. I am proud to bleed with you! Do not fear the coming darkness! Rally to me and envision victory!"

Mighty war cries rippled through the Iron Kai army. Their faith had been renewed and rekindled. Preparing for the worst, the Iron Kai army needed every ounce of courage and with good cause; the army of spliced slaves was drawing near and the time for conflict was quickly approaching.

Shambling forward, the 20,000 spliced slaves presented a new threat. Many of those in the front ranks of the army were suddenly gripped with sadness, a wedge of doubt that filled them with sorrow. A significant number of those advancing slaves were family members and friends of those in the unified army. As Iron Kai soldiers looked out, they could see their mothers and fathers moving forward under the will of the Reaper Kai, willing to kill for the Dark Order. Doubt filled these men as many were brought to tears.

Understanding that some of the soldiers had to fight and kill their own family members, Gunther held his hand in the air, knowing the implications of such actions all too well. "Stand your ground! Have faith!" Gunther yelled. "Hold your fire! We still have a chance!"

Gunther was referring to the covert strike on the production facility in Metalweaver Flats. If Nova 7 could knock out the Splicer relay, the slaves would be free from the control of the Reaper Kai. Without this control, the 20,000 slaves would not be a threat.

Fifty yards out, the entire top of the ridgeline of sand dunes was covered with the advancing spliced slaves. Shaking their heads in despair, the soldiers in the Iron Kai army trembled, seeing their siblings clutching hand weapons, ready to kill for the Reaper Kai.

"I can't do this!" a terrified soldier whimpered. "I can't kill my brother." The soldier was pointing with a trembling outstretched finger at a mindless slave advancing upon them. As the anguished man whimpered, a raw sense of empathy surged through the ranks. A somber reality began to set in. In order to survive, many of the soldiers would have to kill loved ones. It was too much to bear. Many soldiers began to look around for any avenue of escape. This panic rippled through the army and Gunther knew that he was a mere minute away from his entire army fleeing.

"Have faith!" Gunther boomed. The shambling horde of spliced slaves was now only 40 yards out.

"We need to kill them now!" a soldier yelled, terrified at the proximity of the slaves. "We'll be overrun!"

"Hold your fire!" Gunther ordered.

"I can't do this!" Another soldier broke down in tears, seeing his own mother clutching a rusty knife, slowly plodding forward under the will of the Reaper Kai.

Twenty yards out. Restless soldiers began to sweat, their eyes wide with fear. They could smell the dirty slaves now, sensing their filthy odor as they advanced. The Iron Kai were totally outnumbered by the slaves alone but the Reaper Kai had additional Biogtech and war priests in reserve. The situation was grim.

Closing his eyes, Gunther felt tears sting him. Was this it? Was this finally the end of the Iron Kai? Killed by their own families and friends? Shaking his head, he knew that he had to stand strong and have faith. "Hold your fire! We still have hope!"

Only ten yards away, the army of Spliced slaves was almost on top of them.

"What are we waiting for?" a frantic soldier yelled.

Gunther knew that he had to give the order to open fire. Gripped with indecision, he raised his hand in the air, preparing to order the attack. Biting his lower lip, he knew that ordering his soldiers to fire upon their own families and loved ones would be the hardest thing he would ever have to do. As he held out a split second longer, a mighty explosion echoed through the canyon. The boom rolled through the area and both armies held their ground, uneasy and shaken by the enormous blast.

In the distance, smoke curled into the sky. The explosion emanated from the Reaper Kai facility in Metalweaver Flats. Blinking as if in total disbelief, Gunther felt the tears sting his eyes. The explosion was the Splicer relay, the massive computer that was controlling all of the spliced slaves in the valley. Nova 7 had done the impossible once more.

The spliced slaves ceased to advance. The once-blank expressions upon their faces lifted as life returned. Curling up like dead spiders, the Splicers themselves detached from the slaves and fell to the ground, totally motionless. The slaves were free from the taint of darkness, free from servitude to the Dark Order. As the flames in Metalweaver Flats rose from the destroyed Splicer relay, fire leapt in the hearts of all those souls that had been enslaved by the Reaper Kai. Outraged by their enslavement, the freed slaves roared and chanted war cries. Grabbing weapons from the dead, the 20,000 liberated slaves took arms with only one intent: to slaughter the Reaper Kai.

Smiling, and utterly exhausted, Gunther hastily gave orders, forming the army together into a cohesive unit. Providing an addition of 20,000 fresh warriors, the liberated slaves were a beacon of hope. The Reaper Kai were now severely outnumbered and their leader Father Vertigo was slain. Sensing victory, Gunther knew at that moment that it was almost over.

Atop his mount, Gunther stood at the head of the ranks of soldiers and slaves. He held his hand high in the air and ordered the final attack on the Reaper Kai. Riding with his troops into battle, Gunther was the first into the fray, fighting with hope and endless courage.

With stalwart hearts and renewed hope, the Iron Kai army crashed into what remained of the Reaper Kai army. Within the ranks of the Reaper Kai, now without solid leadership and outnumbered, it took only a few minutes for morale to crumble. Sensing their imminent defeat, the Reaper Kai army broke apart and began to flee deeper into the canyon. The fleeing troops were slaughtered, crushed by the might of the Iron Kai army. As their opponents boxed them in, the Reaper Kai had no escape. Pinned against the back of the canyon and totally surrounded, the entire Reaper Kai army was crushed, obliterated once and for all by the valiant Iron Kai army. Not a single Reaper Kai survived the attack. Each and every one was killed.

The war against the Reaper Kai was finally over. Centuries of death and destruction were finally set right. The Dark Order, a hideous cult of evil zealots, was finally crushed. It would be a day long remembered both in the history books and in the hearts of all, and a day not easily forgotten by all those tortured souls who survived the horror of Metalweaver Flats.

Chapter 40
Farewell

Clutching her arm, Mineera was motionless, enveloped by extreme pain. She was lost in a trance, digging her fingernails into her arm, trying to awaken from what she wished was a nightmare.

Standing atop the hill, she stared at the green grass with a somber look upon her face. A soft wind had pushed out of the mountains, agitating the tall grass. With each burst of the wind, the grass pulsed and surged, creating gentle waves that traveled outwards. The scene would normally be peaceful but on this day, it was somber and rife with sorrow.

Below the prophet, in the open valley, a great battlefield was bustling. The thousands of casualties were being buried, ally and enemy alike. Staring at the dead filled Mineera with a renewed sense of sorrow. Wiping the tears from her face, she turned around to face her greatest challenge.

Blinking, Mineera confronted a chilling sight. A mound of fresh dirt rose from a patch of bare earth. A wooden cross rested near one end of the mound. Perched atop the cross was a black hat, Banion's hat. As she stared in disbelief at the grave, she fought back the torrent of tears.

Looking up from the mound of earth, Mineera saw that the entire hillside was filled with the funeral's silent attendants, all of them looking down at the grave with somber eyes.

Tani and Jared stood close to the grave. Tani was openly distressed, the tears flowing down his face so frequently that the tribal had removed his glasses. Snot was flowing out of his nose and down his lips. From time to time, he would be overtaken with grief, breaking down in sobs. Wracked with sadness, Tani stared at Banion's grave with a deep sense of loss and loneliness. In that moment, he felt that death was nothing more than a cruel torture that the living had to suffer.

Jared stood beside his friend and stared at the grave with deep hate building inside his heart. His body was tense and rigid. Gazing around him without a hint of sorrow, Jared was consumed with bitterness. His friend and mentor was dead and gone. The tribal wanted nothing more than to maintain the rage inside his heart. There were no more enemies left to kill but he wanted more. If the tribal warrior could somehow bring his enemies back to life, he would do so in order to punish them again and again. He would kill without end, never able to satiate his sense of vengeance. He wanted more death to settle the score, and felt robbed that there was no one left to kill.

Beside Jared was the beastly Globulus. Standing tall, the enormous hippo hybrid was overwhelmed with sorrow. He was crying, unable to keep his emotions in check. For the mighty hippo, there was the feeling of losing a friend but something much more, as well. The two had known each other for a great many years. Globulus and Banion had performed many missions together to ensure the safety of Rasheed. They were compatriots in arms and good friends. Losing Banion did not just mean the loss of a friend but the loss of an entire, fleeting dream. Banion represented Globulus' last tie to the kingdom of Rasheed and his former home. King Toil, Marion Toil, and now Banion had passed into death, leaving Globulus alone. Globulus had not just lost a friend but the last remnant of his former home in Rasheed. In a sense, the city of Rasheed was an icon to Globulus, a symbol of his life and self-sacrifice for the greater good. The hippo had lost everyone and it left him with a deep sense of loneliness.

Carla Reins stood silently beside Globulus, giving him comfort by grasping his hand in her own to lend him support. She tried to console him as best she could, but Globulus was in a dark place and would continually pull away from her as she tried to comfort him.

Beside Globulus was Emperor Gunther. The mighty leader had wanted to pay personal tribute to the hero of Dune Station.

Standing tall, Gunther was respectful of the proceedings. Nearly 1,000 soldiers from the battle of Metalweaver Flats were stationed behind him, wanting to pay tribute to a real hero who had paid the ultimate price for his convictions.

Standing in the gentle breeze, Mineera took a brief moment to collect herself before saying goodbye to the reckless hero. As she listened to the grass rustle in the wind, a calm came over her. Opening her eyes, she looked at Banion's grave. She smiled down at the mound of fresh earth and said a silent prayer.

Looking up from the grave, she took a deep breath.

"We are gathered here today to pay tribute to a great man." Staring at the crowd, she could sense the sorrow in all of those attending. "It took me considerable time to think of a proper way to pay tribute to Banion O'Neil. At first I thought that I could convey to you all the great accomplishments that he made in life. But the more I thought of Banion, the more I was convinced that I did not need to focus on his life to pay him proper tribute. I decided that the best way to pay tribute to a man like Banion was to focus on how he lost his life."

As Mineera uttered those words, a tense ripple rolled through the crowd. Most were confused but were willing to listen.

"I want everyone here on this day to know that Banion O'Neil was defined by how he left this world. Banion is defined by his deep convictions and sense of love for his friends. In the end, the real Banion stood by our side, a real man, a true hero who paid the ultimate price for his convictions. I want everyone to know this day that Banion loved so deeply that he could not stand to see one of his friends suffer. He is a true hero. Banion lost his life defending his friends; he sacrificed himself to save us all. When it really mattered, Banion chose love instead of hate; he chose to give his own life to save another."

The crowd was utterly silent. Many were staring at Jared of Scarskin, having already heard the tale of how Banion sacrificed himself to save the boy.

Jared was motionless, lost in a haze. The guilt coursing through him was overwhelming. Banion had sacrificed himself to save him, and Jared wished that his friend would have let him die. The thought that his mentor, a man who had meant more to him than his own father, had died because of him was too much to bear. Rage filled him and he wanted more suffering to quench its thirst.

"Banion would not have wanted anyone to shed a tear due to his passing. He would have wanted you all to know that he was finally going home, going home to his lost love, his beloved wife who passed into death so long ago. Do not grieve his death. Celebrate his homecoming. Banion is now with his beloved, beyond the taint of war and suffering. Celebrate his homecoming, not his death. Instead of shedding tears of grief, pay him homage by shedding tears of joy that Banion is with those he loved most."

Her words were soothing. Many did as she said; they began to weep, shedding tears. But instead of grieving Banion's loss, they celebrated his freedom from suffering. They celebrated his homecoming in the afterlife with his beloved wife.

The wind blew gently through the lush, tall green grass. Wave after wave pushed and pulsed as the wind hissed through the land. Spring was at hand, and a cleansing sense of renewal was riding the winds, warming the earth. As the breeze filled the land with a sense of life, those who had survived the war stood and paid homage to a great man. In shared silence, the crowd paid Banion a final tribute by bowing their heads and offering him a moment of peace.

Slowly the crowd dispersed, souls drifting away into the grasslands to find their own inner peace and reflect upon their own lives. In the end, only six people remained near the grave, wanting to stay near the great man.

Jared, Tani, Mineera, Globulus, Carla, and Gunther stayed behind. Standing around the grave, they lingered in silence. As the day wore on, the sun pushed westwards, an event that had occurred long before man ever set foot on the earth. With the last rays of light passing beyond the horizon, darkness settled over the land.

When night overtook the wasteland, Gunther moved over to the foot of Banion's grave. Standing at attention, Gunther saluted the grave and then bowed his head in gratitude. Turning away, the Emperor of the Iron Kai pushed into the darkness.

Globulus knelt before the grave and placed his enormous hand on the soft mound of dirt. Tears streamed down his face as he left a large handprint in the earth. "I will never forget you, my friend." Carla patted him on the back, trying comfort him. Finally, he rose from the ground and moved into the darkness with Carla walking beside him.

Tani collapsed near the grave and began to sob. He pounded his fists on the grave with wild frustration. Shaking his head back and forth, he was barely able to contain his grief, his thoughts frantic. "Banion, I miss you so much. I'm so sorry. I'm so sorry it had to end this way. I am so sorry." He trembled violently. "I want to say thank you. I want to thank you for everything you did for me. Thank you for teaching me what sacrifice is. Thank you for teaching me what it is to be a real man, not just a boy." Tani retreated and could stay no longer. Fleeing into the night, he passed into the shadows.

Jared stood silent, without a single tear in his eyes. He was filled with rage, not sorrow.

"It's not wrong to cry for your loss. It's not wrong to shed a tear for him," Mineera said softly to him.

"Shut up!" Jared yelled at her. "Just shut up!"

"Don't shut yourself down. Grieve for him."

"Don't tell me what to do," Jared shot back.

"You're filled with rage. Anger won't bring him back. Grieve for Banion." Mineera was calm and tried to coax him to surrender to his emotions.

"I want to be angry. I want this feeling!" Jared shouted. "He was like a father to me! Don't tell me how I should feel."

"Don't let the rage consume you."

"Why? Why not let the rage consume me?" Jared asked in a nasty tone.

"The world has seen enough death. Don't lose your way."

"Lose my way? You mean like Banion? He was filled with rage, and he's a hero. Don't tell me not to be like him. Don't you ever tell me not to be like him."

"Banion chose love, not hate," Mineera pressed.

"I choose hate." Jared's tone was harsh. Storming away from the grave, he disappeared into the darkness. The tribal never even said goodbye; he never gave himself the chance to kneel before Banion's grave and say farewell. As Jared blended in with the shadows of the night, Mineera knelt alone before Banion's grave.

A chill blast of air broke from the mountains and pressed on into the grasslands. The wind whipped through the landscape, whistling as it went. Praying before Banion's grave, Mineera paid homage to him for many hours, unable to leave his side. As the night wore on, she grew weary and fell asleep beside the grave of the man who had haunted her dreams for an entire lifetime, a man whom Mineera had deeply loved in life.

Chapter 41
Of Fate and Destiny

An enormous blast of wind roared from the mountains. Moving down quickly from the heights, it picked up speed, rushing across the land to strike the hillside where Banion's grave rested. The wind grabbed at the grass, pushing and pulsing its way through. Wave after wave of the green grass rustled and bent, hissing as the wind whipped through it.

At the edge of Mineera's consciousness, the noise rose in intensity until it sounded like a waterfall. Stunned, she sat up in the darkness, blasted by the frigid wind. She frantically collected her thoughts and stared around in alarm. All about, the grass hissed as the wind trampled it. Staring down at the grave in the darkness of the night, Mineera wished that it was just a dream, that everything she had experienced that day was just a dream. Much to her dismay, it was not. Banion was still dead and gone and now she was more alone than ever in the world.

She settled back and rested in the darkness. As she did, the wind increased once more, howling across the lonely landscape. In the chill, she drew her robes close about her body. Bringing her knees to her chest, she clutched them tightly, warming her chilled bones. She found herself reflecting upon her life, feeling sorrow prick once more at her senses. Small tears began to form as she stared at Banion's grave with anguish.

"I'm so sorry that I failed." The tears began to flow as she whimpered.

In the darkness of the night, a whisper rose from the grass itself, only barely audible over the roar of the wind. *"Mineera..."*

At first she thought it was her fragile mind playing tricks on her. But the longer she lingered near the grave, the more she felt that she was not alone.

"Mineera..." The voice rose from the grass all around her. Stunned, she stood up and whirled around, desperately trying to discover where the whisper was coming from. Mineera's senses were on overload as the grass around her writhed and moved in the strong wind.

Finally, she saw a small pinnacle of light hovering above Banion's grave. Blinking as if witnessing an illusion, Mineera stared uneasily at the glowing object for a brief moment until she finally realized that it was not a hallucination. The pinnacle of light began to flash, emitting bright pulses of white light. With each pulse, the pinnacle grew in size, turning into a shimmering, rotating disk of light. Spinning faster and faster, the disk continued to grow, changing into the form of a spectral being. A head emerged, as did two arms and two legs. Taking a step back, Mineera shielded her eyes from the intense lightshow. At last, the transformation was complete and a shimmering form stood before her.

"Mineera, hear my words for they ring true," the entity addressed her.

Mineera felt at peace in the presence of the spectral form, with which she had a long acquaintance. She had first seen the image in her prison cell after betraying the Reaper Kai. Now many moons had passed and many events had taken place since their first meeting, in which the ghostly form instructed her to save Banion from death at all costs. There had been many such meetings and the communication was always just that: save Banion from death or the entire Darken Realm would be lost to the shadow.

Staring at the ghostly form, Mineera moved forward and bowed before the heavenly being. Mustering her courage, she stared at the being and humbly apologized. "I am sorry I failed you. I'm sorry that I could not save Banion."

"Mineera, do not apologize. Banion met his destiny, his true fate, a fate that was not born out of suffering and misery but rather out of compassion. Do not fret, prophet of Gogoli. All things have been set right."

"Set right?" Mineera echoed in a skeptical tone. "He wasn't supposed to die! I failed him! I did what you said, and look what happened!" She was agitated and wanted to shout at the ghost.

"You did the right thing. Banion met his true fate."

"But I loved him!" Mineera shouted back. "Don't you get that?"

The spectral form fell silent for a moment as it gazed at Mineera.

"I know you loved him."

"All of my life, I dreamed of him, I dreamed of Banion. I knew him even before we met. I saw him every night in my dreams and knew that I have only one true charge in life, to save the man from my dreams. Now everything is done. Banion is gone and so is my soul. I feel that now that he's dead, my purpose is done as well. I have no people, no home, and no purpose." Mineera shook her head in dismay. "I have no hope."

"Your role in this war is complicated. Throughout all of your dreams, the secret of Banion's fate was hidden. From the very first time we met, you have seen images that were true to fate, true not only to your destiny but to the destiny of Banion and the tribals."

"The tribals?" Mineera was confused. "What do Tani and Jared have to do with Banion's death and the fate of the Darken Realm?"

"Jared and Tani had everything to do with Banion's death and his true fate."

"I don't understand. I was supposed to save Banion."

"You did save him. It was your kindness and the innocence of Jared and Tani that saved him, truly saved Banion, not from the world, but rather from himself and the tortured memories that guided his existence. You all taught him compassion, and he was then able to save this world from darkness. But more importantly, you all saved the world from darkness, each of you."

Mineera was silent, staring at the ghostly form, trembling as tears streamed down her face.

"I told you the first time we met that you must save Banion from death, and you stepped outside yourself to do so, saving him from an assassin's bullet in Rasheed. You saved Banion that day so that he could save Jared."

"Save Jared?"

"Yes. Banion lived a tortured life. In his travels with all of you, he learned compassion again. It was that strength, the love for each of you, which gave this world a fighting chance. Banion sacrificed himself to save Jared from death. It was a part of the puzzle that had to fall into place. Without Jared's survival, the Darken Realm would have suffered." The spectral form reached out its hand and placed it on her shoulder. As it touched her, flashes of memory filled and overwhelmed her consciousness.

Mineera was teleported to the time when Jared was believed to be dead, having gone missing after the ship sank on the way to Dune Station. At that time, Mineera was tortured by the thought of Jared's death. She could still remember the conversation she had with the ghostly form.

*   *   *

"Mineera..."   The specter spoke more directly, with purpose.

The being flared and white light poured from it. "What do you want?" she whispered.

"Do not despair, you must maintain your faith if the world is to survive this nightmare," the angel murmured in a calming, soothing tone.

"How can I not despair? Jared died so needlessly," Mineera replied in the dreamlike state.

"It was the will of God."

"How can it be the will of God that Jared died? I don't understand. I do not believe you. How can the needless death of the innocent be divine will?"

"You must believe and hold your faith. If you do not, all is lost..."

*   *   *

The image from the past departed from her mind and she stared at the shimmering form presently before her. Suddenly, it began to make sense to her. She addressed the specter excitedly.

"Jared didn't drown! He went on alone, through the desert. After that point in time, he had the raven totem. Something happened to him out there, when he was alone." Mineera was putting the puzzle together.

"Jared found himself out there in the wilds of the Darken Realm. He learned what true courage was and vowed to continue on alone if need be to stop the Dark Order. He glimpsed images upon the walls of an ancient church that chronicled his life. He found faith in the spirit world with the ancient tribal totem that hangs around his neck. The story of Jared, the story of Navezgane, is part of the greater picture. Jared is a strong warrior who lacked courage and confidence. He learned his true place in this world through his journey and through Banion's teachings. You saved Banion so that Banion could save Jared from death."

Mineera felt a deep sense of awe as the story began to unravel.

"Do you remember in the Iron Gate ruins, when you were overwhelmed by voices in your soul? When evil willed you to kill Jared?"

Mineera nodded. She could still remember her betrayal of her companions due to the demonic spirits that had entered her body, willing her to do evil acts.

"You had seen the true path, but evil had tainted your perception. You had foreseen Banion's death many moons ago but were tricked into believing it to be an evil plot. In the end, Jared did kill Banion in a sense. Banion sacrificed himself to save Jared. The devil himself tried to get you to kill Jared. For if Jared died, the Darken Realm would have been finished, sacrificed to dark powers. But you persevered, resisting the darkness, driving the demonic spirits from your body."

As the being touched her again, the vision filled her senses and she was transported back to experience it once more...

*   *   *

Jared, his sword stained in blood, turned around. At his feet were the remains of Banion. His eyes were filled with hate and he gazed at Mineera in disgust. The strange totem around his neck was glowing intensely, its red eyes hungering for more blood, more suffering.

When Mineera tried to run, her legs would not move. The tribal youth moved towards her, hate burning in his eyes. When she tried to yell, her voice would not sound. The youth moved ever closer, gore-stained blade in hand.

"Damn it, Mineera!" Jared screamed, his cheeks flushed red. There was a crazed look in his eyes.

Mineera stared at Jared dreamily. Her subconscious was screaming that something was wrong. "Jared?" she asked in a confused tone. The hotheaded youth had Banion's revolver in one hand and the mighty Scar Blade in the other.

"Wake up!" Jared shouted angrily. "Snap out of it. We have a job to do."

Mineera looked around and found her surroundings unusual. Old, corroded metal walls and steel girders rose around them. She spun around and caught sight of Tani sitting on the floor, leaning against the wall, a look of shock on his face.

"He's gone!" Jared said in a matter-of-fact tone. "There isn't a damn thing we can do about it now. We need to get moving."

*   *   *

The image faded and wisdom began to fill Mineera's heart. Finally, her dark visions were beginning to make sense.

"Jared was saved by Banion. Through his journeys and through Banion's teachings, Jared was able to persevere against insurmountable odds. His skill and the power of the totem allowed him to slay Father Vertigo. It was God's will that the boat sank that night so many moons ago. It allowed Jared to find himself and the totem. Jared survived so that he could save Tani."

"Tani?" Mineera repeated, still mystified.

"Marion Toil was on the verge of killing you both. Banion saved Jared so Jared could save Tani. Jared killed Marion Toil so that Tani could survive and meet his destiny."

"Tani was the only one who knew how to destroy the Splicer relay..." It finally made sense.

"Indeed. Banion saved Jared so Jared could save Tani. Tani then destroyed the Splicer relay and thus allowed the Iron Kai army to finally annihilate the Reaper Kai."

Mineera blinked as a chill shot down her spine. Every experience in which she had taken part and every vision she had experienced had ultimately led to the destruction of the Reaper Kai. The entire Dark Order had been destroyed by Nova 7, both by nuclear fire and by acts of heroism during the battle of Metalweaver Flats.

"Banion's sacrifice was profound. His compassion saved the Darken Realm from evil."

In the blink of an eye, all of the memories flooded through Mineera from start to finish. The ultimate destiny of Nova 7 was revealed to her. It made her feel awestruck to be part of something so profound, so intricate. "All of this has been planned?"

"No, not planned. Through divination, we have been able to see the end of all things. The holy powers do not force people to do things. The divine only consorts with those worthy of great deeds. The story of Nova 7 has been known to us since the fall of man. The valiant souls of the righteous were simply brought together. God did not save the world of man, God simply brought you all together and helped you to save the world. It was your actions and your courage that saved the world from darkness. Destiny is nothing more than a person realizing their inner strength. It is up to the person to choose how to meet that destiny. Banion, Jared, Tani, and yourself chose to meet your destinies together. Banion's destiny was compassion. Jared's destiny is courage. Tani's destiny is knowledge. Your destiny is faith."

"I was so blind," Mineera said softly, still awestruck by the intense revelation.

"Do not fret, Mineera. You were part of the story. You were all part of the story. You saved Banion. Banion saved Jared. Jared saved Tani. Tani rescued the Iron Kai army from ruin. Full circle, Mineera. The loop is almost complete. You feel empty and devoid of home and purpose. But you still have much work ahead of you in this world, reclaiming the battered earth, saving the lost souls. Do not fret, Mineera; you will always have a purpose in this world."

Bowing before the heavenly vision, Mineera felt a spark of hope enter her heart. The shimmering being began to dissipate, disappearing into the darkness of the night. It took but a brief moment for the spirit to vanish completely. Mineera was left alone again.

Staring down at Banion's grave, she said a silent prayer, bowing before the man from her dreams. Saying goodbye one last time, she paid tribute to a man whose ultimate destiny was not hate and bloodshed but rather compassion.

Moving away from the grave, Mineera passed through the lush, tall grass. As she walked, the wind battered the earth and the grass hissed intensely. Shrugging off the cold chill air, she wandered the grassy fields until the morning sun rose over the wasteland once more, driving away the darkness of the night, bathing the earth in warm light.

Chapter 42
Hollow Rewards and Empty Victories

The sun had barely peeked over the horizon. Chilling desert winds began to dissipate as the earth began to warm, harsh cold air being driven away by dry heat. In the desert canyon, near the scene of the worst conflict of the war, hundreds of soldiers and warriors began to collect. Their goal was not to honor the dead but to be honored themselves for reckless acts of courage and selflessness in dark times.

The column of soldiers had come to attention. Standing tall and proud, they faced forward, rank after rank. Those standing before Emperor Gunther were there for good reason. During the war against the Reaper Kai, many daring deeds and acts of heroism had granted many soldiers their place in Iron Kai history.

The proud warriors were being honored for their service and duty.

"The actions of simple people can result in great things," Gunther's voice boomed. Smiling broadly, he walked back and forth in front of the first rank. He stopped at the end of the formation. Three souls garbed in ragged clothes, three people completely out of place amongst the soldiers, stood before him. Tani, Jared, and Mineera were part of the ceremony, having earned the rank of hero in the eyes of the Iron Kai army. Gunther stopped at the front of the formation, staring at the trio with a smile.

"Today is very special. In the last 400 years, the Military Service Cross, the most revered and difficult medal of honor to receive, has not once been granted. In all of that time, there has not been a single soul that has earned the right to wear the coveted medal. Today, I am proud to say that I will be handing out four such medals."

A shock of bewilderment rolled through the crowd. Not since the days of the civil war had the Military Service Cross been bestowed. The criteria for such a medal were legendarily demanding. Those who received such an honor had sacrificed their very souls for victory. The entire band of soldiers stared in wonder at the trio at the front of the ranks in their tattered clothes.

"The Military Service Cross is given for extreme acts of valor and a dedication to performing well beyond the normal expectations from a soldier for an extended period of time. The person receiving this honor was in harm's way for an extended period of time and deserves the highest honor that this army has to give."

Looking at Nova 7, Gunther grew solemn. He looked at each of them in turn. Tani was reserved, with a sheepish look on his face. The tribal's cheeks were flushed bright red. Gunther could tell that Tani was neither accustomed to such fanfare nor relished it. Next, Gunther turned to Jared. The boy was tense and taut. A nervous twitch filled the young warrior and a sense of fevered rage had settled over him. Gunther did not spend much time looking at the boy, preferring to move on to Mineera. The psychic warrior was standing with her hands folded just below her waist. She seemed to be calm but was engulfed by sorrow. He looked at her and gave her a light smile. She responded by tilting her head back, regarding him with respect.

"The story of Nova 7 will be forever remembered in the annals of history. A group of four people, radically different in thought, came together to do the impossible not only once but twice. King Toil of Rasheed, before his death, issued a command to seven mercenary teams to scour the wastelands and ruins of old to locate a functional nuclear weapon. Of the seven teams, only one team survived the invasion of Rasheed. That team was Nova 7.

"After months of travel and endless hardship, the team persevered and managed to locate a fully functional nuclear warhead. Nova 7 returned to our capital city and the warhead was used on the Reaper Kai. This act alone was an indication of valor and worthy of a place in Iron Kai history. This daring deed would have entitled each of them to a Military Service Cross."

Everyone in the crowd stared in awe at the three tattered heroes standing before Gunther. This ceremony was the stuff of legends, and everyone in the crowd would remember the day forever. The Military Service Cross would not be given again by the Iron Kai order for the next 150 years. The entire crowd was hushed with wild anticipation.

"Come before me." Gunther addressed Nova 7 in a calm, commanding tone. Nodding, they each came to him and turned around so that they faced the audience. Feeling nervous, Tani and Mineera averted their gaze, eyes hastily shifting from side to side. Jared, on the other hand, was hateful and defiant. He would stare at people in the audience for extended periods of time, making them feel uncomfortable enough to cause the audience members themselves to avert their gaze.

"Nova 7 earned a place in history once for their daring deeds in recovering the warhead. But not to be outdone, they volunteered for an even more dangerous mission, a mission that led them into the heart of evil itself, earning them a second place in the history books. Nova 7 was the entry team responsible for the destruction of the Splicer relay, an act that secured our victory on the battlefield, allowing the Iron Kai to once and for all defeat the Dark Order. The destruction of the Reaper Kai order occurred due to the actions of this team."

A hush came over the crowd, and for good reason. Four ornate boxes containing the Military Service award were brought to Gunther by Captain Maddock. When Maddock handed him the first box, Gunther came before Tani and smiled. Trying not to cry, the tribal scholar could barely keep his emotions contained.

"The first Military Service Cross goes to Tani of Scarskin. Tani is the brains of Nova 7. He is the most gifted scholar that I have had the opportunity to meet in my life. Skilled in the ancient lore of this land, Tani is also one of the best demolitions experts. Without his skill, the nuclear warhead would have never been liberated from the vaults of the ancient world. He is also the person directly responsible for destroying the Splicer relay. Tani of Scarskin-" Gunther gave him a serious look, holding the medal in his hands. "I bestow upon you the Military Service Cross for acting above and beyond the call of duty. Your courage and bravery honor us all." With that, Gunther placed the medal around Tani's neck.

Tani could not hold back the tears. All the long months of strife and insecurity suddenly bubbled to the surface. Looking down at his chest, Tani cupped the medal in his tattered hands. Though small, the medal felt strangely heavy. Clutching it in his hands, he thought about all the times he had wanted to surrender, all the times when he felt the impossible could not be done. Openly weeping, Tani began to shake, the gravity of the events that had brought him to that spot fully engulfing his emotions.

Bowing before Tani, Gunther patted him on the shoulder, rubbing it lightly. He then grabbed the second medal from Maddock and moved over to Mineera.

A deathly silence filled the crowd as Gunther reached Mineera. He considered her oddly. The bestowal of the next medal was unexpected, an ironic twist of fate. Collecting his thoughts, he stared into Mineera's bright blue eyes.

"The next military service cross is awarded to Mineera of..." Gunther's words fell short. Everyone knew that Mineera was once a Reaper Kai. It was ironic that a former Reaper Kai would be awarded the most prestigious medal of honor that the Iron Kai army had to offer.

Collecting his thoughts again, Gunther took a deep breath, then addressed Mineera directly. "I don't even know where to begin. I cannot fathom the sacrifices that you have made for the people of the Darken Realm."

Looking out at the audience, he began to speak again. "Courage can come in many forms. When I hear the story of Mineera, I can only think of how hard it must have been to betray her entire race. I cannot fathom what it's like for a person raised in such an evil environment and how such a person comes to terms with their heritage and makes a concrete decision to betray that heritage and do the right thing. It's one thing to praise someone who has fought evil, but to rise from the darkness and change one's life is a monumental accomplishment. Mineera is defined by her deep sense of justice, and her courage is born from fierce conviction. Mineera defined herself during this conflict as the moral compass of Nova 7, the person who did the right thing no matter how hard it was."

Gunther fell momentarily silent once more, shaking his head in amazement. "This is a ceremony of legend. Never before has a Military Service Cross been awarded to a former Reaper Kai. As if that wasn't enough, never before in the history of the Iron Kai has a Military Service Cross been awarded to a woman." Placing the medal around her neck, Gunther bowed his head to her. "I bestow upon you the Military Service Cross for acting above and beyond the call of duty. Your courage and bravery honor us all."

Overwhelmed with emotion, Mineera looked out into the crowd. Instead of being perceived as the enemy, she was viewed as an ally, a person to be trusted and revered. Mineera had lost everything, including her home and her identity, for the sake of fighting evil. For a very long time, she was viewed with disdain both by the Reaper Kai and by those she sought to protect from the Reaper Kai. In that moment, Mineera gained what she really wanted, a place in the world, a new home. No longer was she an outcast. No longer was she someone to be mistrusted. She had paid painfully for her sins but now she was accepted. The raw emotion that she had in her heart spilled out. Holding the Military Service Cross in her hand meant that she had a home again. Weeping openly, she wanted to collapse, gripped by her feelings.

Gunther steadied Mineera. She regained her composure and smiled at the crowd, bowing in respect to them. Many of them bowed back and the rest smiled at her.

Grabbing the third ornate box from Maddock, Gunther came before Jared.

Staring at him, Gunther knew that the youth had changed dramatically since Banion's death. Gunther prepared to speak of the boy as he surveyed him for a long moment. "There is a legend in the wastelands. For many, many months, we have all heard whispers of a warrior, a warrior reputed to kill Reaper Kai unscathed, a mighty witch hunter. I thought that such tales were mere legend. The legends are true. The third Military Service Cross is awarded to Jared of Scarskin."

Whispers broke over the crowd. The rumors and legends of the witch hunter were potent and widespread. It was said that a Reaper Kai slave convoy had been liberated by a powerful witch hunter. It was also said that many Reaper Kai had been slain due to his prowess. All the legends were true.

"Jared is renowned for his legendary battle skill and courage. There are none in this world who have been able to stand toe-to-toe with this legendary warrior. We, the Iron Kai, have for centuries feared Father Vertigo. Ominous tales have been told to our children for generations about this dark priest. Vertigo has plagued our nightmares for too long. It is a great day when I can openly announce to this assembly and to the world that Father Vertigo has been slain, utterly destroyed, and will not be returning."

The whisper erupted into a fervent storm of disbelief. Could it be true? The dreaded Father Vertigo was finally put to death? Amazed, the crowd stared in disbelief at the muscular tribal warrior.

"Jared will be remembered as a great savior of the Darken Realm. His courage and great battle skill have rid this land of Father Vertigo and many Reaper Kai. He is the greatest warrior I have ever known, a person who has devoted his life to the art of battle."

Bowing before Jared, Gunther was somewhat astonished that the youth did not respond. The tribal warrior simply stared at the crowd, glowering at them in contempt. Not knowing what else to do, Gunther placed the medal around his neck. "I bestow upon you the Military Service Cross for acting above and beyond the call of duty. Your courage and bravery honor us all."

It was an odd sight, the golden medal resting next to the worn, burnt raven totem. Clutching the medal in one hand, Jared held the raven totem in his other hand. A strange feeling crept over the tribal. All he had wanted his entire life was to be a hero. Jared had received exactly what he wanted. He would be remembered for all time, throughout history, as a legend. But as he held the Military Service Cross in his hand, he did not feel proud; he felt angry. He felt angry to have lost so much in the name of courage. Instead of feeling happy that he was a true hero, he felt an overwhelming sense of emptiness and loss.

A deep sense of regret filled him as he was honored for his bravery. Standing still, he did not weep; instead, he hated. He wished that there were more foes to kill, more Reaper Kai to slaughter. His rage was defining him and he now had an unquenched sense of vengeance. Jared had been robbed of revenge. He wanted to satiate the empty feeling with more death but there were no more enemies left to kill. If he could bring them back, he would, just to have another chance to punish them for the way he felt, punish them for taking Banion from him.

Gunther sighed slightly after leaving Jared's side. He was concerned for the tribal but knew that he could not help him; Gunther knew nothing could help him. Shifting his thoughts, he grabbed the final Military Service Cross from Maddock. The medal that he held in his hand was not for someone living but rather for someone who had given his life during the war.

"I am proud that we have honored three valiant heroes of the Darken Realm. But where courage and valor are the stuff of legend, brimming with hope, there is no victory without the sting of loss. The leader of Nova 7, a man defined by his struggle against the Reaper Kai, did not leave the field of battle alive. The final Military Service Cross is being awarded to a man who paid the ultimate price to defend us all against tyranny. Banion O'Neil, the hero of Dune Station, will also be remembered as the savior of the Darken Realm itself."

The entire crowd was silent. There was not a single person in the audience who had not heard the harrowing tales of the legendary gunfighter. Many desperate criminals had been captured or killed by Banion O'Neil prior to the start of the war. He was a deadly enemy of evil, a person who administered his own brand of justice with a silver revolver and a fierce persona.

"Dedication to a cause is what Banion O'Neil will be remembered for. Those who knew him understood that he had lost much. Everyone he ever loved was taken from him violently. Banion used this rage to fuel himself. He fought with fierce conviction, battling with true passion. He didn't know how to quit, how to surrender. Using his combat skills and strong will, he assembled and led the legendary mercenary team Nova 7. Where injustice reigned, Banion was there to thwart evil. It has been said that accepting tyranny is easier than opposing it. For Banion, accepting tyranny was more difficult than meeting it head-on.

"He was known as the Hero of Dune Station. When he was a mere boy, his bravery and courage sparked a bloody revolt in which his actions led his people to victory against the Reaper Kai. From that moment onward, he was a gallant warrior who protected the innocent from those who would seek to subjugate them and rule with an iron fist."

Many in the audience were misty eyed as they thought about Banion's death. With the Reaper Kai destroyed and Banion O'Neil dead, it was the end of an age, the end of a dark time in history. In a strange sense, Banion had to die. His life was defined by his struggle against the Reaper Kai. It was a dark symbiosis; one could not exist without the other. Banion was kept alive by his hatred of the Reaper Kai. With the passing of the Dark Order, it was the natural order for Banion to pass on as well.

"Banion will be remembered as someone who loved life and loved us all so much that he sacrificed himself to rid the world from tyranny. At the end of his life, he fought tyranny the only way that he knew: with his very existence. He sacrificed himself so that all of us could live in peace. Banion O'Neil was a great solider and a great man. His loss will be grieved by all."

Tears filled Gunther's eyes. Breathing in heavily, he brought himself under control, resisting the urge to weep. Opening the box, Gunther held Banion's Military Service Cross in his hands. "Banion O'Neil…" Gunther spoke while looking into the blue sky. "I know you can hear me, wherever you are. It is with great happiness that I bestow upon you the Military Service Cross for acting above and beyond the call of duty. Your courage and bravery honor us all."

The entire crowd came to attention and saluted Gunther as he held Banion's medal. Grasping it in one hand, Gunther himself saluted the Military Service Cross, paying Banion one final tribute. Dedicating a moment of silence to the fallen hero, the crowd paid him homage and respect. Banion's sacrifice and conviction had saved them all from darkness.

"As a final tribute to this great man, a statue will be placed in Dune Station. This medal of honor will be placed around the statue's neck, so that all can know his true courage and selflessness."

Somewhere in the crowd, a cheer erupted. The sentiment was shared by all, and that cheer rose to a roar as everyone chanted Banion's name. Shaking their fists in the air, they cheered the fallen hero. No one wanted to celebrate death; instead, the crowd celebrated their freedom. It that moment, they cheered Banion for freeing them from darkness.

The celebration lasted long into the day. There were many war heroes from every race and kingdom in the Darken Realm. It was a celebration of courage, a celebration of freedom, a day long remembered in the hearts and minds of those who had been forced to endure such dark times.

Chapter 43
Homeward Bound

What was left of the great army had fully assembled. The last of the tents were being collected and packed away for the journey home. As the Iron Kai army prepared for the long trip to the north, Gunther lingered in his tent. His aides were packing away his belongings, but he was gripped with a sullen silence. He sat in a chair with his feet propped upon a table. Although his tent was buzzing with activity, his demeanor was lackadaisical.

As he sat motionless, awaiting his next meeting, he toyed with a device in his hand. With a sigh, he looked down at the powerful radio transmitter. Flipping the switch on, he checked to ensure that the device was working properly, then, satisfied with the radio, sighed again and looked around his tent.

Most of the war gear had been stowed already and only bits and pieces of furniture remained. Remnants of the military equipment were being whisked away from the makeshift camp. Gunther looked around the enormous tent with a dismal stare, as if bored with the situation until, finally, his interest was piqued. Tani had emerged through the entrance of the tent and was timidly looking around. Catching sight of the tribal scholar, Gunther smiled and waved to him.

Pulling his feet off the table, Gunther rose to greet the tribal. Tani waved back, a little embarrassed and somewhat mystified, and approached the Emperor of the Iron Kai. Bowing his head in respect, Tani came before Gunther.

"It's good to see you again. I was afraid that I'd missed you and Jared before you left on your journey back to Scarskin," Gunther said.

"We're leaving right after we speak." Tani's cheeks flushed as he spoke. The youth was still unaccustomed to consorting with important leaders.

"Where is Jared?" Gunther quizzed. "I instructed that both of you should come speak with me."

Tani shook his head in dismay and sighed. "I don't know what to say. I couldn't get him to come with me to speak with you."

Gunther raised his brows when receiving the news, unaccustomed to being ignored and disobeyed. "He's still having tantrums, I see."

Agreeing, Tani sighed. "Jared is in a really dark place."

"Aren't we all?"

"Yeah, you're right. I don't know what else to say."

"Me neither. I wanted to thank you both again for everything you've done for us. I am eternally indebted to you. I also wanted to see if you have reconsidered my offer."

Gunther was referring to an amazing proposal. Since Nova 7 had helped the Iron Kai so much, he had offered the tribals and Mineera key positions within the government if they were interested. He had offered mayoral positions to both the tribals and a position in the high courts to Mineera. The offers were lavish and extremely hard to come by, but they were turned down by all three beneficiaries. Mineera cared nothing for politics and the tribals were nearing the end of their Exile and preferred to return home to their village of Scarskin.

"I appreciate the offer, but Jared and I need to be with our people. We need some time to heal and reflect upon the journey we've made," Tani replied respectfully.

"So be it. But if you ever reconsider, you will always have a place in the empire. Your deeds and acts of courage will be long remembered by the people of the Darken Realm."

"Your offer is gracious. I'll always remember your hospitality."

"Well spoken. You have the grace required for public life. Just one more thing before your journey home; I wanted to give you a gift before you leave." Gunther handed Tani the radio device.

Tani blinked in incomprehension. "A radio?"

"Not just any radio. It's a very old piece of technology from the ancients themselves, an extremely rare artifact from the old world. This radio has a 500-mile range."

"What do I need this for?" Tani was still confused.

"I want you to keep it and use it if you ever need it. If you ever need help or aid, use it to contact us. We have listening posts across a great portion of the Darken Realm. I know your village is remote, but our listening posts should pick up your transmission if you ever need anything, and I mean anything. We are forever in your debt and this empire is willing to help you with anything you need."

Tani was stunned. The Emperor of the Iron Kai had just committed to helping the tribals if they ever were in danger or needed help. He was extremely appreciative of the offer and didn't know how to react. Bowing his head in appreciation, Tani felt the gift was too gracious.

"This is too much. I can't accept this."

"You will accept it. I will not have this exchange go any other way. Take the radio and keep it safe. If you ever require aid, simply let us know. This is the very least that I can do for you. I would consider it an insult if you refused this gift." Gunther spoke in a stern tone.

Tani was shocked by his directness and nodded in agreement. "I gratefully accept your gift."

"Excellent." Gunther smiled, taking a brief moment to stroke his fiery red beard. "Now, is there anything else the Iron Kai Empire can help you with before your journey home? Food? Water? Ammunition?"

"No, we're good to go. Thanks for the offer."

"Then I guess this is where we part company." Extending his hand, Gunther gripped Tani's damaged hand and shook it, squeezing tightly. Tani grimaced in pain, feeling that his hand was being crushed. He turned bright red and gasped a bit, smiling through the pain. Releasing his iron grip, Gunther stood at attention and crisply saluted Tani. Hesitantly, the tribal saluted him back.

Smiling once more, Tani bowed to him and turned away. As he was about to exit to the tent, he lingered a brief second, and turned around to wave to Gunther one last time. Gunther waved back and the tribal moved on, looking for his companions.

As he made his way through the camp, every soldier that he passed saluted him crisply. Many others cheered him, shouting war chants as he passed. It was an odd feeling, being a celebrity of sorts, something to which Tani was unaccustomed. As he passed by the ranks of soldiers, he felt a little embarrassed by the ordeal but deep down, he was happy. Deep down, Tani knew that he had made a difference, a real difference in the lives of many. It was a fantastic feeling to know that one's actions had such a positive impact on everyone in the camp. Even though the journey had been difficult, Tani knew that it was worth it. Feeling elated, he would wave back or return the war cries as he passed the soldiers. He had earned a true place in the Darken Realm, and was now a true hero of legend.

Moving to the edge of the camp, the tribal scholar ascended up a small hill on which two solitary people lingered. Mineera and Jared waited patiently, completely silent. Jared was still gripped by his enraged persona and did not even attempt to communicate with Mineera. Mineera was saddened by his sullen attitude. The companions had spent a great many months together and the silence was truly uncomfortable. Mineera was shocked that Jared didn't even want to try to communicate with her. There were so many things that she wanted to say to him, but he would not have it.

Walking in between them, Tani stared at Jared, wanting him to respond. Jared could feel his eyes upon him but failed to look back. He was lost in a dark place and had completely withdrawn not only from Mineera, but from Tani as well.

As Tani took a brief moment to collect his thoughts, a knot formed in the back of his neck. The stress was beginning to take its toll on him, and sorrow washed over him. Tears formed in his eyes as he stood trembling. Mineera, sensing his distress, moved forward to comfort him.

"Tani-" she addressed him with a smile.

Tani, gripped with sadness, could not look back. Avoiding her gaze, he tried to recoil from her. Mineera gently placed her hands on his shoulders, rotating him so that she was looking directly at him. Tani persisted in looking away, a stream of tears rolling down his cheek.

"Tani, look at me," she coaxed him.

"I can't look at you. I don't want to say goodbye. This is really hard for me."

"Look at me."

Finally he looked up and their eyes met. When they did, both Mineera and Tani began to weep. Smiling, they wept tears of joy instead of sorrow.

"I can't believe this is really it. I can't believe that we've reached the end of the road and now we have to say goodbye," Tani said, looking at Mineera.

"It's hard for me, too. You're part of me. I never had a family, but you and Jared are like my family."

Tani smiled at her. "You're like an older sister to me, a *strange* older sister."

"Hey!" she shot back. "Watch it, bookworm."

"Come back with us. You have no home, come back with us," Tani urged her.

"I can't. I'm thankful for the offer but I just can't. I need to find a home on my own. I need to find my place in this new world."

Sighing, Tani was trembling. "I guess this is it then."

Nodding back, Mineera agreed. Looking at each other uncomfortably, they finally yielded to their emotions and embraced, hugging each other tightly. As they did, both of them began to weep once more. Clutching one another for a moment, they prepared to say goodbye, then released each other, their eyes locking for a brief moment.

"I'll miss you," Tani said with a smile.

"I will miss you also."

"One more thing," Tani added, his voice heartfelt.

"What's that?"

"I told you once that there was no God." .

With a look of surprise on her face, she looked at him quizzically.

"*Maybe,* just *maybe*, you're right. *Maybe* there is a God."

Mineera laughed, her face alight. "I told you once that technology is evil. *Maybe,* just *maybe*, you're right. *Maybe* technology will help rebuild this world."

As they smiled at one another once more, Mineera was suddenly aware of Jared lingering just a few paces away, sitting on the ground. She turned to approach him. The tribal warrior failed to acknowledge her presence, purposely ignoring her. He was avoiding his true emotions, preferring to brood in a dark place filled only with death and suffering.

Kneeling down, Mineera looked at him. He still did not respond. Reaching out, she placed her hand on his knee. "Are you in there?" she asked in a soothing tone.

Jared still did not respond, refusing to even look at her.

"I want to say goodbye to you, Jared. I want to tell you how much I care about you. I wanted to tell you how much I admire you, and that I'm glad to have met you." She spoke softly to him, her hand still on his knee.

Jared was like a rock, an emotionless rock. He could hear her voice but his soul was so very far away, still gripped with rage and brooding over Banion's death. He knew that he should respond to her. He knew that this would be the end of their journey together and that soon they would part. Jared knew that he should say goodbye to her but he just couldn't do it. Lost in a haze of darkness, he could not even respond.

"I know that you're in there somewhere," Mineera addressed him again. "Just know that I'll miss you very much. Know that I will always think about you and that you will always be in my heart."

Jared did not respond. Respecting his grief, she looked at him one last time. "Goodbye, Jared of Scarskin. I'll never forget your courage and your peaceful heart."

The mention of his peaceful heart sent a dagger of rage into him. He didn't want peace, not anymore. Jared wanted revenge. Recoiling from her touch, he withdrew even further from her.

Feeling sorrow sting her heart, Mineera retreated back from Jared. She rose to her feet, feeling sad that she could not truly say goodbye to him. Vexed by the exchange, she looked at Tani in concern; he looked back with an equal measure of apprehension.

"Jared," Tani said. "Come on, we're leaving, say goodbye."

Anger flashed through the tribal. "Shut up and leave me alone."

"Don't be like this. Say goodbye," Tani coaxed him.

"No more goodbyes!" Jared shouted. "I'm sick and tired of goodbyes!"

Grabbing his gear, he stormed off, heading toward the open desert, heading toward home.

"Jared!" Tani yelled, but his companion would not listen. "Jared, come back!"

Ignoring him, Jared pushed off quickly, walking briskly away from the war camp.

Seeing him rush off, Tani felt like a wishbone; he wanted to stay and ensure Mineera was taken care of after Jared's rash and rude behavior, but he also needed to be with Jared. Caught in the middle, he was frantic.

"Go to him," Mineera said calmly. "He needs you."

Tani blinked, filled with hesitation. "I'm so sorry," he said.

"Don't be." Mineera smiled. "Go to him, he needs you."

Taking a few shaky steps toward Jared, Tani stopped dead in his tracks, and turned around to rush toward Mineera. Wrapping his arms around her one more time, he gave her another hug. She welcomed the embrace as tears rolled down her cheeks. Finally, Tani released her, speaking to her one last time. "Goodbye, Mineera."

She waved goodbye with her right hand. Her left hand was clutching her quivering lower jaw as she wept.

And so Tani of Scarskin rushed away, moving deeper into the sprawling sands. Catching up to his companion, Tani walked side by side with Jared. Mineera watched them pass into the open desert. She lingered upon the hill until she could no longer see them. As they passed out of view, she said one final goodbye.

Descending the hill, she looked out into the open desert. Tani and Jared were gone, having left her life as quickly as they had entered it. With sadness filling her, she looked down. Tears stung her eyes. The only sign of their passing was a set of tracks fading into the great nothing, through the rolling dunes of endless shifting sand.

Chapter 44
Destiny Beckons Once More

In the few days since the departure of the tribals back to their village of Scarskin, Mineera had been gripped with indecision. She felt somewhat displaced. The majority of the Iron Kai army had left Metalweaver Flats and only a small contingent of engineers remained, still sifting through the ruins of the mighty Biogtech production facility. Gunther's orders were iron clad: destroy the entire metal-works and production facility. He wanted to ensure that future generations would never have to deal with the threat of robotic soldiers. And so his engineers toiled, setting large amounts of explosives, utterly obliterating all computer and production equipment within the facility.

As the soldiers worked, Mineera took time to ponder her situation. Where did she fit into this new world? What fate did Mineera have? Her ruminations had driven her to wander.

Walking amongst the burned-out buildings, Mineera felt a shiver wash over her. The sounds of combat echoed in her soul. Images of dying men filled her mind as she tried to drive away the horrible sensations coursing through her.

The early morning sun cast long shadows amongst the ruins as she wandered. Pulling her blue robes tightly to her body, she rubbed her arms to warm them. Silently she passed through the buildings, feeling ever lonelier as she ventured deeper into the shattered production facility.

Moving to the center of the complex, she stopped dead in her tracks. Ahead of her was *the building*, the very building they had been forced to infiltrate to knock out the Splicer relay. Flashes of recollection filled her as she stared in sorrow. It had only been a few days since the battle, but the memories seemed to have been burned into her consciousness a lifetime ago. As she paused before the building, a chilling blast of wind rolled out of the mountains and passed through the lonely structures. A whistle rose in the air as the wind whipped through the burned-out husks. Shivering in the cold wind, she watched in fascination as the turbid air currents picked up tiny grains of sand. The sand emitted a hissing, rustling noise as the wind battered it. The hair on Mineera's neck stood on end as the cold breeze struck her. In that moment, her feelings stretched outward. Closing her eyes, she felt the warm morning sun on her face and the sting of chilling wind. Smiling, she felt happy to be alive. But the longer she meditated, the more troubled she became.

Something at the edge of her senses seemed out of place. As she focused on the feeling, a sensation of fright passed through her, as if something or someone was watching her. Frantically, her soul and mind tried to focus on the threat. As the panic rose to a peak within her, a loud noise startled her and Mineera opened her eyes.

The sound of a horse neighing loudly brought her back to the conscious world. Stunned by the proximity of the sound, she whirled around and was so startled, she fell backwards, landing on the ground. She pushed herself away to put distance between herself and a host of people who were staring at her with quizzing eyes.

Blinking, she tried to formulate what was happening. Twelve men, all on horseback, had formed a semi-circle around the fallen Mineera. Each man had a serious look upon his face, combining awe and concern. They stared at her and Mineera stared back, both sides unable to speak.

Collecting herself, she rose from the ground to confront the ominous horsemen. As she rose, one of the horses neighed loudly once more, obviously agitated by her presence. Bucking its head several times, it voiced its displeasure with her in ominous fits.

An aged man at the center of the formation dismounted. He was bald, save for long wisps of gray hair that fell away from the back of his head and just above his ears. Moving forward slowly, he stationed himself just a few paces before Mineera. Not knowing what to think, Mineera held her ground and allowed the strange man to speak.

"Do not be alarmed. We mean you no harm. My name is Matthew Moralis." Bowing before her, the Oracle conveyed his deep respect.

"I'm Mineera," she said, some hesitation in her voice.

"Is it really you?" one of the other horsemen asked in a tone of disbelief. "After all of this time, is it really you?"

Unable to respond, Mineera stared back dumbfounded.

"It is her." Matthew Moralis' voice was confident.

Suddenly Mineera felt her stomach lurch. Did the man say his name was *Moralis?* Stunned by the revelation, she felt the hair on the back of her neck begin to rise again. Her pulse quickened as she pondered the strange event unfolding. "Did you say Moralis?" she quizzed the man.

"Yes, my name is Moralis," the aged man confirmed.

"As in Ceibla Moralis?" she verified.

"Yes, Master Ceibla was an ancestor of mine, actually an ancestor of all of us." He held his outstretched hand towards the other horsemen.

"I never imagined that there were survivors." She shook her head in amazement.

"Oh my, yes, there were many survivors of the lost Reaper Kai tribe." He smiled back at her.

"I don't understand," Mineera said with a look of confusion. "Why are you here?"

"We came to this place looking for you."

"Me?" She was shocked once more. "Why would you all be trying to find me?"

"The ghost brought all of us to you. We are to fight by your side in the final battle," the Oracle of Saints explained to Mineera in a confident tone.

"Final battle?" Mineera laughed dryly. "You missed it. Look around you, the war is over."

The Oracles simply looked at each other, appearing to question her words. Their confidence was so strong, Mineera felt somewhat foolish. What did they know that she didn't?

"We were called to you, for the final battle against the darkness. You are to lead us to victory over evil," the Oracle of Valor added, confirming the strange tale.

"But… there are no more enemies…" She felt a crisp sprig of terror erupt from her heart. The feeling was growing quickly, filling her with wavering dread.

"The great beast, the creature born from hell itself, we are to slay it," the Oracle of Heaven contributed.

"Creature?" Mineera echoed, and suddenly the cause of her terror was revealed. A flash of memory filled her. Thinking back to Rasheed, an ominous feeling came over her. A vision of darkness filled her…

*   *   *

The demon was taller than a two-story building and thicker than a bus. Sick green bloated flesh covered its body. At uneven intervals were human faces, screaming and moaning in terror, rising from the beast's sickly skin. For each victim who had been eaten became part of the demon's flesh. The faces of hundreds dotted the belly of the monster. Each was twisted and contorted, and had seen hundreds of years of torment being trapped within the body of the monster. In its right hand, the Abomination carried a mighty black steel cudgel drenched in gore. Its head was grotesque and distorted. A set of yellow, demonic eyes scanned the helpless soldiers. Black teeth smeared with blood and a tongue coated in human flesh topped off its grisly appearance.

The monster strode forth and brought its weapon to bear on the soldiers. None were able to see the monster, but all could feel its presence. Many of the soldiers crawled across the ground in random directions in a desperate attempt to escape. The demon smiled and smashed the helpless soldiers with its mighty weapon. The blade was dull, but smashed the troops into piles of pulp. The beast slowly worked his way across the square, squashing and crushing all he saw.

The soldiers could not look upon the beast, and the sounds of the dying were too much to handle. Many of them fled, while others fired randomly about like blind men, hoping to kill the beast.

With glee it moved. Every once in a while, the demon would grip a soldier and eat him alive. Within seconds after the remnants of the soldier slid down its throat, another new tormented face appeared on the belly of the beast. With each meal it consumed, the Abomination grew slightly larger and hungrier.

Mineera knew she could not face such a creature alone.

"*Flee, Mineera. This is not your day to slay this beast,*" a voice spoke softly in her mind...

                              *   *   *

As she emerged from the strange vision, the feeling of dread in her heart was fully realized. Shaking her head, Mineera could not believe that she could have been so foolish. The Abomination, a creature born from true darkness, had not been killed during the battle of Metalweaver Flats. Even more ominous was the fact that this demonic creature was not even present during the battle. She wondered *where* this evil monster had been hiding.

Finally understanding the threat, she looked at the twelve Oracles before her with renewed interest.

"You will help me kill this beast, then?"

Nodding in agreement, the twelve Oracles confirmed her conclusion. "We are here to serve you, my lady," Matthew Moralis said.

The gravity of the situation was sinking in slowly. Mineera's destiny was far from over. Having found purpose once more made her feel that she truly belonged in the world. Determined to see the gruesome task of slaying the demon through to the end, Mineera prepared herself mentally for one last challenge, one last fight.

"We should set out at once then." Mineera spoke in a confident tone, taking up the mantle of leadership quickly.

"We await your command, my lady. We will follow you."

Standing still, Mineera felt somewhat foolish. She had no idea where to begin to track the monster they sought. Dumbfounded by such responsibility, she confided honestly to her new companions, "I know not where to look."

"We are to follow our dreams."

"Our dreams? I haven't seen such things in my dreams," Mineera said.

"I have," the Oracle of Temperance said. "In my visions, I see the creature slaughtering villagers, high atop a mesa."

"A mesa?" Mineera was in shock.

"Yes, I have seen such things also. There is a primitive, tribal village, protected and sitting atop a giant mesa. The beast is killing at will, slaughtering the defenseless inhabitants."

"That cannot be!" Mineera yelled in shock.

"I am afraid it is, my lady. The divine spirit instructed us that you would lead us to this place."

Looking out into the desert, a chill rolled down her spine. A village atop a mesa being attacked by the Abomination; the vision hit close to home. Frantically, her mind was screaming. The tribals had left several days ago, heading out into open desert.

"Jared! Tani!" Mineera gasped in horror. "This cannot be!"

"You know the village that we seek?"

"Yes..." Mineera shook her head in dismay. "Vertigo must have ordered the destruction of Scarskin before his death, some sort of blood vengeance against the tribals."

"Then lead us to this place. We'll set things right."

"It's not that simple. The village of Scarskin is in the middle of the great wastes, beyond the burning deserts. No one but my former companions knows the way to Scarskin. They left days ago."

"Perhaps their trail is still there? Perhaps their footprints still remain in the shifting sands?"

Frantic, Mineera made haste. Giving orders, the Prophet of Gogoli prepared for the final battle. She rushed back to the camp and grabbed her belongings. When the company scoured the desert sands, the trail left by Tani and Jared was still visible. Rushing off in the tribals' wake, Mineera and the twelve Oracles tracked the vague trail deep into the burning wasteland. Mineera said a silent prayer, wondering with growing dismay if they would ever be able to find the tribals before the terrible monster known as the Abomination attacked the peaceful village of Scarskin.

Chapter 45
The Long Road Home

Tani's eyes were closed. Pulling his knees to his chest, he let the coming darkness wash over him as a chill wind broke across the dunes of endless sand. The wind rose in intensity as the sun pushed beyond the western horizon, an event that had been occurring since before recorded time.

Basking in the solace of his existence, Tani let his surroundings overtake him. His skin prickled in the chilling wind. In his ears, a hiss erupted as the winds battered the sand, picking up small grains, forming new dunes as old ones were withered to nothingness. His palate was dry and his tongue was stuck to the roof of his mouth. Opening his eyes, Tani let the wonders of the world overtake him.

The tribals had stopped their journey for the night upon the ridge of a tall sand dune. Looking westward, Tani saw a broken string of clouds dotting the horizon. Each cloud was lit with the brilliant colors of the setting sun. Fiery orange splashes of color were intermixed with somber purple hues.

He sat in utter silence for many moments, letting the fatigue of not only the day, but their entire journey sink into his weary consciousness. It had been three weeks since the battle of Metalweaver Flats and the tribals had been steadily pushing toward home, traversing the desert in an attempt to find their village of Scarskin, hidden somewhere in the great wastelands. To the east of their position, the moon was rising. Blinking at its eerie wonder,

Tani felt a chill run through him and sighed, barely stirring as the natural event unfolded.

Jared was also aware of the great milestone that was heralded by the rising of the moon. Resting near his friend, Jared was tense. Gripping his knees tightly, the tribal warrior pressed hard, so hard that pain flared in his legs. He continued to push, grimacing in pain but refusing to let go. In a strange way, he wanted to feel physical pain, for when his body was tortured, it seemed to remove some of his mental anguish.

The journey home was not a pleasant one for Jared. He was gripped with a deepening sense of rage that grew with the passing of each day. As this anger grew inside of him, the semblance of his former personality seemed to wither. He was sullen and withdrawn, seeking to ignore any conversation with the tribal scholar. Each passing day led the youth into a strange world, a world filled with dark fantasy.

Banion's death had polarized the youth into a hate-obsessed vision of madness. He had a deep emotional need to punish the enemy, but felt cheated. The Reaper Kai order had been crushed and the war had drawn to a close. Knowing that no more enemies remained filled Jared with a deeper sense of hurt. He imagined killing his enemies over and over again in his mind. He fantasized about brutalizing them in an attempt to get even with them. But each fantasy left the youth feeling more drained and angrier. The more time he spent thinking about revenge, the emptier he felt, causing the process to repeat itself. The cycle was purely destructive and Jared was sinking into a pit of despair.

The situation was so bad that Jared had not spoken a single word in over two days. On several occasions, Tani had directly spoken to him, but Jared would simply continue to move forward, pressing on without a response. It wasn't that Jared was ignoring Tani; it was that he could not hear him, or anything else, for that matter. The tribal warrior was so lost in a daze of hatred that nothing seemed to awaken his senses. He simply plodded onward like a zombie.

The natural event unfolding was something to be cherished, as it marked the end of the road for the tribals. Normally, the rising of a full moon was marked with a celebration. Over the course of their journeys, each full moon was usually a festivity, a time to reflect on the long road that they had walked. But on this night, the rising of the full moon set a somber tone.

Breathing in heavily, Tani let out a loud sigh. As the sun passed beyond the western horizon, the moon made its appearance. A small crescent of holy light emerged from the darkness. Rising over the edge of the earth, its form acted as a beacon of hope, pushing away the total darkness of the night.

Tani nudged Jared. Blinking with a distant look on his face, Jared acknowledged the event and stared at the white orb of light rising in the distance.

Many moments passed and the full form of the moon was revealed, shining over the wasteland, bathing the earth in a warm glow.

"Nineteen moons," Tani whispered. The tribals were now only a month away from the end of their Exile, an inconceivable journey that had begun so long ago. It was a strange milestone. The next full moon that rose would end the Exile and allow Jared and Tani to return home to their village of Scarskin. Returning from the Exile would allow them to become adults and join Scarskin society as full members. It was an honored tradition that now, from his new perspective, almost seemed comical.

Thinking about such an idea and the stress of recent events sent Tani into utter hysteria. He laughed wildly, his belly taking the brunt of the comical fit. Nothing was amusing about the stress that Tani felt, but laughing was a solid way for him to blow off some steam. For many moments he chortled, until he could breathe no longer. As he recovered his senses, his breathing returned to normal.

"What the hell happened to us?" Tani shook his head, speaking aloud but knowing full well that Jared would not respond. In the end, it didn't really matter if Jared responded. Tani was speaking to quell the demons in his own mind. It didn't seem to matter if the crazed tribal warrior took any part in the conversation. "What the hell did we do over the last nineteen months?"

Laughing again, he shook his head and watched the full moon with a mild bout of anger filling him.

"So much death…" Tani whispered, and his mood began to plunge into darkness. A chilling resentment began to take shape in his mind. Thinking about the Exile made Tani feel angry. Wildly, he shouted out, "We were supposed to learn about life and become adults! I never wanted any of this! Damn it, I never wanted any of this."

Jared heard his words but simply stared at the full moon with a blank expression. He was lost in his own thoughts and did not care to surrender any part of his own self pity to aid his friend in an emotional time of need.

"Twenty moons… is that how long it takes to figure out life and become an adult?" Tani began to laugh again wildly. The idea was totally ridiculous to him. Putting a timeline on growing into an adult was outlandish. "I've seen more in this short period of time than most see in an entire lifetime. I've experienced things that no one should endure. But if we return home before the rising of the twentieth moon, we're cowards…" Still laughing, Tani rolled onto his back, staring into the starry sky above him.

As the rattle from his manic fit died down, his thoughts began to settle. Looking at the night sky seemed to fill Tani with a mild amount of peace. His breathing became more regular.

"Do you ever wonder what would have happened to this world if we would have traveled any direction but east from our village?" Tani spoke out loud again. Jared blinked several times; this time, he heard the question. The tribal warrior pondered the solution but chose not to share it. Tani kept going, conducting a private conversation with himself.

"We could have done hundreds of things. We could have traveled north and spent a peaceful Exile in the Primal Lands, working on a farm, tending sheep. But no! We had to travel east, something that had never been done before! We could have spent a lazy Exile. But no! Our actions led us into the bloodiest conflict that has ever occurred on this continent. We were directly responsible for the destruction and mass murder of an entire race of people. But if we return home before the twentieth moon rises, we're cowards, we're nothing, considered children who still need additional life lessons. I've had *too many* life lessons!

"Do they even know what we've lived through? Do the village elders even comprehend the suffering and hardships that we've endured? And yet they can judge us as cowards if we return home before the end of the Exile." Shaking his head, Tani felt better. Venting out loud had allowed him to release pent-up anger.

"What do you think, Jared? Oh wait, I forgot my best friend is a mute now." Tani's tone was sarcastic.

Mimicking Jared's voice, Tani responded for him. "I feel just like you do, Tani. I wish that things would have been different."

Suddenly, Jared turned to Tani, his tone direct. "I don't wish things would have been different. I'm glad we did what we did. Someone needed to step up and we did. I don't give a damn what anyone thinks about us back home. They'll never know the hardships we had to endure. I don't care if they ever understand us."

Tani felt relieved that Jared had finally spoken. It had been a long time since he had heard his friend's voice.

"No regrets?" Tani asked, inquisitive.

It took a moment for Jared to respond. "Just one regret. I wish that I would have killed more of them when I had the chance. I wish that I could have seen more of the Reaper Kai suffer. I wish I could have made them hurt as bad as the suffering that they caused others. I feel cheated. I'll never be able to make them suffer."

The statement was dark, filled with intense malice. Hearing such words made Tani shiver. While only a few minutes ago Tani would have given anything to have a conversation with Jared, Jared's dark speech had changed things. Hearing such malice drove Tani into seclusion. The sentiment was so ominous and evil that Tani could not participate in it. Retreating back into his own world, he fell silent.

"You don't want to talk anymore?" Jared's tone was sinister.

"No, I'm done," Tani responded.

"Good," Jared shot back.

An eerie silence settled between the two friends. Laying out their sleeping mats, they fell asleep under the light of the full moon.

For Jared and Tani, the hardest part of their journey still lay ahead. The voyage back to Scarskin was nearing an end but it was still a long road home, not physically but emotionally. The scars from their journey had formed in a short amount of time, but it would take a lifetime to heal such wounds.

Chapter 46
A Horrible Truth

Jared was crouched on the ground. In his right hand, he clutched his submachine gun, pressing the stock of the weapon against his chest. His left hand was probing the ground in front of him as his eyes nervously shifted back and forth. Tani was a few paces back, weapon ready, having taken cover behind a fallen log.

Breathing heavily, Jared felt a thin line of sweat cover his brow. The pressure and anxiety were building as his hand continued to fumble on the ground. Finally his fingers came in contact with a small cylindrical object resting in the sand. The object was hot to the touch, having been heated by the burning sun. Closing his fingers around it, Jared lifted it so that he could view it properly.

When he glanced down quickly, his worst fears were confirmed. Jared was stunned, the image burning into his mind and sending a shiver down his spine. With a sigh, he whispered to his friend, who was just a few paces back.

"It's a shell casing all right." Jared's voice was nervous. Grasping his gun with both hands, he crept forward, prepared to kill anything hostile that greeted him. He moved quickly, poised to breach the perimeter of the oasis.

Tani was on his heals. Deftly, he charged, catching up with Jared. The two tribals took refuge in a thick green stand of leafy plants. They moved inside the foliage silently, taking cover. Crawling on their bellies, they continued their scouting mission. It took them a few moments to secretly press on into the interior of the oasis, completely concealed within the densely packed plants.

When they finally reached the interior, both their hearts leapt in sheer fright. They were so shocked by the sight ahead of them that they both gasped.

In the center of the oasis stood a large white tent. The light breeze blowing out of the desert moved the flap on the front of the tent back and forth, causing a metal clasp on the flap to rattle against one of the iron posts that supported it. Just above the rattling clasp, a bright red stain, a splatter of blood, marked the tent flap.

The adrenaline hit their systems immediately. For many moments they lingered, concealed within the foliage. Looking at each other in sheer amazement, they both felt as if they had been punched in the stomach. They maintained their covert positions, still reeling from the ominous image of the blood-stained tent, and surveyed the rest of the scene.

A pile of shell casings littered the ground only a few feet from their position. Both tribals saw it immediately. The high number of casings in such a small area meant only one thing. "Automatic weapons," Tani whispered. Jared confirmed his conclusion with a nod.

This new revelation was chilling. During their first crossing out of the great wastelands, they had been surprised to encounter simple weapons such as handguns. But it had taken the tribals many moons to encounter such things as automatic weapons. It appeared that since their departure from the wastelands, things had changed dramatically. Piles of shell casings littered the ground around the abandoned tent. The horror that had initially breached their senses turned to intrigue. Wanting to understand the mystery, the tribals decided to investigate further.

They left the safety and sanctuary of the dense foliage and began to further examine their surroundings. Moving forward, they swept the oasis for signs of life. As they pressed beyond the tent, the scene became more disturbing.

Near a grove of prickly desert trees, the remnants of a bloody massacre were revealed to their eyes. White-garbed desert nomads, the same nomads whom the tribals had encountered on their initial journey through the wastelands, were scattered throughout the area. Their bright white clothes were stained with blood and their bodies were riddled with bullet holes. A thick rotting stench engulfed the area as the spoiled corpses decomposed in the harsh desert sun. The air was filled with a sickly buzzing sound as the bodies were covered in a thick layer of flies and maggots. Reeling from the scene, the tribals held their ground at the perimeter of the massacre. Neither Tani nor Jared was eager to investigate the site further but they felt a certain duty to uncover why their former friends had been so recklessly slaughtered.

Shaking his head in disgust, Tani spoke in a whisper while continually panning his weapon around the area, ready to open fire on any real or perceived threat. "What the hell happened?"

"Automatic weapons, here in the wastelands?" Jared whispered back. "Things have changed since our absence."

"What is that?" Tani suddenly pointed at a fallen log near the edge of the area where the bodies were spread out. Blinking, Jared looked and was also confused by what he saw. A nomad spear was sticking straight up in the air. The point of the weapon was embedded in *something*, some sort of object on the other side of a fallen log. As they rushed quickly to the fallen log, their blood ran cold.

The sight revealed behind the fallen log was an ominous one. The answer to all their questions was lying dead on the ground, impaled by the primitive weapon. The spear was embedded within the chest of a sickly white form. Plastic and high-tech resin covered the chest of the dead monster. Motor oil and hydraulic fluid had pooled around the wound where the spear had pierced a thick metal chest plate. The body was half covered in sand but the tribals knew all too well what lay before them. The remains of a Biogtech confronted their shocked eyes.

Staggering back from the sight, Tani was lost in a trance. He stumbled through the oasis, tripping and falling over one of the corpses of the slain nomads. He crumpled, hitting the sand near one of the bodies as the flies rumbled and took flight.

A swarm of flies circulated around Tani as he stared at the desiccated corpse rotting in the blazing sun. The smell of death wafted through his nostrils as he batted away the angry swarm. The situation was too much for the tribal. The anxiety and sensations coursing through his mind roared, uncontainable. With his stomach constricting, he felt the vomit rise in his throat. Bending over, he began to retch violently, throwing up all over the ground.

The thought of Biogtechs in the wasteland and the dead bodies all around him had conjured horrid memories, memories of war and violence. The proximity of the Biogtechs to their village of Scarskin was too much for Tani to bear. Violent emotions began to course through him as his thoughts turned to his family and friends back home. He was lost in a daze, drool mixed with vomit trickling out of his mouth.

"This isn't fair!" Tani grumbled in a frantic tone. "The war is over! We killed them all! I can't believe this. After everything we've done, everything we've endured, it *still* isn't over!"

"It will never be over..." Jared said. As he looked at the dead Biogtech, he should have felt disgusted, but he didn't. Jared should have been afraid of what he saw but instead, he was elated. The simmering rage in his heart began to bubble to the surface. All he wanted was revenge. He had once thought that his quest for vengeance would never be realized. Seeing the dead Biogtech made him feel that his desires would be fulfilled, after all. If there were Biogtechs, there were Reaper Kai. Instinctively, his hand closed around the raven totem at his neck. The image of Banion's bloody chest flashed into his mind. He could still see his beloved mentor bleeding to death. As the images filled his mind, his body was taut and tense. Fury was building inside his heart. Dark fantasies were taking shape. Images of butchery filled his mind as he envisioned slaying the Reaper Kai, pummeling them repeatedly with his bloody sword.

"What are we going to do?" Tani whined in a defeated tone.

Jared did not respond. A wicked smile had overtaken him. Staring at the dead Biogtech, Jared was thankful that there were more enemies to kill. His sense of bloodlust had not been diminished over the long weeks since Banion's death. Jared hungered for slaughter and death; his dark desires would soon be realized.

"Jared?" Tani called, watching his friend fondle the sinister raven totem.

Shaking his head in disbelief, Tani was shocked to find Jared completely unaware of his surroundings. Suddenly, a noise at the edge of Tani's hearing piqued his interest. For a brief second, he thought he heard a voice in the distance. Retreating from the buzzing swarm of flies, he moved next to his friend. Holding his breath, he listened to his surroundings intently.

His concern was confirmed. Another voice sounded in the distance. Wiping the drool and vomit from his chin, Tani grabbed Jared. The tribal warrior did not respond, still lost in a sinister daydream.

"We're not alone!" Tani said frantically to his befuddled companion.

Jared did not respond.

"Move it!" Tani pulled at him and finally, Jared returned to his senses.

"What?"

"Voices!" Tani pointed to the far side of the oasis. "I heard voices in the clearing. We're not alone."

Snapping back to alertness, Jared nodded in acknowledgment. Taking refuge in the foliage once more, the tribals hid and prepared themselves for possible conflict.

Many moments passed and the sound of human voices lingered in the distance, just at the far side of the oasis. Jared and Tani were completely silent, crouched with guns ready. Although prepared to engage in battle, they were both cautious, especially after having just discovered a destroyed Biogtech in the oasis.

The voices grew in intensity and soon the sounds of dozens and dozens of human voices were echoing around them. Concealed near the site of the massacre, the tribals lingered for many moments, wary of revealing themselves to a possible threat.

Finally a group of over a dozen nomad warriors pressed out of the foliage on the far side of the clearing. They were wearing flowing white robes, and dark-skinned faces kissed by the sun peeked out of intricate headdresses. Each warrior carried a long spear and most were chattering away in a foreign tongue. As the warriors explored the clearing, they quickly came upon the bloody scene. They yelled out excitedly, and soon the entire clearing was overrun. Nearly 50 nomad warriors charged to view the aftermath of the massacre.

The warriors were shouting, obviously angered. It took only a few moments for the nomad chief to arrive on the scene. He was dressed in fine blue and white robes, and brandishing a pistol. Following him was a petite woman garbed in a white blouse with a blue skirt, with an assortment of scroll cases hanging from her belt. Timidly she arrived at the clearing and stared in horror at the dead nomads littering the middle of the oasis.

As Tani and Jared caught sight of the nomad chief and the scribe, they were instantly set at ease. During their initial journey out of the wastelands, they had encountered the nomad tribe and had traveled for many weeks with them. During this time, the tribals had even learned how to crudely speak and understand their language. Wanting to greet old friends, Tani and Jared decided to reveal themselves.

Their emergence from the foliage startled the nomad warriors. Immediately, several warriors raised their spears to challenge the tribals who had risen from the lush green foliage like expert magicians emerging out of thin air.

Seeing their distress, Tani knew that he needed to communicate with them quickly, and called out to them in their native tongue. "We mean you no harm."

Relaxing their aggressive postures, the nomad warriors recognized the two tribals.

Blinking in amazement, the nomad chieftain approached hesitantly. The tribals were known to him but they were different from the last time he had encountered them. An air of confidence surrounded them and their bodies were marked with scars from past conflicts. Instead of two starry-eyed tribals from the wasteland, Jared and Tani were battle-hardened warriors who had more mileage than most people four times their age.

Regarding them with a look of wonder, the chief greeted them as he would one of his own family members. "It has been many moons, Prince Jared and Scribe Tani, since we have been in each other's company. I am happy that we have crossed paths once more."

"It fills our heart with joy to be in your presence once more." Tani bowed before the chieftain. "I only wish that our meeting was heralded by peace and not the bitter sting of war." Tani regarded the dead in the clearing as he spoke.

"We have just arrived in this oasis to meet with part of our tribe. I am frightened by this slaughter. We lost many loved ones. I am confused by what we found in the clearing, a creature made of metal that bleeds oil."

"Much has changed in this world since our last meeting." Jared's tone was ominous. "I think we need to spend some time telling you a story."

Nodding in agreement, the chieftain urged the tribals to follow. They moved to the edge of the oasis, making camp as the warriors buried the dead. As night set over the wasteland, Tani and Jared spent the entire evening spinning a fantastic tale about demons and machines, heroes and tyrants, life and death.

Chapter 47
Scent of Death

An inhuman scream echoed through the labyrinth of stone. The piercing wail was so intense, so frightening, that the nomad scout trembled, clutching his spear with white knuckles. Taking several steps back, he frantically scanned the stone passage, hoping to catch sight of the mutant menace.

The tall sandstone towers of rock around the scout were concealing a creature born from the nightmares of the apocalypse. As the scout tried to maintain his composure, a second scream tore through the air, sending him into a terrified state. Breathing heavily, he looked around and found himself completely alone. All around him, passages snaked off in different directions, fractures in the enormous rocks lined with sand from the desert.

Panic had set in. Whirling around, the scout tried to escape the stone maze forged by the desert. He rushed back into the network of passages, sweat forming around his white headdress while beads of moisture rolled down his cheeks. As he began to move faster, the frequency of the screams increased dramatically. Unbeknownst the scout, he was being stalked through the passages. A creature, a cunning and sinister monster, had made this network of stone passages its home. The monster knew the exact location of every twist and turn. All it would take was a single mistake by the stupid human for it to get stuck in one of the dead ends. Hungering for soft flesh, the monster rushed onward, its inhuman cries driving a wedge of terror into the nomad scout.

As the screams roared and echoed through the rock spires and fractured stone, other monsters took notice, drawn to the scene by the noise of the hunt. More screams erupted all around the scout. He was now outnumbered, with multiple mutant terrors hungering for the kill.

The panic turned to absolute terror. Rushing blindly through the stone passages, the scout felt that his minutes were numbered. He could barely think, overwhelmed by primal instinct. Driven by a need to survive, he stumbled around a corner and almost dropped dead from fright. *Something* was around the corner. The nomad had no time to think and was so terrified that he tripped and collapsed onto the sand. Whimpering, he shot backwards, away from the object, in a crude attempt to escape. When the nomad scout finally collected himself and his thoughts, he found that the *thing* with which he had nearly collided was no creature.

The relieved scout was elated to find Tani standing at the junction in the rock passageway. Tani had become concerned when the scout had not returned from what should have been a brief scouting mission of the badland rock spires. As the minutes passed by, the sounds of mutant Malg screaming amongst the rock spires was all that Tani needed to grab his submachine gun and search for the waylaid scout. After a few minutes of searching, Tani located the terrified scout, and none too soon.

The tribal stood calmly listening to the sounds of the screaming creatures as the calls got ever closer.

"We need to get out of here!" the scout called out frantically.

Tani simply stood still. He clicked off the safety on his submachine gun, blinking several times, thinking about his next course of action. Breathing calmly, he listened to the echoes and prepared himself for the coming conflict.

"What are you doing?" the scout asked, tottering on the edge of his own sanity. "We can still escape!"

"We're completely surrounded." Tani spoke with perfect clarity. "We'll make our stand here."

As he spoke, another piercing scream broke the air. The sound was so close, the hair on the back of the scout's neck stood straight up. Trembling violently, he held out his spear and backed up against the rock face.

In all the chaos, the tribal scholar stood resolute, without a hint of fear. His experiences had driven the terror from him. For Tani, it was just another day in his life. He pressed the stock of the weapon against his shoulder, finding a solid firing position.

Rounding the rock corner, one of the mutant Malg finally revealed itself. The creature was much taller than a human, standing at about eight feet tall. It had a stocky form, covered in putrid white folds of flesh. The creature's skin seemed almost transparent in spots, revealing sickly yellow globs of fat just beneath it. Reminiscent of sausage, the fat appeared ready to burst forth from underneath the thin membrane. One of the creature's arms had a grotesque black nodule underneath the skin, a fatty tumor the size of an apple.

As it caught sight of Tani and the nomad scout, the Malg emitted another wild scream, spewing pus mixed with a thick green mucous from its open mouth. The pus rolled down the beast's chin and landed on its bloated chest.

The monster sized up its next meal, hungry and excited to feed. Its head turned to consider the duo. Only one functional eye looked outward; the other was completely engulfed by another fatty tumor. The black tumor had swollen the creature's eye shut long ago, and the tissue had stretched over part of the Malg's forehead.

The monster was about twenty yards away. As it stood near the junction of rock, Tani wasted no time. Wanting a better firing position, he took several steps toward the beast. The Malg was stunned by the advancing tribal's brash, aggressive action, unaccustomed to such behavior. Screaming, the Malg tried to frighten Tani, to no avail. Tani didn't even blink and continued to bear down on the monster. Finally the tribal was in perfect firing range for his weapon. Steadying the submachine gun, he prepared to open fire, staring down the weapon's barrel.

The monster looked at Tani and took a step backwards. Crouching down, it submissively decreased its size, instinct instructing it to try and appear less aggressive. The creature felt uneasy. Carefully it sniffed the air, trying to catch Tani's scent. As it did, the Malg emitted a soft cry, almost a whimper. Sensing that the beast did not like his smell, Tani moved forward aggressively, his weapon ready to kill the beast in a split second. With his trigger finger firmly in place to make the shot, Tani knew that the beast was panicked.

As Tani drew closer to the Malg, his scent filled the beast's nostrils. What the monster smelled was death. The tribal had much experience killing, and the monster knew it. It could also sense his confidence. There was not a single hint of fear in Tani and this made the Malg extremely nervous. One of the creature's hunting tactics was to terrify its victims, but such tactics were useless with the tribal, who was clearly not an easy meal. The Malg wondered if its life was about to end. Staring directly into Tani's eyes, the Malg cooed submissively, crouching low on the ground, almost whimpering. It could not maintain eye contact with Tani and averted its gaze, shifting around nervously on the ground, backing away without looking at him.

The monster's submissive coos echoed through the canyon. All around them, similar noises were emitted, and it was clear that all of the mutant monsters in the area had gotten the message and were retreating.

The Malg finally turned around and stood up. As it fled from Tani's presence, the mutant would occasionally glance back, fearful that Tani was giving chase. The tribal let the monster go.

After witnessing such an amazing scene, the nomad scout was grateful to be alive and thanked Tani many times. Tani simply nodded and gave out a loud sigh. Nodding in reassurance, he said, "Everything is all right. Let's get back to the others."

Moving away, the duo passed through the labyrinth of stone towers. As they traveled, Tani began to speak in a low tone, still holding his submachine gun ready. "My people call this place the Badland Rock Spires. It is the furthest eastern edge of our domain. To my people, this is the end of the earth, a place haunted by all those youths exiled into the wastelands who never return."

"It is a frightening place," the nomad scout concluded, still rattled from the encounter with the mutant.

"It is said that when the wind blows through the rock passages and tunnels, you can hear the dead whispering, calling out from the void and darkness of death and the great beyond."

"Do you believe such stories?" the scout quizzed him in a nervous tone.

Smiling, Tani responded immediately. "I'm a man of science. Such things don't make any sense and have no scientific backing."

"So you don't believe the stories then?" the scout asked as a calm came over him. The thought of being in a haunted place had made him nervous.

"Oh, I didn't say that. I can't explain the voices and whispers scientifically, but I can tell you, I have heard voices in the wind, whispers from the darkness, pleas for help. The stories of this place are real. It is cursed by the dead and they will forever be trapped here, calling to hapless travelers, urging them for help that will never come." Tani's tone was eerie.

As the words left his mouth, the look on the scout's face became solemn. A chill shot down his spine and he looked around uneasily. "Let's get out of here," he said nervously.

"Good idea." Tani smiled once more.

Passing out of the interior of the Badland Rock Spires, Tani and the nomad scout moved to the eastern edge of the rock formations. As they lingered near the edge of the open desert, they both scanned the area and caught sight of Jared and another nomad scout.

Jared was motioning to both of them as he moved to greet them. "What was with all of the screams?" he quizzed them.

"Malg," Tani supplied.

"I didn't hear any gunfire," Jared said to his friend, mystified.

"I *encouraged* the Malg to leave."

"Encouraged?"

"It didn't like how I smelled." Tani smiled.

"I don't like how you smell either," Jared responded. A serious look then covered his face. Thinking about the more important issue at hand, the tribal warrior resumed speaking, his tone ominous. "You're not going to like this."

"Not going to like what?" Tani asked, concerned.

"Come on, I'll show you." Jared motioned the rest of the team to follow.

A gentle rock formation stood just to the north of the scouting team. Ascending the slope, the four traveled up the rock face, gaining height quickly. After a short climb, the team was standing atop a massive stone outcropping. From their position, they had an excellent view of the eastern wasteland, but their view of the western expanses was blocked by the maze of rocks and stone spires.

Motioning to the team, Jared pointed at a rock spire atop the rock face. He climbed up the steep outcropping, with the rest of the team following. After several minutes of tough clambering, the team reached the top of the stone spire. From their new vantage point, they were able to see the western wastelands beyond the Badland Rock Spires.

It took only a few seconds for shock to set in. To the west of the spires, in the heart of the wasteland only a half day's travel ahead of them, was a sprawling camp. Blinking in concern, the team members looked at each other in fright.

"What is that?" one of the nomad scouts asked, frightened.

"It's an army encampment," Tani replied, shaking his head in dismay.

"An army?" the other scout asked. "An army of what?"

"An army of robots just like the one we found in the oasis. And by the looks of things, there are about 1,000 Biogtechs down there. And where there are Biogtechs, there are Reaper Kai." Jared's tone was dark.

"I can't believe this," Tani said angrily. "After everything we've done and fought for, the enemy still lives and our home is now in harm's way."

"One thousand soldiers? One thousand soldiers armed with guns?" a nomad scout repeated in dismay. "We want to lend aid but we can only muster about 200 warriors. And with our warriors armed only with spears, we stand little chance against such numbers."

"We need more men. We need more firepower," Jared said.

"Yeah, we do," Tani agreed, his gaze distant. As he blinked, clarity finally coursed through the tribal. Wild excitement erupted from him. Tani had an idea. "We need help!" he said excitedly. "And I know just where to get it!"

"What are you talking about?" Jared's voice was dismissive. "Have you lost your mind?"

"No, I haven't lost my mind," Tani replied as he crouched down, fumbling through his backpack frantically. "Remember the radio?"

"What radio?" Jared sounded moody and out of sorts.

"Gunther's radio," Tani said triumphantly, producing the device from his pack.

"That's real nice, Tani, but the enemy is only five days from Scarskin. It would take months for the Iron Kai to get an army here. That radio is useless."

"No it's not…" Tani responded with a twinkle in his eye. "I've got a plan."

"Oh, great." Jared shook his head while rolling his eyes. "Tani's got a *plan*."

Turning to the scouts, Tani addressed them excitedly. "Can you get word to the nomad encampment and call for aid?"

"Yes, but the enemy is too strong in number."

"Let me worry about that. Just get word to the nomad camp and get as many warriors back here as soon as possible."

The scouts nodded in agreement, prepared to help. Having such a strong enemy presence in the region endangered everyone in the wasteland, not just Scarskin. The last remaining Reaper Kai army on earth was still a massive threat to all.

"It's not going to work," Jared said in dismay.

"That army is five days from Scarskin, Jared. Do you know what happens in five days?"

Nodding, Jared knew all too well what would happen in five days. The rising of the twentieth full moon would occur. For the tribals, it would mark the end of their Exile from Scarskin.

"Do you think it's a coincidence that the end of our Exile will occur the same day Scarskin is invaded? There's something more to all of this," Tani said, his mind surging wildly as he thought about the strange convergence of events.

"When did you come to rely on blind faith?" Jared chuckled as if his friend was a fool.

"Mineera taught me that." Tani smiled back. "Mineera taught me to believe in things greater than myself. This plan will work. It *has* to work."

And so the tribals from Scarskin stood atop a rocky spire, staring down into the desert at the last Reaper Kai army on earth.

With hope fading for the village of Scarskin, the tribals braced for the coming conflict. As the nomads pushed away from the Badland Rock Spires to muster their warriors, Tani grasped the radio in his hands. With wild trepidation, he turned on the device. The radio crackled to life and a voice responded on the other side, half a continent away. The gears of war were about to roar to life once more, spinning and grinding, consuming the living in a fury of deathly hunger.

Chapter 48
The Final Call to Duty

Emperor Gunther had a strained look on his face, his jaw clenched. He was standing in the center of the remains of the military camp which had been left behind to explore the ruins of Metalweaver Flats. Shaking his head, Gunther was mumbling under his breath while holding a radio transmitter.

"What's going on?" Mad Dog Maddock asked with a look of concern on his face.

At first, Gunther did not respond; instead, he simply stared off into the desert with a distant look. After several strained minutes, he turned to Maddock with a look of utter defeat upon his face.

"The most bitter of enemies cannot be defeated by a single action. The toughest of enemies must be vanquished by utter persistence and an unwavering, indomitable will," Gunther declared.

His words resonated through Maddock's ears, making him feel as if his stomach had leaped into his throat. "The war is over," he said, voice wavering.

"No, it's not." As Gunther spoke, a chill rolled down Maddock's spine.

"This cannot be!" He was jolted by the reality of the situation while vague details began to play upon his mind as his creativity started to spin fanciful tales of dread.

"A war band of about 1,000 Biogtechs, led by a Reaper Kai raiding party, survived the war. They had orders to destroy the village of Scarskin."

"Scarskin?   The village of the tribals from Nova 7?" Maddock said in alarm.

"Yes, Jared and Tani's village," Gunther confirmed.

"What are they going to do?"

"It's not a matter of what *they* are going to do. It's a matter of what *we* are going to do."

"I don't understand."

"Tani and Jared have paid a debt of service to the entire Darken Realm. Their courage and resolve have saved us all from the fear of tyranny and utter annihilation at the hands of the Reaper Kai. Now, their home stands on the precipice of ruin. One single misstep and their entire world will be plunged into darkness. We have a duty to help them by any means necessary."

"But aid is not possible, my lord. You heard it yourself; their village is in the middle of the wasteland. It would take weeks and weeks of travel to reach it. If they stand on the threshold of ruin, we don't have the means to aid them in time."

"We have an option."

"No we don't," Captain Maddock responded with a confused look upon his face.

"We have the choppers."

It took a moment for the idea to sink in. Blinking, Maddock was still confused.

"The helicopters only have a limited range. They wouldn't have enough fuel to return, the soldiers would be cut off, and our most important war machines would be out of commission."

"I know." Gunther's tone was confident.

"We can't sacrifice our best military asset."

"That's exactly what we are going to do. If it weren't for Jared and Tani, we would never have won this war. First they returned the nuclear warhead and then they risked their lives once more and destroyed the Splicer relay. Their aid directly brought about the end of this war. We owe them more then we can ever give. We'll load up our helicopters with ammunition and troops. We'll travel to Scarskin and kill whatever remains of the enemy."

Maddock listened and nodded in agreement. With a distant look, he let out a sigh. "So Scarskin is truly where all of this madness will end."

"Get the best and the bravest for this mission. With 1,000 Biogtechs, our troops will be hard pressed to defend this village."

"You will get the best," Maddock confirmed.

"Here are the coordinates to their village. Tani said that the village is due west of their current position. Scarskin is set atop a mesa, amidst a sea of sand."

"We'll bring them out of the darkness, Gunther, just as they delivered us all from terror. Your will be done."

With that, Maddock rushed off into the military encampment, rallying the brave for a mission of madness. As he was left alone once more, Gunther inhaled a full breath of dry hot air into his lungs, then exhaled powerfully, his gaze drifting toward the center of the encampment. Twelve green helicopters were on the ground. As he stared at them, dread began to enter his heart. Twelve helicopters might not be enough to quell the invasion force marching on the village of Scarskin. Worry and anxiety filled him once more. Although the Darken Realm was safe, those who had saved the Darken Realm were now in mortal danger.

With mixed emotions, Gunther watched the camp spring to life. Soldiers from all over the Darken Realm had heard the story and answered the call. From the Mord Tech Empire to the battered city state of Rasheed, soldiers answered the call. Steel Crag Mining Guild soldiers mixed with battle-hardened Iron Kai soldiers, charging forward to volunteer for one last battle. Seeing such fervor made Gunther proud. After such a horrific war, it was good to see that courage was still part of the world. While the encampment made ready for slaughter once more, Gunther retreated into the solitude of his thoughts.

In the desert, just beyond a ridge of shifting sand to the south, an enormous series of black clouds rolled across the sky. Driven by intense wind, the dark storm clouds surged, covering the earth in darkness. As they passed over the desert, the light of the sun was driven back, plunging the world into shadow. The heat of the burning sun was beaten back as frigid air blasted the land. A boom of thunder rocked the landscape as lightning erupted from the clouds.

Shivering in the cold air, Gunther rubbed his arms and stared at the natural wonder overtaking the military encampment.

Seeing the darkness of the storm push away the light, Gunther was suddenly comforted. His thoughts about the final battle to save Scarskin surged into his mind as the storm rushed forward. There was a similarity between the coming battle and the storm. Just as the clouds had pushed away the sun, the coming battle would plunge the village of Scarskin into darkness. But the storm that had overtaken the land was but a temporary event. The coming battle of Scarskin was, like the storm, an event that would cause much strife but in the end, the clouds would part and the sun would shine once more. Such is life. Where darkness seems unending, it is something that needs to be endured until the light streams through once more.

Gunther took solace in such thoughts. Even though war was about to erupt once more, he knew that is was a temporary event, something that could be endured until the darkness was once more driven back. Smiling, Gunther stood in the chill wind, staring up at the dark clouds. Closing his eyes, he felt the first drops of rain strike his face. Those in the camp sought shelter, but Gunther remained standing in the rain and the fierce wind. As nature assaulted the Emperor of the Iron Kai, he stood laughing like a madman, taunting heaven, knowing full well that soon the storm would end and he would still remain long after the clouds were broken apart by the brilliant rays of light surging from the sun.

Chapter 49
Master Mogi

The aged man faced his rivals alone. Holding an old worn staff in his right hand, the weaponsmaster stood his ground, clutching the crude weapon with white knuckles. The man did not seem worried in the least about his opponents. Smiling, he took a step back. His right knee popped loudly, creaking as his aged bones whined under the stress of combat.

"You're outnumbered, old man!" a youth called out with a wicked look upon his face. As he spoke, the youth took a step forward, clutching a club tightly in his right hand. Mogi took another step back.

"Outnumbered?" Mogi laughed. "It is you who are outnumbered, by experience."

As the game of cat and mouse continued, the weaponsmaster let out a loud sigh, subtly telling his opponents that he was rapidly growing bored of the game. "If you little brats want a piece of me, come and get it," he laughed at them.

At the sound of the taunt, one of the youths raised his club above his head. Letting out a boisterous war cry, the youth charged the aged man. Mogi watched him rushing forward, timing his advance with perfect precision. Just as the youth was three steps away, the old man sprang into action.

His white hair spun in an arc as his body did the same. Rotating around, the aged weaponsmaster dodged the clumsy attack. Sidestepping the youth, Master Mogi twirled his staff and swept downward, striking the youth's legs. The attack was fierce and well placed, so well placed that the youth crumpled to the ground immediately, his legs buckling under the attack. Gritting his teeth, the youth winced in pain, grabbing his legs immediately and letting out an anguished yelp.

As their companion was taken out of commission, the two remaining youths decided that it was an opportune time to attack. Both let out war cries and advanced immediately upon Mogi.

Hearing them advance, Mogi planted his legs firmly into the sand, pivoting on his right leg so that the heel of his foot dug into the earth. He inhaled deeply, preparing to defend himself once more. Sliding his staff forward, he extended it a few feet beyond his right hand. With a fierce look on his face, Mogi crouched and let the two youths attempt to pummel him.

Launching forward, the first rookie warrior leapt into the air, swinging his club in a wide arc. Mogi was ready for him. Rolling the staff over his knuckles, he swung at the same time, striking the youth in the stomach in mid-air. Groaning, the youth fell to the ground, his face turning purple as he gasped desperately for breath.

Mogi did not stop the attack. With one continuous motion, the aged man brought the back end of the stick around, ramming it into the groin of the third attacker. The attack was so severe that the youth immediately collapsed and began to whimper in agony, clutching his manhood.

Standing tall, Mogi planting the butt of his staff into the sand and shook his head in dismay. "I expect more out of all of you. I am in my sixties and *three* of Scarskin's youth cannot best me? I remember when two such lads could both best me in single combat; now it takes an entire gang and you still lose!"

"You're too quick," the first boy whimpered, rubbing his bruised legs. With each passing second, black and purple splotches were appearing where Mogi had struck him.

"Too quick?" Mogi laughed. "I haven't been quick in thirty years. Do you know why you lost?"

The three youths did not respond; instead, they tended to their wounds.

"You lost because you were so enraged by my taunts and so eager to best me that you forgot all of your training. You know better! Wait until your enemy overextends himself, *then* move in for the kill. I drew you all in and you were all too foolish to realize it. If this were a real battle, all three of you would be dead!"

"Just leave us alone. This isn't real combat. If it were, we would have done better," the second youth boasted, still gasping for air and rubbing his stomach.

"Real combat is what the Exile is all about. When you're defenseless in the middle of the wasteland, you will know what *real* truly is. For your lack of zeal today, you will all give me twenty pushups!"

"Master Mogi!" the third youth called out while trying to stand. "That's unfair."

"Complain again, you worthless whelp, and I will give you another thrashing. Give me twenty pushups, you little runts!" Mogi boomed, and his voice was so fierce, all three of the youths launched onto the burning sand and began to do pushups.

Satisfied, Mogi smiled and almost wanted to laugh at them. When the pushups were completed, he barked more orders at the youths and they all ran off towards the village of Scarskin.

Standing at the training ground, Mogi took a brief moment to suck in a full breath of air, feeling the dry air sting his nostrils and his throat. He grabbed a sheep bladder and drank down what remained of the water that had been superheated by the desert sun. Taking solace in the quiet moment, Mogi resolved to travel back to town.

As he passed down the worn trail, Mogi looked at the foliage around him. Dry yucca plants surrounded the desert trail. Small purple and yellow flowers erupted from crevices in between large rocks, the root systems having sought refuge deep within the earth to dredge out any moisture that could be found in the harsh environment. Grasses, tall and lush, swayed in the distance around the perimeter of the farming fields. Corn stalks grew high in the fields, as did row after row of wheat.

Passing out of the grassy expanse on the northern edge of the mesa, Mogi found himself staring down off the edge of a mighty cliff. The trail skirted the edge of the mesa and as he moved, Mogi watched his footing very carefully. Only a few feet away, the cliff face rested more than 2,000 feet above the shifting sand dunes below. As Mogi passed down the trail, his heart leapt into his throat as it had every time he passed down the trail. Even though he had gazed down the sheer cliff face thousands of times in his life, it still gave him a startle.

After a few minutes of travel, Mogi made it to the village of Scarskin. Smiling, the aged weaponsmaster entered the village. The main street passing through the village was flanked by a collection of whitewashed adobe houses. The burning sun reflected strongly off the pale walls. Squinting in the bright light, Mogi beheld the citizens of Scarskin.

Rushing about the main street, children were laughing and giving chase to one another. A small dog was yapping away, spinning around in circles, barking at the children as they rushed around. Women were huddling in the local marketplace, chattering about rumors and gossip as they shopped. Beyond the market, the local men were milling the wheat by rotating an enormous stone wheel, crushing the wheat into flour.

Halting in the marketplace, Mogi dug into his pocket, pulling a wooden chip free. He handed the chip to a local vendor and grabbed a handful of strawberries. As he continued his travels through the peaceful village, he slowly ate the fruit. The juice from the berries was refreshing, especially after his exercises with the youths of the village. Halting near the Elder Hall, Mogi sought refuge in the shade by the side of the building. He sat down on a bench and exhaled strongly, letting his head rest against the whitewashed adobe wall.

As he rested in the shade, his pulse began to weaken. Relaxing, Mogi began to think about the village. All in all, it was a good home. It would never be a place of great wonders. There would never be fantastic architecture nor would there be advanced comforts, but what it lacked in technological grace, it made up for with charm. The people of Scarskin were a colorful, resolute clan that loved life to the fullest, seeking every opportunity to have a banquet or celebration. A deep sense of family was the core value of the village.

Rubbing his aching joints, Mogi was grateful in that moment to have lived his entire life in peace. It was a quiet life but it was a good life. Closing his eyes, he thanked his ancestors for having had enough wisdom to craft a peaceful society and a safe place to live.

As the afternoon wore on, Mogi rested in the shade, watching the familiar inhabitants mill about, going about their lives.

While he lingered in the sun, his thoughts began to drift to those who had left the village so long ago, exiled from Scarskin as a rite of passage into adulthood. So many had been lost to the desert, so many had died to secure a stable future for the village. For generations, the youth had been sent into the wasteland to harvest lost technologies from the ancients. This process had returned many artifacts to the village, allowing the people of Scarskin to progress beyond neighboring villages. And so Scarskin became the gem of the desert, a citadel against anarchy and lawlessness in the region. Thus far, no army had ever laid siege and successfully breached the walls of Scarskin.

As thoughts of the Exile passed through Mogi's mind, memories of two special youths began to drift through him. He could still remember young Jared, rash and headstrong, taunting the aged weaponsmaster, his arrogance leading the charge. Jared was so damn foolish, so damn prideful that it almost made Mogi sick to his stomach. Brash and irreverent to everyone else's opinion, Jared was a monument to stubborn behavior. Mogi always said that rocks were hard but Jared's head was harder. But while he was full of arrogance, Jared also had great skill. The boy was the toughest warrior that the village of Scarskin had ever produced. Able to handle a multitude of foes at the same time, Jared could make a mockery of the village's most battle-hardened warriors. By the time of his Exile, there was not a single warrior in all of Scarskin, Mogi included, who could stand toe-to-toe in combat against Jared.

Smiling, Mogi snorted as he thought about Jared. With a shake of his head, his thoughts drifted to Jared's counterpart. Where Jared was skilled and arrogant, Tani was wise and reserved.

Jared was a legendary warrior and his best friend Tani was an equally legendary scholar. Tani had grown up at the edge of Scarskin and at an early age, it was readily apparent that there was something different about the boy. Whereas most children were interested in playing in the fields all day, wasting the day away, Tani would rush around the village, borrowing books from anyone he could. Spending the majority of his life reading, he rapidly progressed, soon able to comprehend complex technical documents and ancient texts. While many of the elders excelled at ancient lore, none could rival Tani in sheer intellect. His inquisitive nature also had a dark side. He was brilliant, but there was also an anarchistic streak to his intellect. One of his hobbies revolved around creating and detonating explosives. At a very young age, an accident with a homemade stick of dynamite had blasted several of Tani's fingers off his right hand. Brilliance mixed with a splash of mayhem was a dangerous blend, and the quest for wisdom could readily turn deadly with such a combination.

Thinking about Jared and Tani gave the aged man solace. They represented the best and the brightest that Scarskin had to offer the world. He hoped that they had lived up to their reputations and his expectations on their Exile. The two had chosen to travel east from the village, a dangerous prospect that had killed every exile who had attempted it in the past. Tani and Jared were skilled, but the eastern crossing could kill even the most seasoned.

In his heart he knew that they had made it across the eastern expanse, and that Jared and Tani would return home. With a sigh, Mogi looked out into the sky. The sun was still high and the afternoon was far from over. Mogi had been watching the passing of the sun beyond the horizon for a long time. Ever since Jared and Tani left on their Exile, Mogi had been secretly counting the days, watching the cycles of the moon with great interest, always knowing how many days were left until the two legendary youths would return from the wastelands of the Darken Realm. And as Mogi watched the sun, his heart began to leap. The aged weaponsmaster knew that when the sun set, it would usher in an event that would herald the return of Jared and Tani. The rising of the twentieth full moon would occur that night. It was an event that excited the old man. His imagination was aflame as he wondered what tales and stories the youths would bring back from the great eastern expanse.

As Mogi's mind filled with wonder, thinking about the return of Jared and Tani, his eyelids became heavy. Passing into a gentle slumber, he fell asleep and dreamt about the youths' return. The dream world of an old man would not last for long. As he slumbered, malice and hatred plotted misery and death. Just beyond the horizon, an army stirred, an army born from nightmares. A host of Biogtech soldiers led by a party of Reaper Kai priests charged the base of the mesa upon which Scarskin resided, with orders to slaughter all of the inhabitants. Evil was about to unleash reckless malice on the unsuspecting village.

The drums of war roared to life once more, awakening a restless old man from a world of dreams. There would be no mercy. There would be no remorse. As demonic trumpets sounded in the valley below, the inhabitants of Scarskin watched in terror as an army marched upon their peaceful village. The siege of Scarskin had begun.

Chapter 50
The Siege of Scarskin

"Hold them back!" a tribal warrior screamed, clutching his chest. Blood was pouring from several gunshot wounds he had sustained as he made a frantic attempt to stabilize the gate. With his life force fading, the warrior began to slump down against the wooden beams. A split second later, a deafening boom rocked the battle field. Burning cinders and fragments of the wooden gate were blasted free as the demolition charge reduced Scarskin's first defensive gate to mere rubble.

Screams of panic rose as the attackers began to stream through the gate. Pasty white forms cackled with glee as they pushed through the burning rubble. Chanting war cries, several tribal warriors charged the attackers with spears in hand. Their advance was cut short. A stream of bullets raced towards the charging warriors, pelting them with a hail of gunfire. All three of the warriors were killed instantly. Seeing the completely ineffective attack, the citizens of Scarskin who had witnessed the event began to fall back up the narrow trail, pushing toward the fortifications beyond.

Scarskin was built upon a tall mesa. The entire bluff upon which the village was built was protected by a sheer rock face, with the exception of the southern edge of the mesa. More gentle slopes characterized the southern edge of the mesa, where the villagers had built a road that consisted of a series of switch-backs. At each edge of a switch-back, a defensive gate had been constructed to repel invaders.

The first gate had been utterly obliterated by demolition charges, allowing the passage of the Biogtech army onto the main roadway that led to the heart of the village. As the horde of robotic soldiers advanced, the citizens of Scarskin braced for invasion. Charging up the roadway, the survivors from the first gate sought refuge beyond the second wooden gate, slamming it shut behind them. The battle would be waged further up the edge of the mesa.

The high council had been roused and was watching the terrifying siege unfold from atop the mesa. Ordering dynamite to the second gate, the high council of Scarskin was ready to make a stand by raining crude explosives down upon the Biogtech army.

The Biogtech army was on full advance, hundreds of Biogtechs having already breached the first gate. Slowly they plodded onward, firing intermittently at targets higher up on the ramparts above them. The warriors of Scarskin were used to defensive battles, preferring to crouch behind the stone walls that flanked the roadway. Within minutes, the Biogtech army ground to a halt at the second gate.

With the troops densely packed along the narrow roadway, the bombardiers of Scarskin unleashed hell. Throwing lit dynamite sticks into the densely packed Biogtechs had devastating results. Several blasts erupted in the midst of the enemy soldiers. Over a dozen Biogtechs were mangled in the blasts, granting a small victory to the tribal warriors. As the explosives detonated, a host of warriors stood up from their defensive positions armed with bows and arrows. Firing a volley of arrows into the Biogtechs, the soldiers of Scarskin pummeled the attackers. However, the arrows had limited effect; most ricocheted off the steel plating of the Biogtechs, while others were embedded into the robotic soldiers without causing damage.

Just after the smoke cleared, the tribal warriors ducked for cover, hiding behind the stone walls a split second before the Biogtechs counterattacked with their firearms. The bullets harmlessly bounced off the rock walls, leaving the defenders of Scarskin unscathed. The tribals' defensive tactics were well tested. Over the centuries, not a single army had reached the mesa to breach the heart of Scarskin.

The siege ground to a halt as the last remnants of the Dark Order tried to batter their way through the second gate. While the tribals had great skill, the Biogtechs had great weapons. A Reaper Kai priest from the desert floor took aim at the gate with an anti-vehicle rocket, targeting the thick supports that flanked the gate. When fired, the weapon raced forward and detonated on target, slamming into the support beams that held the gate. The blast was so potent that several defenders behind the gate were blown apart in the blast and killed instantly. Groaning, the wooden beams bowed and the gate began to lurch horribly to one side. The beams popped and splintered, and the second gate collapsed, falling down the steep cliff-face of the mesa.

The defenders were stunned and left totally unprepared for the enemy counter-attack. Attempting to flee, they were cut down by gunfire as the Biogtechs sprayed bullets into the ranks of the tribals. Several dozen Scarskin warriors were shredded by the volley of gunfire as they fled up the roadway toward the third gate.

As the siege progressed closer to the heart of Scarskin, the council members were left dumbfounded. Never before had an attacking army breached the second gate, let alone so quickly. Within a span of less than thirty minutes of fighting, the Biogtech army had pushed deep into the village's primitive defenses.

Mustering a new tactic, Master Mogi conceived a novel plan. Instead of defending the third gate, the council resolved to fortify it with stone. They summoned the warriors, and the strong men began to fortify the gate with large stones, creating a rock wall behind the third gate. They labored intensely and managed to significantly block the third gate from the passage of the enemy army.

Anti-vehicle rockets slammed repeatedly into the fortified gate will little result. The stones behind the gate were holding back the torrent of explosions. As the leadership of Scarskin observed that the gate was holding, they resolved to renew their attack.

The rain of dynamite began in earnest once more. The explosives, hurtled into the massed troops, made a significant impact. Dozens of Biogtechs were killed by the attack, while the Reaper Kai army found no effective way to breach the defenses of the tribal village.

As the red-robed priests tracked the unfolding battle from the desert floor, they watched the sun very intently. Only half an hour of sunlight was left. Ordering a full retreat, the Biogtechs moved away from the third gate, leaving the perimeter of Scarskin's defenses.

Cheers echoed all the way up the cliff-face as the warriors of Scarskin chanted war cries, watching the enemy army retreat back onto the desert floor. But where the tribals felt they had secured a victory, the leaders were not so certain. Instead of withdrawing completely from the scene, the Biogtech army simply regrouped in the valley below, restlessly massing for something...

Gathering the warriors, the leadership of Scarskin braced for a second offensive. The high council amassed troops along the roadway leading into the heart of the village, fueled by a heightening anxiety. Whatever the enemy was planning, they seemed confident enough that it would work.

As the warriors of Scarskin waited, the sun raced toward the horizon, finally dipping below the edge of the world. Darkness began to touch the wasteland. The rays of light dissipated as the sun disappeared to the west. A chill wind rose over the desert, a phenomenon that occurred every night. As the wind broke across the sand, a hissing noise erupted, the tiny grains being pushed by the chill wind. In the desert below, the darkness grew and with each passing minute, the Reaper Kai priests began to chant with increasing fervor. Demonic prayers were uttered as shadow engulfed the battlefield. When the night had fully swallowed the landscape, something wicked began to stir.

A creature of darkness, a demon from the underworld, sought to reveal itself. The monster was forged from dark magic, infused with the darkness of the night. The sun itself was harmful to the creature and it hid from the light of the day. But once the light had dissipated, the demon was free to unleash terror upon the world once more.

In the chill wind and safety of the cloying shadow and darkness, the beast lingered. A tremor rocked the earth. The sand began to ripple. Something unholy was pushing forth from the safety of the sand. A sickly green arm erupted from the earth. As the event unfolded, all that witnessed it were overtaken by a wave of fear. Averting their eyes from the creature emerging from the sand, they sought to escape its presence.

A roar emerged from the desert. Two glowing yellow eyes were revealed as the monster pulled itself free from its earthly tomb.

Liberating itself from the sand, it stood upright, a demon born from unholy ritual. Covering the beast's body were the faces of all those that it had consumed. Gibbering, ranting, and moaning, the faces on the demon's body were trapped in the flesh of the monster, their very souls absorbed by the foul creature, their life force sealed inside the demon and giving it extra strength.

Sniffing the air, the beast roared in anger. "I hunger!" the Abomination boomed in a sinister voice. The creature's scream was so intense, even those at the top of the mesa could hear it. "It has been many days since last I have fed. Give me fresh meat, fresh souls to enjoy!"

In the darkness of the desert, there was only one person who could look upon the creature. Sister Nightshade, hated matron of the Reaper Kai, advanced upon it with a look of dispassion upon her wasted face. The Abomination looked down upon Sister Nightshade with great displeasure as she advanced.

"You owe me fresh souls!"

"Feast as you will, creature of darkness. The village above us is for you. Break down these gates that hinder our progress. Slaughter the defenders and feed your hunger. Unleash misery and suffering. Leave none alive," Nightshade proclaimed in a dark tone.

Smiling, the demon roared in the darkness. It advanced upon the village, pulling down what was left of the first two gates and then made its way towards the third gate. As the creature advanced, the terrified souls trapped inside it wailed in anguish.

"Set us free!" they moaned. "Slay the beast, save our souls!" they cried out.

"I am so scared!" one face wailed in terror as tears rolled out of the eyes bound to the monster's flesh.

An overwhelming sense of fear overtook the defenders of Scarskin. The Abomination was a demon from the underworld with intense supernatural powers. Only a soul that was completely righteous and good or completely filled with evil and malice could look upon the monster. All others were unable to look upon the beast, as they were filled with much fear and terror. Thus the monster advanced upon the village of Scarskin. The defenders were driven into sheer panic as it came ever closer. Unable to behold the beast, the valiant warriors of Scarskin fled from its presence, leaving their fortifications completely abandoned.

Coming before the third gate, the enormous demon grabbed its mighty gore- stained cudgel in both hands. It roared in anger, slamming the gate over and over again with the weapon, battering it with all of its might. The stones behind the gate trembled with each slam. Repeatedly, the beast battered away at the gate. Finally, the stones began to fall away under the demonic might of the Abomination. Bashing through the gate, the creature pulled the rocks away and ripped down what remained of the gate. Screaming in glee, the demonic creature moved up the ramparts toward the fourth gate.

As the Abomination advanced, the Reaper Kai army followed the monster. Using the beast's unholy powers of fright, the army was able to advance without interference from the village's defenders. And so the monster led the last army of darkness against the terrified protectors of Scarskin. Battering and bashing it went, smashing the defenses of the tribal village. Within a matter of minutes, the entire Reaper Kai army was stationed outside the stone walls of Scarskin. The only thing that remained between the enemy and the villagers was the main gate.

Screaming out a war cry, the Abomination slammed its cudgel into the main gate. The trembling villagers of Scarskin could feel the power of the demon as they yearned to flee from its presence. The world was growing darker by the second.

Slam! The gate shook again. Hope was fading. *Bam!* The Abomination struck the gate again. This time some of the wooden beams cracked and popped under the strain of the beast beyond.

As the tribal village was about to be overrun, Master Mogi climbed the wall above the gate. Fighting back the fear in his heart, he crouched behind the wall, breathing heavily. He had a stick of dynamite in one hand and a lit torch in his other. Trembling, Mogi knew that no matter what, he had to make a last stand. Just before he was about to light the stick of dynamite, his gaze shifted out beyond the walls of the village, toward the horizon.

In the darkness of the night, a sprig of light had just erupted. A pure pristine ray of light broke the shadow. In the distance, just behind an enormous dune of sand, the moon was rising. At that moment, everything stood still. Mogi blinked, his heart leaping. The rising of the full moon was an omen of hope for the villagers of Scarskin, and watching it inspired Mogi. Smiling in the darkness, he observed for a moment as more of the moon emerged over the ridge of the sand dune.

A roar of pain resounded below the gate. The moonlight, reflected light from the sun itself, had struck the Abomination. Squinting in the moonlight, the demon was utterly displeased by the latest development. Covering its eyes, it yelled in disgust, "Damn this infernal light!"

The beast ceased its attack for a brief minute. As it did, a chill rolled down Mogi's spine. The light was harming the beast and the moon was not yet full. Maybe there was still hope. Just as his mind was spinning, something curious met his sight. As the moon continued to climb higher into the night sky, a strange silhouette appeared on the top of the dune. Two forms, two people, crested the dune with the moon behind them.

"It can't be!" Mogi whispered as his stomach lurched. He watched in fascination as the two forms climbed the dune, his heart leaping. "It can't be mere coincidence!" With his mind spinning, tears of hope filled his eyes. "The twentieth full moon! Jared and Tani!" he cried out in sheer excitement.

His thoughts drifted back to the night they were both exiled from the village. Jared and Tani represented the best that Scarskin had to offer. Jared was a warrior of legend and Tani was a scholar of renown. The two youths were legendary and had a legendary mission. Never before had any exiles passed on into the eastern wasteland and returned. The two forms on the ridge of the sand dune filled Mogi with hope. As he stared in disbelief, the gate shuddered once more beneath him. The pain the Abomination was feeling from the moonlight had driven the beast into a frenzy. Beating on the gate repeatedly, the Abomination was making headway at breaching the final defense.

Mogi watched in awe as the two silhouettes stood in the light of the full moon behind them. The full moon bathed the wasteland in holy light, revealing a sight which caused Mogi to freeze in shock. Hundreds of mounted warriors atop horses and camels were in the valley below, nomad warriors who had answered the call to battle. Jared and Tani had returned, but not alone; they had returned with an army and the battle skills needed to wage war.

Tears of hope streamed down Mogi's face as he saw the army of warriors in the valley below. It was not just coincidence; it was fate. The rising of the full moon had brought home the two most legendary exiles in the entire history of Scarskin.

War cries erupted in the valley below. The nomad warriors charged towards the besieged mesa.

As they charged into the fray, the Abomination completed its assault on the front gate of Scarskin. Collapsing into a pile of rubble, the gate had been breached. The demon charged into the village, seeking to unleash reckless slaughter. With the front gate breached, the army of darkness was free to pour into the tribal village. Biogtechs, Reaper Kai priests, and a host of Goat Minions clambered to kill.

Mogi crouched upon the ramparts above the gate and watched in horror as the army streamed into the village. Saying a silent prayer to his ancestors, Mogi lit the stick of dynamite. He chucked the explosive into the midst of the enemy soldiers, drew his sword, and prepared to fight with all of his might.

Chapter 51
The Final Struggle

An inhuman scream pierced the night. Cowering in terror, the defenders of Scarskin watched in horror as the main gate leading into their village collapsed. In the darkness of the falling debris and the shadow of the night, the sound of screams rose. A monstrous form strode forth, reeking of death. A deep sense of fear overrode the villagers' need to protect their village from the reckless assault. Huddling fearfully, the valiant defenders could not behold the form of the Abomination. Powerful demonic magic had been branded into the beast and only the righteous and the wicked could look upon it without withdrawing in fear. All others would flee the presence of the demon, unable to look upon its twisted visage.

"I hunger!" the beast screamed as the villagers fled the main gate. Rushing forward, the Abomination charged, grabbing a hapless villager within its green, slime- encrusted claw. A wail of anguish rose from the villager as the beast swallowed him alive. Within a few seconds, a new face appeared upon the flesh of the demon, the life-force and soul of the victim absorbed by the creature's body, feeding the monster with spiritual energy. As the soul of the victim was fused into the beast's body, the face of the newly trapped man looked around in horror, screaming in terror.

The demon roared in glee, flexing its muscles, fueled by a renewed surge of power. As it did, the smell of fear wafted through the Abomination's nostrils. Driven by a deep hunger, with drool trickling down its chin, the beast sought more fresh souls to devour.

Protected by the shadows, the monster was unstoppable. It roared and sought to feed its insatiable appetite, hungering for more warm flesh. But even as it began to rush forward, the Abomination stopped dead in its tracks. The full moon had now risen high in the sky and was emitting a holy glow, bathing the wasteland and village in warm light. Squinting in agony, the demon sought to escape the light. For while the beast was mighty indeed, light was the bane of its existence, especially sunlight. The sunlight reflecting off the full moon was intense enough to drive the creature back. As it retreated into the shadows, the monster's greenish skin had already begun to crisp in the holy light. Smoke was rising off its flesh as it crouched behind an adobe building.

"Damn this foul light!" the Abomination roared in pain. Staring in anger toward the night sky, the demon cursed repeatedly.

And so the mighty beast lingered near the front gate, hiding in the darkness, having been driven back by the warm light of the full moon. But while the beast suffered mild defeat, the front gates were now open to the rest of the Reaper Kai forces. With drums pounding, the red-clad priests yelled out dark prayers, ushering in the forces of evil to ransack and slaughter the inhabitants of Scarskin.

The Biogtech army poured through the front gate, cackling with glee. In the dim light, the red eyes of the robotic soldiers were an ominous sight as hundreds of the death machines streamed into the village. Washed in the white light, their pasty bodies made them look like an army of ghosts on the march. The Biogtechs spread out and began a search-and-destroy mission.

Shambling down the streets off the main square just beyond the gate, the Biogtechs opened fire on any hapless humans foolish enough to pass their way. Sporadic gunfire echoed amongst the adobe buildings as the inhabitants of Scarskin encountered creatures born from fierce ancient technology. The attack on Scarskin had now commenced in earnest.

Near the main square, a host of courageous tribal warriors, dressed in animal skins and with their faces covered in war paint, chanted battle cries. Brandishing spears and crude weapons, they rallied in an attempt to deflect the attackers.

"Drive them back!" a brave tribal warrior yelled, holding a sword above his head, shaking it fiercely as he screamed. His companions joined in the chanting and a hundred proud warriors charged the Biogtech lines.

Rushing down the main street, the warriors ran head-first into a veritable firing squad. It took a few seconds for the Biogtechs to respond to the charge. The robots turned to face the threat. Cackling, they leveled their submachine guns, taking aim and firing bursts of bullets. The front rank of tribal warriors took the brunt of the attack. Screams of anguish arose as nearly a dozen warriors were shredded with a volley of bullets.

Undaunted by the losses, the tribal warriors grew even more enraged, more staunchly devoted to bringing bloody justice to the invaders. Slamming into the massed Biogtech troops, the Scarskin warriors began to hack and bash the robotic soldiers. At such close range, the losses were utterly horrid. Firing their weapons at full auto, the Biogtechs sprayed the warriors at point-blank range. Bullets were ripping through flesh, creating sprays of crimson blood, showering attacker and defender alike. But as the Biogtechs tried to hold back the tide, the frenzied warriors intensified their assault. Rank after rank of Biogtech soldiers began to falter as their weapons were totally drained of ammunition. As the slow robotic death machines tried to reload their weapons, the tribals took the initiative, destroying rank after rank.

The street became clogged with the dead as heaps of humans collapsed amongst the shattered bodies of Biogtech soldiers. After witnessing the damaging effects of the guns, it didn't take long for Scarskin warriors to scavenge them from the slain Biogtechs and return fire. As the villagers were unaccustomed to the weapons, few Biogtechs fell, but the villagers were still holding their own.

While the fierce battle raged in the street, evil plotted the demise of the defenders. In the darkness of the night, creatures born from pure evil slunk quietly, seeking to ambush the tribal warriors. A host of savage Goat Minions skirted around behind the warriors and drew their weapons. Dressed in blood-red robes, the Goat Minions bayed in the night, sniffing the air with quick gasps.

The smell of blood and death was ripe in the air. Sniffing, the Goat Minions felt a sinister rage settle over them as the scent wafted through their nostrils. Almost like a euphoric wave of pleasure, the images of death in the street drove the Goat Minions into a frenzy. They wanted to kill, they needed to kill. Charging into the unprepared ranks of the Scarskin warriors, the Goat Minions crashed into them with devastating results.

Screams rose as the savage Goat Minions began to butcher. Severed limbs and warm blood covered the cobblestone byway. Caught between the Biogtech troops and the savage Goat Minions, the band of Scarskin warriors was trapped. Fighting valiantly was not enough; they were outnumbered and outmatched by superior weapons. In mere minutes, all of the warriors had passed into death.

With a mountain of bodies in the middle of the street, the enemy troops began to bash down the wooden doors of the adobe houses and enter the homes of Scarskin inhabitants. Once inside the buildings, the forces of evil killed all whom they encountered within. None were spared; men, women, and children were all put to death.

All over the village, the situation was similar. The Reaper Kai army was crushing and systematically slaughtering the entire village. The tide of battle had turned to favor the forces of darkness.

As the village of Scarskin stood on the doorstep of ruin, riders from the deep desert appeared. With terror in their hearts, the mounted troops beheld the rear of the Reaper Kai army. Biogtech soldiers were trudging up the long winding trail that led into the heart of Scarskin. Gathering their courage, a host of mounted nomad warriors, the same nomad warriors whom Jared and Tani had befriended in their desert crossing, prepared to purge the violent aggressors from the land. Help was on the way, and the nomad warriors were prepared to pay the ultimate sacrifice to defend the village of Scarskin.

Chapter 52
The Final Seduction

Charging across the sand, the formation of nomad warriors rushed toward the mesa of Scarskin. In the bright light of the moon, the riders were an ominous sight, bounding over the dunes with the intent of causing reckless slaughter. Yelling out war cries, the nomad warriors brandished curved swords, ready to make the army of darkness pay a toll for breaching the desert sands.

The Reaper Kai army was unprepared for the attack. The remnants of the army that had not pushed into the village remained as support forces for the rest of the formation. Within a few seconds, the forces were scattering as the nomad warriors struck them. Like a wedge, the riders slammed into the Reaper Kai forces with devastating results. The nomads, master warriors, tore a wide swath through the rear guard of the army.

The Biogtechs turned to meet the assault head-on but were too late. By the time the robotic death machines raised their weapons, the nomad warriors had ridden over them. The sound of popping plastic and mangled metal echoed as hydraulic fluid shot into the air. Popping like pumpkins being smashed, the robotic warriors turned into a smear of broken parts and fluid upon the sand. Any Reaper Kai priests within the formation had been cut down before they could utter dark prayers to their sinister masters in hell.

With the rear guard of the army crushed, the winding trail leading into the village of Scarskin was open to assault. From the center of the nomad warriors, a grouping of unusual riders pushed their way to the front ranks, led by a woman dressed in flowing blue robes. Twelve riders wielding long spears followed her with looks of unease upon their faces.

Staring at the winding trail leading up the sheer rock face of the mesa, the woman leading the band of holy warriors eyed their destination with a tremble of fear inside of her. Was this finally it? Was this the final battle against the forces of evil?

Closing her eyes, Mineera could hear the sounds of death in her mind. Above, upon the mesa, a battle raged. The citizens fought with desperation for their very lives. The fear inside of them rocked through her sensitive mind. In that single moment, Mineera was not alone; instead, she was infused with thousands of screaming voices, tipping her sanity toward madness. A stream of tears began to roll down her face as she lost control of her senses. The voices and images in her mind were beginning to fully overtake her consciousness.

"Can you hear the screams? Can you feel their terror?" A sinister voice rolled through her mind. *"I enjoy such turmoil, as should you. I know you seek to end this suffering. Do what is right, my child. I am giving you one final chance to cherish your heritage, your true role in this world. Embrace the darkness and aid your brethren in battle. Take up the mantle and lead your people to victory!"*

Trembling, Mineera fought the voice stinging her mind and soul. She had encountered the foul being before many times. A sick, unclean feeling was washing over her.

"Let me in once more, my child. Bask in my glory, bask in my power. Let me cover your flesh with the taint of darkness. Let me in!"

"No!" she whispered, feeling the bile rise in her throat.

"You are my child! Cherish the darkness of your true desires. Take my power. Let it course through you. Unleash bloodshed for me and you will sit at my side for all eternity."

The perverse presence, the same presence that had invaded her body and soul before, was trying to take possession of her once more. The unclean spirit knew that the end was near. Without Mineera, the army of darkness was on the edge of loss.

"Leave me be!" she whimpered.

The Oracles surrounded her and averted their eyes. Each could feel the unclean presence around her and each of the Oracles knew that Mineera was once again battling the will of evil itself. It was a battle with which they could not help her.

"You dare defy me! How dare you!" The Voice roared inside her mind, sending a sickly stream of evil into her. Mineera was rocked with dark energy. She swayed back and forth, her blood turning to ice. *"Obey me, child, or you will suffer. You are an outsider. Heaven's gates will never open for a bitch like you. You will spend an eternity alone, your soul not welcome in heaven, and you will never walk with your true companions in hell. Join me and I will give you dark pleasure in the afterlife. Betray me again and your soul will have no home!"*

Home. The word resonated in her mind. The thought of home had tortured Mineera all of her life. Since she was a small child, she had never truly felt that she belonged. The ideals of the Reaper Kai were fundamentally flawed in her opinion. Even though the Reaper Kai were *her* people, Mineera never felt a part of them. This detachment intensified when she betrayed her own people, branding herself as a traitor. From that day forward, she had no home. The Reaper Kai despised her and all others never trusted her. It was her station, her burden to have no home, no real home. What the sinister entity offered her was the thing that she desired most.

"All I ever wanted was a home, a true place in this world," she whispered with tears stinging her eyes.

"I know, child," the Voice erupted in her mind. *"Come home to us, your true people. Join us."*

The battle raged inside of her. All she wanted was to belong, to be part of something. But in the end what she truly wanted was freedom, freedom from the darkness, no matter the cost. Mineera would never have a home. She had made that decision long ago. It was a conscious choice to defy the temptation of evil in order to allow her soul the freedom to exist without darkness, without suffering. She had no home, no real home. In the end, what Mineera truly wanted was something that she could never have. She was a lost soul wandering the thin line between good and evil, skirting across the barrier between salvation and damnation. If she never had a home again, it would all be worth it. The darkness would never rule her soul again.

"I have made my choice," she whispered.

"Join me," the Voice whispered back seductively.

"I choose exile over excess. I choose freedom instead of the shackles of darkness."

"So be it, fool!" the entity declared harshly. As it did, Mineera's body was wracked with convulsions. Pain, agonizing pain, erupted in her body. Whimpering, she forced warm thoughts into her mind. When evil filled her with sorrow, she thought of happiness: her companions, her friends. When evil filled her with jealousy, she thought of self sacrifice for others. When the darkness made her feel self pity, Mineera found freedom. Focusing on these ideals, she fought back the flood of darkness killing her body.

With every ounce of strength and conviction, Mineera, lost child of the Dark Order, freed herself, forcing back the sinister creature that had invaded her senses. As she pushed the spirit away, it screamed and cursed her, trying to wreak havoc upon her. But though it tried with all its might to possess her, it could not. Mineera was a free soul, bound to righteousness as a choice, not a duty.

And so Mineera removed the shackles of darkness once more. When she opened her eyes, all was quiet. Blinking in the warm light of the moon, she smiled, looking around her. Each of the Oracles bowed to her in respect. All of them knew that she had just fought and won a terrible battle.

"I no longer fear the darkness. I was once the one over whom the darkness did hold sway. Now I understand more than ever my place and purpose. My home is my bond. My purpose is conviction. Although I will never have a people to call my own ever again, I know that I do have a home, a place in this world." Smiling, she looked upon her companions with a sense of duty overtaking her. "We have a job to do."

Sheepishly, the Oracles trembled. In the darkness above them, a scream of anger rose to fill the air. A creature, an unholy monstrosity, was killing at will, feeding upon warm flesh. It was time to face the darkness in battle.

"Do not fear the coming darkness," Mineera said resolutely.

"It's not the darkness I fear, my lady," an Oracle replied in a mild tone. "It's what was forged from the darkness that I fear."

"I will go alone if need be." She smiled at them, totally devoid of fear.

Her fierce courage was both chilling and inspiring to witness. Burying their fears, each of the Oracles nodded at her in turn. Each was ready to face the darkness.

Mineera kicked her horse, directing it toward the stone ramp that led to the village of Scarskin. The twelve riders followed her, heading toward the demon that resided at the top. As they ascended the stone trail, the sounds of combat grew closer and more immediate. It was a time for blind faith, a time for war.

Chapter 53
Leaders of a Desperate Time

As things seemed most dire, an ominous sound arose in the distance—a dull hum coming from the sky. As seconds passed, the sound increased in intensity. Erupting from the night sky came a sight which was frightening to the inhabitants of Scarskin. Unfamiliar, advanced machines emerged from the darkness and began to buzz over the rooftops. Cowering in fear, the villagers were totally unprepared for what was about to happen.

"This is Vulture One Seven," the radio crackled in all of the cockpits of the infantry-packed Iron Kai helicopters circling the village. "Prepare to deploy ground teams on the north end of the village. After troop deployment, I am authorizing all gunships to fire at will."

The green helicopters were hovering in mid-air near the north end of Scarskin. Ropes dropped out the sides of the monstrous machines and veteran Iron Kai soldiers began to slide down them, landing in densely packed squads. Hitting the ground were two heroes of renown, who stepped onto the mesa of Scarskin as they had not done in twenty moons. Jared and Tani readied their weapons, standing in the center of the Iron Kai troops.

"Today, we end this war!" Jared yelled with a fierce look in his eyes. Drawing the Scar Blade, he held the weapon in the holy white light of the moon. Around his neck, the raven totem began to hum, its eyes beginning to glow red, hungering for demonic magic. A transformation had occurred in the youth. Once, a long time ago, Jared had been nothing more than a headstrong, arrogant boy.

Today he was something much more, something menacing. With the passage of time, the youth had seen strife and learned the true meaning of loss. A hero is someone who has lost someone so dear that courage is nothing more than violent rage. Jared was such a youth. He had the combat experience and a deep sense of outrage simmering within him. He was a boy no longer; now he was a man with the skills necessary to bring his people back from the darkness.

With a booming voice, the youth held his blue steel blade in the air. "We have all seen loved ones perish. We have all seen our homes attacked and our very lives put in peril. The enemy that stands before us was born from the darkness. I say to hell with them! To hell with the Reaper Kai! They have taken everything from us and now we send one final message! Leave none alive! Slaughter all of the enemies you see! Death to the Reaper Kai!"

As the triumphant youth spoke the harsh words, the Iron Kai troops felt their hearts erupt in their chests. With blood pumping, they readied themselves for war once more.

Tani clicked the safety off on his submachine gun. "To victory!" he yelled, holding his fist in the air. "Let's send these dogs to the netherworld!"

A fury of war chants erupted from the Iron Kai soldiers. They were also eager to destroy the Reaper Kai once and for all. Readying their weapons, the host of seasoned troops followed Jared and Tani into the heart of Scarskin.

Explosions tore the battlefield. The gunships began to strafe the village, firing missiles into the densely packed Biogtech soldiers still pouring in through the front gate. Heavy machine-gun fire also ripped the air as the helicopters sprayed the enemy troops. The chaos of battle had increased tenfold within a few minutes.

The citizens of Scarskin literally felt as if the end of the world had arrived. Strange attackers made of metal were using unknown weapons. Savage Goat Minions were slaughtering at will. Reaper Kai priests were channeling dark energy, lances of fire erupting from their fingertips. A demonic creature was assaulting the main gate. Finally, strange flying machines were racing over the rooftops of the village. Morale had completely collapsed and the villagers were fleeing out of the interior of massed houses in droves.

Charging forward with a small army, the youths of Scarskin led the Iron Kai troops into battle, trying desperately to defend the village from Reaper Kai forces. As Jared and Tani led the way, they passed through a mass of frightened villagers. At first, the villagers stopped dead in their tracks, eyeing the mass of soldiers with suspicion. But this suspicion was quickly dispelled. Blinking in disbelief, many saw Jared holding the mighty blue Scar Blade in his hand. Shocked, they felt they were dreaming. Hope leapt in their hearts as many caught sight of Tani, the tribal genius. Dazed by the strange events, the villagers simply stared at the legendary youths in disbelief.

"We need to do something," Tani said, sounding overwhelmed. His friend shook his head in agreement.

"Come with me," Jared urged Tani.

Charging forward, Jared and Tani ascended a rock outcropping. Above the frightened citizens, Jared waved the Scar Blade in the dim light of the night. Stunned, the citizens of Scarskin stared in awe at the two legendary youths, two of their own whom they had not seen for twenty full moons. By the time Jared began to rally the villagers, the crowd had swelled to the thousands.

"Fear not!" Jared yelled in a resolute voice. "We are the proud children of the desert, valiant warriors who are masters of war! Do not flee, do not fear! We have brought powerful allies to hold back the tide of death and despair. I need all of you to hear my voice. Trust in me, for I am one of your own. Take up arms, all of you, whether man or woman, whether young or old. This is your home, these are your lives. Defend your families, defend your friends. Follow us into battle, Tani and me. We will not fail you!"

A spike of hope erupted in the villagers. The two most legendary youths ever exiled into the wasteland had returned home, returned from across the eastern wasteland, a task thought to be impossible. Seeing the army of soldiers behind them, the villagers felt that they could withstand the Reaper Kai army. Mustering their courage, mere children picked up rocks. The old brandished their canes. Mothers and fathers stood together, hoisting weapons into the air. War cries erupted. The mob had become an army.

"Death to the enemies of Scarskin!" Tani yelled, leaping off the rock. Jared followed suit and the two tribals charged through the middle of the Scarskin villagers while the crowd opened to allow them passage. Making their way through the clustered villagers, Jared and Tani rallied them further. When they came to the head of the newly assembled army, they charged headlong into the besieged village of Scarskin.

The army descended upon the streets with such speed, the Reaper Kai army was caught completely off guard. Hitting their flank, the Scarskin warriors, mixed with Iron Kai soldiers, cut the enemy army in two, killing hundreds of enemy troops within a few minutes. As the army came to the defense of the village, driving back the enemy, the gunships hovered, spraying the Biogtechs with machine-gun fire. Chaos erupted and the central command of the Reaper Kai army was in complete disarray.

Sister Nightshade, dark matron of the Reaper Kai, could see victory slipping away. Charging through the streets on her mighty horse, she rallied her troops, driving them toward the center of the village. Near the gates, the Abomination could hear the sounds of combat. Still hungry, the Abomination wanted slaughter. The demon charged into the light of the full moon, wincing in pain as its flesh began to burn in the warm light. It shrugged off the pain, craving killing more than self preservation, and stormed toward the center of the village. The final battle would be decided in front of the council chambers.

The forces of good and the forces of darkness both poured toward the center of the village, all eager to resolve the war once and for all. A mob of differing battle forces clashed with horrendous results. Gunfire was being exchanged in the square. Psychic attacks were being flung at the defenders. Tribal warriors were bashing and slashing their way through the Reaper Kai army. Goat Minions, drenched in blood, were savagely butchering all that they encountered. Helicopters sprayed the forces of darkness with machine-gun fire. In the center of the melee, Jared and Tani fought with all of their might, encouraging and inspiring their countrymen with daring acts of courage.

Making a sizeable dent in the enemy troops, the forces of Scarskin had tipped the scale toward victory. Sensing a triumph, the courageous soldiers surged forward, ignoring pain, forging onward. But while victory seemed near, the enemy had other plans.

Striding into the square, the Abomination, body singed by the moonlight, turned the tide of battle. As the demon moved into the square, all were overtaken with a sense of fear. The villagers and Iron Kai soldiers cowered, unable to look upon the creature.

Goat Minions also cowered and fled from its presence. All that remained in the square were the mindless Biogtechs. Taking advantage of the beast's demonic power, the death machines fired upon those fleeing and those who cowered. Unable to fight effectively, the defenders of Scarskin found themselves in real trouble.   Though courageous, Jared and Tani could not look upon the demon, nor could they keep morale from failing.

As things seemed most desperate, a ray of hope erupted from the southern street. An army of horse-mounted nomad warriors drew near and heading their ranks was something curious. A woman garbed in blue robes, riding a mighty horse, approached the square. Behind the woman were twelve horsemen, Oracles of Light, each brandishing a long spear with a silver serrated tip.

As this mighty host of horsemen approached, the Abomination sneered. Racing to meet them head on, the demon was stunned to find that the woman and the twelve Oracles did not flee its presence. Not only did they not flee, but each of them, being righteous, was able to look upon the beast.

Grabbing its mighty cudgel, the Abomination snorted and charged. Mineera of Gogoli, calm and unflustered, held her ground. Duty had replaced terror in her heart. Staring at the charging monster, she calmly extended her right hand. A spark of holy light formed around her wrist, growing in intensity until her entire hand was engulfed with white light. Focusing on the beast, Mineera leveled her fingertips at the face of the Abomination.

"Let's see how you like not being able to see your opponents," Mineera called out in a commanding tone. As she did, a searing beam of light, as bright as the sun itself, erupted from her fingertips. The holy light slammed into the Abomination's face, searing the flesh and producing a stream of thick smoke. The beast screamed and moaned in agony, but Mineera continued the assault. Shrinking back, the demon collapsed to the ground, clutching its face. Mineera's intense attack had effectively blinded it.

"*Yes!*" a face upon the Abomination yelled in glee. "*Slay this monster, free our souls!*"

"*Save us!*" another face wailed, tears streaming out of its eyes.

"Damn you, insolent bitch!" the monster wailed.

"Woe to all those who oppose the will of heaven." she responded in a crisp tone. "Now is a time for destiny, now is a time for triumph." Mineera turned to the twelve Oracles near her. "Do not fear, do not waver. This creature is born from darkness; send it back where it came from."

With that, the twelve Oracles, mounted on their valiant steeds, held their mighty spears at the ready. Spreading out, the twelve men stationed themselves side by side. In the center of the formation, Matthew Moralis, the Oracle of Justice, shouted to the other Oracles, "Send this creature back to hell! Charge!"

All twelve men, Oracles and descendants of the Lost Tribe of Ceibla Moralis, held their spears forward, then kicked their mounts. The horses bucked and raced forward in formation. With Matthew in the center, the twelve Oracles charged forward as the demon lay prone upon the ground. Hearing them advance, the Abomination staggered to its feet. With a wild swing, the beast tried to kill them as they charged, still unable to function after being blinded. However, the attack was futile. Slamming into the beast, Matthew Moralis embedded his spear deep within the creature's chest. The silver metal burned the flesh of the beast as it slashed and eviscerated the monster's insides.

The rest of the Oracles followed suit, plunging their weapons into the demon. Roaring in pain, the Abomination flailed in agony, swinging repeatedly in an attempt to kill the Oracles. It staggered unsteadily, the wounds inflicted upon it having taken their toll. Mortally wounded and still blind, the demon collapsed to the ground, cursing repeatedly. Blood poured from the spot where the silver-tipped spears had struck the monster. As its life-force began to wane, each face upon its flesh, each soul trapped within its body, began to rejoice; their torture was almost over. Groaning, the demonic creature passed onto death.

As the beast finally shuddered one last time, breathing its last breath, a bright sprig of light erupted from the Abomination's chest, rising high into the air. Everyone in the square watched in fascination. The bright, shimmering light then disappeared. But a split second later, dozens of similar lights began to rise from the beast's body. Each tiny light was a soul, the soul of a person who had been consumed by the demon, the very life-force of the being that had been bound into the creature's body. Each trapped soul was finally free and would finally be at rest. The torture and fear of being encased in the demon's body were at an end.

The light show lasted but a brief moment as hundreds of souls were liberated. In the darkness of the night, in the bitterness of a brutal battle, the unusual display would be but a brief moment of solace from the bloodshed.

In the blink of an eye, the fear was gone. The terror brought by the Abomination had ended. Jared recovered his senses and rose from the ground, surveying the courtyard in which a battle had been raging but a few minutes before. The enemy forces were doing the same, looking at the scene with stunned silence. As enemy looked at enemy, the sense of conflict readily progressed to violence.

A spike of hate bolted through Jared. Looking toward the Scarskin council chambers, the youth viewed enemy soldiers preparing to wage war once more. It was that split second between peace and war that would forever change the life of young Jared. Staring through the smoke, the tribal warrior caught sight of something familiar. A band of men, proud warriors of Scarskin, were moving up the street silently, ready to make a sneak attack on the Reaper Kai forces preparing for war.

Jared knew the warrior leading the formation of council guards. The man was Jared's father, Chayton, a proud warrior of the Scarskin tribe. A thin smile graced Jared's lips. It had been twenty full moons since he had last seen his family. As he stared in wonder at his courageous father, a snap broke the air. A single bullet was fired. A split second later, more gunfire erupted. The gears of war started churning and moving once more, grinding away, consuming life in their hungry pursuit.

Still in a daze, Jared heard screams around him, men dying and the sounds of chaos. But he was lost in a momentary trance and the sounds of battle seemed so distant. Fond memories briefly rolled through his mind as he saw his father charging into the fray, ready to kill the enemies of Scarskin. He felt warm for a brief moment, safe even amidst the chaos. The vision of his father gave him comfort and solace in a dark time.

As Jared stared curiously at his father, something perverse filled his consciousness. A deep sense of malice invaded his senses. He shuddered for a brief moment. Something was horribly wrong, Jared felt as if he was being watched. Blinking, he averted his gaze from his father. Turning his head, he caught sight of Sister Nightshade standing on the steps of the council hall, staring directly at him. As their eyes locked, the totem around Jared's neck began to vibrate violently and a brisk chill erupted from the ancient relic. The last of the mighty Reaper Kai looked at him with dark fascination. Smiling, she averted her gaze and looked at Jared's father.

A chill rolled down his spine. A frantic feeling filled him as Nightshade stared at Chayton, smiling in sadistic glee.

"No!" Jared yelled. The battle returned to his focus. An explosion rocked the street and Jared was thrown to the ground. Fear filled the youth. Grabbing the bloodstained Scar Blade, he rose from the ground, lost in a crowd of soldiers and warriors. He pushed them aside, but could not see his father or Sister Nightshade. The panic inside of him turned to terror. Screaming, he pushed his allies aside and charged through the crowd.

For a brief second, he caught sight of the council guards, charging up the staircase leading toward the Reaper Kai command group.

"Don't do it!" Jared screamed, but no one heard him.

A snap broke the air close to Jared. A bullet grazed his skull just above his left eye. Blood flowed from the wound, blinding him. Wiping it away, he pushed his way through the mob.

As he broke free from the battle lines, he caught sight of his father. With spear in hand, Chayton was leading a valiant charge against the Reaper Kai command group. Nightshade ordered her forces to attack the ill-equipped warriors. Drawing a curved blade, the matron of the Reaper Kai prepared to face the warriors head-on. She charged with her evil troops, seeking to end the tribal charge.

Goat Minions and powerful war priests slammed into the tribal warriors with frightening results. Severely outnumbered, the tribal council guards were no match for the forces of darkness. Screams of agony rose as the savage forces of darkness butchered the guards.

As he stared in horror, Jared was knocked to the ground once more. He rose to his feet, and was just in time to see Nightshade charge at his own father. Staggering through the center of the courtyard, Jared tried desperately to save Chayton.

Nightshade raised her left hand in the air. A dark spiral of purple light corkscrewed around her arm starting at the elbow. The purple light grew in intensity, thrusting forward in a wave which struck Chayton in the chest. A sick look of pain covered his face as he stopped dead in his tracks. The spear dropped from his hands and he clutched his chest in agony.

"No!" Jared screamed, still staggering through the kill zone. As he rushed to save his father, a bullet slammed into Jared's thigh and he crumpled, gripping his bloody leg. Unconcerned about his own safety, the tribal warrior rose to his feet once more and limped across the courtyard, moving as fast as he could, his gaze transfixed on Chayton.

Another wave of sick purple light struck Jared's trembling father. The look of agony on his face turned to sheer torture. Falling to his knees, he clutched his chest, tears streaming down his face. Blood trickled from his mouth as he gagged. He began to retch, a stream of blood erupting from his mouth as he lay prone and defenseless. Meanwhile, Nightshade drew closer to him, calm and ruthless.

Jared was nearing the steps to the council chambers when Nightshade moved in for the kill, hungering to end Chayton's life. With a sadistic smile, she looked down at the approaching Jared. "This is how it ends, boy!" she screamed at him.

Taking her knife, Sister Nightshade jammed the curved blade into Chayton's throat. He trembled a brief second after being struck by the blade. With immense fortitude, Chayton rose to his feet, blood streaming from the wound on his neck. He stared into the crowd, his vision beginning to dim as his life-force began to ebb.

"Father!" Jared yelled.

Tears streamed down Chayton's face. He could *hear* his beloved boy Jared screaming to him. But was it just his imagination? Frantically he searched the crowd. As he did, Nightshade moved behind him and plunged her knife into him once more, this time in his back. Wincing in pain, Jared's father kept scanning the crowd.

Finally, their eyes met. A fragile smile graced Chayton's lips as he wept, seeing his son for the first time in twenty moons. Jared smiled back as sorrow filled him. In that moment, nothing seemed to matter. All that mattered in the whole world was the love between a father and son. Flashes of warmth filled Jared as he stared into his father's eyes. A feeling of safety coursed through him.

"Everything will be all right!" Chayton shouted as blood poured from his open wounds. "I love you, son!"

"No!" Jared screamed.

His father's strength had failed. The wounds he had sustained were too much to bear. Chayton, proud warrior of Scarskin, fell to the ground and passed into death.

A hero is someone who feels such bitter outrage, such bitter agony and hatred, that nothing can stop them from attaining justice. A sprig of despair filled Jared as he watched his father die at the hands of the Reaper Kai priestess. But even as the despair filled him, a vision flashed in his mind, a vision of Banion dying. The combined impact of both Banion and his father dying filled the youth with something other than despair. A bright flash of anger rocked him.

The hopelessness and helplessness were gone. He was not feeble and defenseless. Jared let the overwhelming sense of rage fall over him. No more victims, he pledged. Ignoring his own wounds, he knew the answer to his feelings was violence.

He became aware of Banion's revolver in his belt. Pulling it free, he leveled the long-barreled revolver at Nightshade. His aim was quick as he pulled the trigger. Nightshade was stunned by such quick action. Jared's attack left her unprepared and the bullet slammed into her stomach. Reeling back, she called for her brethren to defend her.

"Kill the boy!" she screamed. A band of Goat Minions, hearing the call, charged down the staircase towards Jared.

Unable to move quickly, Jared plodded onward, step by step. With the Scar Blade in one hand and Banion's revolver in the other, he was unstoppable. Jared wanted to be cruel; he wanted them to suffer. As a result, he showed no mercy.

The first Goat Minion that reached Jared was totally unprepared for the tribal youth. The creature attacked hastily, and its aggression was met with more severe force. Jared slammed his blade into the Goat Minion's arm, shearing it off with its weapon still in hand. The stunned creature staggered and fell backwards on the stairs. When it was prone, Jared slammed his sword into its forehead, killing it instantly.

A second Goat Minion charged as Jared's sword was stuck in the skull of the first beast. Without a hint of fear, Jared grabbed the wrist of the second beast with his right hand. Placing the barrel of Banion's revolver against the Goat Minion's chin, he pulled the trigger. The gun roared and the creature's head whipped back as the bullet killed it instantly.

With a grunt, Jared pulled his sword free and continued to slowly plod up the staircase. Time and time again, he was attacked by the savage Goat Minions, but each one that tried died a horrible, violent death at Jared's hands. Reaper Kai priests flung their psychic attacks at Jared with no result. The strange raven totem around his neck absorbed the dark energy, harmlessly dissipating it.

Step by step he moved toward the council chambers. Unbeknownst to the youth, most of the gunfire had stopped behind him in the courtyard. He was lost in a trance, a killing rage that he could not abandon. Without a semblance of emotion upon his face, he killed again and again.

When he reached the landing, Nightshade was lying up against the doors to the council chambers, bleeding profusely from her gunshot wound. The remaining priests and Goat Minions charged the youth. Limping forward, he swung and slashed, dismembering and killing with sinister precision. Dispatching all in his path, he cleared a gruesome trail to his ultimate goal: Sister Nightshade.

In the courtyard below, the gunfire had ended several minutes ago. All remnants of the Reaper Kai army were at the doors to the council chamber, and Jared had butchered almost all of them. A chilling silence had washed over all those who lingered in the courtyard. All had witnessed Jared's ascent up the stairs. All had witnessed the stark brutality and horrendous violence unleashed by the youth. Sorrow overwhelmed the crowd as they stared at Jared kill his way through any opposition.

And so the last of the Reaper Kai, Sister Nightshade, lay against the doors to the Scarskin High Council. Jared approached her with a look of dispassion upon his face.

"You worthless boy!" she taunted him. "I enjoyed what I did! I enjoyed my life and the agony I unleashed! Life is about taking what is rightfully yours and I never wavered, nor let any sense of morality cloud my judgment. I am proud of what I did, what I took."

Jared continued limping towards her. He ignored her words. As he hunched forward like a blood-soaked zombie, Nightshade saw the gore-stained Scar Blade in his hand and knew her death was near.

"I will never be ashamed of my actions! You hear me, boy?" Nightshade taunted him.

Standing beside her, he lifted the Scar Blade and struck her. Without any emotion, he lifted the blade and struck her again. She screamed, but it didn't matter. Like a machine, Jared repeatedly struck her with the Scar Blade. He simply wanted vengeance. He wanted to kill her. Killing a defenseless person didn't seem like murder at that point; Jared had nothing left inside of him. It simply didn't matter to him. He needed to do what needed to be done.

Sister Nightshade, the last of the Reaper Kai, died at the hands of Jared. Her lifeless body lay battered against the door to the council chambers, but Jared didn't seem to notice. With a blank expression on his face, he continued to strike her dead body with his sword. Like a robot, he struck the corpse again and again.

The battle had ended and all the remaining Iron Kai troops, nomad warriors, and Scarskin warriors watched in sorrow as Jared mindlessly battered the body.

Walking up the stairs, Tani and Mineera approached Jared. They found him screaming in rage. "Damn you!" Jared yelled at Nightshade. "Get back up!"

Her body did not twitch or shudder. "Damn you!" he screamed again. Rage overwhelmed him and he kicked the body forcefully. "I hate you!" Shaking, he was exhausted and the very core of his being had failed. Flashes of Banion rolled through his mind. The tribal had not mourned his former friend and mentor. Instead he hid the sorrow deep in his heart. Dropping the Scar Blade, he staggered over to his dead father. As he blinked several times, the reality sunk in. Both Banion, who had been like a foster father to him, and his own father were now dead, consumed by war.

Shaking, Jared collapsed upon Chayton. As he buried his face in his dead father's chest, a whimper rose from the boy. The whimper rose to a wail. All of the stress and sorrow inside of Jared could be contained no longer. The sadness exploded from him as he openly wept, his tears mingling with the blood on his face. As he cried, the tears washed away the dried blood.

Mineera and Tani moved behind him, each placing a hand on his shoulder. He did not recoil nor shrink away from their kindness. Kneeling beside him, they both embraced Jared as he cried and wept. As they lingered with him, their own emotions rose to the surface. It was not a time for war. It was a time to grieve; it was a time to heal. The trio wept together, embracing each other, embracing the emotion, honoring the dead. As they embraced, each thought about the long journey that they had taken together. They thought about triumph and tragedy. They thought about bitter enemies and long- lost friends. In that moment, they were a family, a family that had endured hardship and a host of experiences that changed not only their lives but the lives of everyone.

Chapter 54
Demons of the Past

The day was coming to a close. The sun was pushing towards the horizon, bright flares of color illuminating the sky. In the courtyard, two friends stood motionless next to a fresh grave. Staring down with a mixture of emotions, the two companions felt a fresh salt-air breeze brush across their faces.

The grave was located near the wall of the gardens just outside the befouled Rasheed palace. A wooden cross had been planted in the ground without a name listed upon it. Draped around the cross was a purple swath of cloth.

"No one shall know who's buried here but you and me," Globulus instructed in a commanding tone, staring down at the fresh grave.

"You have my word, Globulus," Carla responded in earnest. "I doubt the inhabitants of Rasheed would be happy to know that their dark queen, Marion Toil, is resting in the palace gardens for all eternity. Especially after all the misery and bloodshed she caused this empire."

A silence broke between them once more. Staring down, the two friends noticed a brilliant yellow rose bush near the grave. The beautiful flowering plant filled them both with hope. Even though the world had been dark and twisted for a great many years, life, beautiful life, had taken root and was casting a ray of hope on the world. It was ironic that the rose bush beside which Marion was buried was the same one that she had tried to destroy in a fit of rage many months before. Even though she hated its beauty with all of her might, she could not stop it from flowering. Now she would spend eternity beside the flowers, a testament to failed hate. In time, the flowers would send roots down deep into the earth, deep into the dust that her body would become. In time, the flowers would draw nourishment from her very body, turning wickedness to light.

"It's finally done," Globulus said, kneeling down before the grave. Stretching out his enormous hand, he steadied the wooden cross as tears welled up in his beastly brown eyes. "May you finally be at rest."

Reaching forward, Carla smiled at Globulus and rubbed his shoulder lightly. He did not recoil from her touch; instead, he reached back and gently rubbed her hand.

"Are you leaving?" Carla asked hesitantly.

It took a brief moment for the enormous hippo hybrid to respond. He was lost in thought and didn't want to answer. Finally he mustered the courage to speak. "Yes, I'm leaving tonight. I can't stand to be here anymore. There are too many memories..."

"I understand." Her voice was almost a whisper.

"You can come with me." He spoke without looking at her.

"No, I can't. You need to be with your people, your true family."

"But you have no one," Globulus responded, turning to look at her.

"I have Rasheed."

Snorting, Globulus almost wanted to laugh. "There's no one here anymore in this cursed place."

"More are returning every day. More people are returning home. In time, Rasheed with be as glorious as it once was."

With fresh tears in his eyes, Globulus whispered, "I hope you're right, young Carla."

"Don't be so sad. I know the way to the marshes. I'll visit you often," she promised with a smile.

"You'd better. I'll miss your incessant chatter."

"My chatter? What about yours? You have become a civilized hippo and are quiet good at conversation," she said.

Chuckling, Globulus felt a little embarrassed and smiled at her.

"But I still wish you would take a bath every once in a while. You stink like a musty river," Carla added with a smirk.

"Hey!" he shouted and tried to grab her. But Carla was too quick and dodged his arm.

"You gotta be quicker than that!" she smiled at him.

Laughing, the two friends took a brief moment to revel in their joy. As they smiled at each other, they both knew that they would miss each other's company. But Carla was right; it wasn't that far from Rasheed to the marshes where Globulus would live with his tribe. They stared at one another for many moments, each too emotional to speak. Finally, Globulus rose to his feet and spoke. "I need to get going."

"You could stay and head out in the morning," she suggested. "It's a long haul through the dark."

"No, I need to travel, I need to be home."

"I understand," Carla said awkwardly. As she stared at him, a silent moment filled the void between them. "I guess this is it then."

"Don't say it like that. We'll see each other soon. I'll visit you as well."

"You're right." She moved forward and grabbed his arm, hugging it tightly.

Laughing, he lifted her off the ground completely and gave her a big hug. She giggled and they embraced for a moment. When they hugged, neither of them shed tears; instead they simply smiled. They were good friends and would always treasure their friendship. It didn't matter that they would be separated by a great distance. They had a true friendship that would endure.

Releasing each other, they stared at one another for a brief moment.

"I'll see you soon." Globulus smiled.

"I'll come to your village in the summer time. That's a *promise*."

"I can't wait."

"Goodbye, Globulus," Carla said with a smile.

"Goodbye, Carla," he responded.

Turning away, he moved out of the gardens and exited the palace grounds, passing beyond into the streets of Rasheed. As he left the gardens, the sun set completely, washing the grounds in an icy blackness. A chill breeze rose from the harbor as Carla stood motionless in the garden. Lost in thought, she lingered for many moments.

Her friend was gone, heading home to his tribe in the great marshes to the south. Smiling, she knew that he would have a happy life there.

As darkness overtook the palace grounds, an unsettled feeling washed over Carla. Something strange was clawing at her senses. Out of the corner of her eye, she perceived a shadow moving near the door leading into the palace.

"Hello?" she called out in a hesitant tone.

Nothing responded.

Concerned, she moved over to the groundskeeper's quarters and grabbed a lantern and her pistol. After lighting the lantern, she moved toward the battered door leading into the dark palace. A cold chill rolled down her spine as she approached, a deep sense of dread washing over her. Trembling, she clicked off the safety on her weapon.

"Hello?" she called out again loudly. "Is anyone there?"

At the edge of her hearing Carla thought she heard a whisper followed by a laugh. But when she craned out her neck to hear better, the whisper disappeared. Anxious about the encounter, she looked around the courtyard and found that she was completely alone. She mustered her courage and took a hesitant step inside the palace. As she entered, all of the sounds around her ceased; it was as if she had plugged her ears.

Nervous, she moved the lantern around, trying to see what was hiding in the darkness. She could see absolutely nothing.

"This isn't funny. Globulus, is that you?"

Through a black archway to the north, she could hear the sound of footsteps on the marble floor, but when she pivoted toward the sound, she saw nothing. Moving quickly toward the sound, she passed deeper into the palace. When she crossed through the archway, she found herself near the stairwell leading into the dungeons. A shadow moved near the stairwell. Carla trained her weapon on it, but it disappeared into the darkness.

A shiver of terror rolled down her spine. A blast of frigid air charged her skin with a deep chill. Spinning around, she heard laughter down a passage leading off into another dark portion of the palace. The laughter stilled just as quickly as it had arisen. In the icy blackness, the only thing Carla could hear was her own heart pounding, resounding in her ears.

"This isn't happening," she whispered to herself.

She heard another series of footsteps clattering upon the marble, as if someone was running. When Carla rushed toward the sound, it moved off down a hallway. With lantern in hand, Carla moved to discover the source of the strange sound. Following the footsteps, she pressed deeper into the palace, quickly moving down a series of twisting and turning passages. Finally, the sounds of the footsteps stopped near a wooden door, at the base of one of the towers.

Carla stood motionless, staring at the door with wide-eyed fear as, with a creak, it began to open. Holding the lantern forward, she could still not see anyone opening the door. She stared at the opening door and the emptiness beyond, mesmerized, her body trembling. As she stood in the dark passage, she heard a skittering noise inside the room.

"Come inside..." An audible whisper erupted from the room.

Unable to comprehend the strange events, she was terrified but curious. Mustering her courage, she stepped forward, toward the opening. As she drew closer, the light from her lantern revealed thick cobwebs in the room beyond. She could also see small forms moving inside.

Taking in a deep breath, she stepped inside the room. As her lantern illuminated the darkness, her stomach lurched. All over the room, hundreds of spiders were climbing on soft white webs. In the center of the room, a desiccated corpse was encased within the wispy webs. Dozens of spiders were skittering across the body.

A scream rose in her throat and she yielded to the sensation. The spiders in the room responded and began to descend from the ceiling, hungering for her. Stepping backwards, she tripped and landed on her rump. She looked up in the dim light to find a ceiling writhing with hundreds of spiders, all spinning webs and descending upon her. On all fours, she scrambled out of the room, and not a second too soon. The mass of spiders were now crawling across the marble floor, skittering toward her with great speed. She managed to get to her feet and began to flee down the passage. As she did, feminine laughter rose from the room, rolling out from the darkness.

Stopping in the hall, Carla stared back in horror at the room. The door slammed shut with a deafening thud. Trembling in the darkness, she breathed heavily, having almost been frightened to death by the ghostly events. She listened to the palace around her, still shaking. A chill rolled down her spine as a blast of frigid air surrounded her, engulfing her with a sickly feeling.

She almost screamed as *something* pulled the hair away from her ear. Frosty air blasted her neck as a feminine, throaty voice whispered in her ear. *"I will always be Queen..."* it rasped. Carla spun around to find a shadow in the shape of a woman hovering in the passage. The light from her lantern could not penetrate the mass of shadows.

Running with all of her speed, Carla bolted past the shadow, trying to escape the palace. As she ran down the dark passages of marble, a feminine laughter rose from the darkness. Again and again, a scream echoed through the palace: *"I will always be Queen!"*

Escaping into the gardens, Carla didn't stop until she reached the gardener's quarters. She looked around hastily and found some wooden boards, a hammer, and several nails. Taking the materials back to the shattered palace doors, she pulled the splintered wood together and began to hammer the wooden planks, sealing the doors into the palace tight.

Backing away from the entrance to the palace, she looked across the garden, focusing on the fresh grave near the wall. As she stared at the grave in disbelief, she knew in her heart that although the dark Queen of Rasheed was dead, she was not forgotten. A horrible stain, a sick stain, would forever haunt the palace as she continued to wail in the darkness, urging the foolish to explore the gloomy passages.

Carla escaped unharmed from the palace, but a terror was wedged within her soul. She vowed to never again enter the palace, for it was a place of great evil. Hundreds of people had died there during the Reaper Kai invasion. The betrayal of the dark queen had permanently tainted the palace with great malice and evil.

Unable to sleep, Carla sat outside the gardener's quarters, staring up at the palace. From time to time, she would hear voices roll out from the darkness. Shadows flickered in the windows. Shaking her head in dismay, Carla knew what must be done. When the sun rose over the palace of Rasheed, she exited the palace grounds. Contacting what remained of the Rasheed militia, she ordered that the palace gates be sealed. The militia acknowledged the order and acted with no hesitation, sealing off the palace of Rasheed and allowing no one entry.

Carla was disturbed by the events, but resolutely shook off the feeling. Although she had experienced a wicked occurrence within the palace, she resolved never to disclose what she had undergone, especially to Globulus.

As she stood in street outside the great palace, she vowed once more to never enter the cursed ruins again. Shaking off the chill in her heart, she turned away from the scene and viewed the busy streets of Rasheed. Life was returning to the city. Merchants were already setting up a makeshift market place. In the distance, a man was shouting that he had fresh fish for sale. Just a block down, a juggler was entertaining a group of children. Smiling, Carla resolved to spend the rest of the day wandering through the market.

She remained in Rasheed and took up residence near the harbor. Charming and charismatic, she had no difficulty finding new friends. Enjoying the freedom from war, she lived her life in peace, spending her days fishing on the ocean and her evenings by the harbor with her friends, looking out into the ocean and watching the waves crash against the shore. At last, Carla was home.

Chapter 55
Among the Marshes

A crisp chill rolled from the mountains to the north. With a look of hesitation, Globulus stared at his surroundings as his stomach lurched. It was finally time for him to return home.

His past had been mired in a series of unusual events. The gracious King Toil of Rasheed had saved the Crushing-Fist tribe from certain death by providing food to the starving tribe. When the gentle king was contacted, the only payment he requested from the tribe in return was that one of their male children be provided to the Toil family, to be raised by the royal family and act as their protector. The chief of the hippo tribe could not in good conscience send a child away from the tribe unless it was his own. Making a tough decision, the chief sent his eldest son, Globulus, to live with King Toil in Rasheed.

From that point on, Globulus had felt like an outcast, forced to leave his village to live with a human royal family. This set of events had sculpted and changed him into a fierce warrior leader, but had kept him from contact with his own kind, his own race.

Now that the war was over and the entire Toil family was gone, Globulus resolved to finish his life in the company of his own kind.

His travels had brought him through the mountains to an area below the enormous snow fields and glaciers. In this secluded valley, the desert had flooded, forming an enormous marsh fed by the snow fields from the mountains to the north. This lush valley was where Globulus' kind had made their home.

As the cool air from the mountains brushed his face, he was filled with anxiety. Standing knee deep in the marsh water, he almost wanted to flee from the valley. He knew that he was part of the tribe, but his past alienation made it difficult for him to want to reassimilate back into their ranks. Globulus had led his people in war, but it seemed more like a dream than reality. He was a warrior, bred to fight. Now that the world was at peace, what would be his place in the tribe? Would he still be accepted?

This and many other questions plagued his senses and he was hard pressed to deal with such emotion. Standing at the edge of the marsh, he resolved to move forward, to be with his people.

As he passed through the tall reeds, a sense of happiness began to replace his sense of dread. Images from his early childhood flooded his mind. It *felt* right to him, to be back home among the marshes. Flashes of joy filled him. Images of his family entered his mind as he pushed toward the village at the center of the marsh. Familiar smells wafted through his enormous nostrils. The warm water against his battered skin felt wonderful. Giving in to his emotions, he submerged his enormous body into the marsh. It felt refreshing to feel the water around him.

Instinct kicked in and he began to swim through the waterways, between the reeds. Swimming in the warm sunlight made him feel even better. Following his old memories, he passed through the water, knowing the way home.

It took only a brief period of time for Globulus to reach the outskirts of the village. The closer he got to home, the less anxiety he felt. Deep down, Globulus wanted to be with own kind.

His advance remained unnoticed as he neared the village. Reaching its perimeter, he unceremoniously crawled out of the water, exposing his enormous form. Walking upright, he began to move toward the center of the village, toward his father's lodge. As he moved, the citizens, proud members of the hippo tribe, noticed his arrival. They looked dreamily upon Globulus without saying a single word. Since the death of his father, the tribe had been leaderless. Globulus' arrival sent a tremor of hope back into the citizens, whose faces broke out in wide smiles. A procession began to follow him as he advanced toward the house in which he had lived as a small beastling.

Globulus noticed the silent procession and simply smiled broadly, his enormous tusk-like teeth erupting from his mouth. His anxiety was gone, replaced by sheer joy. His stomach no longer lurched but rather was filled with excitement.

The entire village knew of his arrival. Everyone clambered to see the legendary Globulus return home. He reached the door to his father's lodge and stood still for a moment. His beastly brown hand reached forward, touching the worn wood. As he did, he closed his eyes.

In that moment, a vision of his father flashed into his mind. The day was warm and his proud father was lifting young Globulus in the air, spinning him round and around. Young Globulus was giggling with joy. In that moment, the world was perfect, father and son playing in the sun. "My boy!" Chief Stoneskin boomed in a warm voice.

The image disappeared as Globulus opened his eyes. Smiling, he knew that he was finally home, finally at peace. Taking in a full breath of air, he prepared to address his brethren and fellow members of the tribe. With exhilaration filling him, Globulus turned around and looked out at the hippo tribe before him.

With amazement, he saw thousands of his kind staring back at him, tears in their eyes. The tribe was just as happy to see the legendary Globulus as he was to see all of them. For a moment, silence was the only sound. His heart was pounding as he witnessed their joy.

A hippo at the front of the crowd bowed to Globulus in a gesture of respect. The tribute started a tidal wave of movement. Every citizen of the village bowed before Globulus, acknowledging his homecoming. After all had bowed before him, Globulus returned the gesture and bowed to the tribe in return.

A yell erupted from somewhere in the crowd. "All hail Globulus, Chief of the Crushing-Fist!"

The proclamation was followed by a flurry of cheering. Globulus had returned home and his people welcomed him with open arms. He was now the chief of the tribe, a wonderful honor, especially since peace had swept over the land. The cheering crowd surged forward, hoisting their new leader into the air, carrying him on their backs. The cheers lasted for many moments. When they ended, the village rallied and a grand banquet was given that very night in honor of Globulus' homecoming.

Although his life had been filled with strife, the mighty warrior Globulus had endured the hardships and emerged victorious. The strife in his life was over. It was a time for celebration and joy; it was a time to simply live life in the marsh, in the company of friends and family.

Chapter 56
The Last Emperor

Magistrate Riches was dumbfounded. He sat motionless in his chair, overseeing the official proceeding. As he listened to Emperor Gunther speak, a chill rolled down his spine. What Riches was witnessing was the end of an era for the Iron Kai Empire. With trepidation building in his heart, he stared in wonder at their valiant leader.

Gunther stood before the court with a reserved look on his face. His expression was confident, but conveyed a hint of sadness. Looking around the room, he knew what must be done to protect the future of the Iron Kai Empire.

"During the course of this war, formal charges were brought against me. I was charged with treason for ordering a covert strike against Reaper Kai operatives within the empire. I recklessly abandoned the laws of this nation in an effort to secure the safety of all. I knew what I did was against the law but shirked that responsibility. I am here to formally admit my guilt for these charges." Gunther spoke in a bold tone, gazing around the room.

A hush rolled over the courtroom. Everyone present knew of Gunther's criminal conduct but no one wanted to see him charged for breaking the laws of the nation. If it were not for Gunther's guidance and leadership during the war, the Iron Kai would have been crushed and the Reaper Kai would have secured a victory. Everyone knew that Gunther was the key to the empire's survival. Where once the crowd had been ready to convict him and send him to the gallows, today no one wanted to see justice served in this instance.

"I think it goes without saying that you have been absolved of all charges due to the service you have given in securing the safety of this empire. No one in this room wants to see you suffer for the laws you've broken," Riches pleaded with Gunther.

"I am not admitting guilt so that I can be punished," Gunther replied. "I am admitting guilt so that change, real change, can be created."

"I don't understand," a councilman responded in a confused tone.

"In times of old, sweeping witch hunts killed thousands of innocent people. We instituted laws against covert actions aimed at the populace to ensure security. If I had acted against the interests of this nation, we would be in a much different set of circumstances right now. I could have aided the enemy and our nation would have fallen."

"But you didn't act against this nation," Magistrate Riches protested with a look of concern.

"The point is that the position of emperor in this nation wields too much power. One person should not be able to control the entire military. A balance needs to be instituted so that corruption cannot take root within this nation. There exists an imminent danger with one person wielding so much power," Gunther explained.

"I'm not following what you are proposing."

"In my last act as emperor of this great nation, I am proposing that the position of emperor be permanently removed. I propose that since the emperor's vote is the most powerful in this nation, three additional representatives be added to the government so that the power of the military can be dispersed to prevent corruption."

The audience was stunned. The most beloved and powerful leader that the Iron Kai Empire had ever produced was pushing to have his power removed. An eerie hush gripped the audience as they watched in amazement. This was a true turning point in the administration of a nation.

"You're giving up your power permanently?" a representative asked, as a sense of awe filled him. "You understand what you are proposing?"

"Yes, I do," Gunther said in a confident tone. "The representatives of this nation are to act in accordance with the wishes and interests of the populace. The position of emperor within this nation is contrary to these beliefs. I am attempting to abolish the position of emperor in an attempt to return control of the nation back to the people."

Blinking in amazement, Magistrate Riches felt emotion course through him. Gunther's words made sense. The power of one man should not exceed the interests of the masses. With a shaky hand, Riches banged his gavel once to obtain the attention of the audience.

"The proposal at hand is to abolish the position of emperor in this great nation and to replace this position with three representatives so that the populace has greater control of this nation. Please record the motion and votes."

The voting proceeded and each representative in turn approved the motion, agreeing to the conditions at hand. Finally, it was Gunther's turn. As the vote came to him, he added an additional provision.

"Part of our heritage was a dark heritage. The Reaper Kai order was part of our history. Now that it is clear that we no longer require an emperor to govern, I propose that our nation be renamed so that we can move on from the tortured past that we have all endured. I propose that the Iron Kai Empire be renamed the Dakota Nation at this time, and this day will act as the first step toward a free society, a society that will be governed by the people."

His final proposal as emperor was quickly approved by all others. Finally, the vote came down to Gunther. All he needed to do was to approve his own resolution and the empire would no longer be an empire but rather a free society governed by the people. A silence rolled over the courtroom as the valiant leader stood in front of them all. Taking a silent moment, Gunther thought about his life and the great service he had given to his nation. With a broad smile, he looked out into the audience and in a confident tone, affirmed his own proposal to abolish the position of emperor and to rename the nation.

"I, Emperor Gunther of the Iron Kai Empire, fully support the motion to abolish the position of emperor and to change the name of the Iron Kai Empire to the Dakota Nation."

With that, the proposal was accepted unanimously and Emperor Gunther, the last emperor of the Iron Kai nation, stepped into legend and into the history books. With a resounding cheer, the audience rose to their feet and yelled in support of Gunther. He was emperor no more, but it didn't matter to him; all Gunther had ever wanted was for his people to live in freedom from tyranny and fear.

Wearing a proud smile, Gunther felt tears sting his eyes as he looked out into the audience. He knew that the long road through the darkness was finally at an end. His people were safe, and he knew that the torture his soul had undergone was well worth the reward of rescuing his people from oppression.

In that moment, Gunther was truly happy, truly at peace. Smiling, he yielded to his emotions and bowed before the audience. "I lived only to serve you all. Leading this nation was the greatest honor of my life. I am proud to have served you all," he declared while waving at the crowd.

As he spoke, the crowd simply cheered louder. With boisterous yells, many in the room rushed forward and grabbed Gunther, lifting him off the ground and onto their shoulders. Cheering and chanting his name, the rest of the crowd followed, rushing Gunther out of the courthouse and into the streets beyond. As they cheered his name, more and more citizens rushed into the street to join them. The parade travelled through the city while everyone rejoiced.

It was the end of an era for the Darken Realm. The Reaper Kai had been defeated and the land was brought back from the brink of ruin. Peace had returned and the Dakota Nation was ready and willing to help rebuild the ruins.

Gunther would always be remembered for his fierce temperament and his unwavering duty not just to the people of the Iron Kai Empire, but to those of the entire Darken Realm.

Chapter 57
Home at Last

He felt strange as he stood in the darkness, letting all of his senses come alive. Opening the door to his small room, Tani stood in silence and awe for a few moments. It had been over twenty moons since the youth had beheld his tiny room. Shaking as he stood in the gloom, he felt the tears well up in his eyes. Tani fought back the emotion, trying to keep from collapsing.

"Are you all right, son?" a soothing voice emerged from the hallway as Tani's father eyed him with concern.

"I'm fine," Tani lied as he quickly brushed the tears away from his eyes. Placing his wire-rim glasses back on his nose, he took a deep breath and entered his tiny room.

Closing the door behind him, Tani lit a candle on the desk, sparking a flicker of light from the darkness. In the dancing light of the flame, the scholar took a brief moment to survey his belongings.

A giant stack of old-world books rested near his small wooden desk. Moving over to them, he openly wept, overjoyed to finally be home. As he stood near the stack, a strong smell of chemicals wafted through his nose. Tani smiled, his tattered hands grabbing for an earthenware jar. Pulling open the cork stopper, he peered inside. Leaves with medicinal properties filled the jar. Reaching for a leaf, he pulled it free and sniffed it quickly. A pungent odor greeted his nose but it brought back such fond memories.

Dropping his backpack on the floor of his room, he unshouldered his submachine gun, resting it next to his desk. Tani sat down in his worn chair, eyeing the gun with a distant look. The weapon was out of place and didn't seem to belong. In that moment, he realized that his life was never going to be the same as it had been.

A long time ago, a timid scholar had emerged from his room to meet the world head-on. After twenty full moons of experiences, the youth would never be the same. He had been to the edge where life and death mix and mingle. He had gone through the very limits of fatigue and emotional distress. The youth had seen and experienced more in his Exile than the entire village had experienced collectively.

The fragile-minded boy had learned to trust in himself and his own instincts. He learned never to surrender and to always have hope. Tani learned that in the end, self sacrifice is the only thing that really matters when the world is falling apart. The fragile boy had changed and grown well beyond his years. And although he was young in appearance, his body was worn and battered. Scars covered his form and his eyes spoke volumes. Whereas once he had been carefree and wonderstruck, the look of awe had been replaced by a calm, conscious gaze.

Staring at the submachine gun on the floor, he removed his belt and placed several hand grenades next to the submachine gun.

"So the old me has met the new me," Tani whispered, seeing his possessions of war resting near his beloved books. Tani was a soldier and a scholar. He was a great philosopher but also a killer, someone who had taken lives to protect not only himself but the entire Darken Realm.

As he reintroduced himself to his old belongings, a deep sense of sorrow washed over him. Flashes of violence rolled through his mind. Screams and blood spatters erupted in his memories. He shook uncontrollably as the visions tore at his very soul. Focusing back on the long journey he had made, he realized that he had done some horrible things in the name of being a hero. He had murdered and deceived. He had seen his countrymen and friends die beside him. Shaking his head, he tried to force the horrid thoughts out of his mind.

As he struggled, he wanted to give it all back, all the hurt, all the madness. In that very moment, he wished that he could relinquish it all, all of his experiences, all of the sorrow. Wiping the tears from his eyes, he shook his head in disbelief. Even as he fought back the hurt in his heart for what he had experienced, he knew deep down that it had been the right thing to do.

In the end, Tani had persevered and struggled to save not only himself but the entire Darken Realm. He had seen horrendous things but he had also witnessed countless acts of heroism and courage. He had seen bloodshed but had also seen love and compassion. Shaking his head, Tani knew that he wouldn't take back any of it, not even a single moment. He had lived on the edge and had experienced everything that the world had to offer. If he had to go back, he would have walked the same path again.

That startling revelation gave him peace, real peace, something that Tani had not experienced since leaving the village of Scarskin so many moons ago.

"And here you are, Master Tani, here in your room once more," an aged voice emerged from the darkness beyond the boy.

Spinning around, Tani saw Master Mogi standing in the doorway to his room. He was limping severely, having been wounded in the siege upon the village. Bowing in respect, Tani motioned the aged man to enter the room.

"When last we spoke, I urged you not to pass beyond the eastern reaches of the wasteland. I urged you not to sacrifice yourselves to the cruel wasteland. Now you stand before me, a mere boy, but with memories that are beyond even my own. So how does it feel, young Tani? How does it feel to have defied the entire world and returned from the brink of madness?" Mogi quizzed him.

Tani held silent for a brief moment, biting his lower lip. Finally he let out a sigh and looked directly at Mogi. "It feels wonderful. I feel wonderful. I did everything in my power to make things better. I fought with everything inside of me and I made a difference. Everything inside of me mattered. Everything I am was good enough. I succeeded where so many others had failed and I emerged victorious. Master Mogi, even though I will never be the same and have seen such horrible things, I would never take any of it back. In the end, I lost part of my soul but I made a difference.

When the world was falling apart, I helped bring it back from the edge."

"You did indeed, Master Tani, or should I say Councilman Tani?" Mogi smiled and slapped the youth on the back.

"What?" Tani asked with a look of surprise on his face.

"Being appointed to the high council of Scarskin requires leadership and strong character. Everyone on the council agrees that you have what it takes to lead this village."

"Me?" Tani spoke with a surprised grin on his face. "A member of the high council?"

"Yourself and Master Jared. You have both been selected to lead the village of Scarskin as full councilmen."

Blinking, Tani smiled. Being a member of the high council was the highest honor that any tribal could aspire to hold, a colossal achievement.

"But I'm too young. No one has ever been elected to the council at this age. I'm barely eighteen years old!" Tani frowned.

"Eighteen with eighty years of combat and leadership experience." Mogi laughed. "So, what say you?"

Frowning, Tani averted his gaze and stared at his weapons on the floor next to his books, troubled, then looked back at Mogi. "What did Jared say? What did he say about joining the council?"

Mogi sighed, replying in a dull tone, "He needs some more time to think about it."

"More time?" Tani blinked in amazement. "But this is what he always wanted, to be on the high council."

"I'm not sure what he wants, Tani," Mogi said with a hint of sadness. "He needs some time to himself. He has been through a lot."

Nodding, Tani agreed. The death of Jared's father wasn't the only tragedy he had been forced to endure. Jared had lost more than any member of Nova 7. Banion's death was the first in a chilling line of losses for the tribal warrior. Jared had then been forced to witness his father's death in the battle of Scarskin, and to make matters worse, when the smoke cleared and the battle had finally ended, the blood-smeared warrior reached his former home only to find further loss. His entire family, including his mother and sister, had been killed in the battle. Jared was now a lonely mass of worn leather. His soul had been chaffed and battered beyond recognition.

"I agree, time is what he needs." Tani nodded back and let out a heavy sigh. "I'm worried about him."

"We all are." Mogi nodded back, then changed the subject. "It is good to see you back in one piece, Tani. Get some rest; the inauguration is tomorrow. You'll need all of your strength if you are to help lead us out of this mess and help rebuild the village."

Tani nodded, and Master Mogi moved out of his room, shutting the door as he left.

Exhausted, Tani put his feet up on his desk, looking around his room lazily. Finally his eyes landed upon his enormous pile of books. In the center of the stack, a title caught his eye. Reaching forward, he liberated the ancient book from the stack, opening it gently. He looked at the first page, smiling as the eyes behind his wire-rimmed glasses began to move back and forth, hungrily absorbing each and every written word.

The scholar of Scarskin was finally home, sitting amongst a stack of books. Tani spent the rest of the evening reading in his ramshackle room, still littered with broken electrical devices and jars of chemicals. The boy who had been timid had grown to a man in the span of twenty full moons. He was no longer scared to voice his opinions or to act on his instincts. The boy had grown into a leader, someone who could shape and mold the minds of others around him. He had succeeded not only in surviving, but in meeting the challenges of adulthood.

Tani fell asleep that night at his desk, as he had done countless times as a child. With his face buried in a book, he slept soundly, slumped awkwardly in his tattered chair. The scholar of Scarskin was finally home and finally at peace.

Chapter 58
Fond Farewell

"Tani!" Mineera called out excitedly, waving at the young scholar. Standing on his tiptoes, Tani looked through the crowd and found her after a few confused moments.

"I thought it was you," Tani said as he moved toward her. With a warm smile, he hugged her tightly. She responded to the affection and held him close. They let go and stared at each other for an awkward moment, neither of them knowing what to say.

"I wanted to congratulate you. You must be proud to be part of the high council," Mineera said.

"It hasn't really sunk in yet. Last time I was here in Scarskin, I was a child. Now it seems that I'm finally home, but the home I left will never return. So much has changed, but more importantly, I've changed."

"Changed for the better." Mineera's tone was confident.

"Maybe..." Tani responded with a distant look in his eye. "Part of me seems gone forever."

"You're a compassionate person, Tani. Don't ever let anyone tell you otherwise."

"Thanks," the scholar replied. "It seems so strange, being on the council, able to change Scarskin for the better. I'll be able to change policy and sculpt how future generations live. It's an amazing feeling, but scary, too."

"Scary?" Mineera laughed. "After everything that we've experienced, being a politician is scary to you?"

"Well, if I was scared before, I could just lob a hand grenade at whatever was trying to kill us. Something tells me lobbing hand grenades during a session of the council wouldn't go over very well." Tani laughed.

Mineera smiled, but her eyes were wary and there was concern locked behind those peaceful blue globes. Looking quickly over Tani's shoulder, she seemed to be scanning the crowd for someone.

"He didn't show up to the inauguration," Tani said gravely, knowing who Mineera was looking for. "I think Jared still needs some time. He needs some time to heal and to be alone."

"I know," Mineera responded. "I'm worried about him."

"Don't be." A confident voice emerged from the crowd right beside them. Jared was moving toward them, a look of sheer exhaustion on his face. "I'm doing fine, really."

"Jared," Mineera said warmly. "It's good to see you." Her words were heartfelt and she smiled in earnest at the young warrior. When last they met, Jared had been utterly hostile, consumed by bitter rage. He seemed exhausted now, but was not overtly hostile towards her.

"It's good to see you too," Jared responded in an appreciative tone, then looked away, seeming suddenly self-conscious. He had been a bitter fiend to Mineera last time they had been together and guilt was beginning to affect his demeanor.

"Congratulations, Jared. Being a member of the Scarskin council is a great honor."

"Honor?" Jared laughed. "Yeah, I guess so."

"Would have helped if you'd have shown up to the ceremony," Tani mused, his tone sarcastic. "You're the first member of the high council in the entire history of Scarskin that missed the inauguration. You are a legend once more."

"Legend?" Jared smiled and shook his head in disgust. "There's nothing legendary about me." He laughed to himself and shifted his gaze from his friends.

"Well, I congratulate both of you again. Your village is lucky to have two great leaders to help in rebuilding and shaping the future of your tribe," Mineera said, encouraging.

"Listen."   Jared sighed and shifted the conversation immediately away from the inauguration. "I'm sorry," he blurted out.

"You don't need to apologize," she responded.

"Yes, I do. I was an asshole. I let my emotions get the better of me. I let rage guide my senses. I shouldn't have left without saying goodbye." Jared spoke with a sheepish look on his pale face.

"Banion's death hurt you deeply."

"It hurt us all deeply," Jared responded. "It was so personal to me. I felt so responsible for his death. If my gun wouldn't have jammed, he would still be alive. I was responsible for Banion's death."

"The only ones responsible for Banion's death were the Reaper Kai," Tani declared firmly. "It wasn't your fault."

"I don't see it that way," Jared said with tears in his eyes. "He died saving my life."

"He died because he loved you and couldn't stand to see you hurt or killed. He sacrificed himself because he loved you," Mineera countered.

"But why me?" Jared asked, bitterness in his voice. "I would have rather died that day than to let him die. Why couldn't I have died that day instead?"

"You feel ashamed of what happened because you're just like Banion," Mineera stated, her voice confident.

"What?" Jared asked in confusion.

"You're suffering because you are selfless, just like Banion. You wished you would have died, and that's what makes you like Banion. When you were in danger, Jared, Banion only thought about your safety. Just like you wished you could trade places with him, Banion felt the same way about you. You would have sacrificed yourself to save him and Banion did the same for you. You're ashamed of what happened because you're just like Banion. You're selfless. You are like Banion," Mineera concluded, and Jared felt a sting of sadness hit him.

"Just stop it," he said. "I didn't deserve his charity."

"Yes, you did," Tani said with tears in his eyes. "You did deserve his charity."

"Stop." Jared wept.

"You've suffered enough, Jared. From the beginning of this journey, you have suffered."

"But we all did," he countered.

"Yes, we did, and in a sense we all deserve each other's charity. We are a family, a team that went well beyond all sense of sanity and reached deep within ourselves to do what was right, no matter the cost to ourselves. Each of us has suffered on this journey and will never be the same."

"Why didn't you just give up on me?" Jared asked, bitterness in his voice. "I'm not happy with what I've become. I've done unspeakable things. Why didn't you give up on me?"

"Because you never gave up on me," Mineera replied and reached out, grabbing his shoulders with her soft hands. "When I was lost to the shadow, lost to the darkness, you found forgiveness and learned to trust me again. I tried to kill you, Jared, but yet you forgave me. I can't give up on you since you never gave up on me."

"I'm such a fool." Jared spoke in earnest. "When we left the village at the beginning of our Exile, I wanted to be a hero, a valiant adventurer. But being a hero isn't about fame or gratitude; it's about heartbreak, it's about suffering. I always looked up to Banion and wanted to be like him. And now, I am him."

Nodding in agreement, Tani and Mineera looked at Jared in silence. It was absolutely true. A blinding act of violence had torn Banion from life, robbing all of them of a father figure and mentor. That act of violence had polarized Jared into a vicious killing machine with the skills to bring about the destruction of the Dark Order. And just like Banion, Jared had suffered great loss at the hands of the Reaper Kai, losing his entire family to violence. He was broken. He was alone. He was lost in anger. Jared's ultimate fate was the same as Banion's, consumed by bitterness and rage that led to violence.

"I'm sorry for missing the inauguration," Jared concluded, changing the subject. "It was childish."

"I think everyone understands," Tani replied.

"I hope you're right." Jared laughed.

For a brief moment, the remnants of Nova 7 stood in silence, listening to the world around them. Hundreds of tribals were moving about, reconstructing their homes, repairing the damage done during the invasion. There was not a single family that had managed to avoid loss during the invasion. Each family had lost loved ones, but it didn't seem to matter. To the people of Scarskin, the invasion now seemed like a trial, a harsh lesson to learn. Each member of the village was suffering inside but each person knew that they had to push onward. The industrious work to rebuild their world was, in a sense, helping repair the loss in their hearts.

After a brief moment of reflection, Jared turned to Mineera.

"What are you going to do?" he quizzed her. "The war is over and you're the last of your kind."

"I'm going to start over." Mineera spoke with exuberance. "I'm going to settle in the Frontier, start a monastery and help heal the heartbreak caused by this war."

"Start a monastery? What are you going to do there? Pray to your *God*?" Tani spoke with a hint of sarcasm in his voice, which was not lost on Mineera. Instantly she answered his challenge.

"What are you going to do, Tani? Hang out in a library? Maybe roll around in a pile of paper? Smear ink all over your face?" she shot back.

Tani laughed. "You win that one, Mineera. That was really nasty."

"Thanks." She smiled back. "No, really, I think I have a great opportunity to teach others and to help rebuild the world. I don't have a home, but I'll make one for myself and others."

"You could always stay here, with us," Tani offered.

For a moment, Mineera grappled with the offer. It would be a peaceful life, living in the village of Scarskin, far from the politics of civilized society, away from strife and intolerance. But living in Scarskin would be the easy path and Mineera had never walked such a path in all of her years. Although the offer was gracious, she could not accept.

"Thanks for the offer," she responded. "But there are others with great need. I can help more people if I leave and settle in a war-ravaged area." Looking around at the ruins of Scarskin, she adjusted her comment. "Or rather, a *more* war ravaged area."

"I know you wouldn't have it any other way," Jared replied with a smile.

"So this is it then," she declared in a cryptic tone.

"Huh?" Tani responded.

Moving forward, she grabbed Tani with one arm and Jared with the other. Pulling them close, she hugged them tightly. For many moments, she hugged them without a word. Finally, she released them, smiling and bowing before them. "I now take my leave. Farewell, Jared and Tani of the Scarskin tribe."

"Farewell? You're leaving now?" Jared asked, astonished.

"Yes, we have several hours of sunlight left before sundown and many miles to go." She pointed toward the front gate of the village, where a host of nomad warriors, Iron Kai soldiers, and the twelve Oracles were waiting patiently for Mineera to join them on their journey away from the village of Scarskin.

"You can't leave now!" Tani whined.

"I have to go." Mineera's tone was resolute.

"Then get back here," Tani said, opening his arms again. "I want to hug you one last time."

Smiling, she moved back to Tani and they embraced once more. As they did, Tani and Mineera both began to weep. Embracing each other, Tani and Mineera felt at peace. After releasing one another, they wiped the tears from their eyes and exchanged a smile.

Jared then stepped toward Mineera and grasped her hands in his own. Squeezing them tightly, he felt tears sting his own eyes. Looking at her soft blue eyes, he smiled and spoke in a whisper. "I'm glad that I knew you, Mineera."

"I'm glad to have known you also, Jared. I'll think of you often and keep you in my heart for the rest of my life." Squeezing his hands firmly, she moved forward and hugged him tightly. Jared responded and embraced her in turn. They separated and Mineera turned away, pushing through the crowd of tribals busily rebuilding the village.

In the soft light of the afternoon sun, Jared and Tani watched Mineera move to the front gates of the village. Climbing atop a horse, she pulled her blue hood over her face and directed her horse towards the gate. The rest of the formation began to move out. When she was almost outside the gate, Mineera reined her horse to a halt. The horse responded to her command. Looking through the crowd, she stared at the tribals one last time. Removing her hood, she smiled at both of them. She gently kissed her hand and then flung it toward them, gesturing that she was giving them one final kiss goodbye. Jared and Tani smiled back at her, each of them waving to her.

Turning away, Mineera urged her horse onwards, pressing outside the front gate of the village of Scarskin. In the blink of an eye, she was gone. Jared and Tani stood in silence for many moments, staring at the spot where Mineera had disappeared from their lives. Both felt a hint of sadness at her passing, but that emotion was overwhelmed by a feeling of warmth as they thought about her. Mineera was gone from their lives but Jared and Tani would always hold a special place in their hearts for her.

"Farewell, Mineera," Tani whispered.

Jared smiled and slapped Tani on the shoulder. "Come on, Councilman Tani, we have a village to rebuild."

Chapter 59
The Sanctuary

A warm, gentle breeze was blowing through the northlands. The grasslands danced as each pulse and push of the wind touched the green stalks of grass. Viewing the breeze gently touch the grass was soothing, almost hypnotic. In the midst of this scene, a woman sat in silence and solitude, watching with warmth filling her heart.

Mineera had returned to the heart of the Frontier with the twelve Oracles. In the center of the Frontier, upon a ridgeline, stood a monastery overlooking an ancient river that snaked through the lush plains. Brick walls surrounded a courtyard filled with saplings of exotic trees that had been donated by many towns and villages within the Darken Realm. New monks tended the growing gardens, breathing life into the courtyard.

Beyond the courtyard was a stone church, built with care. Behind the church was a dormitory and eating hall for the monks. Rising from the base of the dormitory was a solitary tower, soaring several stories off the ground. It was in this tower that Mineera had made her home. With a modest wooden desk and a simple bed, the holy woman was at peace, true peace for the first time in her life. She ran the newly constructed monastery and for the first time, felt like she had a home, a true home.

As Mineera reflected upon the strange events of her life, singing arose in the courtyard below. Monks, both men and women, were singing in the gardens as they tended to the green plants. As the gentle wind brushed the grasses beyond the walls, Mineera listened to the peaceful melodies and smiled.

War, the bitter threat to all life, had finally ended. The Darken Realm, just like Mineera, was finally at peace. Instead of fear ruling the minds of the populace, hope had made a welcome return. As peace and hope filled her emotions, she reflected upon her life.

Her road to her current life at the monastery had been an extraordinary one. Born into the Dark Order, Mineera was raised with the teachings of the Reaper Kai order. The fundamentals of evil taught her to focus on her own aspirations and to use violence to further her goals. Evil was about strength and punishing the weak for their failings. Immersion in such a wicked climate led Mineera down the wrong path; a child raised in such an environment believes that evil is the only way of life. When everyone around the child is acting in a violent, evil manner, there is little hope that the child can see the light, the true path. Without healthy, positive role models, there is no hope for children.

The Dark Order was a horrid reality of this sort, an entire race of people who worshipped selfishness and fear. When such malice and hatred take root in civilization, it is almost impossible to uproot such ideas. In the case of the Reaper Kai, their twisted desires and teachings were so contrary to the beliefs of others that war was the only option for peace. The Reaper Kai would never yield nor negotiate; their lust for power and control was absolute. To surrender to their warped worldview would have led the Darken Realm to ruin under the rule of the Dark Order. All semblances of truth and justice would have been torn asunder. If the Reaper Kai had won the war, it would have taken centuries to dislodge the ideals of evil from the land, if such a possibility even existed. With the tight, tyrannical control they would have maintained over the Darken Realm, it was entirely possible that evil would have flourished unchecked for many centuries.

The subtleties of the Dark Order occurred in stages. Being cautious at first, the Reaper Kai used their wicked lies to beguile the Darken Realm. Mineera spearheaded this assault on the Darken Realm, in her role as the principle diplomat who ultimately led to the weakening of the entire continent prior to the full-scale invasion. The propositions of the Dark Order seemed benign at first. Small changes in the mindsets of the populace were planted like wicked seeds in the tainted earth. As each small subtle ideal played on the minds of the Reaper Kai's enemies, the Dark Order would then bolster these wicked ideas in such small increments that no one seemed to notice.

The death of liberty occurs in small stages. One is taught to believe by a tyrant that change is needed to secure the future. But this change is often cloaked by fear. Terror and mistrust often fuel the loss of liberty. The populace is taught in subtle increments that their freedom is being taken in order to protect them. The Reaper Kai knew that such a strategy was the only true path to victory and so they lied and lied, spreading false hopes of peace when what they really hungered for was death.

Using their crafty ways, the Reaper Kai managed to infiltrate every large government in the Darken Realm. Once these entities had been compromised, the Dark Order used subtlety to spread fear. By the time their evil plans were unveiled, it was too late for many of the free peoples of the Darken Realm to act.

The only true way to fight evil is to meet it head-on and to force it back. Lack of vigilance, or a feeling that someone else will deal with the spreading of evil, is a perfect way for darkness to take root. Once the darkness has gained a foothold, it festers in silence, spreading like a cancer until it rears its ugly head. Anyone who can act to prevent evil has an obligation to do so.

Mineera was such a person and met the challenge of fighting evil head-on. She knew in her heart that something was deeply wrong with what she was doing. Her dark diplomacy had led to death and suffering and she knew that such activities must stop. And so she enacted a plan. Betraying the Dark Order, Mineera took much of the Reaper Kai's plans for domination to the Reaper Kai's enemies. Her betrayal gave the majority of the Darken Realm the time it needed to put a plan in place in order to fight the tyranny lying in wait.

Branded as a traitor, she was marked for death, cast out from her entire race as a holy pariah. But even though she lost the only home she had ever known, Mineera felt more at home by betraying the Dark Order. Her heart was able to transition toward the light. However, even as she yearned to free her heart from the darkness, evil had other intentions. On many occasions, Mineera was assaulted spiritually. Dark forces battered her heart and soul, willing and urging her to return to evil. Fighting back the voices in her mind, she managed to free herself completely from their seductive call. Once free, she walked the righteous path, leading herself and others from the shadow.

With the Darken Realm free from tyranny, Mineera could now lead others away from the darkness and the stain of death that had marked the land. Her true reward for her vigilance and kind heart was to teach others the way of peace and truth. It was a profound reward for her. Already she had made a positive impact on dozens of people since the monastery doors had opened. While fear is infectious, so is hope.

Mineera had a home at last, within the walls of the monastery. Able to live her life in peace, she knew that the suffering she had endured was well worth the reward. She had resisted the taint of evil with formidable will and had won a major victory over her evil upbringing. Even though she had had a tortuous childhood, being immersed in evil, Mineera found the true path from the darkness. Everything she knew of the world she learned through suffering. But in that suffering, Mineera learned truth and ultimately peace. Sometimes the hardest thing that someone can do is to survive their parents, to survive a dark heritage of suffering. Mineera learned how to survive such strife and therefore win a victory over the darkness. She would not let her upbringing destroy the rest of her life.

Mineera's life was a testament to an iron will and the need to do what was right. To truly lead, one must often abandon the hurt and rage associated with suffering. The wealth of knowledge attained in learning to rise above one's own personal pain can prevent others from suffering. Mineera survived to teach others how to survive.

Sitting in the tower, Mineera closed her eyes, feeling the gentle breeze rush across her dark skin. Tickling her cheeks, the cool wind invigorated her soul. She listened to the sounds around her, hearing the melodious strains of singing rising from the courtyard as the monks tended to the lush gardens. Life, beautiful life, was all around her. Smiling, she breathed in and smelled the aroma of flowers.

Mineera, last born survivor of the Reaper Kai order, was finally at peace. In the warmth of the sun she lingered, letting the sounds and smells of her new world surround her. The warmth of the sun permeated her very soul. Mineera was at home, a true home for the first time in her life, and it felt wonderful.

As she opened her eyes, a beaming smile was on her face. Rising to her feet, she grabbed a pair of worn leather gloves and a garden trowel, and stepped into the courtyard, joining the monks tending to the garden. There was work to be done, life to be lived. And so Mineera worked in the garden with her brethren, making things grow, spreading the warmth of life so that others could bask in its glory. As she worked, Mineera felt joy, true joy in her heart. She had triumphed over evil and had finally found her place in the world.

Chapter 60
The Exile

Trembling in fright, the boy looked back and forth, sweat rolling down his face. With shallow breaths, the youth tried to get himself under control. But the more he thought about his situation, the more he lost control. Looking to his left, he saw another boy who was also nervously staring in wonder at the vast crowd just below the platform. The boy then shifted his attention to his right and caught sight of his long-time friend. Nervously, the boy chewed on his lip, sighing from time to time, unable to look into the crowd.

In the night sky, the brilliance of the full moon shone down upon the village of Scarskin with ominous intensity, bathing the village in a primitive glow. The three youths upon the stage were beginning to lose their minds.

The Exile was created ages ago and was a rite of passage into adulthood. The youth of the village were cast out for the duration of twenty full moons, unable to return beforehand or else be labeled as cowards and forced to live on the lowest rung of Scarskin society.

The tradition of the Exile was the strongest part of Scarskin culture. Sitting behind the frightened tribal youths was the high council of Scarskin. At the center of the council members sat Master Mogi, the aged weapons-master of the village. Master Mogi had been responsible for training the newest Exiles. He sat motionless, his mostly bald head reflecting moonlight off his scalp. White wisps of hair trailed down from the base of his skull, snaking down his shoulders. He was dressed in ceremonial robes, his hands folded across his chest and his face projecting a menacing look.

Flanking Master Mogi were two seasoned warriors. Tani and Jared sat on the stage, watching the Exile ceremony unfold around them with a lump in their throats. It was difficult for Jared and Tani to watch the Exile ceremony, let alone be part of it. When last they had experienced the Exile, it had been Jared and Tani who were forced from the village, exiled into the wastelands for twenty moons. That fateful night several years ago was still present in the thoughts of each of them.

The sound of drums pounding filled the night sky. Dancers dressed in primitive garb, covered in feathers, danced around the perimeter of the stage. In the darkness beyond, a host of tribal warriors were chanting war cries, adding to the tense tone of the ceremony. Half of the audience was drunk, having imbibed the strong and potent fermented cacti brew. The ceremony was rapidly drawing to a close and the feast was done.

"Are you ready?" Mogi asked Tani, his voice solemn.

With a hesitant nod, Tani replied, "As ready as I'll ever be."

With a bold gesture, the tribal scholar stood up quickly and moved over to the podium in the middle of the stage. Pulling in a full breath of air, he shouted in a fierce, commanding tone, "All be still!"

The crowd, surprised by the scholar's mighty presence, was stunned into silence. Staring at their new leader upon the stage filled them with awe. It seemed just like yesterday to many in the crowd that Tani and Jared had been Exiled. It was somewhat disconcerting to see a young person such as Tani taking part in the high council, much less leading the Exile ceremony.

"As it was in times of old, so shall it be this night." Tani spoke in a low, eerie tone. A chill rolled down the spines of the three youths seated upon the stage, who were staring at Tani in terror.

"We, the tribe of Scarskin, were born from the mistakes of a civilization long ago. We, the tribe of Scarskin, were born from the desert. We, the tribe of Scarskin, are all children of the desert." As Tani's haunting voice resounded through the silent crowd, the youths' terror began to seep into the crowd. The rite of passage into adulthood was frightening. Everyone in the crowd had been affected by the Exile, having loved ones that returned or, for many, knowing the loss of sorrow and retaining fond memories of those Exiled who never returned alive.

"Wisdom from our ancestors has taught us to learn and grow from the desert. So shall it be this night. We are about to send our young into the fray. We are about to cast out some of our children so they can learn from the desert and return as men." As Tani spoke, whispers rose from the crowd. Many of the villagers were reciting the ceremonial Exile creed.

"The ancients left great wealth in the desert. They left their knowledge, and this is our heritage. Not only are the youths to learn and grow to become men, they are to return with knowledge of the ones that gave birth to us so many, many moons ago." The three youths upon the stage hid their fear deep inside, their terror masked behind their silent eyes.

"So let it be. So let it be known the three youths that will leave this night are Darin of the Dune Wisp Clan, Rigal of the Dune Wisp Clan, and Morti of the Jagged Knife Clan." With their introduction, the three trembling youths hesitantly rose to their feet and moved toward Tani.

"As custom permits, the elders of this great tribe will in turn give each Exiled a single gift to help them on their journey." Smiling, Jared rose and brought the gifts to the Exiles.

Taking the lead, Jared nodded his head towards the three youths in a slight bow of respect. Grabbing the first item, he came before Darin. "Your studies as a youth predominantly included geography and understanding the world around you. It is no surprise that you have chosen to walk the same path Tani and I walked on our Exile. Your goal is to cross the forbidding eastern wasteland. To help you on your journey, the elders have crafted you a map of the eastern expanses, copied from Tani's maps of the Darken Realm. This map should aid you in your desert crossing, allowing you to find water and shelter as well as noting many dangerous regions in the desert." Jared handed the finely crafted map over to the starry-eyed youth.

With a deep sense of appreciation, Darin smiled and accepted the gift. "Thank you," he said in a serious tone. Jared simply nodded back and smiled.

"The Iron Kai soldiers that fought by our side in the invasion of Scarskin left many items to aid us in the future." Holding up a thick vest, Jared showed the high-tech body armor to the crowd. "This item is military body armor, made from old-world technology. The armor will be given to Morti, who has studied combat his entire life." Handing over the body armor to the youth, Jared solemnly declared, "May this armor protect your life and bring you back home to us."

Stunned, Morti accepted the gift and immediately donned the armor. Standing with a proud look on his face, he held his spear at the ready and looked prepared for any conflict.

Finally, Jared approached the last youth, a small boy with a weak appearance. Fidgeting nervously, he eyed Jared with terror in his eyes, then stepped back, trembling. "Rigal has spent his life studying the stars and gazing into the heavens. To help him on his journey, this tribe gives Rigal a telescope, so that he can further his studies and to aid him in looking toward his future." Grabbing the compact, old-world telescope, the trembling youth was set at ease.

The presentation of the gifts was completed. Jared's demeanor changed immediately, his expression turning stern and somber. With a serious voice, he turned to the three youths and began to recite the ancient Exile ceremonial creed. "I, an elder of the Scarskin tribe, acknowledge the rites of old. It is with happiness and great sorrow that I cast three of our young into the desert. We must pray to our ancestors that they find the strength to be brave and strong." As Jared finished the passage, an eerie silence flooded the night. In the darkness, the wind rose and a gentle breeze wisped across the top of the mesa. The enormous bonfire shifted as the flames were buffeted by the breeze. Light and shadows danced and for a brief moment, Jared was caught in a trance, staring at the fire. A strange sense of loneliness washed over the tribal as he stared at the bonfire, motionless. The tribe was also caught in a trance. The last time youths were cast out of the village was when Tani and Jared left the village.

Finally, a whisper rose from the audience. A tiny boy at the front of the crowd spoke in a somber tone. "All be it with them." The meek voice resounded in the blowing wind with an ominous tone. Jared blinked several times and averted his gaze from the fire, continuing with the ceremony.

"As we are children born from the desert, when we die we return to the desert. Let us pray that the young ones return to us before they return to the desert."

"All be it with them," the crowd hissed in a haunting whisper.

"It is an act of love that I now turn away from you, so that you acknowledge that you are not welcome before my presence until twenty full moons have passed." With that, Jared stared at each of the Exiles in turn. He took but a brief moment to survey each of them. So much fear and indecision were on their faces, so much terror. With a heavy, burdened heart, Jared turned his back on the Exiles, acknowledging to them that they were no longer welcome in the village of Scarskin. As Jared turned away, so did everyone in the village.

In unison, the entire tribe whispered in the light of the full moon, "All be it with them."

Standing by the podium, the three youths were terrified. The only home that they had ever known was casting them out into the wasteland for the duration of twenty full moons. They shook their heads in dismay, the gravity of their situation finally sinking in. Each of them now had to find the courage to survive the Exile. With heavy hearts and fear gnawing at their senses, the three youths passed away from the crowd now shunning them.

Passing down the lonely streets of Scarskin, each of the boys said a fond farewell to their home. As they passed the whitewashed adobe houses in the light of the full moon, they each noticed that the homes were strangely quiet. Taking a brief moment to stop in the middle of the street, the leader of the trio hesitantly addressed his companions.

"Are we ready for this?" Morti asked in a reserved tone.

"No, we're not ready for this," Rigal replied meekly, still clutching his telescope.

"No one is ever ready for this," Darin said with a sense of clarity.

The other two nodded in agreement.

Trembling, Morti dug deep down into the very pit of his soul and mustered his courage. He looked up into the night sky, where the full moon shone brightly. With a sigh, Morti realized that the moon was now their enemy, a watchful guard keeping them from the only home they had ever known. Shaking his head in dismay, he urged his companions onward, towards the desert and the unknown world beyond.

Morti took a step forward, moving toward the gate and out of the village of Scarskin. His companions followed and their Exile began.

As the three youths trudged onward into their futures, the Exile ceremony came to an end. The somber crowd was already dispersing, heading home for the evening. Tani was on the podium, staring around at the audience with a sense of accomplishment. "That wasn't so bad, Jared," he said with a smile. "Our first Exile ceremony and I think we did just fine."

No one responded. Turning around, Tani was stunned to find Jared missing. "Jared?" Tani called out, concerned, scanning the crowd. Jared was nowhere to be seen. "Jared?" the scholar repeated, but no one responded.

During the chaos at the end of the ceremony, Jared had slipped away into the night. Passing down a worn trail, the tribal warrior had slunk off into the darkness of his own accord. Making his way across the top of the mesa, Jared quickly reached a rock outcropping, resting over one thousand feet above the floor of the desert. He sat down on the rocks, letting his feet dangle over the edge. Staring out into the desert, Jared smiled. From his vantage point, the tribal warrior could see the three Exiled youth making their way across the shifting dunes of endless sands that comprised the great eastern wastelands.

"And there you are, young Jared, after all these years, still staring eastward." A familiar voice rang out behind the tribal.

Knowing the voice of Master Mogi very well, Jared didn't need to turn around to know who had joined him upon the rocky precipice.

"You told me that we would never return from the eastern expanse. I guess we proved you wrong," Jared said in a deliberately arrogant tone.

"Deep down, I knew that you would return to us, both yourself and Tani. I just wanted to remove some of that smug arrogance that you so lovingly exhibit."

Turning to view the aged weapons-master, Jared had a look of sadness upon his face. "I learned my place and found humility, true humility."

"I know you have, Master Jared." Mogi approached Jared and placed his hand on his shoulder. "I'm glad you returned to us before you returned to the desert."

"Me too," Jared replied as tears welled up in his eyes.

Seeing his distress, Mogi resolved to leave Jared in peace. "My aged bones are aching. It's been a long day; I am going to get some rest."

"Good night to you," Jared responded.

Mogi climbed down from the rocky precipice and moved off toward the trail that led into the heart of Scarskin. The tribal warrior was left alone in his thoughts. In the dim light, Jared began to feel a strange tug at the edge of his soul.

Letting his thoughts wander, the youth was taken back to the very night that he and Tani had been exiled from the village. He could still remember the tremor of fear in his heart. He could still remember the wild excitement that rolled through his being at the thought of exploring the unknown. He could remember the feeling of loneliness.

His journey throughout the Darken Realm and through life was bound inside of him. His experiences and his heart were now inseparable. He smiled in the darkness, his hand unconsciously moving to his neck. Fidgeting with the strange raven totem around his neck, he was strangely at peace. His other hand moved to his belt and he grabbed Banion's silver revolver. Holding the two objects in his hands, he began to daydream.

Jared imagined walking across the battered landscape, moving across the endless dunes of shifting sand. What was beyond the horizon? What secrets were hiding below the shifting sands of the desert? In his mind's eye, he traveled through the burning deserts, across the distant snow-covered mountains, into the wild canyons, explored the forests of the northlands, walked across the beaches of the western coastline, and rushed through abandoned tunnels beneath the earth. He smiled, his heart torn. His home was no longer in Scarskin. He had no family left. The only thing that filled him was an inescapable sorrow that overwhelmed his senses.

As this sorrow pulled at his soul, his thoughts shifted to darker emotions. He imagined being in combat, fighting desperate life-and-death struggles. He saw his enemies die at his hands and a strange feeling of exhilaration filled him. He felt the pull of battle and the adrenaline pumping through his veins. He craved the struggle and the excitement. Even though he had lost so much, something had changed in Jared forever. He could never be happy living a peaceful existence; he needed something more. He needed the thrill of the hunt and the lure of the unknown.

As Jared stared down into the desert, he saw three figures passing into the eastern wasteland. In that moment, Jared envied the youths. He envied their innocence and also their ignorance. What a wonderful feeling it was to be carefree and have a sense of wanderlust. Jared clutched the raven totem tightly, overcome by a sudden sense of rage. He was dissatisfied with his life and his existence. Clutching Banion's revolver, Jared looked down at the weapon with a feeling of emptiness inside of him.

The trauma Jared had suffered had changed him forever. He no longer had a home. As this feeling welled up inside his heart, he felt broken and empty. He needed more. He lusted for combat and strife. He needed the unknown to awaken his consciousness once more. He was addicted to the struggle and drama of war. He was obsessed with the lure of the unknown. Rising from the ground, he knew what must be done.

That night, Jared crept back into the village of Scarskin. Without any notice of his passing, the tribal warrior grabbed his belongings and passed beyond the village gates. Into the desert he moved, traversing beyond the safety and sanctuary of the village. His heart was broken and to heal his heart, he needed to live in the wilds of the Darken Realm.

Passing into the wastelands, Jared, Elder of the Scarskin tribe, sought to find his destiny. His ultimate fate was the same as Banion's, forced to live alone in a world of strife and reckless adventure. The unknown tugged at Jared's senses and he moved forward with fervent intensity to meet it. The whole world was ahead of him and it felt wonderful. What would he find over the next hill? What secrets would he discover? His whole life was ahead of him, filled with endless possibilities. Escaping from the village of Scarskin, Jared disappeared into the open desert. With a smile, he was at peace, wandering the wilds and ruins of old, seeking adventure, unlocking the mysteries of the Darken Realm.